Long is a Mouse's tail

Roy E. Stolworthy

Copyright © 2022 Roy E. Stolworthy

Roy E. Stolworthy asserts the moral right to be identified as the author of this work in accordance with the copyrights, designs and Patents Act 1988

The characters and events portrayed in this book are fictitious. Any similarity to real persons, living or dead, is coincidental and not intended by the author.

No part of this book may be reproduced, or stored in a retrieval system, or transmitted in any form or by any means, electronic, mechanical, photocopying, recording, or otherwise, without express written permission of the publisher.

For Tommy
For the many hours we spent together

CONTENTS

Copyright
Dedication

CHAPTER ONE	1
CHAPTER TWO	12
CHAPTER THREE	25
CHAPTER FOUR	34
CHAPTER FIVE	49
CHAPTER SIX	74
CHAPTER SEVEN	85
CHAPTER EIGHT	97
CHAPTER NINE	111
CHAPTER TEN	123
CHAPTER ELEVEN	131
CHAPTER TWELVE	158
CHAPTER THIRTEEN	169
CHAPTER FOURTEEN	176
CHAPTER FIFTEEN	185

CHAPTER SIXTEEN	194
CHAPTER SEVENTEEN	203
CHAPTER EIGHTEEN	205
CHAPTER NINETEEN	212
CHAPTER TWENTY	222
CHAPTER TWENTY-ONE	240
CHAPTER TWENTY-TWO	259
CHAPTER TWENTY-THREE	278
CHAPTER TWENTY-FOUR	295
CHAPTER TWENTY-FIVE	311
CHAPTER TWENTY-SIX	324
CHAPTER TWENTY-SEVEN	334
CHAPTER TWENTY-EIGHT	342
CHAPTER TWENTY-NINE	354
CHAPTER THIRTY	375
CHAPTER THIRTY-ONE	392
CHAPTER THIRTY-TWO	401
CHAPTER THIRTY-THREE	412
CHAPTER THIRTY-FOUR	422
CHAPTER THIRTY-FIVE	428
CHAPTER THIRTY-SIX	441
CHAPTER THIRTY-SEVEN	458
CHAPTER THIRTY-EIGHT	462
Books By This Author	465

CHAPTER ONE

What is relevant then is relevant now.

One day, you're the dog, and the next, you're the lamppost, were the first words Anton Page learned during his prison sentence. It came as a great surprise because he didn't believe everything happened as it was supposed to. Accused of murdering his wife, after serving a twenty-year sentence, at last, he was free to go.

On a brisk cold autumn day in mid-November, he drew back the worn cuff of his jacket and glanced at his wristwatch. An eighteenth birthday present from his mother, the watch face had yellowed, making it difficult to see the hands. A few scattered stitches prevented the leather strap from falling apart. He'd forgotten the days he'd promised to fix it, and today was no different. Eyes darting left and right like a camera registering all it saw, at one minute to 9 am, the moment he'd dreamed of had arrived. Less than a solitary step from freedom, he waited for the ecstasy to explode within him, followed by the overriding urge to laugh, cry and scream. Instead, his mind abandoned him. A tremor edged his lips, and he did something he'd never done before; he prayed to God for strength. Flinching at a licking breeze, he turned his back on the burly prison warder holding the gate open and stepped from the prison into the arms of freedom. The expected feeling of elation remained absent. Instead, in its place was a man aged fifty-seven with little else but bits of leftovers from another world.

Dressed in the clothes he'd worn the day of his sentence, he pulled the collar of his jacket tight to his neck and wondered what purpose it would serve to turn a blind eye to the past. Who in their right mind could expect forgiveness for a fifty-seven-year-old man who murdered his wife? Worse, how could the world possibly see into his mind how deeply he grieved the events of twenty years ago? The sight of his beautiful wife lying on the cold concrete drive, her lifeless emerald eyes staring into the night sky indelibly stained his mind. Death can end a life but never a relationship.

Overhead, dark clouds wandered freely as colourless daylight cloaked the streets and buildings. His heart thundering and shivering in an open doorway, he gazed at a world he hadn't set eyes on for twenty years. The falling snowflakes reminded him of Christmas time in the village where he was born and raised. Workers gathered around a hot brazier—green fields hiding beneath a blanket of snow. To the delight of small children's imagination, odd-shaped wintry pillars acted as snowmen. From out of nowhere, an unfamiliar gust of wind slapped the side of his face sending his frail body staggering sideways. Arms flailing, he stumbled and fell, wincing as gravel bit into his hands and knees. A heavily built man wearing a red anorak and dark blue baseball cap slowed and offered a helping hand, then changed his mind when his mobile phone warbled a childish tune and he disappeared into the crowd with the telephone jammed tight to his ear. On his knees, nostrils flared Page murmured an incantation hopeful God would set fire to the phone.

Struggling to his feet and ignoring the pain he swept his eyes over a world full of slow-moving vehicles—crowds of pedestrians swirling around in a graceless dance rushing to different destinations. Nothing changes. The human race remained locked in a time warp, predictable and boring, like looking at the world through the wrong end of a telescope. Caught unaware by a stream of warm fluid trickling from his nose, he sniffed and wiped the snot away with the cuff of his jacket. How many times he'd told himself that nothing in life should be feared; it is to be understood, he'd lost count long ago. But deep down he knew events were far from over. It would never be enough to retreat from the world and refrain from looking back.

Threading a path through the careening crowd he made his way to a low brick wall separating the street from a pay-and-display car park. As arranged with Cate, his daughter, during the last prison visiting hours, he'd wait for her to take him home.

Seated uncomfortably on the wall with his hands pushed deep in his pockets and ankles crossed, a sign displaying directions to the northbound M1 motorway acted as a reminder he must remain patient. Cold and shivering, his head began to throb as a puzzled expression creased his face. So profound was his despair; he worried if he possessed the necessary balls to pull the plug on the past. Where was the sense of seeing himself as a source of shame when at his time of life, he should be sitting in a rocking chair watching life pass by mocking his existence until death set him free?

Perhaps the absence of logic warned him not to wait for Cate. What if she'd forgotten or couldn't be bothered? He wouldn't put either past her. Maybe it would be wiser to take a taxi to the railway station and find his way home alone. But common sense prevailed, and he decided it made sense to wait. A nondescript man with thinning hair and less than medium build, he barely possessed the capacity to make life more unpleasant than it already was. That and he hated the Underground. Once, he'd been on a train during rush hour. Crammed tight among the hot bodies the train had stopped between stations for no apparent reason. It was in the summer, and the heat was stifling. At the time, he thought it might be better if he were dead. But that was then; things were different now.

From feverish to despondent and back again, like a clock's pendulum, his mind swung unchallenged. It always happened when he least expected it to, the rising nightmare forcing him to become a reluctant witness to moments of high drama and sadness while entrenched inside the bowels of the prison walls. Etched clear in his mind, rows of plastic tables with metal legs bolted tight to the floor—fluorescent lighting burning twenty-four hours a day—the ever-present air of violence like a rabid dog waiting to attack. The sound of slamming cell doors never ceased to rattle his brain. Prison warders, in pairs watching everything and missing nothing, waited eagerly to move in with batons ready at the slightest hint of trouble. Eight hundred and five prisoners of different nationalities and religions crowded into spaces built for half the number, seventy-three serving life sentences. Each waking moment filled him with dread knowing he didn't have the strength to ignore the coming day. How could he avoid the disastrous contents that came with it—the constant crescendo of threats made against other inmates pressing unmercifully against his eardrums? Crude expletives echoed off the walls—the stench of tattooed sweating bodies poisoning the air leaving him gagging for fresh air.

Why he continually thought of these things, he failed to grasp. If nothing else, he put them down to a lack of strength born out of stubbornness to ease his mind. But time never lies. It was over; he'd served his sentence, and now he was free to sit on the patio of his country bungalow surrounded by soothing quietness where he could read in peace and tranquillity. Spend early evenings dead-heading wilting geraniums. Tenderly prune the fading roses in the rear garden beneath a cool summer breeze. With autumn pushed aside to make room for winter he'd watch chevrons of geese with beating wings heading south for warmer climates. Best of all, he could continue to operate as a qualified vet in the surgery situated at the rear of his bungalow overlooking the beautiful verdant English countryside. Nothing bad could happen to him anymore. The nightmares that convulsed him into uncontrollable fits would eventually become something from another world. Time is a great healer; he'd learn to live with an untroubled conscience. But that was easier said than done. The force of character that once lived within him had dwindled like a burned-out candle.

With little else to do but wait, his mind returned to the shameful memory of the day the world robbed him of his freedom. The media had a field day describing the murder of his wife as worse than gruesome. More chilling was the weapon, a garden spade with the price tag still attached, leaving the victim's head almost quartered. Crime experts from across the UK gathered to make up a panel on TV. Their job was to condemn or justify his actions before a live audience. Page's deceased wife, Lizzie, a stunning woman of great beauty, led some to suspect it was a crime of passion. Jealousy over another man had propelled her husband to murder, a popular choice among the masses. Put to the vote; the majority chose a different route describing him as cold-blooded and evil. Endless suppositions continued to headline the daily rags until he stood alone and bent, facing the hawk-nosed judge in the Old Bailey dock. With the chips heavily stacked against them, his be-wigged counsel did their best to describe him as a loyal and hard-working husband. A qualified veterinary surgeon devoted to easing the suffering of sick animals. A generous man, not afraid to help the needy whenever possible. They were wasting their time. Their posturing and protracted ramblings cut no ice with a jury of twelve just men and women.

One of his defence lawyers, a be-wigged woman wearing black stockings with seams running up the back, sent his imagination into overdrive when he envisaged his head between her legs. That one solitary moment was the only time he'd thought of himself as a man in months. After a three-week trial, the jury voted unanimously he was a homicidal maniac best locked away from the public. As the flint-eyed judge passed a sentence of twenty years, Page's features were devoid of remorse as he pulled himself upright and remained silent. *Take him down; the* words echoed like cannon shots throughout the court. After fifteen years, maybe less, he'd be free to walk the earth if he kept his nose clean, his solicitors informed him. How wrong they were. During the early years of his prison term, he became prone to vivid nightmares. He saw things that were never there. When questioned about the murder, he constantly insisted he had no memory of the event. Psychiatric treatment failed to jog his memory. Convinced he was lying, he served the entire twenty years before being considered fit to return to society.

At last, a dark blue saloon pulled to a halt a few metres from where he sat. A smile creased his face as he opened the rear passenger door and climbed inside.

"Thank you for picking me up," he said, his smile widening.

Seated behind the steering wheel with her eyes hidden behind dark sunglasses, Cate, his daughter, made no offer of a friendly greeting. Instead, staring at the road ahead, she tapped her fingertips on the steering wheel while Page hunched down in the back seat as if trying to hide from the world.

"No problem," she said, turning her head and looking into his soulless eyes. "Are you ready for this?"

"Yes, I think so. I'm fine," Page hesitated, expecting a friendlier greeting. "Take me home, please?"

"Your bungalow or my place?" she replied, swallowing the lump in her throat and leaning forward to turn the radio on. Then changed her mind.

"The bungalow will be fine," Page said softly.

Eyes squeezed shut, Cate leaned back against the soft leather headrest and sighed. She wished she'd worn jeans instead of a skirt and jacket but didn't know why. What on earth was she supposed to say? Why should she bother to dress up? How do you greet your father after he's spent twenty years in prison for murdering your mother? Since childhood, she'd longed for parents who loved her and stood at her side during the weeks, months, and years leading to adulthood. It wouldn't have mattered that they argued and fought over minor things; at least they'd be there. But events had taken a different road turning her life upside down. No matter how hard she tried, she could never change the past. Her mother was no more, and her father, a convicted murderer, left her mind scarred forever. Initially, she refused to believe the news of her mother's death. But eventually, newspapers and TV coverage slowly knocked the wind from her. Over the years, she gradually recovered. As bursts of energy and strength flowed through her, she gathered herself, determined to be her father's loving daughter.

"Okay, let's go," she answered, opening her eyes and slipping the car into gear.

*

Surprised by the short journey, the miles rapidly disappeared on a gleaming new motorway. No code of behaviour existed between them during the trip. Low in the rear seat Page rested his head against the door pillar and stared through the window at the autumnally washed scenery. All forms of conversation absent throughout the journey, Cate struggled against the temptation to stare at him in the rear-view mirror. Instead, feeling her heart beating in her throat, she concentrated on the icy road ahead. When they reached his bungalow he struggled from the car and waited for her to join him. But she had other plans, and pushing the vehicle into gear pulled away without a word. Lips curved humourlessly and arms hanging by his sides in a pantomime of helplessness, he watched the car disappear past the walled orchard into the narrow village streets. Motionless, disappointment flooded his thoughts as nausea washed over him. He'd expected her to gather a few of his friends as a welcoming home party, sandwiches, perhaps a bottle of his favourite chilled white, but it wasn't to be. But nothing mattered anymore. He yearned for sleep, somewhere he could hide from the nightmares and dreams and see the world as he wanted it to be, free from the maniacal voices haunting the recesses of his head.

CHAPTER TWO

Through half-raised eyelids and lips turned down at the corners, Page turned and stared at the bungalow where he'd spent most of his adult life married to Lizzie. With shaking hands, he inserted the key into the front door and entered. Remembering the ghosts of the past, he ducked to avoid hitting his head on the low exposed beams. Cold air and stiff doors accompanied by creaking floorboards heralded his homecoming where he'd spent many wonderful moments as a husband and father. Tugging off his overcoat and sweeping the woollen hat from his head he sat on the edge of the bed he'd shared with Lizzie. Hopeful of catching a whiff of her perfume, he inhaled a deep breath through his nose. Then angrily shook his head recalling the latter years when she treated him with open contempt for reasons he failed to understand. His mood worsened and he clutched his face as hot tears burned his eyes. Outside, a fading winter sun trickled through the windows exposing a mess of familiar objects scattered around the room, each a broken memory. Alone in the unlit recesses of the dank and dusty rooms once called home, he peered through the window at the softness of the green countryside: fields, the railway arches, the tall chimneys of the cement works reaching up into the sky like thin bony fingers. A ripple travelled across his shoulders and down into his belly. The pain in his head stole the colour from his sight. An unforgiving past trespassed deep into his mind of the times when locked in his cell he cried himself to sleep with his head buried deep in a pillow. Wiping away the tears, he recalled the cold lonely nights he prayed to God to be struck down with a heart attack or killed by a prisoner driven to madness from constantly locked away in a tiny cell. Even a botched suicide attempt to give him a minor release from his torment would be welcome; it wouldn't matter how or why; all that mattered was when.

*

Page had never met an honest inmate who confessed to his crime during his time in prison nor expected to. Each prisoner harboured a festering wound somewhere deep in their history. Some possessed no money, others no trade and a few were unable to read and write. Rather than soil their hands, they stole from others without shame. Clever men with good jobs lost them through greed. Worse of all was the violent murderers given to unpredictable outbursts of temper. Glued to their faces expressions of hopelessness as they shuffled from one part of the prison to another. To stave off the rising threat of insanity, he made friends with those he thought he could trust. The one tangible thing they shared was a deep sense of forbidding nomadity. Even though he couldn't assume their character, he could attempt to conceal his own and walk amongst them without friction. Whenever possible, he shrank from all forms of contact.

Finally, the sun disappeared over the horizon leaving the bungalow enveloped in darkness. A particle of elation briefly cheered him when he flicked the switch to light the rooms. Stuff tipped from upturned drawers lay strewn over the floor. Spider's webs occupied every space. Kitchen cupboards yawned on tired hinges. A thick cream bedroom carpet lay damp and moulding on creaking floorboards. Windows swung on broken hinges allowing freezing air to banish the musky nose-clogging atmosphere. Next to a worn green velour sofa covered in tea stains, a matching chair with a fractured leg leaned at a crazy angle. Hardbacks and magazines explaining animals' origin alongside well-thumbed thrillers lay covered in dust in a creaking bookcase. Someone had stolen the toilet seat. Outside, constant raindrops beat an irregular tattoo on dirty windows. Clouds of crisp brown leaves shuffled noisily across the patio as if possessed by a life of their own.

Minutes after winding the hall clock, it struck five o'clock. The sudden breaking of silence startled him. Filled with despair, he counted each chime. A third of his life staring at a prison cell's bare grey walls, memories of a solitary past became an unwanted companion he struggled to rid from his mind. Life had become like a diver underwater in the murky darkness feeling his way inch by inch until his fingers touched something solid.

On unsteady legs, he entered the bathroom unable to understand why Cate hadn't raised a finger to clean the place ready for his homecoming. Hands gripping the sink, in pressing silence, he raised his head and gazed into the mirror at the reflection staring back. Something about his expression made him nauseous. It wasn't him; the man in the mirror was someone else, a grotesque caricature of what he'd once been. He'd lost weight. Shadows lodged deep beneath his raw eyes, his skin pale as cold morning porridge. Unable to bear the sight of himself, his frail ego disintegrated; humble and ashamed, he turned away.

After a wet shave he cleaned his teeth, re-entered the bedroom and once again glanced out the window. The sky had turned a granite grey. He didn't care. A lashing pitiless rain beat an even tattoo against the windows. He didn't care. The world had gone mad, and tomorrow promised to be worse. He didn't care. Rain would follow more rain. He didn't care. Instead of a brick cell wall, he watched the wonder of nature unfold before his eyes. Then everything changed. His face set like concrete. Today was Sunday, 15th October; by no coincidence, it was the twentieth-first anniversary of the evening when he was arrested and accused of the brutal murder of Lizzie. The intensity of the memory frightened him. Try as he may, he lacked the inner strength to smother his feelings. He no longer wanted collaboration with the event. He wanted something else. It's finished, he pleaded silently; please let it be over. Undergoing an internal struggle his eyes settled on the spot on the driveway where he'd found Lizzie dead following an anonymous phone call. A cut-and-dried case of first-degree murder they called it. No matter how hard he pleaded his innocence, he failed to dislodge the unsettling fragments that scraped beneath his skull that he was as guilty as charged. Straightening his shoulders, he turned his attention back to the windswept countryside. A mist had rendered the country invisible beneath a cloak of darkness. He didn't care.

*

Halfway through the following morning, the sound of a car door slamming shut jerked him from the stillness. Cate had returned. Regardless of her mother's constant objections he'd named her Cate after an Australian actress whose surname he couldn't remember. There had been a time long ago when Cate doted on him. He was her hero, the saviour of injured animals. She wanted to be by his side, away from her mother's continual complaining. Shocked at the news of her mother's tragic death, she refused to believe her father would do such a thing and fervently clung to the memory of the good times. Yet her senses strained to help her find a sense of harmony that would lead her from the darkness. Twenty years later, her blood had dried in her veins. Still no nearer the truth her heart had gone to sleep.

An overwhelming urge to return to his crumpled bed filtered through Page's mind. Instead, seated at the kitchen table, he raised his gnarled hands and counted the liver-coloured blotches on the back of his right hand. He thought it vital to keep an eye on such things; locked in a cell, age had a habit of playing tricks with the mind. Tomorrow, God willing, he'd count the blotches on his left hand. There was no point in rushing things; he wasn't going anywhere he hadn't been before.

The sound of high heel boots crunching up the gravel path grew closer, followed by the scratching of a key searching for the tumblers on the locked front door. The moment Cate entered through the front door his breath stuck in his throat.

She watched him, aware of the change in his

expression. His eyes were empty and lifeless, his appearance shabby and worn. Gripping her shoulder bag with hands trembling, what else should she expect from a man just released from a twenty-year prison sentence? She tried to imagine the thoughts that ran haphazardly through his mind. Then turned her gaze to the small bunch of carnations arranged in a glass container she'd brought two days previous. The idea that flowers might add cheer to the occasion suddenly seemed ridiculous. Her face reddened. It wasn't the kind of welcome for a man released from forced captivity. A liveliness sprang into his eyes. She knew she was her late mother's image and reminded him of the past. The sensation exhilarated her. Her raven black hair cascaded over her shoulders, her features chiselled to perfection; deep brown flashing eyes took in everything. Dressed in jeans and a short brown leather jacket over a tight-fitting white silk shirt, she looked anything but a teacher of history.

"Did you sleep well?" she asked quietly.

"No, I can't get used to the silence."

"You'll get over it in time," shrugging as if she didn't care. "Are you hungry?"

"Thank you for not selling the bungalow and picking me up outside the prison," he answered, ignoring her question.

"Not my property to sell, is it? As for picking you up, it was the least I could do."

His heart opened; he wanted to hold her. Tell

her he was sorry for being the worst father a girl could have and beg forgiveness for taking away her mother. But he couldn't do that; no words existed to soften the loss of a daughter's mother.

"Do you mind if I sit? Are you sure you're not hungry?" she asked, sensing a sudden empathy.

"Help yourself to a seat. No, I'm not hungry; I need time alone to become accustomed to freedom. I feel so tired," Page smiled vaguely.

His words left her confused. Despite her forced tact and kindness, she felt worthless.

"Yes, of course, I understand. I've filled the fridge and pantry with food. The land phone in the hall works. I'll leave my mobile number next to the phone if you need me. And would you mind getting dressed?"

"Thank you, you have been very kind," he answered, looking down at his thin bare legs poking out a pair of baggy grey underpants.

"And will you please stop talking to me like I was a stranger?" Cate snapped.

"Sorry."

Silence fell, interrupted by the ticking of the hallway clock.

He watched her run her thumb around her right index finger. She was nervous. Glancing up, she looked into his eyes and then quickly turned away. Darkness rumbled through him; he knew what was going through her mind.

"What was it like to be arrested for murder? You must remember something about the night?" she asked in a hushed voice.

His mouth set in a grim line Page knew what she meant. His mind wandered back to her childhood. Beautiful and full of fun, if she had a fault, she never stopped asking questions regardless of whether they were hurtful.

"I remembered everything as clearly as if it happened yesterday," he said, his voice soft as if he was speaking to himself.

The skin on her forehead stretched tight.

"So, it is true, you admit to doing it?"

"Doing what?"

"Killing mother, what do you think I'm talking about?" she said, her nerves on the brink of snapping.

"I never killed your mother. I couldn't have. She was already dead when I got there."

Cate looked at her father as if she had never set eyes on him before. Her mind became more and more entangled with a mass of questions.

"But you were found guilty. At least have the decency to tell the truth after serving your sentence. It doesn't matter to me anymore."

"I was in bed with Tracy Harmon smoking weed the night of your mother's murder. I knew nothing about it until I received a phone call telling me Lizzie had been in a serious accident and would I go home as soon as possible."

Fury stabbed Cate's chest as she tried to make sense of his words.

"What, you were off your mind on weed?

What were you, a junkie? And with Tracy Harmon, how could you mix with that tart?"

"Mind your tongue; I've known Tracy since we were at school together. If your mother could fool around, then so could I."

"Then who called you, and why didn't you tell this to the police? It would have put you in the clear?"

"I don't know who called me. I left my phone at Tracy's and never saw it again. Tracy said she was engaged to be married to a policeman, and I didn't want to be the cause of any trouble."

"So instead, you served twenty years in prison for something you say you didn't remember doing? Tracy Harmon immigrated to Canada two months before your trial began, and she didn't marry a policeman," she said, staring at him in stunned disbelief. "What kind of a man are you? How you could be so stupid leaves me speechless?" The words tumbled from her mouth.

"Now that it's all over, perhaps I should tell the police what happened," Page whispered.

"Good God, what's the point?" Cate said, enraged. "After twenty years locked in prison, what good would that do?"

"But whoever killed your mother is still out there."

There was something obscene about his response and Cate's confidence shattered into pieces. Spots of red flared on her cheeks—the agony of disappointment plain on her face.

Page wanted to free his mind and force the darkness from his heart. Each time he closed his eyes, the darkness inside him intensified. He began to sweat, listening to the blood roaring in his ears. Perhaps he'd die unmourned and forgotten. He never heard the door slam shut when Cate trounced from the bungalow.

Early the following morning, the cold northeast wind that often found its way through the worn window frames had disappeared. Grubby lace curtains hung damp and limp instead of continually buffeting against the side of the bungalow wall. After tying his shoelaces, Page reached for the plate of cold mashed potatoes and cheese uneaten from the night before and shovelled the contents down his throat using a tablespoon. Hunger satisfied, he sneezed and blew his nose on the pink cotton sheet. Seated on the edge of the bed, time came to a halt before he remembered where he was. But old habits linger. After twenty years in a cell, taking deep breaths helped settle his nerves and brought his mind to order.

With little interest, he watched a skinny ginger Tomcat wander into the bedroom, then jump onto the wicker chair and fall asleep. Its body twitched as if dreaming of unsuspecting rats searching around the wheelie bins for food scraps. Unable to rid his daughter's image from his mind he moved to the window sensing his self-pity crying out for attention. Childish panic crept up his spine like a schoolboy caught smoking in his bedroom while doing homework. Had he done the right thing telling Cate he wasn't sure if he'd murdered her mother? Although visibly shocked by his words, she'd remained adamant that things must stay as they were. But the question remained: the natural killer was loose, and if he wasn't the murderer, who was? Ignoring his heart beating against his ribs, he opened the wardrobe. The first thing to confront him was a full-length mirror. God, he looked awful. His body was almost devoid of flesh; his protruded bones stretched his skin to breaking point. He looked like a walking skeleton. Then he stared at the clothes hanging neatly on hangers, and a lifeless smile strained his face; for once Cate had thought of everything.

Thoughts pushed aside; his mood lightened, and feeling as mad as a flag in a breeze, he selected dark blue tracksuit bottoms and a lightweight grey sweatshirt. Dressed and in a better mood, he went to the front door and gazed over the cold frosty countryside. A dry wind picked up small crisp golden leaves and rolled them across the pavement like an invading army. Halfway between him and the horizon, a red tractor pulling a trailer moved slowly across a cropped cornfield. A passing passenger aircraft bound for an exotic destination drowned out the sound of singing birds. Less empty and less afraid, he felt ready to take the short walk to the village and meet old acquaintances.

He hesitated two paces from the front gate, aware that the village people were narrow-minded and lacked intellect. Their imagination was vivid but not creative. Returning to the safety of the bungalow and fumbling with the key, he told himself he cared little what people thought of him. But who was he to make such harsh judgments? Of course, they'd talk to him, like they did when he'd treated their sick pets and never asked for payment from the needy. Why should they feel different now? Later perhaps, when he felt more assertive, he'd venture out and plunge himself into the mercy of the villagers. Or maybe he wouldn't. Right now, he wasn't sure.

CHAPTER THREE

During one of her regular visits to the prison, Page recalled Cate mentioning she'd become engaged to an electrician named Luke. At the time, he'd smiled inwardly, wondering if he and Luke would ever become friends. Probably not, he mused. What kind of family wants their son married to the daughter of a convicted murderer?

His thoughts remained fixed on his daughter. For seven years she'd taught history at the upper school on the edge of the village overlooking plots of allotments where kids found the cabbage patches an excellent place to hide when wagging classes.

Unmarried and in her late twenties, those who barely knew her might believe her to be an unflattering woman. After all, history is about events long out of sight and covered in dust fit to block the lungs. But she was far from that. Tall and attractive, she could turn the heads of men with ease. During her visits, she rarely spoke of her mother's death. Their conversations were so stilted and incoherent that she could only pick out certain words. Overshadowed by grief at the twenty-year sentence, she steeled her nerves and promised to visit her father every week without fail. To her credit, she kept her word, never judging or condemning him but deeply disappointed at what might have been a happy family. Long before his release date was due, she begged him not to return to the village, but her words fell on deaf ears. Face free of expression, he stared back at her without uttering a word. With no other family apart from her, he cared little about what the villagers thought of him, he told her. Then added his stubbornness and lack of a sense of guilt were strong enough to overcome their whispering pettiness. Stiff with anger at his words, she climbed to her feet and, with stilted legs, walked out.

*

For the remainder of that day until early evening, Cage felt more and more irritable. The luxury of being a free man weighed heavily on his mind. Like it or not, eventually, he must venture into the village and face his demons. After five minutes of pacing the room, he opened the front door, smiled and stepped into the cool evening air.

A tall man with a Labrador on a red lead stopped on the opposite side of the road. Both men studied each other. Page remained rooted to the spot. The dog sat obediently by his master's feet.

"You've got a bloody nerve showing your face around here, you murdering bastard. They should have strung you up and left you to choke," the man shouted loud enough that anyone in the street couldn't fail to hear his words.

Page's face turned to one of bewilderment. His breathing came in short pants like a dog chasing a cat. Sweat dripped inside his shirt. Confused, he returned to the bungalow and pulled the curtains shut. Cate had warned him not to return to the village, but he'd remained adamant he would never leave. He was wrong, and she was right. His head tumbled. Why him? If he hadn't murdered his wife, then who did? Who called the police minutes after phoning him and leaving him standing over the body with the garden spade in his hands? It wasn't a good marriage; he'd agree wholeheartedly to that. People said all she wanted was his money. After the first few years, the more he tried to put his arms around her, the more she pushed him away and began to treat him like dirt, constantly criticising everything he did. Forever telling him all he was fit for was wiping dog's arses. The dreariness of married life suffocated her.

The domesticity of paying bills and raising her daughter was too much for a woman of her intellect, she told him at every opportunity. He knew of her unfaithfulness and suffered the embarrassment of wagging tongues in silence. But murder her, no, he'd never do that. Hands clamped on his lap, he stared up at the ceiling looking for the spider that scuttled from one wall to the other the night before. When he saw no sign of the spider, he half-smiled. Was this the path the remainder of his life would take? Where he'd expected to find peace and comfort, there was nothing. The shrill sound of the phone playing a tune he didn't recognise jerked him back to reality.

"How are you? Are you all right?"

Recognising the voice, he sucked in a deep breath.

"Yes, Cate, I'm fine, thank you."

"I've just come from the mini-market. The words all over the village that you are out of prison. Some villagers are distributing leaflets ordering shopkeepers not to serve you. I warned you it wasn't wise to return, didn't I? Why won't you consider moving away where people don't know you?

Page balled his fists and tried to flex the stiffness from his hands.

"Damned if I'll be chased out of my home by a bunch of wagging tongues."

"For God's sake, your stubbornness will ruin you. You know those wagging tongues will make your life a misery. Stay where you are. I'll be round within the hour."

Page blinked, trying to clear his thoughts.

"There's no need. I'm fine. Can't it wait until tomorrow?"

Before she could complain, which he knew she would, he dropped the phone into the cradle and slumped onto the sofa.

Misery shuddered through his bones; where was the sense of it? Why did the villagers treat him this way? Had they forgotten his donations to the village council to help make minor improvements? Renovate the village hall, clean and repair the cenotaph honouring those who fell in two world wars. Provide caps and sweaters to help form the cub and guide movement for the village's children. He'd willingly paid for those and much more out of his veterinarian surgery profits without complaint: his reward, the deep cut of betrayal. Too much water had flowed under the bridge and things could never be the same again. The taste of disappointment curdled the saliva in his mouth. He'd been a fool and stared at the worn photograph in a gilt frame above the fireplace. It was the last picture he'd taken of his parents before they set off on a trekking holiday in Peru. Two months later, after rushed calls from the Foreign Office, it came to light that his parents were captured by bandits seeking a ransom for their return. Following a six-month search, their mutilated bodies were found half-buried at the foot of a mountain. Page took the news better than most expected and threw his energies into the animal surgery.

Absorbed in his work, people thought it was his way of dealing with the sudden shock and decided he was best left alone. The upstart was that his parents had left him two properties in Bournemouth which he sold at top price. That and cash in the bank had left him a wealthy man.

A sharp rap from the front door interrupted his thoughts. After a small interlude, the rap came again, this time louder. Nervously licking his lips, Page climbed to his feet convinced the villagers had arrived in force to tell him they didn't want a murderer in their midst, especially one who killed his wife for what might seem to some as a few measly discretions. Sucking in a deep breath, he strode to the front door ready to defend himself. When the door swung open the words readily formed on his lips disappeared.

"So lovely to see you again, Mr Page," the elderly woman said softly, steadying herself with a worn ebony walking stick. "It's my Donny; there seems to be something wrong with his legs. Would you mind taking a look?"

Taken aback, Page wasn't sure how he should answer

"I'm sorry, I haven't practised for years," he stammered, running his fingers through his hair

"Oh, come along, Mr Page, surely you recognise me even after all these years. It's me, Holly Foyle; I used to drive the mobile library van. I visited your bungalow twice a week when you lived with your wife. Of course, I no longer drive the van; it's my eyesight. Blind as a bat these days; I am; old age, I suppose it comes to us all."

Page stared at her. Everyone in the village knew Holly Foyle. She won the annual village pancake race for as many years as he cared to remember.

"Of course, how silly of me," he muttered. "It's been a long time since I saw you last."

"Yes, that's all done and dusted now. Best we forget our past discrepancies, I always say. Life goes on, you know. Now, will you take a look at my darling Donny? I can pay you."

Mrs Foyle raised the lid on a wicker basket to reveal a cocker spaniel puppy.

"Say hello to Mr Page, Donny. He'll have you up and running in no time."

Unsure how to respond, Page lifted the pup from the basket.

"It's his front left that seems to be the trouble," Mrs Foyle said, bursting with relief.

"Yes, I can see that. It's infected and swollen. He needs a course of antibiotics and the pus cleaned out. Not much I can do; I don't have the medication."

But Mrs Foyle wasn't for turning and stared into Page's eyes.

"Surely you can reduce the swelling and clean out the infection. Are these so-called antibiotic medicines so essential? We never had such things when I was a young girl," she snapped.

Page looked perplexed.

"The animal needs proper treatment; I'm sorry, I cannot help."

"You must be able to do something. I couldn't bear another night listening to him crying in pain."

"I'm sorry, I have no medication available."

Mrs Foyle's toes curled in her shoes. Donny was ill, and little else mattered.

"Oh, come along; I'm sure a trained vet can treat an animal without modern medicine."

For a moment, they stared at each other. Mrs Foyle's expression remained unmoved. Page's frown creased, and his left eye began to twitch.

"Very well, you had better come in. I'll do what I can."

Mrs Foyle needed little prompting. Pushing Page aside, she placed the wicker basket on the kitchen table and stepped back with folded arms. Left with little choice, Page bathed Donny's injured foot in warm water and removed the pus to help reduce the swelling. Using cloth torn from a pillowcase, he bandaged the dog's foot.

"Thank you, Mr Page; how much do I owe you?"

"Nothing, I hope the dog recovers, but I advise you to take her to a vet for a check-up."

"I shall do nothing of the kind. Three days from now, I shall call on you to take a look at Donny. Now let me give you some advice Mr Page; open up your surgery and get the villagers back on your side. Goodbye, it has been nice to talk to you again."

CHAPTER FOUR

The following day Page woke from his dream feeling he couldn't move. His eyelids felt so heavy he wondered if he was dead and if someone had placed pennies over his eyes to pay the ferryman who transported the dead across the River Styx. It had been the best part of twenty years since he last enjoyed a whole night's sleep. During this time, he'd barely closed his eyes and slumbered peacefully. Like always, the memories were present; the never-ending sense of guilt had never entirely gone away. Only at night did it fully reveal itself, no longer like a shadow but looming as though taking a physical form of its own.

Over a breakfast of burnt toast dripping with marmalade, he considered the last night's events and Mrs Foyle's words. Get the villagers back on your side, she'd said. Why should I? He countered silently. What have the villagers ever done for me? Collecting payments from the surrounding farmers had been like squeezing blood from a stone. Then he remembered Cate had promised to drop by. He wondered if it would be so bad if he opened his surgery again. It would have given him something to do rather than moping around, feeling sorry for himself.

After purchasing the property, he'd extended the rear for surgery to treat sick animals. Now it stood empty and useless.

Nevertheless, the more he thought about it, the more the idea appealed to him. He'd ask Cate for advice; she'd know what to do; she always did.

Interrupted by the familiar sound of a car door slamming shut, he checked his watch. He smiled a wan smile and wondered why Cate was so heavy-handed. He'd always considered her to have a gentle nature.

"Hi," she said, casting a raised eyebrow over the sink full of dirty plates and utensils. "Don't you ever tidy up after you have eaten?"

Page changed his mind. Perhaps she wasn't so gentle after all. Or maybe he was the problem?

"How are you keeping? Not too busy to use a little cleanliness, I see," she snapped.

Instantly on edge, Page wanted to tell her to show more respect for her father. But the words died in his mouth; the last thing he wanted was an argument. Instead, sensing his confidence rising, he gazed into her eyes.

"I've decided to buy a car and re-open the surgery," he said boldly.

Cate felt her lips numb. She hesitated for a second before answering.

"Bit sudden, isn't it? What's brought all this

on?"

Taking his time he told her of Mrs Foyle's visit. Before he'd the time to finish, she waved her hand dismissively.

"Don't you think you're biting off more than you can chew?"

Page restrained himself—anger brewed in his bones.

"We all know what a crackpot Mrs Foyles is," Cate continued. "Always lost up some country lane in that library van. It's a wonder anybody ever had something to read."

"She brought her sick puppy to me. That's all I need to know about Mrs Foyle."

"Oh dear, not the start of an old-age romance, is it?"

Angered by her sinister observations, Page's mind turned to the safety and privacy of his cell, where he could hide and separate his mind from his thoughts. From the beginning of his prison sentence it always had been there, but not this time. Unable to stand Cate's laughter he clasped his hands over his ears.

"Yes, I killed your mother, is that what you want to hear," he shouted. "Or do you prefer the gory facts?"

Page's face beamed bright red as he fell to his knees. Head tilted forward, exposing his balding head and arms draped out sideways with palms flat on the floor he looked like a grandad playing with his favourite grandchild

Cate paled and stumbled backwards against the kitchen table. Page crawled into the bedroom on all fours and slammed the door shut. Moments later, he heard Cate's car skidding as she drove away from the bungalow. What had possessed him to say something so stupid? Hadn't she suffered enough hardship since her mother's death and his imprisonment while still a child? Grandma Simmons, her mother's mother, had taken her in and given her a home. Unknown to Grandma Simmons, Cate stoically bore her situation and insults from other pupils throughout her schooling until the day she left and trained to be a teacher. Growing up, she entered the world of adults. The cutting insults turned into words of encouragement. People smiled and wished her well in her new profession. Weeks after Cate started at the local village school, Grandma Simmons's health declined and she passed away. Heartbroken, Cate became convinced that families weren't necessary. A handful of good friends would suffice.

Unable to see through her oncoming tears Cate pulled onto the grass verge in Wagons Walk, known locally as The Green. Only weeks ago, the prison Chaplain warned her that her father might become unpredictable and, at times, cruel. Now she realised how quickly a promise could bow its head under pressure. As for herself, she'd tried her best to remain kind and unselfish, always ready to give her father the support he needed to help him acclimate to everyday life. Learn how to turn her feelings and thoughts into the words he desperately wanted to hear. Instead, she'd spoken to him like she would a problematic pupil during lessons. Continually disagreeing with every word he uttered wasn't the way forward. She knew he didn't mean what he'd said. He'd spoken the words out of fear and temper. Slowly but surely, she was beginning to understand that life hung on him like an unwanted burden that couldn't be shaken loose. Re-starting the car, she gripped the leather wheel with both hands. She loved to feel the power between her fingertips, sense the buzz as she drove through the curves and twists of country roads. The faster she moved, the deeper her thoughts became. What she'd feared most was happening; she was turning against him. Her caramel eyes dried and softened when she pulled to a stop and, closing her eyes leaned her head on the steering wheel.

Overcome with guilt at the treatment she'd handed her father she promised herself she would learn to accept the past. Spend quiet weekends with him. Encourage him to open his surgery and assist him in any way possible. It was the least she could do. Foot pressed flat on the accelerator, she started the car and yanked the wheel hard to the left to avoid the sudden appearance of a red tractor. The vehicle skidded against the wet tarmac, crossed the road and thundered into a wall of trees. Slammed forward, her face disappeared into the exploding airbag before flung back in her seat.

*

Five times in as many minutes, Page stared through the window at the spot where Cate parked her car. Each time it was empty. Deep in his gut he'd expected nothing less. He shook his head and failed to understand why he'd uttered those cruel and stupid words. If failure was the precursor to success, he must learn to control his feelings and prevent the past from poisoning his mind? Perhaps a breath of fresh air might help him to think straighter. Passing through the remains of his surgery he stepped into the rear garden and sucked in a long deep breath. Tall evergreen trees with emerald green leaves reached upwards towards the blue sky. An enormous Oak with naked white limbs sat in the middle of the lawn, its branches like giant tentacles extending everywhere. Plants and flowers slept through the coming months until the arrival of the following spring. Thanks to the continuous visits from a greedy heron, the small pond was without the multi-coloured fish. Covered with algae, it served as a haven for frogs and the nocturnal creatures of the night. Amid the peacefulness of nature, Page's shoulders relaxed. Little by little he allowed his mind to relinquish all thoughts of the past. He knew it would be difficult for him to fit into society. Mixing with old acquaintances and chatting with newfound friends sounded all very well but hardly possible. Alone with his thoughts he sat for two hours until the phone's ring tones interrupted his thinking. Quickly on his feet, he entered the bungalow hoping it was Cate demanding an apology. He'd decided to remain silent while she berated him without mercy for threatening to kill her.

"I'm so sorry fo…" he began before being interrupted by a woman's voice he failed to recognise.

"Mr Anton Page?"

"Yes, this is Mr Page. Who is this?"

"Doctor Emma Parker from St Mary's hospital, I'm afraid your daughter Cate has been involved in an accident with a tractor."

"Oh, my God, is she seriously hurt?"

"She's shaken but fortunately not too badly injured."

"Is it possible to visit her today?"

"Better if she wasn't disturbed. She is on drugs at the moment, and rest is vital. Ring tomorrow morning. Hopefully, we'll have more information. I'm so sorry."

"Yes, of course, whatever you say, thank you for letting me know."

The familiar black shadows lurking in his heart's unseen corridors danced throughout his body—anxiety, like a torrent of rushing water from a mountain stream, pulsed through his veins. Throughout the night until the early morning, he tossed and turned. Sleep impossible. When he cried out in vain for company, no answer came. Like the times locked away in his cell, he was alone with only his shadow for company. Spittle formed on his lips. He must confront his demons. The time had come to embrace the present and not worship the ashes. With all the strength he could muster, he sealed his mind shut and loathed himself for his weakness. When he next opened his eyes, bright sunlight lit up his bedroom. His head tumbled with memories as he played with a loose button hanging by the tiniest threads on his shirt. The beginning of another day filled with misery had dawned.

*

Unlike December, the dark early morning clouds had disappeared, leaving the sky with bright sunshine. With the image of Cate in a hospital bed clear in his mind, he knotted the hood of his anorak over his head and headed for the local garage, hopeful it still sold second-hand cars. Twenty years had passed, bringing changes. The name above the double garage doors read J Gurnhingam & Son. Across the road, vehicles and minibuses lay rusting between large clumps of weeds. Glancing around the forecourt, he sighed with relief at the row of second-hand cars marked for sale. Parked on the front in prime position, a white Range Rover with a black top caught his eye. Tucked beneath the wiper-blades, the paperwork read 23,500 miles, a full MOT, and ready to drive away.

"Real bargain that beauty. It used to belong to the president of the Conservative Club in town. You'd think he was the President of Russia the way he carried on. You're welcome to a test run," a voice called from the open doors.

"I'll take it now, a cheque, okay?"

"You can't say John Gurningham doesn't do a fair deal. I'll have to check with the bank first if you care to step into my office, sir."

A grossly overweight man, Gurningham was the kind people quickly disliked. With close-set twitching eyes and a heavy paunch from continually pouring pints of lager down his throat, he reeked of stale alcohol.

"Get out the way, you useless mutt," he sneered, aiming a foot at an old German shepherd dog sleeping by the entrance to a small untidy office, "About as much use as my missus lying around on her fat arse all day."

Documentation completed, Page sat behind the wheel sensing his exhilaration warming his bones. He'd killed two birds with one stone. First, he'd ventured from his bungalow and then purchased a car on the same day. But his day was beginning. How would Cate greet him in the hospital? Maybe she wasn't well enough to see him or didn't want his company. Crouched behind the steering wheel with the black hood of his anorak covering most of his face, he smiled as he passed the village's familiar sights. The butchers, the bakers, the newsagent, and the small corner mini-market all brought a plethora of memories of happier times when everyone tipped their hats and smiled as he passed on his way to treat a sick animal or deliver an awkward calf from a belated mother. Past the cold, forbidding cemetery with lines of silent tombs standing to attention like soldiers on parade. As far as the eye could see, the dead leaves of autumn haunted the countryside with disquieting persistence. Then came the rolling moors with dense woods lurking in the valleys overlooked by bare hills. Opening the window, he pulled the hood from his head to allow the fresh air to enter his lungs. His face wrinkled into a broad smile for the first time since stepping from the prison gates.

Twenty years since he drove a car, parking became a problem. After ten minutes of sweating and reaching for his breath he finally found a space easy to park. When he entered the hospital milling bodies barred his way. Afraid of being recognised, he shrank against the wall and stared at the ground. Nurses hurriedly pushed beds with patients covered by a solitary blanket. Men in white smocks with stethoscopes dangling around their necks strode purposely down the crowded corridors smiling as people stepped aside to let them pass to attend to the sick. An elderly man dressed in a pair of creased pyjamas and pushing a walking frame stopped every few seconds to check his bearings before making his way to the exit and took a sly drag of a cigarette before returning to the ward and disapproving glances from nurses. Behind the glass partition at the reception desk, a woman with purple hair and pink butterfly-shaped glasses looked up and smiled.

"Can I be of assistance, sir?"

Hesitating outside the ward where Cate lay seriously ill, Page's nerves gradually began to get the better of him. A pang of overriding guilt had replaced every thought in his head. It was his fault Cate lay in a hospital bed; therefore, it was only right he'd enter and make his peace. Filled with unease, he reached out and pushed open the door leading to the ward.

"Sorry, sir, visiting hours have just finished. Come back between 3 pm to 4.30 pm."

Page turned to a small petite young woman trimly erect in a creaseless nurse's uniform.

"Oh, dear, I am sorry. I believe my daughter Cate Page has been admitted following a road accident.

"Miss Page? Yes, sir, she is asleep in the bottom room while we await the results of the X-rays."

"May I see her?"

"I'm afraid not. Call back after two hours. One of the doctors will speak with you. Thankfully she doesn't seem as badly injured as we first believed. Now, please leave, sir; we are rather busy."

*

Crestfallen, Page made his way back down the cramped hospital corridors. He needed an alternative, something complete with calmness to help settle his nerves. The nagging thought of being recognised crowded his mind. Already he'd braved the arms of society to visit Cate. Now he needed to act in a manner free of anxiety and avoid his judgment's fallibility.

Hunched behind the wheel of his car, he searched his mind for anything, no matter how small, that would end his enduring fear of a world after prison. Wide-open spaces left him frail and vulnerable. Constantly fighting against a rising panic, the words of Mrs Daly sprang to mind. Of course, what was there to stop him from practising his veterinarian skills again? Why waste all the years of studying when he could relieve sick animals? Calmness warmed his body. The town where he bought drugs and medicines for his surgery was a little more than a fifteen-minute drive away.

The journey took a further ten minutes than Page expected. Successfully negotiating the industrial estate's narrow roads, he halted outside the storage unit. Nothing had changed. The vertical roll-up door was open. Seconds after leaving the car, he paused at the sound of voices. Caught in the open with nowhere to hide, the sudden pressure of the unknown became unbearable. The voices became louder. A man in a shabby ill-fitting grey suit emerged from the secured animal pharmaceutical unit pushing a wire trolley filled with boxes of medicines for sick animals. For a brief moment, he slowed and stared at Page. Page's shoulders stiffened. His hands began to tremble. Then, another man appeared, taller than the two; he stopped, cocked his head to one side and studied him carefully.

"Bloody hell, Anton Page, I never thought I'd ever set eyes on you again," he said. "I thought a twenty-year spell in nick would see you off within months. Mind you, I never for a moment thought you were guilty. Don't just stand there gawping like a nut that lost its bolt; come inside, and I'll put the kettle on."

Page kept his head, trying to recall ever knowing the man. When the man smiled, he displayed a set of teeth so perfect they had to be false.

"You don't recognise me, do you?"

Page shrank back.

"No, I'm afraid I don't."

"Steve Weir, I used to be the assistant manager."

Page blinked and shook his head. A tiny smile spread across his face.

"Yes, how foolish of me not to recognise you," he stammered. "What happened to your boss,

David Cross, if I remember correctly?"

"That's a long story. Don't just stand there; come on in, and I'll tell you all about it over a brew."

They were past their second mug of tea when Weir finished explaining the events of the last twenty years.

"It seemed Mr Cross had his fingers in the till. He might have got away with it until the Pakistani owner ordered a second audit without his knowledge. Bagged a right few quid, he did, as crooked as a corkscrew he was. Course, the Pakistani fired him on the spot and threatened court action. Cross disappeared and hasn't been seen since. Right pissed off; the Pakistani threatened to sell the place and return home to Pakistan. I asked him to hold fire and consider the four people, me included, that had run the place from the first day it opened. To cut a long story short, he agreed to let me run the place and take fifteen per cent of the profits instead of a salary. The rest I'd send to him. Bit his hand off, I did. This place is a goldmine if run properly. More tea?"

Page's heart soared at having a civilised conversation with someone who didn't threaten to rip his head off. He felt whole again and wanted the conversation never to end.

"Well, I suppose you'll need some supplies if you intend to set up business again."

"What made you think that?"

"You wouldn't be here for any other reason, would you? I run the place like a supermarket now—no more hanging around in queues like in the old days. You're a licensed vet, take what you need, and I'll see you at the till. Good to have you back, Page; this area is calling out for good reliable vets. You'll need to read up on new procedures after being away. I have some pamphlets you might want to check out."

"Thank you, do you mind if I call back later in the week? I have to tidy up the surgery and attend to a few things," Page smiled.

"Of course not; pop back when you are good and ready. It's good to see you."

CHAPTER FIVE

Cate had given up trying to sit up in the uncomfortable hospital bed. Instead of trying to work out which part of her body hurt the most, she laid back and closed her eyes in a futile attempt to block out a searing headache.

"Ah, you are awake, good. The doctor is on his rounds and will be with you shortly. Are you suffering any pain?" The petite nurse asked

"Not really, apart from a violent headache."

"I'll get you some painkillers."

"Thank you," Cate said, forcing a grin.

"At least you are in good spirits; always a good sign."

Later that day, after being cleared by the doctor to leave the hospital, Cate had just finished dressing when her father entered the ward.

"Your daughter will be ready to leave in a few minutes, Mr Page. Thankfully she wasn't as bad as we first thought, and the doctors gave her a clean health bill. She's still suffering a few minor scratches and a headache. Best she rests when she gets home," the nurse said.

Few words were spoken during the drive to Page's bungalow. Cate chose to sit in the back, fearing her safety jeopardised with her father behind the wheel. Her attitude became increasingly agitated each time he fumbled nervously with the gearstick. When they finally reached the bungalow, she left the car and let herself in without commenting. Page followed and remained silent as she made coffee.

"Thank you for picking me up," she said.

"No problem," Page answered. "It was the least I could do. Don't you think it would be wiser to stay here for a couple of days?"

"I don't see why. The place is a pigsty."

Page felt the hairs on his neck bristle.

"Don't be so damned ridiculous. No thanks to you; it's a damn sight cleaner than when I moved in."

"Doesn't look like it to me."

"Try spending twenty years cooped up in a cell. You'll soon learn to look after your possessions. Damned cheek, don't you have an ounce of respect in your body?"

Promises made earlier were quickly pushed aside as Cate shuddered at the look of glistening spite in his eyes. She could only imagine what lurked within the depths of his mind. Hard as she tried not to, she couldn't help but feel uncomfortable in his presence from the moment he'd left prison. A barrier had grown between them. Separated for twenty years, she hardly knew him; his traits and habits were alien to her. He didn't feel like her father but more a distant acquaintance she must learn to tolerate. When her mobile phone trilled, she glanced at the caller's name, forced the phone back into her pocket and busied herself stirring two cups of coffee. Feeling foolish, she racked her brain for something that might ease the rift between them. Unable to think of something suitable, she watched him gaze from the window at the overgrown garden realising he'd been through enough pain to make him angry at the slightest hint of provocation. Reluctantly she recalled the arguments between him and her mother that occasionally threatened to turn to violence. She hated her mother for the names she called him. Cringed at the insults no wife should call a husband who loved her. Instead of retaliating, he stood upright with a sheepish grin as if it were some sick joke. Yet, despite the brutal nature of her mother's words, she knew he never stopped loving her.

"I'm going to re-open the surgery," he said quietly and reassuringly.

She looked at him, struggling to find the right words to answer.

"Well, what do you think?" he continued, waiting for her response.

"Er, yes, that's a good idea. It will help keep your mind off things and give you something to do with your time."

"Yes, that's what I thought. I'll have to give the place a good cleaning first. Tomorrow I'll go to the mini-market and buy cleansing materials and disinfectants. Probably need a lick of paint to smarten the place up to, shouldn't be a problem," Page said, in a confident air.

Her face creased into a smile.

Confident she would offer to help, Page waited for her answer. Nothing came. She hadn't changed since childhood. His mood shifted, and he looked to the floor at the worn carpet. Why worry? He didn't need her to make a life for him. An hour later he drove her home in silence.

*

Seething with anticipation, Page rose early the following day. With no thought of Cate to trouble his mind, he began the short drive through the village to the Mini-market. Heavy lorry tracks had churned the earth where once children played. Old worn tyres, plastic bags, chocolate bar wrappers and out-of-date newspapers fluttered in the breeze across what had once been a football pitch. He failed to understand why the railings around the football pitch and basketball court had been ripped up and piled to one side. The twisted remains of children's swings and climbing frames lay covered in rust. Despair riddled his brain. He wished he was somewhere quiet where people didn't exist.

Stepping on the accelerator, ten minutes later he stopped and left the car with the engine running and gazed over the countryside on the outskirts of the village recalling the glorious spring days when the orchards were in full bloom—buds seeking light to display their beauty, daffodils bobbing gracefully above the grass. He recalled the days when he and Lizzie would seek out a pleasant corner in the fields and while away the hours dreaming of the day they would be married. The sound of laughter as their children ran around a large lawn chased by pet dogs. Colourful regiments of garden flowers standing upright against a warm summer breeze filled his mind with an everlasting hope.

Like a bad dream his thoughts came and went, separated by fear of what he should do next. If he couldn't find a suitable solution to his misery, would his life be worth living? But people, like places, are prone to change. What happened twenty years ago was history. Most of the old guards he knew as friends were probably dead and buried, leaving just a tiny minority of those he once knew. A sense of harmony felt out of the question. But hope is a good thing; it lingers and never dies. Minutes later, he pushed open the Mini-market door, picked up a wire basket and began patrolling the aisles for cleaning materials. Sweat trickled down his back and gathered at the top of his trousers.

"Hello, Mr Page. I heard you were back and planning to open the pet's surgery," an elderly lady said.

He didn't recognise the lady and floundered searching for a suitable answer.

"Er, yes, I hope to be up and running in a few weeks, thank you for inquiring," he stammered.

"Good to have you back; shame everyone doesn't feel the same. But you know what some people are; only happy when they have one foot in someone else's grave."

"Yes, it would seem that way. Such a pity."

"Well, ignore them and go about your business."

"Thank you; I shall try my best."

"Good day to you then; nice to see you again."

He watched the elderly lady walk to the till before continuing his shopping. In the next aisle, he smiled and stepped aside in a display of good manners to allow another lady to pass. Tall and arrogant, there was no mistaking the malice in her eyes matched by the curling sneer contorting her face.

"Found your way back then. You got a bloody cheek; I'll say that for you. Bold as bloody brass, some people are."

"Excuse me, do I know you?" Page said quietly, feeling a familiar anger rise inside him.

"Bloody ought to; I served you in the newsagents enough times. Your missus might have put herself around, but she didn't deserve what you did to her. And that daughter of yours is just as bad wearing her knickers around her ankles."

Page sucked in a significant intake of breath. Shock evident on his face he stared into the eyes of the woman and spoke so quietly that the woman barely heard his words.

"Would you mind telling me where you heard these accusations?"

The woman sucked in her bottom lip. Page's grip on the shopping basket handle increased turning his knuckles white. Pressure swelled in his head. He couldn't calm down. Chewing the inside of his mouth he felt his eyes might burst from their sockets. Then, remembering the times in prison when faced with violence, he turned away and made his way to the till.

"That will be £17.56," she whispered, staring at the counter to avoid his look.

"Thank you, keep the change," he said, handing her a twenty-pound note.

Outside in the street, billows of white smoke drifted over distant housetops. Someone had lit a bonfire. Why should he care? It wasn't his business; people could do what they wanted. It wouldn't have bothered him if the village had gone up in flames.

Sleeves rolled up to his elbows, Page began the tedious job of cleaning out the surgery. Scuffed and scratched paintwork quickly benefited from a shiny new coat of paint. Shelves were cleared of heaps of yellowing papers. As evening fell, his shirt became soaked with sweat from his exertions, and the hen smell of paint stung his nose. Worse, his back ached.

At last, he'd finished what he'd started. Caught up in his achievement he failed to see Cate enter the bungalow until she appeared clutching two mugs of hot coffee. With a treacly smile, she nodded her approval at his efforts.

"My my, you have done well," she said.

Page wasn't foolish enough to consider her words a sign of encouragement and dismissed her comment as little more than sarcasm. The intensity of his disgust for her knew no bounds, and he longed for the day when she returned to her flat in the village leaving him to live in peace.

"If you have a moment, I have something I'd like to discuss with you," she said, ridding her face of the treacly smile.

"It will have to wait until I have showered and changed my clothes?"

Appalled at being told to wait, she shrugged her shoulders and shot him a stern look.

"No hurrying you is there, never was where I was concerned."

Startled by her words, he purposely took his time before he answered.

"Come on then, let's have it. What's bothering you that can't wait two minutes?" he grunted.

"I have been talking to Xander Pennywise."

Had things been under normal circumstances, Page might have listened. But not today. The mention of the word Pennywise sent a shiver spiralling down his spine.

"For God's sake, how many times have I warned you to stay away from that bunch of degenerates?"

"They're not so bad when you get to know them. Nelson comes across as quite intelligent."

"Bullshit, what are they after?"

"They're after nothing. I want to join the Pennywise Hunt."

"The Pennywise Hunt?" Page exploded. "Hasn't it ever sunk into your thick skull that I am a vet, and I have no intention of chasing halfway across the county to put down a deer ripped to pieces by a pack of starving dogs? You are aware hunting is against the law."

"Quite the brain-box for someone who has been away for the last few years, aren't we?"

Disgust twisted his features. He swallowed hard and pulled in a deep breath.

"I think it better if you went. I need time to get my head around life outside of prison."

"As you wish. But I still intend to join the hunt if they will have me."

"What's that supposed to mean if they'll have you? They are a bunch of over-rich toffs with little else to do but break every rule in the book and get away with it. What in God's name do they want with the likes of you? You'll be nothing but a plaything passed around from bed to bed. The horses cost thousands of pounds. Then there's the stabling, the feeding, and the vet's bills. Don't look at me to be a part of this stupidity."

As he spoke, a dark hole inside his chest began to open. It would make him dizzy if he were to stand, so he remained seated. Where he hoped to find comfort and peace, there was little else but darkness. The clock radio blinked its neon numbers. He wondered where it would end.

Alarmed by his outburst, she stared at him through bulging eyes. At first, she thought he was having a mid-life crisis; then, it dawned on her. The terrible simplicity of it was that he didn't care for her. Locked up for twenty years, what did he know about her or her needs? At seventeen, she left school and spent the next four years qualifying as a history teacher. She hated the job and the monotony of village life and yearned for a better life. She wanted excitement and thrills. Meet men and be swept off her feet in Monaco, New York or the French Riviera. He could think whatever he liked; it mattered little to her. Damn him. She'd join the Pennywise Hunt to spite him.

With a furrowed brow, Page struggled to understand. Whatever it was, he knew he could never satisfy her needs. Outside, high in the trees, a crow cawing a rasping message echoed in his ears.

"I need a drink of water," he said in a low voice.

Drained of words, Cate glared at him.

"You need something stronger than water," she snapped, storming from the room.

Once again, the front door slammed shut like

so many times before. Seconds later, the sound of her car died in the distance.

"Damn that child," he said, rising from the chair and entering the kitchen. "Damn her to pieces."

*

Head thumping like a hammer beating on a blacksmith's anvil, it took Page four hours to compile a list of medicines and cures needed for sick animals. At last finished, he shuffled from the bungalow and cast his eyes over the unkempt garden shaded by the falling evening sun. A cluster of women had gathered on the opposite side of the road. A tall woman wearing a bright yellow anorak and red bobble-hat stopped talking and smiled at him pityingly through pinched lips. The pupils of her eyes hooded by tight lids, she raised a fist and shook it at him while the other women stared silently in judgement. Cold dread ripped through Page's body. Nothing brought people together quicker than a common enemy. With what little breath remained, he retreated to the safety of the bungalow.

Like many times before, everything became blurred. The ringing phone in the hallway threatened to convulse him into a fit. His mind looped over the last hour that had led to the argument with Cate. Locked in prison, he'd never heard her cry for her absent father each night. Images of her as a child spooled out before him. Silence pressed against his ears as he sank into the squalor of his own making. What kind of man produces children but never becomes a father? The words rebounded through his mind. He'd struggled with the nightmare for the last twenty years but never found an answer that made an ounce of sense. Damn the phone, let it ring.

*

At 10 am the following day, Cate passed through the tall wrought iron gates leading to the Pennywise Manor. Following the long winding tarmac drive flanked by rows of mature trees standing like rows of sentinels, she slowed to marvel at the grazing deer before pulling to a halt on the gravelled forecourt. Forearms resting on the steering wheel, she admired the dancing waters of a large four-tiered Victorian fountain in the centre of the forecourt, surrounded by wooden benches and trees waiting to burst into blossom. A Union flag hung limply above the castellated turrets of the large manor. Stepping from the car, she rummaged through the contents of her shoulder bag before donning a pair of sunglasses. Built three centuries ago for a local cotton magnate, the manor lacked the undercurrent of power and excitement she expected from such an imposing building.

Pushing back the wispy curls of hair fluttering across her face, she shivered; it wasn't a place where she'd choose to linger. Filled with uncertainty, she checked her watch and recalled the reason for her visit. When Lord Pennywise's youngest son, Xander, discovered her yearning to join the Pennywise hunt, he promised to arrange an interview with his father if she agreed to have dinner with him one weekend. She accepted against her better judgement, aware he was a spoiled brat still in his late forties with a penchant for oppressing women. Shoulders tight, crossing the forecourt she read the Latin words chiselled above the large oak double doors. It was common knowledge throughout the village; the words translated into English read PENNYWISE-POUND PERFECT. An apt motto for the Pennywise family, known for their meanness with all things of a fiscal nature. Eyes rolling in scorn, she reached out and pulled the chain and listened to bells jingling inside the Manor. Then stepped back and tugged down the hem of her skirt that barely covered her pert backside. Minutes later, the double oak doors swung open revealing a small thin man with eyes like pickled onions. Dressed in a worn shiny black suit and matching bow tie, the man gave the impression of a coiled mouse ready to leap onto a sliver of cheese. Cate's eyes narrowed at the smoothness of his skin and delicate hands with long fingers. Something dainty about him puzzled her.

"Miss Page, I assume?" he said in a squeaky voice inclining his head forward in a well-practised nod.

"You assume correctly, in which case you know why I am here."

"Yes, Miss Page, indeed I do," he said, his large eyes peering through thick brown-framed glasses. "I know everything that occurs in Lord Pennywise's residence. It's what he pays me for."

"Then I can assume you know your stuff?" Cate smiled.

He hesitated and ran his eyes down the length of her body. Then, with a white-gloved hand, gestured theatrically.

"If you care to follow me, Miss Page, Lord Pennywise is waiting."

"Do you have a name?" she asked.

"Onions, Miss."

Cate clamped her teeth together to stop the laughter threatening to fall from her mouth.

"Do you have a first name?"

"Just Onions, Miss."

As they walked, Cate gazed open-mouthed up at the magnificent vaulted ceiling adorned with exquisite mouldings. Hand-painted wallpaper hung from the walls. Large open high doors led to a ballroom fit for a queen's attendance. Flushes of heat burned her face followed by a sudden burst of anxiety as she realised she was out of her depth.

When Onions stopped and pulled open a high door, he took a step back and ushered her into a room with another theatrical wave of his hand.

Seated at the head of a long table with his back to a large window shielded by heavy brocade curtains, an elderly man chewed the remains of a sausage roll caring little where the crumbs fell. An open fire grate with dancing flames licked greedily at dried logs on one side of the room. Gloomy, with little lighting, the mustiness teased her nose threatening to make her sneeze. Dressed in a red quilted dressing gown and slumped in childish adolescence, Lord Pennywise seemed oblivious to her presence. Without speaking, Onions withdrew.

"Lord Pennywise?" she asked in a nervous voice.

"Yes, who in God's name did you think I was? Sit down, girl, here on the sofa where I can see you," he said in a reedy voice, then turned and blew his nose on the heavy brocade curtains. "Damn colds, I hate autumn and winter, can't for my life see the reason for them. Nothing grows apart from Brussel sprouts. Blasted things give me wind enough to re-float the Cutty Sark."

Cate remained silent, studying him through intense eyes.

His dressing gown flapped open when he rose from the table without warning, revealing a thin chalk-white chest. Seated before her he leaned forward and stared at the tiny gap between her legs without a hint of shame. What a fool she'd been to wear a short skirt thinking she could get what she wanted by practising female tricks on a man with one foot in the grave.

"So, tell me," he said abruptly. "Where do you keep your horses?"

"I don't have any horses," she answered, fighting to maintain her dignity.

"Don't have horses. For god's sake, where did you learn to ride?"

Cate's face whitened. The stoic expression on her face began to crumble. A strand of black hair fell across her forehead, and she pushed it back in place.

"The riding school in Beltip is the best in the country. I was hoping I might borrow one of yours."

Lord Pennywise closed his eyes and placed his hands over his ears.

"It's a trick. One of those useless sons of mine put you up to this, didn't they? It's their way of revenge because I refused to increase their allowances. They think they have made an old man of me. Did you know they took away my guns? They won't let me drive my Bentley to the gates and back. Course you didn't; how could you know such things? They hide every drop of whisky that comes into the house. Come on then, girl, which one was it, eh, Xander, the womaniser who enjoys thrashing females? Or was it Wellington? I wouldn't put anything past him. A year older than his brother Xander, he is what we used to call queer as a nine-pound note in my day—not allowed to say those words in this so-called modern country today. He loves to dress as a Nazi officer when he's with those of his ilk. I'll discount Nelson; he's too young and intelligent for such nonsense. The silly fellow can't open a door without bombarding everyone that the blasted door handles came from Italy or some obscure country no one has heard of before. Come along, speak up; the cat got your tongue?"

Seconds passed before Cate answered his questions.

"I don't know anything about that; I want to join your hunt. Meet people with whom I can engage in intelligent conversation. Have a meaningful social life."

He stared at her through meaningless eyes. Then once again fixed his eyes on the tiny gap between her legs. Parting his legs, his right hand slid beneath his dressing gown. Without moving his head, his eyes rolled upwards in their sockets. Seconds later, he began to breathe heavily. He was masturbating. Out of sheer devilment, she opened her legs wide enough for him to see her black lace underwear. His moans filled the room. Spittle slipped from his mouth and dribbled down his chin. Spent, he slumped back on the sofa. Ashamed at her actions, she looked out the large window marbled by a cold light to hide her face. The sky had turned a shade of white threatening snow. She'd made a mistake. It would have been wiser if she'd left when he began to fondle himself. Confused, her thoughts turned to her schooldays and Mr Hughes, the handsome young geography teacher.

"Cate, please stay behind. We need to discuss your homework or complete lack of it," he told her.

Sat at her desk until the rest of the class had left; she knew what he wanted.

Within minutes she had his penis out and left without a word after deftly relieving him. Men, they're all the same, she laughed, joining her school friends. But the man before her wasn't a young man. In his late eighties and a multi-millionaire, he was a different kettle of fish altogether. Her lips turned to a pout. There was nothing clever about what she'd done, nor was it against the law. She'd merely exposed her knickers, hopeful it might help her cause.

"Do you know how I made my fortune?" he cleared his throat.

"Something to do with medicines, I believe," she answered in a brittle voice.

"I designed a small implement to help people with asthma breathe easily.

"How noble of you," intrigued why he felt it essential she should know.

"Like an inhaler, but with a small rechargeable battery to rotate a fan. Put the inhaler in your mouth, turn on the fan and breathe normally; it clears the airways making breathing easier. Sold millions worldwide and still selling at £145.99

each. Could you do something like that? Do you have the intelligence?"

"No, why should I when I can clear your airwaves by showing my knickers? Hardly intelligent, is it? Perhaps I should charge you £145.99 for services rendered."

His eyes settled on her face, and it seemed an age before his smile wrinkled the skin on his face.

"So, you want to join my hunt? Then I'm afraid I have to disappoint you. Believe me when I tell you there isn't any way you could fit in."

His rebuff angered her. Her large round earrings shifted. Every inch of her skin grew hot. Anger swelled within her as she fought to maintain her composure. Who was he to turn her world upside down? For years she'd dreamed of riding with the Pennywise Hunt. Now her dream shattered like pieces of broken pottery on a stone floor.

"I understand you are the daughter of that veterinarian fellow. Is that true, the same one sent down for murdering his wife?"

"It's no business of yours," she snapped at him.

"I knew him and his charming wife, you know. Such a pity; I never thought he had it in him," he said, ignoring her sudden change in attitude.

"Really, and what makes you think my mother was so charming?"

Over the years, Cate had learned to read

people. After a few minutes of face-to-face interaction, she felt confident she could reach a verdict that would stand her in good stead. Pennywise began to fidget. She couldn't guess how long they stared at each other without uttering a word. Suddenly she couldn't bear to look at him for a moment longer, and, dropping her gaze, she busied herself with the contents of her shoulder bag before climbing to her feet.

"Oh dear, I have disappointed you," he said. "Come here; I have something I want to show you."

Leaving the sofa aided by a walking stick, he shuffled awkwardly to the large window overlooking a small paddock.

Curiosity had the better of her. Reluctantly, Cate followed him to the window.

"There, beneath the two oaks," he said in a low voice. "See the bay horse."

"I've seen horses before," she pouted, losing the battle to calm herself after being refused point-blank what she wanted more than anything else.

"Not an animal like that, you haven't."

"Really, and what is so special about that horse?"

"It's bred from the finest dressage horse's money can buy."

"How interesting, I think not."

"Do you smoke?"

"No."

"Do you exercise regularly"?

"Yes, I do; why all these silly questions?"

"I'm looking for a competent horse person to run my stables. If you want it, the job is yours."

Cate turned and stared at him.

"I know little about caring for horses."

"Then learn."

"I already have a job, thank you."

"I will double your salary and all expenses paid. Think about it and let me have your answer seven days from today. Good day Ms Page, Onions will see you out. Thank you for an interesting morning. I feel certain we shall meet again."

"Before I leave, why choose me to care for your horses?" she said calmly, waiting by the door.

"The men around here are lazy, stupid and untrustworthy. You are feisty; I like that in a woman. If you apply yourself, I feel you can get whatever you want from life. You are comfortable around horses, and I believe you will learn quickly. Trust me, Ms Page; the rewards far outweigh trotting around the countryside on a knackered old horse. The choice is yours. Please close the door behind you and be kind enough to tell Onions I wish to see him."

Not the type to remain confused for any length of time, Cate's way was to fight the battle head-on until victory belonged to her. But today, things were different. When she left the manor and crossed the gravel drive, her mind remained fogged, and her face distorted into pantomime concentration. Fatigued, she'd strained at the leash of utter boredom like an untrained dog. Her dream of joining the Pennywise hunt lay shattered at her feet. Instead, Lord Pennywise had offered her a job running his stables. But why? There were plenty of experienced horsemen in and around the village. Frustrated, she closed her eyes and began hurling obscenities at the windscreen. Hidden from view behind the brocade curtains, Lord Pennywise watched her from his window, then turned and bellowed.

"Onions, tell Mr Xander I want to see him immediately."

The second youngest of Lord Pennywise's three sons, Xander Pennywise, suffered a violent headache from the previous night in the Crooked Stick Inn. Late last night, with the sole intention of getting his leg over, he'd taken a local girl down the towpath by the canal. When she refused to cooperate with his sexual activities, he became violent. Two men working on a narrowboat late into the night overheard her screams. A foul-mouth quarrel started. Xander suffered a bloodied nose and sore ribs from a vicious bout of kicking while lying doubled-up on the ground. Immediately after Onions delivered his father's message, white-faced and silent, Xander hurriedly dressed. To keep his father waiting was a mortal sin. Sour-faced, he lurched from side to side waiting for his father's usual double broadside of insults.

"Good grief, look at the state of you. You look like you have been in a brawl and come out worse. What in God's name have you done this time?" Pennywise thundered.

"I was set on by a couple of the local ruffians who didn't know how to fight fair."

"Fair, there's nothing fair in a fight. It's winning and coming out on top that counts."

"Yes, father, of course, I shall remember that in future."

"Remember? You couldn't remember your birthday unless it smelled like a woman's fanny."

"Yes, father, as usual, you are right."

"Don't get funny with me, boy," Pennywise hissed. "What do you know about that Page woman, Cate, they call her?"

"I knew her slightly a few years ago. We went to the same junior school. Her father has just finished serving a twenty-year sentence for killing her mother."

"Knew her slightly, you say; that isn't what I heard."

Xander stiffened and stopped rocking back and forward on his heels. His eyes opened wide as if threatened with a painful death.

"I don't know what you mean," he stuttered.

"Oh, of course you do."

Xander gasped and began to chew his bottom lip.

"I have asked Cate to run the stables."

"But father, you said I could do that. You promised."

"Rubbish, I know better than to promise anything that concerns you and your useless brothers."

Anger boiled in Xander's chest. Used to his son's irritability Lord Pennywise ignored the coming pantomime and continued.

"I want you to get to know her better. Find out what makes her tick. She has all the hallmarks of a social climber and the looks to climb into any man's bed."

Xander held his breath, trying to understand his father's reasons. At the same time to remain cautious. He'd learned long ago that it never paid to intimidate his father. One wrong word and he'd toss him out on the street like an unwanted dog.

"Yes, father, I shall do as you ask," he said quietly.

Lord Pennywise cleared his throat and looked his son up and down as if he saw something that didn't sit right on his mind. There was something vulnerable about the boy. He was like a child struggling to come to terms with life. Sometimes, he'd feel afraid to communicate if the boy did something utterly stupid. However, for better or worse, he decided to tell Xander of his meeting with Cate and how he pretended to masturbate while she watched.

"Really, how did she react?" Xander grinned.

"Like a mongrel on heat, she takes after her mother, that's for sure. Remember what I said; you may go now."

CHAPTER SIX

At last, the grey clouds cleared, leaving a reluctant sun to brighten a dismal world. From the moment Page opened his eyes, the glare of the early daylight left him dazzled. 9 am, still fully clothed, he'd slept through the night stretched out on the sofa. Not that it bothered him, today, he planned to go to town and stock up with medicines necessary to run a successful veterinarian surgery.

Two cups of hurried coffee sufficed for breakfast. The thought of a civil conversation with Steve Weir raised his morale. Yet, like always, the element that haunted him for years still lurked menacingly in his mind. Try as he may, there could be no ridding himself of the past; dread and blackness swirled within the fiery stigma of guilt. Once a con, always a con, the old lags in prison told him. Like a kiss from Judas, it haunts the soul for as long as you live, they added. He'd given the remark short thrift; nine-tenths of what he heard in prison was bullshit, but the irrational tenth was different. It was like a heron flashing into a lake and rising with his catch. I must try harder to mix, he silently scolded himself. But true freedom comes at a premium. Cursed with the thought he couldn't do as he pleased, he became cautiously fearful of doing something wrong without knowing and being dragged back into prison.

He left the car on the outskirts of the town for no particular reason other than it promised a fine day. From a bridge above a slow-moving river, he watched the water wind on its way through banks of thick bulrushes before disappearing beneath an old stone bridge. On either side of the river, tall trees interspersed with regal weeping willows shivered in the breeze. Brown leaves drifted from the low branches of an old gnarled oak tree. Nettles choked the paths blocking the pathway to a park where kids played during summertime. Behind him, the spire of St Luke's pricked black against the clear blue sky. Tomorrow, as a qualified vet, he'd be doing what he knew best: healing sick animals. Spirits soared like an eagle searching for thermals of air; an unforced smile settled on his face as a thin, silent mist rose from the water and crept along the edge of the bridge. A warm feeling of maturity of thought and positivity grew within him.

*

Five hours later, seated in his surgery, Page studied the list of words he'd written in a blue-covered notebook the night before. Although he'd packed his car to the gills, he needed more animal medication and would return to the warehouse tomorrow. Spooning sugar into a mug of fresh coffee, an image of Cate sprung into his mind. The gulf between them had grown more expansive.

"To hell with her," he said out loud.

Were the truth known, he didn't know how to deal with her constant criticism that led him to the unwavering edge of anger each time he dared to open his mouth. He thought his frailty abhorrent, a deplorable submission that he could overcome with little difficulty. But he was kidding himself; she was too strong for him and, at times, too cruel.

A loud rap of the front door knocker dispelled his thoughts. Before he'd got to his feet, the rap came again—noisier than the first time.

"Alright, alright, I'm not deaf," he shouted, striding down the hallway and tugging open the door.

"Hello, Mr Page, going a little deaf, are we," Mrs Foyle said. "I must remember to knock louder next time. So sorry I never came round earlier as promised. But I thought I'd pop by and tell you that thanks to you, Donny has recovered and running around like a newly born puppy."

"That is good news, Mrs Foyle. Anytime I can be of service. I'm re-opening the surgery in the next few days. I'd be most grateful if you cared to spread the word."

"I shall indeed. Goodbye, Mr Page. God bless you."

*

The following day the wind had dropped to a slight breeze, and the sky had turned the colour of a vanilla milkshake. Council workers finished mowing the grass before winter was upon them. Some, the hardier, leaned on wooden rakes smoking hand-rolled cigarettes. The air was sweet and fresh, spoiled only by the curling smoke from a chimney on the opposite side of the village.

As far as Cate was concerned, it might have been the eye of an arctic storm. After explaining her meeting with Lord Pennywise to Luke, he stared at her in disbelief. Then burst out in uncontrollable laughter.

"You idiot, I wouldn't go near that family with an electric cattle prod. I thought you had more sense."

Cate's eyes flashed.

"How dare you call me an idiot? Stick to changing fuses in plugs; that's all you are fit for."

"Come on, Cate, act your age. I thought you had more sense than to get mixed up with that crowd. Don't tell me you're still intent on joining the Pennywise Hunt."

"Get out, get out and don't come back," Cate shrieked, hurling the cup of coffee at Luke's head.

Luke's laughter turned to a sneer as he dodged the cup.

"No problem. Hadn't you better run to daddy and see who he's murdered today?"

"You disgusting pig, I never want to set eyes on you again."

"My pleasure. You and your kind are more suited to that bunch of Pennywise Neanderthals. I wish you luck. You will need it," Luke said, slamming the door shut behind him,

Cate's eyes burned. Gripping the edge of the wooden chair she fought to force her anger under control. Instead, her temper increased. Blood roared in her ears. As hard as she tried, she couldn't calm herself. Then, suddenly she felt purged. The blackness drifted away on an invisible cloud. When she'd finished cleaning the coffee-stained carpet she felt saddened by how she and Luke had spoken to each other. During her father's absence, Luke had been her rock, steady and caring, ready to provide a sturdy shoulder when things got too much for her. The sound of the door chimes upped her temper a notch. If he thought an apology would suffice, he was out of his tiny mind. Yanking the door open, she gasped, rooted to the ground.

"Alexander, what the devil are you doing here?" she hissed.

"Alexander?" he grinned, "I remember when you called me Xander. By the way, I just passed your boyfriend in the street; he didn't seem too happy. Well, aren't you going to ask me in?"

"One minute, then clear off. And get rid of the

piece of hair hanging from your upper lip."

As he stepped inside, a hint of daylight came through the windows and settled on his face. He looked worn and tired since the last time they'd met—the wispy moustache adding to his demise.

"Well, what is it you want?" Cate asked.

"Father asked me to drop by. He wants to know if you intend to accept his offer."

"I don't know. I haven't had time to think about it."

"Do it, Cate. Get out of this backwater dump before it's too late."

"Don't tell me what to do. Get out of here and tell your father to stick his job where the sun doesn't shine," she said, her voice rising angrily.

"I'm sorry you feel this way after the good times together," Xander answered, stepping towards her with outstretched arms.

Caught off guard at his sudden movement, she slapped him hard across his face. The muscles in his jaw worked. He paused, then turned and reached for the door handle. Cate faltered, knowing he wouldn't hesitate to strike her back.

"Don't you dare think of laying a finger on me? How often must I tell you, get out?" she spat at him.

"All right, I'm going. But think hard on father's offer," he said, slamming the door behind him.

Cate's breath sucked at her heart like a greedy sponge as she struggled to find order in her mind for a moment, then gave up. Behind the wheel of his car, Xander smiled. He could easily control her whenever it suited him; he always could. Seconds later, his phone rang. The name on the illuminated mobile phone screen read, *Father*. Immediately, his adult mind disappeared, replaced with a child's irritability. A message from his father meant trouble, and he could count on being the font.

"Get home, now," his father's reedy voice came. "And I mean now. Not when you feel like it."

Xander's laugh stuck to the back of his throat. Nothing ever changed where his father was concerned. The sky was never blue or white. Clouds never existed. Flipping the phone onto the passenger seat, he started the engine, shoved the lever into drive and headed for Pennywise Manor.

Seated by the window overlooking the village green listening to Elvis croon Suspicious Minds on the radio, Cate's life felt like a storm at sea, dipping one way and then rising the other. At times she felt like a small monkey swinging through the trees, the next a coconut falling from a high branch and smashing to the ground. Quiet sobs racked her body. No matter how hard she tried to hold everything together, the strain of the past was beginning to take its toll.

*

By the time Xander reached Pennywise Mansion,

the sight of two police cars parked on the gravel drive rapidly relieved him of all sense of humour. Fear became paramount as he racked his memory, trying to recollect any misdemeanours he'd been involved in recently. Probably one of the local girls had sworn on oath to the police that he'd raped her and was the father of her illegitimate child. When Xander entered his father's office, he raised an eyebrow and grinned at his father dressed in pyjamas.

"Hello, father," he said, breathing in the aroma of fresh coffee. "Is something wrong?"

"Something wrong, I'll give you something wrong. What the blazes have you been up to this time?"

Instead of answering immediately, Xander busied himself pouring a cup of black coffee. When he'd finished stirring in three sugar lumps, he turned his attention to the man and woman standing quietly by the door.

"Now, perhaps someone will tell me what seems to be the problem?" he asked, pleased at his father's annoyance.

"Detective Inspector Isobel Mattress," the tall thin woman said in a gravelly voice, "And this is Detective Sergeant Down. I understand you had a run-in with a couple of men the night before yesterday on board a barge down by the cut."

DCI Mattress was unlike any policewoman Xander had ever seen. Six feet tall with brown beady eyes, she hovered over him, perfectly groomed and coiffured; she reminded him of a starving vulture waiting to strike. Everything about her struck of discipline except her shoes. Instead of police issue, she wore a pair of dirty white trainers.

Xander fought to keep the distorted amusement from appearing on his face.

"Yes, that's correct," he said. "They were working on a barge when my girlfriend and I passed by. She can get quite boisterous when aroused. I can't blame her when she's around me; I'm quite the lady's man, you know. The men thought I might be harming her and set on me. A bad experience, I can tell you. I have a body full of bruises to prove it."

"The men weren't working on the barge, sir; they were stealing it. When your lady friend started hollering, the men were worried she might attract unwanted attention."

"Do you recall the lady's name by any chance, sir?" Det/Sgt Down interrupted.

Xander shrugged and stared into the gangly policeman's steely grey eyes.

"Her name is Jenny Irons," Xander snapped, looking away from the policeman.

"Would that be the same Miss Irons that came into the station a few months ago and accused you of raping her? Think very carefully before you answer, sir."

"Oh no, not that old ruse again. My two brothers and I only have to glance at a woman to have that lie levelled at us. She's after a quick settlement out of court. A couple of hundred quid usually shuts them up."

Det/Sgt Down's large Adam's Apple bobbed as he fixed his glare on Xander's face. He wanted to laugh at his wispy moustache hanging like burnt candy floss from his top lip; instead, he kept his amusement under control.

"We have both men in custody, and each has made a statement stating you were helping them steal the narrowboat. They swear it was your idea to steal it."

"Utter nonsense. What would I do with a narrowboat?"

"Sell it, perhaps?" Det /Sgt Down said, casting his eyes around the room professionally as if seeking a clue that might bring the meeting to a favourable conclusion.

"If I were to do that, it would be all over the county within minutes. Anyway, I hate water."

"Tell me, Inspector, do you intend to arrest my son?" Lord Pennywise interrupted.

"No, sir, not at the moment. It isn't the first time a narrowboat has gone missing in the last few months. Thank you for your time, sir."

"And the girl's accusation of being raped by my son?"

"I'll have a word with Ms Irons. If she insists on pressing charges, I suggest you find a good solicitor. Goodbye, sir. Thank you for your time."

"Can't you ever keep out of trouble?" Lord

Pennywise hissed at his son.

Xander stared at his father. The pale yellow skin and jigsaw of broken veins just below his face seemed more noticeable. A grown man, Xander resented the influence his father had on him, forever treating him like a gormless adolescence

"I told you, father, I haven't done anything wrong," he snapped, his voice like the crack of a whip across a horse's flanks.

CHAPTER SEVEN

Excitement surged through Anton Page's body. With everything slotted neatly into position, the Veterinary surgery was finally open and ready for business. Spick and span, cupboards laden with everything needed to treat sick animals were full to the brim. Two rows of galvanised steel cages with fresh blankets awaited animals too ill to be loose in the great outdoors. The small waiting room smelled of a hint of lavender. Next to the window, he looked out into the street at passing pedestrians huddled beneath umbrellas battling against a sleeting wind. Not the kind of weather people ventured out with sick animals for treatment, he mused silently. After an hour, he'd given up hoping someone might ring the doorbell and enter as instructed on a small metal plate attached to the wall. Perhaps he was silly to expect a sudden rush of whimpering dogs and hissing cats. Besides, he'd barely spent time advertising the surgery was open for business. Suddenly his thoughts began to melt; drumming his fingers on the tabletop he stared morosely into the mug of tea. Had he made a mistake by rushing things?

Left with no alternative but to shut the surgery and spend more time studying new diseases, it could be months before he re-opened. Eyelids drooping, he sat for a moment. Then drawing in a great breath, he stood upright and reached for the keys to the surgery. Everything he'd worked so hard for had drained into nothing. Perhaps things might be more favourable later, and he'd start again, but time waits for no one. The one redeeming factor he clung to had disappeared into a distant cosmos. The cold sword of failure sliced a path through the fibres of his being. The overhead fluorescent light flickered and buzzed. Seconds later, the surgery became plunged into darkness. He was down and out before he'd started.

Sickened and confused, he busied himself washing the mug under running tap water. When the doorbell rang, he thought loneliness was playing tricks on his hearing. When the doorbell rang again, he turned off the running water tap and headed to the surgery door.

She couldn't have been much older than fifteen. Her hair plastered to her face from the sleeting rain. Dressed in a dark blue anorak, as fashion demanded, there were holes in her jeans. Her features were strong but not coarse. Her mouth was well shaped, her eyes piercing blue and exceedingly precise. Yet, in the greyness of the morning, some might find her beauty meaningless. Tucked under each armpit were metal crutches to help keep her slender body upright.

"Are you the vet man that heals sick animals?" she asked, peering through pebble-lens glasses with pink plastic frames. "Can you make Warrior better?"

Page rocked back on his heels. She looked too young to be out alone in this weather.

"I think you had better come in out of the rain before catching your death," he said, stepping back and pulling open the door.

At first, she hesitated. Then manoeuvring the crutches, she squeezed past Page out of the rain.

"Give me your coat. I'll hang it over a radiator. Wait here while I go and get a towel to dry your hair. Do your parents know you are out in this weather?"

Pale and cold, she looked insubstantial as a small puff of wind. Leaving the question unanswered, she cast her weight to one side on the crutches and unzipped her soaked anorak. Seated on a wooden surgery chair, she took the towel and began to dry her hair. Page took in her chewed fingernails, her frozen hands tinged blue around her knuckles.

"How far have you come?" Page asked.

"Not far, about a mile on the other side of the village."

"What! You walked here alone on crutches through the storm?"

"It's Warrior. He keeps crying."

"Crying? He must be in pain?"

"I don't know, I think so."

"Where is he?"

"In my coat pocket."

"Then you had better get him out and let me look at him. What kind of animal is he?"

"A hamster," she said, searching through the pockets of her wet anorak. "Promise me you won't hurt him?"

"No, I won't hurt him," Page said, holding the animal and peering at him closely. "Hmm, nothing too serious, a case of runny eyes. I'll flush his pouches out with warm water and administer eye drops. He'll be as right as rain in a couple of days. Don't feed him soft food. By the way, do you have a name?"

"Of course I do; everyone has a name."

"Yes, of course, how silly of me," Page smiled patiently.

"I don't think you are silly, and nor does Warrior. My name is Willow."

"An unusual name."

"They all say that," she said, glancing around the surgery. "You don't have many sick animals; do you make them better quickly?"

"No," Page smiled. "I've just opened the surgery, and as you are my first customer, there won't be any charge."

"Thank you. When you have lots of sick animals, can I come and help? I love animals, and they seem to like me. I can clean the place, answer the phone, groom and wash sick animals before surgery."

"Oh, I think it's a bit early to make plans like that. I'll have to have a word with your parents first," Page said, treating her remarks as fleeting. "As soon as you are dry, I'll drive you home. You can't go out in this weather."

"No need. I can find my way," she said sharply.

"How far is to your home?"

"I don't know. How long is a mouse's tail?"

Puzzled at her words, Page couldn't make up his mind to smile or frown.

"What kind of an answer is that?

"It's something I say when I don't know the answer to a question."

"Sounds silly to me."

"Do you know the answer to everything? Do you know how long a mouse's tail is?"

"No."

"Then you can't say it's silly, can you?"

"Wait here until I get my car out of the garage."

Head cocked to one side, she looked at him, wondering why he couldn't understand her words.

"Okay, I'll wait."

When he returned, she was gone. Why would a young girl in her condition venture out in a storm to have a hamster treated, he wondered? Disappointment in having someone to talk to disappear foolishness struck him square in his face. He'd been a fool, not just any fool, but a silly old fool for attempting to seek solace in a child. Shrugging the thought aside, he turned his mind to more important things. Tomorrow he'd purchase a new fluorescent tube for the surgery. It seemed a good enough reason to converse with people to help halt the loneliness gradually eroding his mind.

Like most nights, he found it difficult to sleep. Under cover of darkness, with the bed quilt over his shoulder, he made his way to the lounge and lay on the sofa, listening to the creaking floorboards. His mind on autopilot his thoughts returned to the night he was accused of murdering his wife. Words blundered around his head like black shadows. No matter how hard he tried not to, his memory remained vivid— the sight of her lying on the drive with blood pouring from the head wound. For no particular reason, he stooped and picked up the shovel seconds before the police arrived with sirens blaring and flashing lights. Forced to the ground and handcuffed, a police officer he couldn't see read him his rights. After that, everything descended into a blur and remained that way for the following twenty years. Lately, weeks after his release, he felt nothing had changed.

Late the following afternoon, he woke and feasted on cheese on toast. The weather had turned colder. Convinced nobody would turn up with a sick pet he lit the fire in the lounge.

Eventually, day drifted into the night. Trapped in a world devoid of people, he asked himself, 'What am I doing here?' Then chastised himself. It wasn't something he should dwell on.

Throughout the following night, sleep escaped him. At 7.30 am, dressed and showered, he ate a hearty breakfast for the first time in weeks. The eastern wind had dropped. Of the ginger cat, he'd seen neither hide nor hair for days. Perhaps he'd found a new home, one warm and full of cheer.

Startled by the rapping on the front door, he stiffened.

"Hello," he said, opening the door. "Can I help you?"

"Maybe you can, and maybe you can't. People around here tell me you are a vet," a heavily built man with a broad Irish accent said, pulling off his hat and unwinding his scarf. "It's my dog here. She always seems tired these days she does. She doesn't want to walk anymore. That's not like her, usually fit as a flea in a bat's ear."

Page racked his brain trying to recall if bats suffered from fleas in their ears.

"Best bring the dog inside and let me take a look," Page said, clearing his throat.

Seconds after running his hands over the black Labrador's back and belly, Page gently squeezed the dog's ears.

"Nothing to worry about, sir. She's pregnant."

"Is she now? They'll be going the same way

as the others, in a cloth bag with a brick to send them to the bottom of the river. I can't afford to have dogs running all over the place. Be over in seconds. They won't feel a thing," the man grunted.

It had taken Page twenty years to learn the importance of self-control. Antagonising other prisoners was a surefire invitation to violence from which he might never see the daylight again. What he'd just heard fired his temper so utterly he struggled to get to his feet. Upright and with open contempt, he stared at the man standing before him.

"Leave the dog here until she gives birth. I'll take the pups and find them a home. Now get out."

The man licked his lips and smiled.

"Suit yourself. You can keep the dog for all I care."

Page rubbed his sweating palms down the side of his trousers. In no mood for an argument, he considered the subject closed.

"Lady, that's what I call her. She ain't no lady, that's for sure, I reckon."

*

"Enough, enough," Lord Pennywise hissed, slamming his fist down on the unused leather blotter sending piles of paper fluttering in alarm. Leaning across the desk with his face almost touching Xander's, his long drooping eyebrows concealed rheumy grey eyes, and he reeked of brandy. "Now you listen to me," he snarled, saliva gathering in the corners of his mouth. "God knows how long I've tried to reason with you, but I'm usually wasting my time. Who can reason with a moron?"

"I can't help if Cate refuses to speak to me," Xander snapped, irritated. "Talk to her yourself; I have her number."

*

Pennywise didn't get the opportunity to finish his usual tirade of insults. Instead, white with anger, Xander turned and stalked from the room. Seething with rage, Pennywise turned his attention to his youngest son Nelson.

"And what have you been up to, sitting in the library eating books, I suppose Or trying to work out how a flea can make a whale pregnant," Pennywise grunted.

"On the contrary," Nelson answered in a soft voice. "I've been studying how to win a gold medal in the Olympic Dressage competition. It makes fascinating reading. Perhaps you should lay off the brandy and read it."

Ignoring Nelson's last remark, the anger melted from Pennywise's face.

"By cheating, you mean? There's nothing wrong with that; they're all at it, especially the Russians."

Nelson gave his best lop-sided grin. At last, he'd gained his father's attention and had no intention of letting go.

"More, tell me more," his father said eagerly.

"I haven't finished my studies yet. I'll give you all the necessary information as soon as I have it."

"And how long will that be, for God's sake?"

"Soon, I hope, father, soon."

"Soon? That's no use to me. I need to know now, not next year."

"Yes, father, of course, I understand completely."

"Good, here's your monthly cheque. And give this to your stupid brother Alexander when you see him." Pennywise said, handing Nelson two cheques and waving his hand dismissively. "You may go."

"Yes, thank you, father. May I ask why this money isn't paid online into our accounts?"

"I've no time for those portable knick-knacks. Now stop your blathering and get out of my sight."

Pennywise waited until Nelson closed the door before turning his attention to Wellington, his eldest son.

"And I suppose you've been goose-stepping over the graves in the village cemetery dressed as Hitler. Or whatever it is you do with your bunch of illiterate cronies."

"Father, how could you talk to your eldest son and heir?" Wellington said in a melancholy tone.

"Son and heir, what in the blazes gave you that idea? What would you do, eh, wear skin-tight leather shorts and march on Buckingham Palace with the rest of those degenerate weirdos you call friends? I'll see you hung drawn and quartered first."

"Father, how can you judge me so? It's not fair."

"I know precisely what you are, a homosexual needing constant care and supervision. Be warned my boy. Bring disgrace to this family, and I'll have you dropped in the English Channel with a bucket full of arse cream tied around your neck. Now take your monthly cheque and bugger off out of my sight."

Smarting with anger, Wellington pulled himself up to his full height, gave a smart military about-turn, stamped down his foot and minced from his father's office.

"The old bastards in a bad mood today," he said to his two brothers waiting in the corridor.

"He hasn't been the same since old man Page got out of jail," Xander said.

"Yes, I noticed that too. The old boy seemed rather more agitated than normal. The cock and bull story about winning the Dressage at the next Olympics might help keep him quiet for a few days."

"You mean it was all a pack of bullshit?"

"Of course it was. I had to keep the old boy sweet until we had our cheques, didn't I?"

"Do you think he has a connection with the death of Page's wife?" Wellington asked.

"Twenty years ago, who knows what the old bastard got up to during all that time? Best ask, Onions. He reckons he's the font of information," Nelson said.

"Leave it. It's none of our damn business, Xander growled.

"Ooh, touched a nerve, have we?" Wellington laughed.

"How would you like a smack in the face? You jumped up perve?" Xander snapped, his face red with anger.

"Come on, boys, the last one in the Crooked Stick get the first round in," Nelson giggled.

CHAPTER EIGHT

Business at Pages surgery finally began to show an improvement. Slow at first but gradually improving as time passed, without subterfuge, owners with sick pets confided in the various ailments of their beloved animals. His regular contributors were mainly elderly people who looked upon their pets as their last link with life. Familiar with most of them, Page quickly found himself the oracle of village gossip on who did this and said things they ought not. After producing five healthy pups Lady the Labrador followed him everywhere. Three of the pups were promised good homes when they reached the age of ten weeks. Late one evening, Wellington Pennywise visited the surgery. Hearing puppies were going free to good homes, he promised to take the remaining two to roam free on the Pennywise estate. Happy to consent, Page felt compelled to ask Wellington to stay for coffee for reasons he couldn't explain. Adrenaline coursed through his veins when Wellington accepted the invitation. Most of the time, Wellington went into great detail informing Page of his father's improvements on the estate. When the time arrived to leave, Page gripped his hand and stared into his eyes as if there was something he should know. It had been a long time since he had felt so vitalised. An hour later, Cate turned up unexpectedly.

"Wow, all those people with their pets, and so soon. Well done you," she cried

Page's face spread into a wide grin, aware he must stay focused. Formalities dispensed, Cate tugged Lady's ears and told her what a clever doggy she was to have such a beautiful family of gorgeous puppies.

"By the way, there's quite a crowd in Sanderson's field. Someone or something has butchered a horse. I think it best you get over there as soon as possible. Forget the local hostilities, and remember you're the local vet. I'll drive you there if you like."

Page nodded his assent.

"I'll get my coat and bag."

Forced to duck to avoid a spiky bush before emerging into an open field, Page gasped and stood rooted to the spot. Anger twisted deep inside him at seeing a horse lying covered in blood and staring placidly up at the sky. After carefully examining the horse, his rage rose at the comments aimed at him from the local villagers crowding around for a better look.

"Get away from here, you bunch of bloodthirsty arseholes. Go on, get back in your caves," Page roared.

"You heard the man. Go home, now," a uniformed policeman shouted.

"Thank you, Constable," Page said, wiping dried blood from the horse's neck with a small towel.

"Dogs again, I reckon; the village is full of them wandering around loose," the policeman said.

Page had often been called to heal a sick animal and found it cold and dead. But this time, it was different and unnatural.

"I don't think so. See these marks on the neck? They were made with a knife. Someone stabbed the horse to death and cut out the heart while the animal was still alive."

The Policeman removed his hat, revealing a thatch of neatly cut straw hair.

"Makes you sick. The same thing happened a couple of years ago. They never found out who was responsible—dropped after a couple of weeks, lack of evidence, they said, bloody shame. These wild horses have grazed here for years. They help to keep the woods and land in good condition."

"Yes, I agree. Someone hunted this horse down and butchered it for no reason," Page answered thoughtfully.

"The locals believe it's witchcraft. Weird sods these villagers are. I wouldn't put anything past them. I'll call the station and tell them what you have told me. Be a great help if you stayed until someone turns up from the station if you don't mind, sir."

"Yes, of course, and have the carcass removed as soon as possible. A great deal of flesh is missing from the horse's front legs. Could have been a fox."

"Or somebody looking for a free meal," the policeman grimaced, sending a message on the radio attached to his tunic collar.

Det/Sgt Down had barely said a word since his appearance. Instead, in a manner suited to a dutiful police officer, he stared around the paddock and then swept his eyes at the nearby woods as if seeking a hidden clue.

"Seen this twice before during the last six or seven years. Used to think it was travellers, but they wouldn't treat horses this way," Down grunted. "I'll have men search the woods for anything that might help find the arsehole responsible for this. Pound to a penny, we won't find anything."

"Did you ever find the person responsible or suspect anyone?" Page asked.

"No, always strange goings-on up at Pennywise Manor. Bonfires and loud music were nothing unusual. Some of the villagers reckon they have seen naked people prancing around."

Page wanted to question him further. Instead, he remained silent. It was common knowledge Pennywise Manor was off-limits to the police.

Anyone caught snooping around the grounds would receive a heavy fine in the local court. Many in the village beggared belief why Pennywise held such sway over the police.

"There's been reports of a crazy wild man living in the forest. We'll investigate the death of the horse, but I don't hold out much hope. Thank you for assisting Mr Page," Down said, watching DCI Mattress struggle from her car.

"Everything under control, sergeant?" she said, watching Page stride away.

"Yes, ma-am. Strange fish that Page. I ran a check on him the minute he returned to the village. Do you know he passed with honours at a top veterinary college and turned down job offers from London Zoo and animal sanctuaries worldwide, apart from a year in Africa? He made quite a name for himself inside the nick. Once the prison governor discovered he was a vet, he brought his two Labradors in for Page to look over. Prepared to do anything to keep the lid on the boiling prison, he allowed prisoners' wives to bring in their sick pets once a fortnight for Page to treat. As his popularity increased, the prison governor approached Page to give a talk to the prisoners about sick pets and the simple ways to avoid expensive vet bills. Once a week, prisoners crammed into his classes. It made Page quite a celebrity, especially with the real hard nuts and lifers. Nobody dared to bother him for fear of reprisals. Before his internment, he'd hardly left the village unless to treat a sick animal. He did a bit of woodcarving until he married Lizzie Clark, the village beauty. It was thought a bad match with her family steeped in witchcraft and his wealthy family on friendly terms with Lord Pennywise. Did you know the Peruvian police held his parents for stealing holy Inca relics while trekking in Peru? When they were released, they kept defiling sites for artefacts until they were captured and killed by bandits."

"Really? And what about now?"

"Right now, Page isn't popular with most of the villagers after the death of his wife."

"And the rest?"

"Most jump a mile at the mention of his name."

"Probably scares the life out of them knowing he's done time and has the ear of some right nutters."

"He's a strange character. Twenty years inside for murder, and he acts as if butter wouldn't melt in his mouth."

"Hmm, best keep an eye on him."

*

Eager to know more, Page questioned Cate about the horse's death during the ride home.

"What do you think happened?" he asked

"Who knows? Thousands of people visit the forest each year; it's common knowledge it's steeped in witchcraft. That's what attracts many of them in the first place; the sense of the macabre. The police won't do much. An increase in their presence will only frighten away the tourists, and that won't go down too well."

"So you think it is something to do with witchcraft?"

"I don't know what to think."

"Thought any more about Lord Pennywise's offer?" Page asked, changing the subject.

"I'll give it a miss. I don't want to get too close to Pennywise and his family," Cate answered, her face reddening.

"A wise decision."

Cate's face twitched into a frown. She remained silent, choosing not to reply until they pulled onto Page's drive.

"Looks like you have a visitor, a kid on crutches. She looks as if she could do with a sit-down."

"Hello, Willow. Can I help you?" Page said.

Willow fidgeted with her crutches before answering.

"I've come to see how Lady's getting on with her new puppies."

"She's fine. I've found homes for the pups. Why do you ask?"

"Because she is my dog, not my dad's. He had no right to give her away."

Page sensed the irritation in her voice.

"No problem. You can have Lady back as soon as the pups are ready to go to new homes. How does that sound?"

Willow didn't have time to dwell on his words. Grabbing at fresh air, she lost her balance and fell, striking her head against the concrete step leading to the front door. Page quickly stepped forward and, taking her in his arms, pushed open the front door, entered the bungalow and laid her on the small dining table as Cate entered the room.

"Oh my God, what happened?"

"Her crutches gave way, and she fell and struck her head."

"Does she need an ambulance?"

"I don't think so," Page said, pulling Willow's hair from the wound. "Fortunately, only the skin is broken."

"Just the same; I'll take her to A&E. Best make sure she's okay."

Three hours passed before Cate returned with Willow's head wrapped in a bandage.

"Nothing serious. According to the doctor, she'll have a headache, after which she'll be fine. You do know she doesn't have a home address?"

"Really," Page answered, stepping back from a blinding shaft of sunlight slicing through the coloured glass of the front door. "She must live somewhere."

"Well, I couldn't get it out of her, nor could the hospital."

"Stop worrying. I'll be fine in a minute; can I see Lady and the pups now?" Willow said, staring at him, her coyness evaporating like dew beneath a rising sun.

"Later," Page said. "Best you sit still and take it easy. How about I make you a cup of tea?"

"Don't mind," Willow answered, tucking a lock of hair behind her ear. "Seeing you're so interested, I live in a caravan with my dad on the other side of the village. People call us travellers."

Startled by her words Page dropped his gaze. Cate remained silent stirring teabags in hot water, then absently added sugar regardless of who wanted it.

"You shouldn't stir teabags in hot water. Taste better if you left them to fuse for a minute," Willow said. "I thought everyone knew that."

"Well, pardon me for being so thick," Cate grinned. "How long have you lived there?"

"Three weeks. We'll leave soon; dad wants to return to Ireland for his brother's funeral."

"I'm sorry to hear that."

"Don't be. I don't like drunkenness, fighting, and singing dirty songs. Be a month before they stop. It's no way to see a man off."

Page turned and, tugging the curtains, peered outside. He knew how it felt to be somewhere you didn't want to be. Restless, he turned and faced Willow.

"When you have finished your tea, you'll find Lady with her puppies and Tommy in the surgery."

"Tommy, who's Tommy?"

"A big ginger cat who wandered in some time

ago and stayed. He and Lady have struck up a friendship and become almost inseparable."

"Oh, how wonderful, a cat and a dog caring for newborn puppies," Willow said, her face alight with genuine pleasure.

Rushing to get to her feet, she lost her balance. Cate's reaction saved her from falling.

"My my, are you always like this," Cate laughed.

"It's animals. I love animals. I'm so sorry for being so clumsy."

*

It took Cate two hours to prize Willow from the surgery floor. Lady lay fast asleep with her head on her chest. Tommy was curled up between her legs while the pups crawled over her.

"She certainly has a way with animals," Cate smiled.

"It would seem so." Page answered, nudging Willow's arm. "Come along, Willow. Time to get you home."

"Can't I stay a little longer, please?"

"No, your father will wonder where you are."

"He won't be bothered."

"Bothered or not, I'm taking you home. You can give me directions to your caravan."

Willow rose, grabbed her crutches and made her way to the front door.

"I can find my way," she said hurriedly. "It's not far."

"In the car, please."

It was plain to Page that Willow had a mind of her own.

The rain had ceased by the time they arrived at her caravan. Page applied the handbrake and looked around. A small copse surrounded by trees and overhanging bushes was eerily silent —the occasional sound of birdsong the only disturbance.

"Follow me," Willow said quietly. "Dad prefers to keep his distance from people."

Page watched her tug at broken branches until she'd cleared a narrow pathway.

"That you, girl?" a loud booming voice called.

"Yes, Dad, and I have a visitor with me."

"How many times have I told to keep away from folk? Troublemakers, the bunch of them," the booming voice turned to an angry roar.

"It's the vet you gave Lady away to."

Startled by the sound of breaking branches, Page stiffened, fearful for his safety. Unearthed decaying bodies weren't rare in the woods. Since the days they were inhabited by the Romans, Vikings, and Saxons, strange things have happened in the woods hundreds of years ago. Even today, rumours of untold secrets lay hidden below the earth, obscured from sight.

Page stared at the heavily built man who'd left Lady at the surgery. He'd grown the makings of a beard tinged grey on the fringes, and he looked larger than Page remembered.

"Oh, so it's you; she keeps running off to see.

Like young women, do you?"

Pages eyes narrowed. His heartbeat quickened. Charlie Dot, a lifer in prison, had taught him how to drop a man using the index finger pushed behind the breastbone, but force was the last thing on Page's mind.

"Stop it, father, leave him alone. He's not like that."

"Get in the caravan. I'll deal with you later, girl."

"Beat her, will you," Page growled, surprised by the precision of his words. "You look the type to pick on defenceless young girls. How about picking on someone your size? There's been a spate of break-ins lately. I reckon you might be just what the police are looking for."

"Get in the caravan, Willow; I won't tell you again. How often have I told you this happens when you mix with this kind?" the man sneered.

"No, father, I'll run away again. You can't stop me."

"Not if I bust those tin crutches, you won't."

Page reacted as if something unworldly had taken control of his tongue.

"Get back in my car, Willow. We're leaving," he growled, watching and waiting for what might happen next.

"You're welcome to the clumsy cow. I found her fast asleep in the woods a few years back. Only took her in because she had nowhere to go, or so she told me."

Page stared at him, and plucking up the courage, he grabbed Willow and guided her back to his car.

"Wait," Willow cried, turning to face the man she'd accepted as her father, "Thank you for looking after me."

A cloud passed over the man's face. Glancing at the ground, he poked the loose earth with the toe of his boot.

"No need to thank me, girl. Go with the man and start a new life. The open road was never meant for the likes of you."

"I'll never forget what you have done for me."

Willow wasn't, by nature a timid person. Regardless of her condition, she could fight her corner. But today, tears streamed down her face, her crutches slipped from her grasp, and she slowly sank sobbing to the ground.

"One day, you'll grow up and find a man who will help you walk again," the man said quietly."

A blackness spread throughout her body like spilt ink on paper. The world and all its glory held no curiosity or memory; all she'd ever known was silence and solitude. Page stumbled forward and lifted her in her arms. Surprised by the frailness of her body, he laid her gently on the rear seat of his car. Then turned at the sound of breaking twigs and faced the man Willow called father.

"She'll need these," he said, handing Page Willow's crutches. "Give her the life she deserves.

I was of no use to her. A month after I took her in, she told me she couldn't stand without support, so we got a pair of crutches from a second-hand shop. I'll be gone by morning. Make sure she doesn't try to find me."

Page's eyebrows rose. The muscles in his face jumped. Without bothering to answer, he started the car and drove away.

CHAPTER NINE

With a face like a stone gargoyle, Lord Pennywise glared at his three sons gathered before him. Filled with recrimination bordering on naked dislike, he speculated whether he had grown too old and brittle to handle the stress they brought him. Like hungry vultures, they gazed back, waiting to hear what he had on his mind —no sign of humbleness or slightest shadow of humility present in their expressions. The mere sight of them clenched his bones. Inside he seethed with anger wondering why he didn't drown them at birth. To his way of thinking, the blame lay squarely on his late wife, who had been dead for the last sixteen years. A cold and arrogant woman, the daughter of a bankrupt Earl, she made it plain to those who could hear that she was unwilling to breathe the air of ordinary people less it tainted the nobility of her lungs. After a month of marriage, he horsewhipped her to instil a fraction of sense where only foolishness existed. She spat in his face and walked naked from the waist up around the house to show the servants how their master treated her.

"The police are appealing for witnesses to an attack on a horse in Sanderson's Field. The creature was stabbed to death following a similar incident eighteen months ago. Residents from neighbouring villages are demanding a meeting with the police for reassurance it won't happen again. I don't suppose any of you three know anything about it?" Lord Pennywise said.

Braving a broadside of unwavering anger, Wellington spoke first.

"Why do you automatically think we are involved whenever something goes wrong around here?"

"Because it is exactly the type of event I would expect from a poof like you. Does that answer your question?"

"That is so unfair, father," Nelson burst out angrily.

Pennywise drained the remains of a glass of whiskey and water down his throat before answering.

"Unfair? Having to tolerate you bunch of whining misfits, that's unfair," Pennywise bellowed. "For God's sake, the three of you are past thirty and still living under my roof. Well, I warn you, things are about to change. I want you out of here by the end of the month. I shall transfer one million pounds to each of your accounts, after which I shall add a further million for each legal grandchild you produce over the next three years."

Nelson, who always sought solitude and considered himself the steadiest of his brothers, couldn't believe what he'd just heard.

"Isn't that a bit severe, father?" He gulped.

"Severe, more like criminal. If mother were alive, she'd stop this nonsense," Wellington roared angrily.

Xander smelled the fear permeating from his brothers. It struck him as funny and did nothing to prevent his grin from widening.

"These grandchildren you mentioned. Must we be married to their mothers?" he asked.

"I'll have no bastards in my house," Lord Pennywise's face twitched. "Show me birth certificates verifying their existence, or you'll not receive a penny. And as for you, Wellington, if your mother were alive today, I'd throw her to the dogs for giving birth to the likes of you. Now get out of my sight."

Seated on a wooden bench in the rear garden behind the freshly painted gazebo, Wellington fought to control the tremor in his hands. His anger churned like mortar in a cement mixer. The encounter with his father had affected him more than he'd expected. Eyes like hot coals, the thought of murdering his father strengthened until it occupied his mind like cancer. But he wasn't foolish enough to realise that whatever his inner thoughts might be, he'd have to pull himself together before he crossed swords with his father.

"Fuck him. The old bastard doesn't deserve to live. Billions in the bank, and he treats us no better than the servants. It's time it stopped, and we each get what we deserve. If not, I swear I'll kill him with my bare hands," he growled, glaring at his brothers.

"Deserve? You jumped up ponce. Just what is it you think you deserve? And as for killing him, you lack the bottle, Beaky," Nelson laughed aloud.

"Stuff you, you shiny-arsed pen pusher and don't call me old Beaky. You know how I hate the name."

"Stop being a Prima Donna. There is nothing wrong with being called old Beaky after the Duke of Wellington; Judging by the enormous size of your nose, you should look upon it as an honour."

"Bullshit."

"Well, good luck, boys; I'm off to find a wife. A million quid for every nipper? Money for old rope," Xander laughed, bending down to rub Barney's labrador's ears. Barney raised his head and sniffed the air, his face puzzled and alert.

"Trust you to find it amusing. One day your cock will rot and drop off and serve you right," Wellington sneered.

*

Cate was still at the bungalow when Page arrived accompanied by Willow—wrapped in a ball of silence, barely a word passed between them during the journey. Due to his interference, he had no choice but to provide Willow with a roof over her head. The problem remained; it was his duty to contact social services. The mere thought he might be breaking the law raised the hairs on his arms like the quills of a porcupine.

Entering the bungalow, Page explained to Cate what had happened. Cate remained silent before answering with a shrug of her shoulders.

"So you have rendered Willow homeless. She'll have to be put in a home until she is old enough to leave?" Cate said.

"That's not true," Willow interrupted. "I'm eighteen years old and free to go and do as I please. No need to worry over me. I'll leave first thing in the morning."

"Sixteen years old?" Page blustered, "You don't look a day over fourteen."

"Lucky me," Willow snapped.

"All right, all right, arguing won't get us anywhere," Cate shouted. "Run her a bath, and Willow, stay in the bathroom until I return. I have clean pyjamas at home you can wear overnight. In the meantime, I'll put your clothes in the wash."

Page and Willow still hadn't moved when Cate slammed the door shut and left.

Eventually, Page managed a forced smile.

"Right," he said. "I'll run the bath and get the bed ready in the spare room. A right old lark this is if you ask me."

Willow remained quiet. Happy would be too strong a word to describe her mood. Now, more than at any other time during her life, she hoped, at last things might change for the better. She viewed Mr Page as a kindly man who cared for sick animals, whereas others would have the creature euphonised to save the cost of treatment. His daughter Cate was the most beautiful woman she'd ever seen. Leaning forward with her chin resting on her chest, she whispered a small prayer that she might be allowed to stay. And, who knows, perhaps help Mr Page care for the sick animals.

"Okay, your bath is ready. Cate will sort you out when she returns. She shouldn't be too long."

"Sounds nice," she answered bluntly.

Page opened his mouth and laughed. He'd yet to hear her say thank you. Not that it bothered him. He found it amusing.

Two hours had passed when Cate prised a shivering Willow out of the bath and told her to try on a pair of her old pyjamas. She laughed when Willow told her it was the first time she could remember having a bath.

"We only had a lukewarm shower in the caravan. Dad said we couldn't afford hot water," Willow told her, then raised her hands to her lips. "I keep saying that, but he wasn't my real dad?"

"Maybe he wasn't, but never forget all the things he did for you," Cate answered in a firm voice. "Right, the pyjamas fit a little large, but that isn't a problem. Best you go to your room and dry your hair, in the meantime I'll put your clothes in the wash. Tomorrow, we'll go shopping for new clothes for you. Would you like that?"

Willow's eyes shone.

"How long is a mouse's tail," she answered quietly.

*

The following morning Wellington sat with crossed legs in the old hay barn opposite the church cemetery. The two pups he had taken from Page sat before him with wagging tails staring into his face.

"Right, boys. I need a plan to eliminate that old bastard who calls himself my father. What do you suggest? Dylan, what about you? Do you have any ideas? There's a big bone in it for a foolproof plan."

Dylan licked his lips and wagged his tail."

"No, Just as I thought, nothing to say? How about you, Thomas? What are your thoughts on my dilemma?"

Thomas stretched out his front legs and lay on his belly with his chin resting on his paws. Then yawned and rolled over on his back.

"Hmm, I suppose I should have known better than to ask. Let's see if you can catch rabbits better than think up murderous plans."

Bristling with urgency, Wellington strode towards the Manor. Wet mud sucked at the soles of his boots, threatening to pull him down and swallow him into the earth's bowels. Find a wife and produce children, he'd father had said. What in God's name was wrong with the stupid old fool? His father made no secret that he hated women, whatever their age. He said he found them dirty, constantly bleeding from the most unnatural places each month. As for children, their mere thought shook him to the core and threatened to turn him into a suitable candidate for the nearest asylum. Growing grumpier by the minute, Wellington's mind turned to the ridiculous. Perhaps he could produce a child if he closed his eyes rather than gaze into a woman's face. But that wouldn't be enough for his father. He had to marry the bitch to boot. If that weren't enough, no doubt she'd lay claim to half his money when she found out the real reason for the marriage. He'd speak with Beelzebub. They'd spoken before whilst under the green magic, or perhaps he'd try something more substantial. A line of 'coke' would do fine. The thought stopped him dead in his tracks. Why should he go through all this with his future at stake and his legacy unfulfilled? A gun, knife, or thick cudgel would provide a more straightforward answer to his prayers.

*

Cate was happy to take a few extra days off from teaching. Since her father's return, her nerves had become fragile, and her physical resources drained like a squeezed sponge. Perhaps a long lazy bath with a bottle of red would help to hasten her recovery.

The morning light was the colour of milky coffee when she woke still wearing her dressing gown. Recently she hadn't felt her old self, but after sleeping solidly for ten hours she felt better than she had for a long time. Showered and refreshed, she pulled back the curtains surprised to be confronted by the countryside full of snow. The scene gave her a sense of security as childish images of Robins, Christmas trees, and Holly flashed through her mind. The uneasy understanding of being manipulated differed from volunteering for events that didn't sit easily on the mind. Remaining close to her father had failed to leave pleasant memories. People whom she considered to be good friends began to shun her. She was paying for her father's mistakes. Willow, the young traveller girl, had entered her life, adding further complications. Hunched over a freshly made cup of coffee, she watched the breeze whip up a snowstorm through the kitchen window. Minutes passed before the phone rang.

"Willow mentioned you were taking her to town to buy her new clothes. Is that right?" Page asked

Cate pulled the phone from her ear and took a deep breath.

"Yes, is that a problem?" she snapped, pulling

the phone back to her ear.

"No, I'm just asking."

"Well, don't," she said, thumbing hard on the red button killing the call.

Seconds later, the landline phone rang.

"Yes, who is it? And no, I don't want to buy it."

"It's me, Xander. Father wants an answer to his offer today."

"Really? My kneecaps are trembling with fright."

"You can be a real awkward bitch at times."

"The answer is no. I don't want to work with your father's horses now or any other time. Is that clear enough?"

"Clear as a bell. By the way, you wouldn't consider marrying me and giving me children. I can make it worth your while."

Rooted to the spot, she burst out with laughter.

"You are one sick bastard, Xander. Have you lost your senses?"

When the line clicked, dead Cate wished Xander was here so she could open his testicles using the electric can opener fixed to the kitchen wall. Or press her thumbs into his leering brown eyes and split them open like ripe grapes.

The thought of her father flashed into her mind. It had been her idea to take Willow into town, and the last thing she wanted was her father tagging along, offering advice on how to dress a girl of eighteen.

Roads packed tight with snow, and filthy sludge made the fifteen-minute car journey to her father's bungalow twice as long as usual. With hardly enough time to get the car heater working, she shivered with cold when she entered her father's bungalow. Immediately she noticed the look on Willow's face. It wasn't a smile nor a grimace but more a glimpse of grim determination. Trouble was brewing.

"It's nice you came. I knew you would," Willow said, pushing a lock of straw-coloured hair away from her eyes."

"I always keep my promises; where's father?"

"He's cleaning the floor in the surgery."

"Good, come on, let's get out of here. Bye, Father, see you later," she called, smiling and ushering Willow out the door.

*

In the privacy of his bedroom, Nelson reeled from his father's words. What did he know about women, worst still making babies? Other plans, lists and agendas filled his mind, including reading the massive pile of books inches from the ceiling. The gothic romance he planned to write had stuttered to a halt in the second chapter while he laboured over a violent love scene. The pleasure and anticipation of his trip to Venice had vanished like smoke into the fresh air. Wellington had been correct; his father must go if he wished to continue his life of ease and learning. But it would be easier said than done.

The thought of bloodshed set his legs trembling.

Nevertheless, the thought helped to brighten his day. Sat back in his comfy armchair with arms folded, he considered the best way to be rid of his father. Once he'd made the first move there could be no turning back. Great care to cover his tracks and avoid suspicion would be vital. Better still, if he could make it appear that someone else was guilty. Discussing the matter with Wellington was one option. But Wellington could be foolhardy and impatient. He'd want to dance on his father's corpse seconds after taking his last breath. Then there was Xander, who relished the thought of producing children at a million pounds each. While tapping his toes on the hardwood floor, his mind went into overdrive. The idea of murdering his father was becoming a drug. A strange look covered his face. Grimacing and smiling simultaneously, he swallowed the last mouthful of coffee and wiped the saliva from his mouth with a table napkin. For the first time in his life, he felt alive.

CHAPTER TEN

When Willow finally chose which pair of jeans suited her best, breathless and relieved, Cates's role as a fictional fashion expert lay in tatters.

"I think four hours to choose a pair of jeans is excessive, don't you?" Cate said, wiping her brow.

"How long is a mouse's tail? My Dad taught me to get value for money."

Cate cocked her head to one side and stared into Willow's face. Willow covered her mouth with her hand and giggled.

"Sorry, I keep forgetting he wasn't my father."

After two hours, a warm rush ran through Cate's tired body. The shopping expedition had finally reached its climax. With two pairs of jeans, a pair of trainers, a couple of sweatshirts, and underwear safely in the car's boot, she and Willow headed for Page's bungalow. Willow's shoulders sank back into the leather seat. It was a dream come true. She couldn't wish for more with new clothes and a roof over her head. Forty-five minutes later, her mood turned to shock. Someone had sprayed the word 'murderer' the length of the bungalow. Paint cans lay leaking and splattered over the pathway and garden. Willow blinked and reached out to grab Cate's hand, hoping it might make the sight disappear.

"Bastards," Cate spat, wiping a hand across her mouth. "I'll make it my business to find the scum that did this.

Willow remained as still as a concrete statue with tears streaming down her face.

"Don't worry. We'll have it cleaned away in minutes," Cate said soothingly.

"But why? Who would do such a bad thing?" Willow whispered.

"Good-for-nothing morons who have nothing better to do with their pathetic little lives."

The front door swung open without warning, and Page stepped out onto the garden. Pale and bent, bitterness soured his throat as he ran his eyes over the bungalow.

"I saw who did it," he said hoarsely. "It wasn't someone young. He was elderly and gasped for breath."

"Did you see his face? Would you recognise him if you saw him again?" Cate said quickly.

"No, he had one of those balaclava things the SAS wear over his face. He was halfway down the garden pathway when I opened the front door. He got into a black van with another man behind the wheel."

"Did you get the registration number?"

"No, I forgot all about that."

"That's a pity. Let us go inside, put the kettle

on, and make a fresh pot of tea. This is far from over."

"Let me make the tea, please. I want to help," Willow said, placing a reassuring hand on Page's arm as Lady bounded out the bungalow door.

Page didn't feel the heat from the orange embers glowing beneath a layer of grey ashes in the fireplace. Nor did he turn away as Lady shook the loose snow from her coat. Cate raised and dropped a tense shoulder.

"I think it best I call the police," she said.

"No, no, that won't be necessary. I'll deal with it," Page snapped.

Goosebumps rippled up Cate's arm.

"What do you mean; you'll deal with it?" Cate's voice rose and broke. "It's a bit late to install security cameras?"

"Don't you ever listen to anything I say instead of questioning everything?" Page said quietly.

Cate looked away wishing she hadn't spoken. Discounting the past twenty years he'd spent locked away in prison, she knew he wasn't the kind of man who lost his temper quickly. She glanced sideways at him; he looked different. His eyes had taken on a hint of grey she'd never seen before. His jaw was thrusting and set. He wasn't the man she knew as her father; this was a man manufactured from the depth of prison life. Something dark and sinister.

Cate's gaze jumped back and forth between them.

"Okay, we'll do it your way. Do you mind telling me what you have in mind?" she said in a level voice.

Page hesitated before answering.

"I'll tell you what I intend to do when the time is right."

Darkness had fallen by the time Cate left. The hours spent drinking coffee in silence had amounted to nothing. Without uttering another word, Willow disappeared into her bedroom. Ten minutes later, she appeared dressed in the clothes Cate had purchased.

She looked so small and vulnerable, her face was pink, and her hair was tousled.

"Well, that is a big improvement," Page nodded. "Quite a beauty behind all that grime, aren't you? You mustn't worry about what has happened tonight. You do know that, don't you?"

Willow shifted her weight from one crutch to another, hopeful of gaining some small comfort.

"I want to help."

"No need for that; I can manage."

Although his voice sounded profound and soothing, Willow felt her neck tighten. Teeth clamped tight together she exhaled a long sigh. They were in this together, and regardless of her condition, he could rely on her.

"Would you mind leaving? I have some things I need to deal with?" Page said with a dismissive wave of his hand.

Willow frowned.

"Don't mind if I do," she said sullenly.

Inside her bedroom, tears sprung into her eyes. Every ounce of strength in her muscles dissolved. No longer capable of holding her body upright with the make-shift crutches, her shoulders sagged and her head drooped. Quite a beauty, he called her. Nobody had ever said that to her before.

Page ceased drumming his fingers on the arm of the chair. If the villagers wanted a battle, he'd give them one they wouldn't forget in a hurry. One that would make today's events dim like a vicar's picnic. He extracted a small notebook from a drawer and flicked through the pages containing memories of his time in prison. Names, telephone numbers and addresses of those he chose as friends neatly written in pencil as clear as the day he wrote them. He recalled their crimes, GBH, murder, arson, drug lords, and rapists. He knew them in a different light. The one thing they had in common was the constant struggle with prison life. After their incarceration, those he considered friends told him that anytime he needed help, he was to contact them. For a brief moment, he dismissed the thought as ridiculous. There were more compelling reasons than to set the wheels of hatred rolling out of control in the village. In sudden reflection, he reached down and patted Tommy's ginger coat.

"Decided to return, have you. Well, it's good

to see you, my friend," he smiled, turning his attention back to the notebook.

Curled blissfully on Page's lap Tommy closed his eyes. He'd lived a good life and hadn't the remotest intention of wandering off into cold nights and frosty mornings for longer than necessary.

The fire in the room had sunk—the ash sighed as it dropped into the grate. Flecks of saliva gathered on Page's mouth when he re-opened the book. To hell with it, he thought, without shame or merit. Damn them. Someone must pay for defacing his home. It took seconds to choose the man's name he intended to contact the next day. Satisfied he'd made the right choice, he lay back and closed his eyes feeling more tired than he'd first thought.

*

Like most nights Page still found it difficult to sleep. That night was no different. Sleep came in short bursts full of strange dreams and flashing nightmares. At 5 am, as daylight probed through the windows he'd had enough of trying to sleep. Dressed, he entered the kitchen, then stopped and listened to the sound of heavy breathing echoing off the walls

"Oh, sorry if I woke you. I need to exercise, and the bedroom is too small."

Surprise and relief hummed beneath Page's skin at the sight of Willow stretched out on the kitchen floor. Her blue eyes shone like wet pebbles, and the plain metal clip in her hair glinted each time she shifted her position.

"Help me up and pass my crutches, and I'll leave you in peace?"

Page bent and gently raised her to her feet, then passed her the crutches.

"Have you seen a doctor about your legs?" He asked.

" No, the man I called dad said I would grow out of it."

"Utter nonsense. I'll ring the village doctor first thing in the morning."

"That would be nice. It's already the first thing in the morning?" she giggled.

Page grinned.

"So, you are a comedian as well?"

"Not at all. I see things as they are. Didn't you notice the sun coming through the windows? " she answered. "Why are you always so unhappy? Don't you like people, or don't they like you? I think you are a nice man."

Page blushed, trying to brush away her questions. Since returning to his bungalow, he'd suffered from prolonged fits of melancholy. He often talked to himself, pretending that Lizzie was alive and loved him dearly. Willow's honesty had jerked him out of a dark shadow. Aware that most villagers would never accept him back into the fold where he longed to be, anger lurked next to muffled violence waiting to explode. The time had come for him to seek revenge

Exhaling a sigh, he left the room, entered the hallway, pulled the small notebook from his back pocket, and studied the list of names. After two attempts, the person he wanted to speak to eventually answered his call.

CHAPTER ELEVEN

A cluster of cottages around the Crooked Stick Inn provided easy access to those who found a lasting companionship in alcohol. The ivy-clad walls were crumbling, and the rooms were damp with a cold, wet winter air invasion. Wildly out of control, the once carefully tendered garden lay hidden beneath the onslaught of choking weeds. Legend had it a dead witch killed by a warlock for her power haunted the building. Villagers laughed at the tale but used the story to frighten away unwanted wealthy tourists looking to buy a second home.

Arthur Parrot, the landlord, a tall, gangly man with prominent elbows between long thick muscular forearms, was known affectionately as 'Polly'. A microscope would be necessary to detect the fuse leading to his quick, brutal temper. On the verge of puberty, his sons, Elvis and Jerry Lee, named after two early rock'n'roll stars, hated their father with a twisted vengeance. Only the naked fear of his legendary temper kept them from repaying the endless hidings they'd received with monotonous regularity as children. Their common denominator; was their mother, Doreen, a whippet-thin woman with a stare to make Jesus blink. Her thoughts kept to herself; she found solace in a large Bulldog named Peggotty. An ugly mutt as unfriendly as a hungry snake in a cage full of mice responded to no one but her. Drinkers learned to keep a wary eye on the animal since a regular had his ankle chewed to the bone after exposing himself in the lady's toilet. Regardless of this, discounting it was the only pub for miles around and the atmosphere of a cemetery, it was well attended on weekdays and brimming full weekends.

Four days before Christmas Day, to the sound of a sixties rock'n'roll song accompanied by growling guitars and thrusting drums from a chipped wooden jukebox, a tall thin man dressed in black and wearing a large wide-brimmed hat, the type worn by Spanish flamenco dancers, concealing the upper half of his face entered the inn. Raising an aluminium walking stick, he rapped sharply on the bar.

"Is anyone serving, or are they busy discussing life insurance?" he hollered. "Or perhaps have I entered a home for geriatric zombies?"

The jukebox relinquished its attack on the senses, and a hush fell over the room. Polly

Parrott forced his mouth full of saliva and ran his tongue around his lips.

"Wait your turn. You'll be served when I'm good and ready," Polly growled.

The man in black smiled, displaying a set of perfect gleaming white teeth below a thin pencil moustache.

"Now, listen to me, you country bumpkin. I demand to be served now."

Hands impulsively balled into fists, Polly's breath quickened. The muscles in his thighs tightened as his feet pressed tight against the stone floor; no man spoke to him in this manner and walked free. Temper aroused to breaking point, he approached the man in black and stared directly into his eyes. For reasons unknown, blood thumped in his ears. The skin on his bare arms prickled and burned. The man in black looked taller than he did seconds ago. With remarkable speed, the man's piercing eyes changed from a soft brown to dark red. Polly's rage subdued as he stared wildly about him before clearing his throat.

"What do you want to drink, you impatient bastard?"

The man in black smile widened.

"Watch your manners, my friend. Single malt whiskey and a jug of water, and be quick about it. And I want a room for a few days."

"We don't do rooms this time of the year."

"A well-aired room overlooking the village

green and fresh sheets."

"You deaf or plain stupid?" Parrott said sharply.

"Have the room ready in thirty minutes."

Polly's left heel tapped a wild tattoo on the stone floor. Sweat sprouted from his forehead; something about the man unnerved him. Aware the eyes of every man in the room were settled on him; he felt unsure of what to do next.

"Get yourself upstairs, Polly, and get the man's bed ready," a voice from the crowded bar called.

Heads turned to face Mrs Parrott, holding Peggotty, a huge great Dane, tight on a leather lead. Men grabbed their drinks and shrunk back away from the bar fearing the dog might launch its salivating jaws into the crowded drinkers. Twisting and turning like a nervous snake ready to strike, it hurled itself at the man in black. Mrs Parrott tightened her leather leash a notch, preventing the dog from reaching the man in black. Immediately the man stepped forward and, leaning at the waist, punched the dog full in the mouth. The dog squealed in pain and fell back on its haunches, blood leaking from its mouth.

"Bring that mutt near me again, and I'll bury it alive," the man said. "Now, please show me to my room."

Polly Parrott wasn't altogether wrong to work on his state of mind. Events over the last few minutes left him confused where once there had always been routine. His reputation as a man who brooked no nonsense from any man alive had been swept away on an irresistible tide of shame. Drinkers from every corner of the Inn shook their heads, muttering words of disappointment. Others smiled as taunts came thick and fast. The muscles in his face jumped. He couldn't think straight.

Mrs Parrott's timely intervention saved him from further embarrassment.

"A room will be £55.00 per night, evening meal and breakfast extra. No smoking or women allowed in the room, and mind you pull the chain after using the toilet. Your room will be ready in twenty minutes. And if that doesn't suit you, you can bugger off and sleep in a hedge."

"That will be fine," the man answered.

"Good, now follow me and sign the register."

"That won't be necessary."

"No signature, no room; it's as simple as that."

In a small office behind the bar, the man in black picked up the pen and signed his name as Mr Legges.

"First name, please. We have strict rules here," Mrs Parrott said, scrutinising his signature.

"For God's sake, woman."

"If For God's Sake is your Christian name, please sign it next to your surname."

Sniffing deep, the man grabbed the pen and wrote his first name in the register.

"That's it, is it, Mr Beau Legges? I'd keep that to

yourself if I were you," she said, her face cracking into a rare smile.

"I'd advise you to do the same and refer to me as Beau," Legges grunted.

"You ever lay a finger on my dog again? I'll have you out of here quicker than a shadow disappears in the shade. Tell me, Mister Beau Legges, why are you here?"

"You'll find out soon enough."

Her smile stiffened. Lips pressed tight, she left the office with deep furrows on either side of her mouth. After years spent behind a bar, she knew trouble when it walked in.

*

9 o'clock that evening, Beau Legges strode head high into the bar. Still dressed in black, he cut an awe-inspiring figure, and drinkers parted to allow him a clear path to the bar. A Belgique who'd served nine years as an unarmed combat instructor in the French Foreign Legion before being jailed for nearly killing a British officer in a public house in Aldershot, Legges could feel the silence in his bones. Fear and dislike spread throughout the bar like yeast on dough when he threw back his head and swallowed the whiskey in one gulp, then slammed the empty glass on the bar and demanded another. Someone whispered words he missed, then another, followed by another. His faint smile went unnoticed. He had them where he wanted them. The time had arrived to spread anxiety

and confusion before bending them to his will.

Duncan Redbreast revelled in his reputation as the village hard man. A big, broad, aggressive man, he never used two words when one would suffice. It was easy enough to see why he lacked the art of conversation during his solitary job loading bricks onto pallets ready for transport to various building sites. Hands the size of shovels, he rejoiced in clapping people on the shoulders and laughing as they fell, spinning to the ground. Aware disgrace would haunt him for the rest of his life if he failed to confront the stranger dressed in black, something warned him it would be folly to mess with this man.

"We don't take kindly to strangers acting as if they own the place. Get your business done and sod off," Redbreast grunted.

Legge's smile spread across his face.

"Are you a religious man, my friend?"

"Religion, what has religion to do with anything?" Redbreast snorted.

Because if you are, pray to God; you are not the man I'm looking for."

The colour drained from Redbreast's face. He blinked and shook his head trying to make sense of the words—nothing of substance, however small, gelled in his mind. For the first time in his life, he knew he was in the wrong place at the wrong time. Like a rat in a corner, he searched for an avenue of escape, but nothing existed. He'd have to rely on his ignorance and brute force.

"This man you are looking for, does he have a name?" he asked nervously.

"All men have names; perhaps it is yours that fits the bill," Legges said, his eyes turning from red to black as he watched Redbreast ripen with fear.

Redbreast's eyes flickered with uncertainty. Why should a man like Legges fill him with fear? He didn't know him or recollected ever meeting him. But there was a malignancy about him, something that thinned his blood and set his heart thumping against his ribs. Aubrey Crabtree, son of a fruit picker, picked up his small banjo with an alligator strap and made for the door; certain trouble was in the air. Someone at the back of the room started a slow handclap. Seconds later, a chorus of handclaps filled the Inn. The crowd was baying for blood. Gathering confidence, Redbreast swung a fist at Legge's head. Legges ducked and weaved like a dancer as Redbreast's efforts met with fresh air. Redbreast repeated his action three times before staggering to a halt and gasping for breath with his arms hanging loosely at his sides. Pulling a small knife from his pocket, Legges forced Redbreast's right hand on the bar and severed his little finger. Redbreast stiffened. Upright and with eyes like marbles, he stared at the severed finger on the bar. Like soft cheese, his feet crumbled as the strength drained from his legs. A hush descended over the bar and mouths dropped open in disbelief.

"Listen to me, and listen well; I want the names of those responsible for defacing Anton Page's bungalow. Each day, until I have the names, one of you present here will have their small finger cut from their hand. Be warned; I do not joke. Should anyone wish to inform the police, I shall sever the little finger from each hand."

A cloak of silence hung in the air. Not a muscle stirred. The crowd stared at Redbreast's unconscious body spread over the stone floor. Then, like a crashing wave rushing for the shore, they swarmed for the exit. Legges smiled with satisfaction. The quicker he was out of this dump, the happier he'd be. He hated the countryside, and it hated him back. The feel of the fresh air and serene atmosphere caused his nose to run and fill his eyes with tears. Crowds crammed together like sardines, and the smell of petrol fumes and the acrid stench of cigarettes were medicine to his lungs. Behind the bar, 'Polly' Parrott stood trance-like, unable to tug his eyes away from Redbreast's dismembered finger. There had been no mistaking the edge of warning in Legge's tone. Something told him it might have been better for the village if Anton Page's bungalow had been burnt to the ground with him in it.

*

A fading sun dropped slowly over the horizon

casting long shadows when Dr Reuben Bone spoke in a low voice as if he wanted no one else to hear his words.

"The scan shows there is nothing serious. The hip joint isn't aligned properly. Nothing a short operation won't put right," he said.

A lifetime of unshed tears welled up in Willow's eyes. Her heart thrummed. Her squeal burst into laughter as she threw her arm around Page's neck.

"Steady on, girl," he laughed. "We have a way to go yet."

"You will, of course, learn to use a walking frame to strengthen your legs and help keep your balance," the doctor interrupted, "It will be weeks before you can walk unaided. But I shall see you before that to monitor your progress."

*

In Page's bungalow, Willow could barely get the words out concerning Dr Bone's prognosis as Cate laughed and clapped her hand at the good news.

Willows's joy and infectious smile raised the conversation to a different level.

"It's Christmas in a couple of days. Are we having a tree and decorations? I've never had a Christmas in a real home."

"Why not?" Cate laughed. "We'll go all the way, mince pies, Christmas crackers and a turkey. What do you say, Dad?"

"Yes, of course," Page answered softly.

She'd called him Dad. He wanted to reach out, crush her in his arms. Tell her how much he loved her and filled him with pride. But he didn't. He didn't think it was the right thing to do.

*

The evening sun had disappeared, leaving a dark sky home to a few far-off twinkling stars when Charlie Waterman, the forty-nine-year-old lock keeper, tugged the chain securing the locks. Satisfied everything was in order, he checked the water level before returning to his small canalside cottage. The next few seconds happened so fast that he barely had the time to lodge the event in his memory. Blinded by the spray on his face, the sharp pain in his right hand lingered as the fear of the unknown weakened his legs causing him to fall to his knees, gasping for breath. The sight of his small severed finger lying on the grass verge unhinged him, and he screamed like a slapped child. Struggling to his feet, he grazed his head against the heavy wooden lock gates. Ignoring the blood streaming down his face, he slowly walked to the Crooked Stick. Drinkers with pint glasses raised to their lips froze at him at the sight of him swaying in the doorway. Like a forest fire, fear travelled through the Inn. As he made his way to the bar, Waterman wrapped both hands around the brass bar rail with loud obscenities gushed from his foaming mouth.

"I warned you he'd do it, didn't I? I never painted his bloody bungalow, so how come he picked on me. Whichever of you bastards did it, go and tell him, cos if I find out, I'll tell him myself. Might even tell him a few names whether they did it or not."

"Don't talk rubbish. I took Mr Legges a tray of coffee not thirty minutes ago. It couldn't have been him." Polly Parrott stammered.

Waterman's curses surged from his lips.

"You bloody great stupid clown, what do you think this is, a bullock's teat?"

Polly stared at the severed finger. Darkness shrouded his mind. Seconds later, his eyes shivered in their sockets at Legges entering the bar.

"Whisky, and don't be slow about it," Legges said quietly.

Waterman clasped his injured hand so tight that blood ran through his fingers.

"You got some nerve showing your ugly mug in here after what you've done, you twisted bastard," Waterman hollered.

Legges tipped back his head and sniffed.

"Strong words," he said. "Perhaps you can enlighten me."

"Enlighten you? I'll enlighten you, alright, with both barrels of a shotgun. You know what I'm talking about. Not ten minutes ago, you cut off my little finger."

"Ten minutes ago, I was naked after a lukewarm shower. I'm afraid you have the wrong man."

"I heard you threatening to cut off a small finger until you have the names of those who damaged Page's bungalow. Well, you picked on the wrong man. I'm reporting this to the police tonight."

"That'll do; I'll have no police on my premises after last week. All of your brats sniffing shit and drugs in the toilet nearly got me closed down," Polly Parrott snapped. "Drink up, the bloody lot of you; I'm closing early tonight."

"What about my finger?" Waterman howled.

"Grow another and stop whining. Blame it on the witches." Polly snapped.

"Witches, it had nothing to do with the witches. What makes you think it was them?"

"Seems strange you should have a finger cut off by a man who says he was naked in his room at the time. It could only have been the witches."

Emotion swelled into confusion as Waterman made his way to the pub's exit.

"You'll not catch me drinking in this place again. You can be sure of that."

"You'll soon change your mind when the thirst takes you."

It took ten minutes to clear the bar before Polly finally managed to lock the Inn's doors. Jaw set firm, he walked behind the bar and filled a small glass with brandy from a row of optics.

"Who are you, Legges, and what do you want?"

"I told you what I want. And I won't leave

until I know the name of the cowards intent on making an old man's life miserable."

Polly's voice sounded strained as he stared at Legges through narrowed eyes.

"You're barking up the wrong tree looking for answers here. You'll find what you want to know at Pennywise Manor. Ask for a man who calls himself Onions. A weasel of a man who reckons he knows everything that happens in the village. And that's all you'll get from me."

"I might just do that."

"So, you are friends with Anton Page. In prison together, I assume?"

"Why should you assume that?"

"Easy enough to see you have the whiteness of a man recently confined from daylight. Your eyes have a look of emptiness. Page must, at one time, have been of great comfort to you."

Legges shrugged.

"For your information, I served a prison sentence with Anton Page. He prevented me from turning insane whilst I was inside for cutting off the hands of a Russian who beat his wife half to death."

Polly nervously ran his tongue over his lips before answering.

"So Page is an expert in human nature and a vet?"

"No need for the sarcasm; Page spent a great deal passing the time explaining the ailments of animals to me. It gave me something to think about, apart from my time in prison and my past stupidity. After a time, other lags heard and came to learn about the ailments of animals. They listened to the stories of animals, and it helped to comfort them. Strange the way the mind works. After finishing their sentences, they told him he only had to contact them if he wanted help. Anton Page has the ear and might of some real bad-uns. Be warned; do not cross this man."

"I'll bear that in mind. Another whisky?"

"Why not. Tell me more about this man called Onions."

*

After feasting on turkey and wearing paper hats pulled from crackers, Christmas Day at Pages turned into a dull affair. Page, complaining of tiredness, chose to take a nap. Cate left to visit old friends in the village. With Lady the Labrador fast asleep at her feet, Willow poured over books and magazines related to the welfare of animals.

*

Legges pushed the key into the car's ignition and fired the engine. Christmas meant nothing to him. It was little more than another day for people to fill their stomachs, get pissed, and continue long-standing family arguments. His interest lay in the man they called Onions, and he had no intention of leaving the village until his curiosity had been satisfied.

At the far end of the drive, rain from a sudden

thunderstorm dripped from the soggy leaves and formed puddles beneath a group of trees. The air changed. Legges shuddered violently at the cold breeze penetrating his clothing. Perhaps he'd leave and come back tomorrow. Or maybe not. The reassuring shape of the knife handle in his pocket comforted him and brought a tiny smile to his lips. Why do tomorrow what you can do today? With his black wide-brimmed glossy hat perched at an angle on his head and starched neck collar crisp and white as a penguin's bib, he approached the large double doors of Pennywise Manor and tugged the metal chain. He'd have to be as deaf as a stone not to hear the ringing bells before the doors swung open. Staring at the man standing before him, shock and surprise crumpled the skin between his brows. Something cold clutched the pit of his stomach. Onions stared back, his face as white as Arctic snow. Legges recovered first.

"Rita Peters, you bucket of shit, so this is where you have been hiding," Legges growled.

"I beg your pardon, sir. Can I be of help?" Onions stammered, stepping backwards.

The two men stared at each other. Legges face steady. But not Onions, his eyes twitched and red spots burned his cheeks.

"Did you think I wouldn't recognise you? Remember, I was sent down for four years because you grassed me up. I know men who would pay thousands of pounds to know where you disappeared after stitching up half of London's East End. A copper's nark, your carelessness in matters of conscience knew no bounds. You'd look good floating face down in the Thames with a slit throat."

Hot breath squeezed through Onion's constricted throat. Aged forty-two, for thirteen years, he'd relied on the thick walls of Pennywise Manor to keep him safe from discovery. Now, drowning in incomprehension, he tried to work out how the man standing before him had tracked him down to the tiny insignificant village on the edge of nowhere. Naked fear pushed him to the limit.

"I'm afraid you have the better of me, sir. Have we met before?"

"Oh, indeed we have. Dressed as a man with your hair shaved to your scalp isn't going to help you."

Face etched in the colour of chalk; fear stabbed Onions like the blades of a hundred knives.

"My name is Onions, sir. May I ask who the devil are you?"

For the second time that night, Legge's hand gripped the cold handle of his knife.

"Stop this stupidity. The name, Legges, does that ring a bell?"

"No, please leave Lord Pennywise's property, or I will be forced to call the police."

Onion's throat closed as the blade of Legge's knife lay cold on his left cheek. His bony white fingers scraped the wall behind him.

"This is what you are going to do, you slime-bag. Tomorrow, you and your cronies will clean the paint off Anton Page's bungalow. Fail me, and I will find you and cut out your heart while you breathe."

Onions took out his handkerchief and wiped the sweat from his brow.

"Page, was it Page that sent for you?" Onions stammered.

"Page could have sent any of the worst criminals walking the streets. Be grateful it was me."

"I don't understand how a man like Page could hold such sway with the criminal world."

"He taught prisoners how to care for sick animals and helped them pass the time in prison, and they idolised him. Funny how a man couldn't give a shit for human life but blubber like a child over a sick pet. I wouldn't have believed it if I hadn't seen it with my own eyes. But let's not dwell on that. I know a few people who will be happy to know your whereabouts."

Onions closed his eyes. Legges wasn't a man given to idle threats. When he opened his eyes, a white frost had settled across the parkland, and fog drifted through the upright trees like a long-lost ghost. Of Legges, there was no sign.

*

The next day Page stared wide-eyed at the four men outside his bungalow armed with a steam cleaner.

"Compliments of the villagers, sir," a small dumpy man with a prominent Adam's apple scraping against his collar whenever he spoke said. "We'll soon have this mess cleared up. Bloody vandals everywhere these days."

Page nodded vaguely

"That's very kind of the villagers. Please convey to them my deepest gratitude."

"I will, sir. You can be sure of that."

His smile barely noticeable, Page turned and entered his bungalow. He didn't believe a word the man had told him, but he did have complete trust in Beau Legges. His smile widened. It wasn't over, not yet.

*

Christmas passed with barely a shadow to mark its presence. A New Year hovered in expectancy. To Lord Pennywise's angst, Onions, exposed by Legges without his knowledge, had lost his air of precise purpose. Like a silent shadow, Onions made a point of keeping his distance from the family and spoke only when spoken to. Disliked by the villagers as aloof and on the strange side, life as he knew it was edging towards destruction. His one avenue of escape was to be rid of Legges. Something far easier said than done, but not necessarily impossible. Borne away on an irresistible tide of hate for Legges, he realised he had to think up something quickly if he wished to survive. But getting rid of him would constitute a miracle in which he held little faith. Of course, he could use Pennywise's three sons to do his dirty work. As much as he dreaded them, they could obliterate all sense and feeling of life for what they'd describe as nothing more than a childish prank.

*

Stretched out on the bed in the Crooked Stick Inn, Legges slid his thumb down the cutting edge of his knife and grinned. After debating what part of Rita Peter's body he'd cut off first, he settled on her tongue. A fitting way for a police informer to be silenced, he smiled thinly. Over the next few evenings, he regularly visited the downstairs bar. Seated at the end of the bar with a whisky and packet of salted cashew nuts, on more than one occasion, he attempted to turn the topic of conversation to Onions, known only to him as Rita Peters. Taking care not to reveal her natural gender, he casually enquired amongst the locals about the places Onions frequented during his days off from Pennywise Manor. It took little time to establish that he wasn't exactly the month's flavour and drew a blank on all fronts. If he wanted Rita Peters, he'd have to find a way inside Pennywise Manor. Hardly a problem for a man of his capabilities. For a passing moment, he fought against an eye roll. Peters was no fool.

*

Seated in front of his television trying to raise

interest in a boring mid-day programme, Page basked in the villagers' change of heart. He'd visit the Crooked Stick Inn. Meet with old friends and acquaintances. Chat about this and that, the things he regularly did before being imprisoned. Instead, he changed his mind and watched Willow pouring over books explaining sick animals' remedies.

"Would you like to become a vet?" he asked her casually.

The speed at which she answered surprised him.

"I want to own a zoo," she said firmly. "With Penguins sliding down icebergs while waving umbrellas. Camels dressed in tutus dancing to ballet music. A chorus of donkeys singing opera. A tiger swinging on a trapeze with safety nets spun by beady-eyed spiders."

Page laughed.

"Sounds wonderful."

When she threw her head back and joined him in the laughter, her wire-framed spectacles slipped from her face and fell at Page's feet. Page leaned forward and, picking them up, looked through the lens. Willow sat unmoving, staring at his frown.

"Read me something from one of the magazines without your spectacles," Page said.

Without hesitation, Willow read from the back page word perfect.

"The picture on the far wall, can you read the

title?"

"Yes, it says, The Hunt."

"Good God, I have a job to read the words wearing spectacles. You know the lenses are made of plain glass and not prescribed?"

"Dad told me I must wear them or go blind. He said he knew where to get the spectacles. Sometimes he made me wear large sunglasses to hide my face."

Page frowned. Something inside of him urged him to know more.

"Tell me about your past and the man you called, dad?" he said softly.

Instead of getting up off the floor, Willow raised herself onto one elbow. She thought it was an odd request. Not that she wasn't willing to answer his questions, but she didn't want to get into specifics.

"Don't mind if I do," she shrugged. "You'll find out soon enough anyway. I suppose you'll send me away after I've told you. I was adopted as a baby and ran away on my sixteenth birthday. The family had a son older than me. At first, he used to bully me, then asked me to touch him in his private places when I grew older. I refused and told my adopted mother. She called me a slut and locked me in my bedroom. That night I ran away. Two days later, the man I called Dad found me asleep under bushes. He said I could stay with him if I did everything he told me. He was kind to me, said his name was Julius O'Ceasar, and lived in a Roman Palace in County Cork. He told me stories of Ireland and promised to take me home to meet his family."

Page remained straight-faced.

"This is the same man we met in the woods?"

"Yes, I think he was lonely and wanted me for company."

"What of your real mother?"

"Not much, only that she lives abroad."

"How did you know that?"

"The lady who adopted me threatened to send me back to her if I didn't behave."

"Did you misbehave?"

"Sometimes. Instead of going to school, I spent the days with the horses on the edge of the woods. The goats were my favourites. They made me laugh. Are you going to tell the police and send me away?"

Page wasn't sure how to answer. He needed time to consider all the options.

"What, for liking animals? I don't think so. Anyway, I'm interested in this zoo you intend to open."

"Thank you, and you won't be sorry; you'll see."

The sound of the front door crashing open startled Page.

"You'd better come immediately. There's been a bad accident in the village," Cate cried, struggling for breath.

"What's that to do with me? Call the police?"

"The police are already there. Remember that butler, or whatever he was, the man that worked for Lord Pennywise called Onions?"

"Yes, of course."

"He was driving a white van, lost control and mounted the pavement and knocked down a man wearing a black wide-brimmed hat and almost mowed down an old lady walking her two dogs at the same time—the man isn't expected to survive. The lady is fine, a little shaken up. The police want you to look at the two dogs. There's blood everywhere. I think you'll have to put them down."

"I'll get my bag."

It took nine minutes in Cate's car to reach the crash scene. A billowing black smoke obscured the entry to the small village post office. Accompanied by a uniformed policeman, firefighters ordered onlookers to stand back and go home. Those cursed with a morbid curiosity refused to move. Some protested against foreigners being allowed to enter the village. The two dogs, both yellow Labradors, were still breathing below a tartan blanket someone had kindly provided. One lay dog silent, its rear end squashed beneath the van's wheels—the other unmarked and whimpering with fright.

"Get this damn crowd back," Page yelled to the policeman. "I'll have to put the dog under the wheels to sleep. Poor thing must be in agony. I'll need the other dog in my surgery where it might have a chance of living."

"You heard the vet. Get back, all of you; there is nothing more to see," the young policeman shouted, forcing the crowd back.

"Always asking questions in the pub about Onions, he was. That was Onions driving the van. They knew each other, that is for sure. I always thought there was something fishy about the pair of them.

"On top of that, we've got a murderer looking after the animals." someone in the crowd called.

Groups of people walking by made scornful remarks aimed at Page's presence.

"Yeah, you're bloody right there. I daren't let my kids out with him on the loose," a voice called.

Page looked up, searching for the man who spoke the words. A dozen pairs of slitted eyes stared back at him, each full of malice. He fumbled with the needle before pushing the tip into the dying dog's front leg. He thought the village residents had begun to forgive his past days ago. Yet, the same people were gawping at him with curled lips contorting their features, a stark reminder that the past never dies. The taste of salt covered his lips.

"I need help to get the injured dog to my surgery," he mumbled.

"We'll use my van. Damned if I'll see the dog suffer," A burly man with a bushy beard said.

Revenge and anger blinded Page. Before he

could respond, the burly man pushed him aside and, gently lifting the dog, carried the still body to Cate's car.

"I've told you a dozen times, get out of this damned village. It's full of hate, and nothing will change that," Cate raged at her father. "You knew the man knocked down, didn't you? Who was he, one of the jailbirds you mixed with while inside prison? Couldn't have been anyone else, could he?"

*

It turned out to be a lucky day for the dog. Apart from minor abrasions and a splint on the left fore to help the knee joint knit, the animal would be as good as new with patience. When Page suggested the dog remain in one of the cages, Willow asked if she might spend time with the nervous animal. Soothe him after the shock of the accident and get him to eat. Page nodded and entered his bedroom. Stretched out on his bed, he closed his eyes, wishing he could do the same to his mind. The villagers hated him; that was abundantly clear. Yet, as much as he dreaded them, he still longed to be their friend. But that could never be; the sticky ignorance of rumour blended with fact captivated him so utterly that it was all he could do to bear the insults. Tears squeezed between his eyelids. His mind became distorted. Common sense tossed aside, he wished he was back within the freedom of prison, where he knew the veins and arteries of a simple life. There, content to perform the tasks others disliked had at least earned him a flimsy respect.

Now alone and lost in the world to drift in whichever direction the wind chose to blow, how silly of him to think the world would forget a murderer. If he wanted peace, he must find it and lodge it deep in his mind. Sinking into the bed, he watched the last light of the day slide down the wall. He knew where he must begin. Somewhere foreign to him. Somewhere that had always been there, yet he'd hardly ever noticed. A place made and blessed for sinners.

CHAPTER TWELVE

On the first Thursday of the New Year, hands pushed deep in his pockets; Page peered at the fading words on the signboard outside the Church of St Luke. Rural legend had it that thirteen witches had attempted to burn the church to the ground four hundred years ago in revenge for one of their own being burnt at the stake. Struck by a massive bolt of lightning, the church had been to piles of ashes. Some believed it to be an act of God. Whenever a violent storm erupted, elderly inhabitants swore they heard the witches' screams. Hence the name St Luke, the patron saint of lost causes. Page managed to raise a smile; his life had amounted to little more than a series of lost causes, each worst than the one previous. Maybe it was a mark of religious respect that made him take his hands from his pockets as he approached the west side of the church and pushed open the heavy oak door in need of oiled hinges. The smell of burning candles and sour incense burned into his nostrils. Candlelight fluttered around the small altar. On top of the altar, next to a small chalice, a thin white wafer lay abandoned. Page swallowed noisily as the impulse to return home grew more vigorous. To one side, seated on a dark carved wooden seat, a large man with rounded shoulders accustomed to carrying worldly souls sat with his hands resting on his lap.

"Can I help you?" a deep voice boomed.

Page turned to face Father Kevin Wrapson. A tall bear of a man with a round face and a fixed smile tattooed on his face, a misshapen nose caused his wire-rimmed spectacles to tilt at a precarious angle

"I don't know," Page stammered. "I'm not sure of anything anymore.

"Page, isn't it, Anton if my memory serves me correctly? I understand things haven't gone well since your return to the village."

"You know of my past? I suppose I should have known."

"We live in a small village. God moves in mysterious ways and sees all."

"Pity at times he doesn't move in the right direction. " Page retorted.

"I take it you are here to chastise God for your mistakes in life?"

"No," Page said, his voice dropping to a whisper. "I don't know why I'm here. I feel I have nowhere else to go where I can be at peace."

"Peace comes from within. Yet, the mind

tends to decay and sees things that aren't there. It changes life into something we recognise as good. Without it, faith in all men fails, and God is destroyed. Speak with God, tell him of your trespasses, and perhaps he will find it in his heart to help you find the peace you seek. If you wish to pray, the church will remain open until you need to leave. Yet, I fear you will not find the answer to your problems overnight."

The words pressed into Page's head threatened to crush his skull, each word displaying the pages of his life clearly in his mind. The loss of his parents. His wife's unfaithfulness, a plethora of scars he couldn't erase from his mind no matter how hard he tried. His only child, Cate, had been raised without a father while incarcerated in prison. He'd taken in Willow, a waif and stray, without considering her future. Worse, seeking revenge on the innocent by using Beau Legges as an instrument of violence resulted in Legge's death. His mind became fuddled; there was more, but he couldn't remember. A dream-like quality descended upon him. Thirty minutes ago, he'd stood watching the ever-depressing world news in front of his TV. Now, before a crucifix, he stared into the transparent face of Jesus. He had come to find peace with misery, his only companion.

*

Xander Pennywise's voice crackled through the intercom fixed to the wall of Onion's bedroom.

Swinging his legs off the bed, Onion wiped his glasses clean, uttered a curse, scowled at the ill-timed intrusion, and pressed the in-coming button.

"Yes," he grunted.

"Ah, Onions, if you have a moment, please join me in the kitchen," came Xander's voice.

Onions features sagged.

"Can't it wait till morning? I've just returned from the hospital?"

"No time like the present. What I have to say won't take a moment."

With rolling eyes, Onions released his finger from the button and placed the computer on standby.

"Uncaring little bastard, the best part of him ended up over his mother's belly button," he mumbled loudly, wincing at the pain in his legs. "More than likely he doesn't have the brains to figure out how to switch the kettle on."

Dusk hadn't yet fallen, and after a long and slow painful walk, Onions entered the kitchen and slowed to a halt at the sight of all three brothers swigging red wine from the bottle. Whatever the brothers had in mind, he knew no good would come from the meeting when he'd recovered his breath.

Xander rose from the table and gestured to a wooden chair with a theatrical wave of his hand.

"Sit down, Onions, or should I say Miss Onions?" he guffawed like a donkey with a sore throat.

Onion's lids slipped over his eyes. His secret was out, and he felt grateful he'd had the sense to pack a bag ready to leave.

Unsure of his feelings at being outed as a woman, things hadn't been too bad at Pennywise Mansion. A roof over her head. The annual salary was more than enough for her needs. Conditions couldn't be better. The only downfall was the three brothers from hell. Greedy, uncaring, and lacking in manners with a bent for cruelty, he could name a dozen men who would revel in slowly pulling out their fingernails.

"So you know the truth from my hospital records. Not a problem. I'm packed and ready to go. A pity I can't say it's been a pleasure."

"Go, go where. Who mentioned anything about leaving? We need you more than ever now," Wellington said, raising a wine bottle and checking the contents.

"If I were you, I'd leave before it's too late," Nelson said hastily.

"Oh, do shut up, you little wet shit," Xander scoffed. "So, Miss Onions, do you mind telling us your real name? I can assure you your secret is safe with us?"

A stab of shame and exhaustion added to Onion's leg pain. Her cover blown; nothing mattered anymore.

"My name is Rita Peters; I am an informer in the pay of the Metropolitan Police. Should you wish to know more, please get in touch with the nearest police station. I'm certain they would be interested to hear your reasons for doing so."

Three blank faces stared in disbelief. Wellington reacted first. His smile sickly, as if he'd just eaten a dead badger's arse. Xander's gulp slapped the silence. Nelson sat as stiff as a cardboard cut-out. When he opened his mouth to speak, his lips refused to part. Every muscle in his body told him to go and fill his lungs with fresh, clean air. Instead, his legs refused to obey his mind. For most of his adult life, he'd avoided confrontation, preferring to have his nose in the pages of a book. No matter how long he gazed at Rita Peters, he felt convinced he was suffering a nightmare made in hell. Leaning his fists on the table, he pretended it was a bad dream, then burned with embarrassment when she caught his eye.

Surprise and anger never occupied Wellington's mind. Brimming with excitement, he leaned forward and accidentally knocked over the bottle of half-filled wine. With unbridled amusement, he watched the contents trickle over Xander's trousers.

"Look what you are doing, you clumsy oaf; you've wet me," Xander spluttered.

"Oh, be quiet, you were wet the day you were born, and little has changed since," Wellington said, roaring with laughter.

Rita Peters drew a breath and allowed her gaze

to fall to the floor.

"You remind me of the three stooges. Now tell me why you called me here?"

Once again, Wellington took the initiative.

"Okay, I'll come straight to the point; we're planning to kill father and thought you might have some good ideas?" Wellington said. "Of course, after what you have revealed, you won't be here much longer, more the pity."

Rita Peters laughed a little too harshly. Not one to mince her words to people like the three idiots seated shoulder to shoulder like a pack of cards, it took her seconds to realise she had the upper hand. And there lie her choice. She could leave Pennywise Manor or work out a plan from which she might benefit. She chose the latter.

"Hmm, I think I should warn you I have been preparing a dossier on all three of you. For years you have been tormenting and terrorising the villagers. Now it's time you paid for your crimes. All three of you will be in the frame if anything should happen to me."

"Are you aware that the man called Legges died in the hospital? Why did you kill him? Was it because of something you did in the past?" Wellington sneered.

Rita Peters exhaled a sigh of relief and sat upright.

"Ask your father. He knows why I am here," Rita Peters lied, clenching her fists beneath the table.

Three pairs of eyes crammed with suspicion stared at her. The tide was fast turning against her. She had to act if she wanted to keep the upper hand.

"Out of interest, if I were to help dispose of your father, what's in it for me? Merely a hypothetical question, of course."

Xander looked up and cast his eyes over the copper pots and pans attached to the wall by hooks.

"One million pounds, cash," he said evenly.

Rita Peters watched him through experienced eyes. She could spot a liar in seconds.

"One million pounds each, and you have a deal."

Nelson's face turned white as a freshly laundered pair of virgin knickers. Wellington's Adams Apple bounced in his throat. Xander's mouth twisted into a bead

"Agreed," Wellington smiled.

*

After leaving the church, Page's breathing raced as he made his way home through the rounded corners and rise and fall of the village streets and lanes. Angry drivers honked their horns and shouted at him to get off the road. A passing car threw rainwater, soaking his trousers. Trapped in a strong breeze, thousands of damp golden leaves flashed across the grey sky and wandered through the trees, shaking the branches. Had he been inside the church, or was his imagination playing tricks like it had done many times while in prison? He felt no different from before; no visible marks on his body to prove God had touched him. No cleansing of his soul after kneeling before the makeshift altar whispering for forgiveness from the Almighty. For a lingering second, he felt cheated. Then something unexpected happened. With evening preparing to fall, the rain stopped so abruptly that he found it hard to remember it was ever there in the first place. The clouds opened to reveal a bright warm sun. He blinked as a shaft of silver light broke through the greying sky. A soft mist rising over the village concealed the houses below. Any doubt hidden away in the crevices of his mind melted. He'd become a man of God.

During the journey home he decided not to reveal his visit to St Luke's church. Cate was bound to scoff, call him a silly old fool, and create another argument. On top of that, he was tired and struggled to place one foot in front of the other. When he entered the living room, Cate was seated by the fire balancing a hot cup of coffee on her lap.

"Where have you been? I was about to search for you," she said, a worried look creasing her face.

"Nowhere, just taking the air and clearing my head. Where's Willow?"

"Where she usually is, wrapped around the dog you treated. I'm sure that girl would rather be an animal than a human being."

Page found Willow on the surgery floor with her arms around the sick dog's neck. Her eyes were wide and wet, her face glistening with tears.

"How's he doing?" Page said, kneeling, pulling back the dog's eyelids, and peering into his eyes.

"How long is a mouse's tail?" she answered in a low voice.

He waited before answering, his eyes searching her face.

"That isn't what I asked you."

"I don't know how he is, except he is sad and in pain."

"What makes you think he is in pain, the length of a mouse's tail perhaps?"

Willow raised her head and looked at him.

"No, of course not. That's something I say out of habit."

"So, when you don't know the answer to a question, that is your stock reply?"

"S'pose so."

Page looked at her briefly, then, climbing to his feet, left the surgery without another word. Willow remained and covered the sick dog with a thin cloth. Struggling to her feet, she grabbed her crutches, entered the sitting room, pushed a couple of logs onto the wood burner, and watched the flames jump greedily at the intrusion.

"That should keep us warm," she said, with

her back to Page.

Page remained quiet.

"May I ask what you intend to do with me?" Willow continued, turning to face him. "Please tell me the truth."

She heard the creak of worn floorboards as he approached and gently embraced her. She stiffened. Sensing her uneasiness, he dropped his arms and stepped back.

"I shall purchase a computer and teach you to become a vet. Each week, I shall ask you questions about the common illnesses contracted by animals and pets. Use the computer to find the answers and memorise them. At the end of each week, I shall test you on each subject I put to you. Remember that we are dealing with living creatures and not changing a wheel on a car. You alone will hold their life in your hands. The slightest mistake and the animal will suffer and die. Could you do that?"

Yes, yes," she cried, throwing her arms around his neck. "Thank you. I won't let you down."

"No, I don't think you will," he smiled.

CHAPTER THIRTEEN

Grey clouds moved across the sky like dancing ghosts dulling the countryside's colour and contours. The facade was over. Onions no longer existed. A shadow of fiction born of necessity had disappeared into thin air. Rita Peters strained to find a direction in his place as she stared from her bedroom window. It was like looking at the world through a pair of smudged spectacles. Had it been worth the going up for the coming down, she asked herself? Thanks to the three brothers from hell, the world would never be the same as yesterday.

There had been times when she'd willingly crossed the lines of decency having innocent people jailed for inventing false information. Trapped between truth and make-believe, she was fighting life the only way she knew and losing the battle. But chameleons have an advantage over lesser creatures. They learned to adapt to their surroundings and remain unseen beneath their chosen camouflage. Confident that the three brothers were mocking her anger twisted deep in her belly. She'd never trusted those who thought they were better than her. Over and over she revised everything that had happened in the kitchen down to the smallest detail.

At last, a rush of admiration touched with pride glowed inside her head. Could she get away with another murder? Fumbling in her closet for a suit and clean shirt, she dressed and left her room. Rain bounced off the sills when she entered Lord Pennywise's sitting room. The windows looked fluid as day turned to night.

" Onions! what are you doing at this time of the night, after time off, I suppose?"

"No, sir, not at all," Rita Peters answered; removing her jacket and undoing the buttons on her shirt, she released her bra and revealed her small breasts.

Pennywise's hands started to shake. Tea slopped from his cup into the saucer and dribbled over his spotless riding breeches.

"Good grief, don't tell me you have had one of those operations women have to make their bits and pieces larger. And you, a man, I thought you had damned well more sense.

"No, sir, I am not a man. I am a woman and have been since birth."

Pennywise squinted through one eye. Mouth gaping open he couldn't think of what to say. Instead, he wondered how on earth he'd failed to notice before.

"I suppose you have a pussy?" he said.

"Yes, of course, sir. Would you like to see it?" Rita Peters answered, struggling to keep her voice under control.

"Look at it. What's the point in looking at it? A pussy should be put to use, not ogled at like a chimp in a zoo. Do my sons know of this?"

"They do."

"Tried it on, I'll wager. That cretin Xander would shag a gatepost if someone hung a pair of knickers on it. Anyway, why are you telling me all this now?"

The moment had arrived. Fearful of Pennywise's response Rita Peters struggled to concoct an excuse to retreat from the room. About to dip her toe into a great lake of water, she knew that one mistake and she would be sucked to the bottom.

"I've struck a deal with your three sons to help murder you. Nothing personal, of course, merely a financial arrangement," she exclaimed, nervously balling her fists.

Anger swelled within Pennywise; his face turned a deathly white until it occupied the whole of his body. He'd always known that one day this hour would arrive, that his sons wanted his money and love and loyalty were never a part of their make-up.

"So now you have shown me your boobies, I suppose you will shoot me and claim your financial arrangement?" he said, twitching the muscles in his face.

"On the contrary. I was hoping for a counteroffer; now you know our intentions."

Rita Peters had played her hand, and now she must await his answer. A giant rat appeared, scuttling along the skirting board and disappearing through a floorboard hole.

"I suppose I should ask your real name, but under the circumstances, I think it best I don't know," Pennywise said, rubbing his cheek with a gnarled hand. "You mentioned a counteroffer. What exactly did you have in mind? That I should leave the country or fake my death?"

"No."

"Then explain what it is you have in mind?"

"It's obvious that your sons want you dead. They have asked me to help them rid themselves of you for two million pounds each. Might it be wise to be rid of them before they kill you? How does ten million sound if I save your life by ridding you of your sons?"

"Rather harsh. And damned expensive."

"It's you or them, your choice."

"And if I refuse your offer?"

"Then, you leave me little choice but to kill you."

"You seem quite confident in your abilities. I presume you possess the nerve to do such a thing?"

"I shan't kill you, but believe me, I can call on

people who will burn this place down within the next twenty-four hours." Rita Peters answered.

"Hmm, you have left me with quite a dilemma. Leave it with me, and I'll give you my answer in good time. Now please cover yourself and leave me to think in peace."

She stared at him. Surprised by his coolness, her nerves started to tingle. She'd said things she couldn't take back and wondered if he had fully understood the situation.

"You have until the morning," she said, glancing through the large window as the sun slipped over the edge of the darkening countryside. "No later."

Without waiting for an answer, she turned and left, gagging for fresh air. Out in the night air, the rain had stopped. Cows grazed. Stars hung pricked against the moody sky. After twenty-five minutes had passed she shivered, wishing she'd worn something warmer. Noises were an everyday occurrence in the darkness, and she paid little attention to what sounded like light footsteps. Then, as if possessing a sixth sense, she turned to face the direction of the noise. She saw the gun muzzle first. A split second later, the grim face of Wellington Pennywise appeared through the gloom.

"You stupid, greedy woman," he growled.

The flash of gunfire startled her. Moments before she fell to the ground, she heard another shot.

Darkness bulged with the sound of groaning, growing fainter by the second. Like flailing paddles, Rita Peter's hands frantically searched her body for signs of leaking blood. Coldness penetrated her inner parts, and her body shook uncontrollably. How could she be shot twice at point-blank yet feel no pain? Another voice, softer than the man who attacked her, drifted through the darkness.

"Get up. Take this money, get as far from here as possible, and don't ever think of coming back," Nelson Pennywise grunted. "I'll have no part in the murder of my father. I shot Wellington in the foot, and he's hobbled away to lick his wounds."

"I don't understand. Why aren't I dead."

"After being summoned by father, Wellington intended to kill you for trying to double cross him, so I took the live rounds from his pistol and exchanged them for blanks. Now go before it's too late. There's fifty grand in used notes in the envelope, the keys to your car, and your passport and credit cards I took from your room. Thank the lucky stars you escaped with your life after trying to extort money from my father. Now get away from here and never return."

Rita Peter's pulse thundered as she fumbled the key into the ignition and started her car. A twisted sneer distorted her features. She'd lost her self-esteem and felt less of herself for failing. Driving from the estate, the image of Wellington's face remained clear in her mind.

"Damn you, Pennywise, you haven't heard the last of me," she muttered.

CHAPTER FOURTEEN

Eyes open wide, Willow relished the look on Anton Page's face. Beaming with pride, she brushed aside the hair falling over her eyes with a sweep of her hand. She felt she'd done something right by answering each question correctly for once in her life.

"Well done. We'll make a vet of you yet," Page said.

"Thank you, it wasn't easy without using the computer," she answered shyly.

He smiled at her, taking in her wide grin, ears' shape, and the width of her nose. He'd learned that when she was nervous, her eyes blinked rapidly.

"Very good indeed," he said. "You answered the questions without consulting the computer. That means the answers are stored in your head permanently. Remember the questions in the future, and the answers will come naturally."

"I'll try."

"That's enough for today. How's our patient

doing?" Page asked, referring to the sick dog.

"He's stopped whimpering and sleeping better."

"It's been six weeks since the accident. There's still some time before we remove the splints. Time will tell."

"The owner called and asked if it would help the dog recover at home if that's okay with you."

"Not a problem; he can pick the dog up anytime, along with the painkillers to help the animal sleep."

"I'll miss him."

"I know you will. It's best never to get too attached to the animals."

*

Willow was busy in the surgery disinfecting the table on which Page used to inspect injured animals when the rattling of keys in the front door heralded Cate's arrival.

"Right, no arguments. We're going to the pub for a drink tonight, just you and me. It's time you got out and about instead of being stuck in here day after day," Cate laughed.

"I've never been one for drinking," Willow answered quietly.

"It isn't all about the drink, but mixing with people and relaxing. And make sure you don't take off your clothes after a couple of drinks."

Willow's hand flew to her mouth.

"Oh my God," she shrieked. "Mr Page will surely throw me out if that happens."

"I'll pick you up at eight o'clock. And try to look nice," Cate laughed out loud.

*

It had passed eight o'clock when Cate made an appearance. Instead of making excuses for her terrible time-keeping, she stared at Willow in jeans revealing her long legs' contours. A loose white cotton shirt struggled to hide the shape of a young woman approaching her prime. Her cheeks were pale, highlighting her piercing blue eyes.

"Wow, you look all grown up," she laughed.

Willow blushed. Unsure whether to believe Cate, the words offered her much-needed confidence. Seconds later, her eyes flickered over the pair of crutches propped against the wall by the fireplace. Cate followed her gaze, desperately searching for the appropriate words. Her own life hadn't been without hardships—her mother murdered by her father leaving her abandoned to live with her grandparents. But there was no purpose in resurrecting the past; no use wishing day was night and darkness never turning to light. With a faint sigh, Willow reached out for the crutches.

"I'm ready when you are," she smiled at Cate.

Cate glanced at her hand and, twirling the small ring on her finger, promised never to allow Willow to drift away from her.

When they entered the Crooked Stick Inn, apart from an elderly man with a stubbly grey beard and a collie asleep at his feet, the bar was deserted.

Behind the bar, Arthur Parrott frowned at Willow struggling on crutches.

"Find a chair, miss, and I'll bring your drinks over."

Cate raised an eyebrow at Parrott's kindness and ordered a gin and tonic. Willow remained adamant that fruit juice would suffice. Apart from the occasional small talk, the conversation quickly became stilted—both waiting expectantly for some mighty event to set the night on fire. When Xander walked in, Cate frowned and sucked in a deep breath. After begrudgingly acknowledging each other, she looked the other way to avoid eye contact. An hour later, Xander left the bar and, without invitation, sat opposite Willow.

"Hello, where have you been hiding this beauty?" he chuckled, glancing at Willow between mouthfuls of ice-cold lager. "Am I going to be introduced? Or must I do it myself?"

Cate's tone would be nothing if it weren't acid.

"Go and sit somewhere else, you silly little prick. You never could hold your drink, could you? You should stick to mummy's milk."

Xander's mouth gaped open ready to respond to Cate's insults. Cate raised her voice, adding to her scorn.

"It's gone nine o'clock; isn't it past your bedtime?"

Xander's eyes narrowed; his voice was as cold as a dagger's blade.

"One day, my dear, you will open your big mouth, and someone will tear out your tongue."

Cate clenched her hands. Determined not to let him get the better of her, she shuddered. He still possessed a subversive attitude, ready to revolt at a moment's notice.

"You disgust me. Finish your drink, Willow. We are leaving."

Willow smiled.

"Don't let me interrupt your conversation. I'm enjoying every moment.

"Well said, young lady. Don't be bullied by her. Did I hear the name Willow mentioned? Rather apt for a slender young filly. We must get together sometime."

"Why not? You can carry my crutches for me. Of course, if you lay me down and have your way, you will have to help me up again. Or would you rather I lathered your loafer?"

Cate's mouth dropped open.

"Good grief, Willow, don't talk like that to the likes of him," she stammered.

Locked in intimacy, Xander and Willow continued their conversation.

"Hmm, sounds interesting. Would you like me to lay you down and have my way with you first?" Xander chuckled.

"You will have to tell me how long is a mouse's tail first."

"And how the blazes would I know that?"

"Find the right mouse and measure its tail, and I'm yours."

"And where will I find this mouse?"

"I don't know. You'll have to search in the right places."

"How will I know if it's the right mouse?"

"No need to worry. I'll know."

"Give me a clue where I might find this mouse."

"Oh no, that would be cheating."

Xander began to lose his patience. Her beauty was alive and inviting, and he wanted to feast on her body.

Cate's face broke into a grin at the bewildered look on his face. She recalled someone once saying there is no such thing as a lapse of confusion; it's just a whisper on your conscience. Willow had tied him into knots, leaving him struggling to make sense of her words. Whatever the emotional pain that grew within him, Cate knew it could only be satisfied by sexual violence.

"Come on; we're leaving," she said, snatching Willow's drink from her hand.

Without complaint, Willow rose and pulled on her anorak.

"Let me know when you have the mouse," she smiled at Xander.

His eyes danced with anger.

"Stuff you, and stuff your mouse," he barked,

watching Cate and Willow disappear through the door.

Outside, a cloak of quietness had settled over the small village. Cate battled with her deepest thoughts. Aware of how Willow cracked Xander's colossal ego, she found it difficult to stop her smile from forming. Willow was an enigma; there was no doubt about that. She knew it wouldn't be the last time she'd bear witness to her rhetoric.

*

Late the following day, Willow stood with all the calm of a cat in a dog pound listening to Page read the letter from the hospital out loud.

"Don't look so surprised," Page laughed. "Who knows, perhaps in ten days from now, you will be able to walk unaided."

Willow opened her mouth to answer. When the words wouldn't come, she sat on a wooden chair and, in silence, allowed her tears to flow freely onto her lap.

"Well, I have things to do. Stay here until you feel ready to join me," Page said quietly.

During the few weeks Willow had spent with him, he'd come to care for her like he would his daughter. She'd changed. Her once dull and tired eyes sparkled with fun and laughter. More surprisingly, he found it difficult to accept the sudden change in his demeanour. Fondling the crucifix around his neck, he smiled knowingly. It was all part of rebuilding a new life for himself.

*

Gradually, as the days and weeks passed the welcoming heads of Snowdrops began to appear, followed by blankets of swaying golden daffodils. Springtime, the season of living, was at last upon them. The cold, soggy world of grey skies and drizzling rain soon became a thing of the past. Page's sleeping habits became more peaceful. The frail white look from being locked up in prison had almost disappeared.

He watched Willow eat through two plates of buttered toast followed by a full breakfast at the Tuesday breakfast table. More than he'd eaten in a day, he smiled. The operation on her hips had proved a great success. Allowed to discard the makeshift crutches and move around on two walking sticks until her legs gained strength; she battled to contain her excitement when the day arrived and she could move about unaided.

Cate and Luke had sorted their differences and once again became an item. Both agreed that all talk of engagement or marriage was strictly off the menu. Content in each other's company, they enjoyed occasional visits to friends for meals. But Luke sensed a change in Cate and knew it was something to do with the Pennywise family. Occasionally she seemed distant as if she wanted to be elsewhere. Afraid he might lose her again, he remained silent.

It was lunchtime when Page dropped his bombshell. When the bungalow received a complete overhaul, he announced and began by calling in a local firm to replace all windows one room at a time, leaving him and Willow free to care for the sick animals. Last on the list, the front and rear gardens would be landscaped. He smiled each time he overheard Willow ordering the workers how she wanted things done.

CHAPTER FIFTEEN

Later that evening, while pondering the best way to change the garden, Page noticed a spiral of smoke rising from the woods south of Pennywise Manor.

His thought hadn't mellowed with time. The village would be better a better place if the manor burned to the ground. Those who lived there had much to answer for. For months Page had buried his nerves, but what stays in must eventually come out, and Cate's constant accusations were becoming more and more belittling. Willow's non-stop chatter stripped his nerves to the core. The surgery's smell and Willow's constant clumsiness annoyed him more daily. Having to clear her mess away took his mind off the injured animals.

"Why must I constantly re-live the past when I should be considering my future?" he muttered beneath his breath. Then releasing the contents of his lungs, he drew in the chilly air through his nose. "It's my life, and I'll live it any way I choose."

A stoic expression replaced his worried frown; with shoulders squared and chin thrust forward, he turned and headed home. Since attending the church, he was no longer a doormat for others to wipe their feet on. He felt whole again, a man in charge of his destiny.

His first thought was to have things done his way instead of being ordered around. Invigorated by his attitude, his mind became focused like a pickpocket ready to make a dip.

When he entered the bungalow, Lady was the first to greet him. Silvery saliva hung from her gums as she leaned her front paws against his chest.

"Good boy, good boy," Page said, rubbing the dog's ears and looking at Cate sitting at the table reading a woman's magazine." Is tea ready?" he asked.

"There's something in the oven left over from last night," she answered without looking up.

"Really?" he snapped. "In which case, get off your arse and throw it in the bin. Then cook me a fresh meal."

Her smug look of satisfaction slid from her face, and she stared at him in astonishment.

"I beg your pardon. Did I hear you right?"

"You did, and don't sit there staring at me. I'm tired of having to do everything around here. Do as I ask or clear off back to your flat."

Before Cate could answer, Willow prodded

open the door to the surgery with her walking stick and sent the door crashing against a small coffee table.

"I can't find the flea powder," she snapped impatiently.

"Then open your eyes and look again, or did you expect it to jump into your hand?"

"You can do the dog yourself if that's how you feel."

"You insolent young woman, who do you think you are talking to?"

"No idea. How long is a mouse's tail?"

"Get out of my sight," Page shouted. "I'm sick and tired of the mess you make—half-eaten food left on plates, rotting apple cores and empty crisp packets over your bedroom floor."

Shocked at the lash of his temper, up until now, she'd done as she pleased. Helped herself to food between meals leaving him to clean the surgery whenever the dogs needed exercising—never replacing medicine bottles in the cupboard. In stunned silence, she leaned her weight onto the walking sticks and stared at the ground.

"There's no need for this kind of behaviour." Cate interrupted.

"And you," Page hissed, turning to face Cate. How dare you treat me as if I was your servant. I've had enough of your school exercise books littering the place. You do next to nothing to help keep the place clean."

"If you need a cleaner, hire one. Plenty of women in the village are happy to earn a few pounds each week."

Page stared at her, inhaled a sharp breath and spread his feet.

"Clear up your mess every night and keep this place clean. Is that clear?"

"Perfectly, and If I don't?" Cate snapped.

His eyes widened, his reply defiant and to the point.

"Then you can get your things together and get out."

Eyebrows half raised and lips turned down at the corners, Cate stared at him. He'd never spoken to her in this manner before. By the look on his face she knew he was serious. Since his release from prison, she'd trampled his words, mangled every sentence he uttered, and spoken to him like he was a badly behaved child. Feeling ashamed, she settled her eyes on Willow sitting like a figure of misery ready to burst into tears. Page waited. Whatever the outcome, he wasn't going to lose the argument.

"I'll go and clean the surgery," Willow said quietly.

"And I'll get my things together and head off home," Cate said falteringly.

Page waited for the sudden surge of compassion to envelop his body. Many times in the past, he'd backed down. But not this time, this time he was clear-headed and decisive.

Instead of being pushed into a corner, he was ready to fight back. He lay on the bed in his bedroom staring up at the ceiling. It wasn't the first time he'd felt the urgent desire to attend church. Like a mysterious urge that must be obeyed after nightfall, he'd go and rest his head on the front pew and ask God if he'd done the right thing. Not that he expected an answer. But he'd ask anyway. Best to be on the safe side.

On the way back to her flat, Cate searched her mind for words to explain her father's behaviour. In one sense, she admitted he was right. She'd barely shown him an ounce of compassion since his release from prison. Instead, it seemed natural to her to doubt every word he spoke. Deep in the pit of her stomach was the same nagging question, did he murder her mother? Memories of her mother shouting and screaming insults at him built up beneath her diaphragm, pressing so hard against her ribcage it seemed they might force through her skin. Again, the stirrings in her belly told her he didn't do it. How could he? He wouldn't harm a hair on her head, regardless of how badly her mother treated him. She knew that as sorrow swept through her. She imagined what it must have been like to spend twenty years locked in prison. Her thoughts were so intense the hairs on her arms pulled away from the skin. Yet, through all of this, she struggled to summon up a vague disoriented affection for him.

That night Page made his way to the church with his tongue clamped firmly between his teeth.

Father Kevin had finished replacing burnt candles while humming *'Onward Christian soldiers.'* when Page entered the nave.

"Good evening Anton," the Father said.

"Good evening Father," Page answered. "What have you for me today?"

"I'd be grateful if you'd brush the dust from the hassocks. It would be a great help, can't have worshippers with dusty knees."

"Of course not. Show me where the brushes are, and I'll make a start immediately," Page smiled.

"Thank you, Anton; you have been a tremendous help to me in the last few weeks."

Page allowed himself a wan smile. For twenty years he'd yearned for a friend—someone who cared nothing for his past. Loneliness had been a way of life for him. Naturally, there had been times when he preferred it that way; no one to burden him or depend on him. But Father Kevin was different. He was regular in his habits, steady and systematic. Best of all, he took Page as he found him. They quickly became firm friends and discovered they had much in common. Page knelt in the aisle for two hours, ensuring the small dust clouds never settled on the seats. After he'd finished, Father Kevin suggested he stay for coffee and a chat. Page waited for life to creep painfully back into his calves before climbing to his feet.

"It's late," Page said. "I need to get back and feed the sick animals."

"Of course, how silly of me to forget, God; go with you, Anton."

For a moment, Page hesitated, then turned and left without speaking."

He recalled the Father's words as he made his way through the narrow lanes and rises. God go with you, he'd said. Then he remembered how cruel he'd treated Willow and Cate. Maybe they would forgive him, and maybe they wouldn't. After all, God knew everything he'd said was true.

Before pushing the key into the lock and entering his home, he paused, wondering if Willow had run back into the woods where he'd first found her. And Cate, she was so headstrong he dared not think how she would respond.

On reflection, he decided to allow Willow to choose the paint for the surgery walls. She'd like that; it would prove that he trusted her. As for Cate, she was, after all, his daughter and his only remaining family. With hands trembling, he turned the key clockwise. When he pushed the door open, the place was in darkness. As if teasing his troubled mind, the ever-creaking floorboards remained unusually silent. Something soft struck his brow, followed by another, and then another.

"Miserable git, miserable git," the singing pounded in his ears.

When the lights flashed on, he stared in shock at Cate and Willow armed with pieces of food ready to throw at him.

Cate burst out laughing. Willow shrieked with pleasure as she hurled pork sausages at him.

"Dinner is ready, sir. If you care to take a seat, Madame Cate will serve you with her speciality of the night, a mixed grill seasoned with dust and the tantalising aroma of a flea-bitten dog," Willow laughed.

Page shrank back and raised his hands. Shocked by Cate and Willow's actions, he slipped and struck his head against a small coffee table in the hallway. Blood leaked from his head. Willow's face twisted with horror. The sausages fell from her hand. Cate, clasped hands clasped over her mouth and stared in shock.

"Get out of here before I call the police and have you thrown out," Page shrieked.

Tears streamed down Willow's cheeks.

"I'm so sorry," Cate whispered, her eyes dancing with fear. "It was meant to be a joke."

Page shoulders slumped. The long, endless winding days spent searching for trust and respect were nothing more than a shadow flitting throughout his mind. Convinced life would never be as he once knew, he climbed to his feet.

"Please go away and leave me alone," he said,

sucking in a great breath.

CHAPTER SIXTEEN

The salesman in the small run-down garage offered Rita Peters a quarter of the value of her car. Angry, she didn't know whether to laugh or punch him.

"It's worth more than three times that," she sneered.

"I've offered you the book price. I can't do any more than that."

"How about part exchange and cash?"

"Take a look around; let me know if you fancy anything, and I'll see what I can do."

Forty-five minutes later, she pushed the Honda into gear and set course for Milford-on-Sea, a small resort on the south coast.

Minutes short of an hour's drive, she pulled into the village on the south coast and booked into an Inn close to the village centre. Not bothering with dinner, she satisfied her hunger with fish n chips at a beachside cafeteria. Back at the Inn, showered and changed into jeans and a white sweatshirt, she stood before the full-length mirror and gazed at her reflection. Forty-eight years old, under the circumstances she hadn't weathered too bad. A little on the small side, not demure but still in possession of a trim figure. Her pale features, nothing a dose of fresh air couldn't correct. If there were one thing she'd like to change, it would be her stick-out ears. With a dismissive nod, she made her way to the bar. Spring was in the air, and the flocks of elderly summer holidaymakers seeking peace and tranquillity hadn't yet arrived to clog the bars and tea rooms.

Two gin and tonics later, she sighed and watched the sun drop behind the Isle of Wight. She needed rest—time to figure out how to spend the remainder of her life. To return to London after blowing the whistle on Serbian Ravi Jekov's three sons and a two-ton delivery of drugs would be plain stupid. Jekov made it simple that he would have his revenge for all three sentenced to fifteen years each. When the police offered her a safe house, she burst out laughing.

"I wouldn't last twenty-four hours," she told them.

*

Not for the first time in his life, Anton Page's fragile conscience required attention. For a man who regularly attended church, he continually viewed himself as a failure. It was not that it mattered what he thought or how he positioned his thinking; he received little encouragement for his troubled mind. Everywhere he looked, the faces of Cate and Willow were clear and present in his mind. All decisions concerning his life had been out of his hands for twenty years. Now his moods alternated between irritation and a pang of growing guilt. In one sense, he was right; Cate and Willow were untidy. But Cate was his daughter, and he was guilty of depriving her of her mother. As for Willow's noisy efficiency, he regarded her as a second daughter.

Business steadily improved in the surgery and the surrounding farms. With spring in the air, farmers forgot their differences and keen their cattle and sheep be ready for the market. Gradually, as the nights became longer, he was forced to work into the early hours of darkness to fulfil his promises. He never ate properly and constantly missed meals. Forever worrying over Cate and Willow, sleep became difficult. With her feisty nature, Willow could be like a gun going off before someone pulled the trigger. Would they see each other again? He didn't know. If they did, he didn't think of the consequences. Instead of time hardening him, it softened him and made him jump to conclusions about their well-being. Each time the phone trilled, his hand hovered over the button like a bird of prey about to strike before he answered the call. His shoulder drooped in disappointment at the sound of voices he'd no wish to hear. It became a struggle to control his temper at the sound of yapping dogs seeking attention. He considered throwing in the towel more than once, selling up and living somewhere quiet and peaceful. Nurturing another violent headache, he viewed life in a small cottage by the sea where he could ease his mind at the sound of crying seagulls flying overhead and a flowing tide crashing onto a sandy beach.

The trouble had begun several days previously. After checking everything was secure and the animals fed, the room swirled. Arms outstretched, Page staggered from the surgery to the lounge, trying to remember where the decorators had left their ladders and tins of unopened paint. Chairs were no longer in their usual places. Unable to find his way, he waited for his condition to pass. As abruptly as it started, his illness disappeared. The following morning a rap on the front door brought him to his senses.

"Good morning Mr Page. I wonder if I might have a moment of your time concerning the young woman Willow. Shouldn't take too long, just a routine call," DCI Mattress said, forcing her practised smile.

Page shrugged. Why was the policeman wearing a voluminous grey overcoat and a hat with the brim pulled down on such a fine morning?

"I'm afraid the place is a bit of a mess. I've got the decorators in," he mumbled.

"Not a problem, sir. We can continue down the station if you wish."

Page's heart sank to rock bottom. From the first day of his release he prayed he'd never have to listen to those words again or be forced to enter a police station. Visions of a damp cell filled his brain as he recalled the hopelessness and loneliness. His skin crawled as if he'd fallen headfirst into a pit of biting insects.

"Willow? You'd better come in."

Mattress followed Page into the bungalow and looked around for somewhere to sit.

"The young lady not at home this morning?" she asked.

"She helps out in the surgery during the daytime. Has she done something wrong?"

Mattress cast the question aside.

"I assume she lives here with you; is that correct?"

Page was close to losing his temper.

"For God's sake, stop asking silly questions and tell me what you want to know.

"She's been seen wandering around the woods close to Pennywise Manor. Don't you think that strange?"

"No, I don't. Pennywise doesn't own all the land around here, even if he thinks he does."

"Four men dressed as medieval archers were also reported seen close to the woods."

"I know nothing about these things. I don't know where Willow is; she's probably out walking the dogs," Page lied. "Best you come back and speak with her later."

"Yes, of course; sorry to have bothered you. We'll call back later."

*

Page spent the following hour feeding the hungry animals and administering medicine to those needing extra care. Disturbed by the visit from the police fear of his future and the unknown oozed from his pores. It seemed unfair that the ease with which his past could be fitted into one event could define his life—things he'd never given any thought to enter his head. He and Cate had never grieved her mother together or laid flowers at her grave. Enough was enough. He no longer needed to be reminded of the past.

It promised to be a fine day. The sun resembled a freshly washed lemon against the pale blue sky. The kind of day he'd dreamed of while locked in prison. Buds were sprouting on shrubs and trees. Flowers and plants sprang from the earth, eager to parade their beauty. For the first time in twenty years, he admired every leaf and petal with tears in his eyes.

During the next few days, he handed back healed animals to their owners and happily received others needing medical attention. Few stopped to chat. Some asked about Willow. Others asked if they could pay the bill next week. Page smiled and nodded. The welfare of the animals concerned him more than money

At last, the bungalow basked in a fresh coat of paint. All that was missing was the sound of Willow's constant talking and singing to sick animals. Page stifled his thoughts and went about what he was best at, making dogs wag their tails and cats purr while smaller creatures like hamsters, mice and other pets turned into happy balls of furs. Busy with the animals, he missed the chats with Father Kevin. The times he sat and listened for hours as the Father espoused evangelical subjects he once considered trivial. But something was absent, a vital ingredient that gave meaning to his life. Something he realised he'd never find in this small narrow-minded village.

*

Rita Peters loved thrillers, the cut and thrust of who did it excited her. Halfway through the latest paperback, she'd already checked out the villain and thought the hero too wet to be true when her phone dinged a ridiculous tune for children. Recognising the voice of Lord Pennywise her cheeks flared.

"What! Are you for real? If you paid me triple wages, you two-faced gilded reptile, I wouldn't work for you. And I don't care how lonely you are."

She changed her mind about telling him never to call her again. If she wanted revenge on Wellington, it would prove prudent to have an excuse to visit Pennywise Manor. That and things might turn out better than she'd expected with a newfound ally in Pennywise Manor.

"I'll think about it," she said, pressing the red button on her mobile before he could answer.

Bored with the paperback, she scowled and tossed it into the waste paper basket. Then started to read another about a couple of pensioners trapped in a block of council flats trying to escape the wrath of a murderous cockatoo whose only means of survival was drinking human blood. Later, if the mood took her she'd visit the bar downstairs and for the second night try to remain awake over a couple of gins and tonic while listening to the barman's tale of the time he caught a three-foot shark using a ham sandwich as bait. Aware her time would be better spent working on a plan to eliminate Wellington and Xander than listening to a load of boring crap she decided on an early night. The thought that Nelson, a harmless young man with a zest for learning was her ace in the pack swirled around in her mind. If it weren't for him, she'd be dead.

*

Willow knew she'd overstepped the mark by making fun of Mr Page and lived in constant fear they'd no longer be friends. Without him, the lessons on treating sick animals would cease to continue. In hindsight, she should have shown more gratitude for how he'd treated her; a saint couldn't have been kinder. Since her first encounter with him, everything she'd dreamed of had come true, and her future held no boundaries. But that wasn't all; something else lay deep in her heart. She looked up to him for showing her respect for the first time in her life. He treated her as if she was his daughter and she revelled in his attention and kindness. When allowed to accompany him on outside calls to attend to sick animals beyond the village's limits, stiff with amazement she watched as he went about healing and caring. Convinced he knew everything there was to know about cows, horses, sheep, goats, dogs, and even birds, along with a farmer's wife, she cried when he lifted an almost dead parrot from the cage floor and blew into the bird's mouth and then replaced it in the cage. Seconds later, the parrot hopped onto its perch and began squawking words unsuitable for lady's ears.

"Indigestion," Page grinned.

CHAPTER SEVENTEEN

As 4.15 pm approached the last of the owners had collected their animals. Most gave Willow a barely perceptible nod. None bothered to inquire after Page, who suffered a violent headache in his bedroom. Filled with anger, Willow cringed at the villagers' ignorance and how they treated Page even though he'd waived payment from the less fortunate. When the last of them had left after helping themselves to a cupboard full of dog food, Willow locked the doors of the bungalow. With Lady trotting contently by her side she made her way back to Cate's flat.

That evening, before bedtime, Cate glanced across at Willow with her head stuck in a magazine. Aware of how close Willow was to her father she felt guilty not having the same feelings.

"I'm selling the flat and buying a house on the new estate a couple of miles away on the edge of the village. I've had a look at a few houses. Close by is a cinema, supermarket, and rows of new shops. I'm sick to my teeth of this damned village and miserable shits that live here."

Willow stopped rubbing her red-rimmed eyes and looked up abruptly.

"Will you help me find the man I used to call dad before you go, I think he'll have me back, and can I keep Lady," she said, her voice barely a whisper.

Cate stared at her.

"I was hoping you might stay with me. I don't want to be alone."

"But what about Luke? Won't he mind?" Willow struggled to get the words out.

"No, he likes you. He says you are good for me; he says you stop me from being argumentative. Goodness knows what he means,"

Unable to stifle her feelings, sobbing, Willow flung herself at Cate.

CHAPTER EIGHTEEN

Seated on the sea wall with legs outstretched, Rita Peters watched the shifting colour of the sea ebb and flow over the sandy beach. Beneath a sky filled with gulls' cries and shrieks, a mist hung low over the blue water slab like dry ice on a disco floor. The thing she dreaded most had finally reared its head. Thirteen years stuck in the decaying dump of Pennywise Manor had been enough to drive anyone to the edge of insanity. Pretending to be Onions had been like throwing petrol on a fire to distinguish the flames. She'd forgotten how many times she'd considered jumping from the roof and bringing everything to an end. Since birth, nothing in her life had been of note. She had no particular destiny to guide her or a mentor to show her the path leading to a life of joy and fulfilment. Condemning people to prison by lying to the police could never be as attractive as opening the gates of heaven. Not that any of this was an affliction; she'd done it simply because she could, and the police paid for the information. Although the money was barely enough to buy a second-hand clothes horse, her actions had driven her from her beloved London for her safety. Had she stayed and the villains found out she was the grass responsible for having half the East End villains banged up in prison, there was no doubt in her mind she would die a painful death.

Nevertheless, with a passion for tidiness and order to help shape those principles that remained in her life, she continued to do as she pleased regardless of the outcome. But things were different now; she'd grown older, more mature in her thinking. And so, it went on, her thoughts rebounding from her skull like a kid kicking a ball against a wall. Would it be wise to return to London? One thing was certain; she wouldn't grow fat eating humble pie. The glory of foolhardiness finally won the day—there was no point in wasting the rest of her days hiding behind a blade of grass. For the last few days, she'd distracted herself, certain her one hope of salvation lay with the vet, Anton Page. Like others, she believed that Page had been badly represented at his trial for the murder of his wife. Thanks to Mr Legges, she knew Page had the ear of Britain's worst criminals during his twenty-year prison sentence. All he had to was pick up the phone and ask for help, Legge told her. And that is where her salvation lay.

Make friends with Page, offer him a shoulder to lean on, and then use him and his bunch of criminal friends to clear a path back to London. Perhaps she might delve into the night Page was supposed to have killed his wife and help clear his name: a long shot but worth aiming for. But first, she needed to rid the world of Wellington Pennywise and, after him, his brother Xander.

*

In the early morning light Willow dressed noiselessly and, forcing her stiff legs forward entered the kitchen. The pain in her hips subsided, helping to redouble her efforts to walk without the aid of the crutches. Seated on a chair beneath a large window overlooking the village, Cate watched her and smiled. It wasn't an easy smile, but more one forced against her natural feelings. Each time Willow slipped into one of her moods Cate knew she must tread carefully. She'd learned it was best to humour her and wait until her mood had passed.

"I've just about finished the packing. A couple of days from now we can move into the new house. How are you at gardening?" she asked Willow, hoping for a civil answer.

"How long is a mouse's tail?" Willow answered morosely.

"Did I ask you anything about a mouse's tail? No, I didn't; I asked if you were good at gardening. And I wish you'd stop answering a question with that silly remark."

Willow stopped struggling with the crutches and glanced at Cate.

"No need to be so grumpy. It depends on what kind of garden you want. Concrete slabs to make a large patio or a garden full of shrubs and flowers surrounding a lawn. Depending on your feelings, you can have both; I prefer the lawn, personally."

"Good, that's settled. I'll leave the planning for the garden to you. I'm off; I have a school meeting this morning' I'll see you later."

Absently staring through the sunlight filled the windows. Willow wondered why she was different from other girls her age. She'd admit she was selfish and self-centred. She'd given little thought to anyone but herself until she met Mr Page. He was a kind man who thought of others before himself. Casting aside the crutches, she reached for the walking stick. With a look of pain glued to her face, placing one foot in front of the other, she crossed the room to a chair where a pile of Mr Page's notes dating back to the early days when he decided to become a veterinary surgeon lay scattered. From these books and notes, plus assistance from Cate's computer, she devoured every word to help her understand the requirements of a lifetime of caring for sick animals.

*

Page knew why he couldn't sleep. Excitement shuddered in his bones; why hadn't he thought of it before? Minutes after the clock tolled midnight, he pulled on his anorak and tugged up the zip. At last, he could leave the bungalow and wander freely throughout the village without fear of sneers and abuse from the inhabitants. Twenty minutes later, he stepped into the darkness of night and softly closed the door behind him. With his breathing deep and irregular, eyes wide open, staring into the gloom, he realised he needed the toilet. To the hell with it. He'd find a gateway and piss on someone's garden. It didn't matter whose; they were all as evil, ignorant and bad-mannered as each other. Warmed by a sense of well-being, his rubber-soled shoes gently squeezing the pavement became barely audible as his breath began to ease. He'd start in Woodcote Grove and make his way to the village centre free from interference. Ignoring the crisp night air cooling his flushed neck, he congratulated himself for realising he could come and go as he pleased under the cloak of darkness. With his eyes crinkled into a smile, he imagined Lizzie's warm hand resting on his arm like the old days when they walked arm-in-arm beneath the dancing stars. During the daytime, the church had become his bastion where he could find peace. At night he could walk with Lizzie tight on his arm. At long last, he had something to help him escape his past. Under cover of darkness, he weaved his way in and out of the large puddles formed by a torrential downpour earlier that afternoon. Beneath a large Oak tree with heavy creaking branches, he took temporary shelter from the sudden downpour and peered along the road to ensure no one was present. Satisfied he was alone he darted across the street and entered the mouth of a wooded lane.

"Come along, Lizzie," he whispered. "Try to keep up. We'll go along Hackle Street until we reach the village centre. Not much to see, I know, but I'm certain it will bring back happy memories."

Seconds later the night lit up like a colossal candle as a lightning bolt pierced the darkness. The wind rose followed by streaming rain battering his face. Without warning it changed direction, soaking his neck and sending tiny rivulets of rainwater trickling down his back. Desperately sucking air into his lungs he ran into the woods seeking cover. Close to the edge stood a large brick shed, flat and square with no windows and a dark opening where once a door hung. Inside, something beneath his feet moved. Unable to keep his balance he fell to the ground. The sound of a low growl turned his blood cold. At least six dogs stared at him through feral eyes. With no idea what to do, he waited, fearful of being torn to pieces by the dogs. Suddenly the rain ceased, and everything turned quiet. Head tilted, he looked at the dogs wagging their tails and sighed with relief. It was common for villagers to put their dogs out at night to act as guardians. Climbing to his feet, he began the long walk to the safety of his bungalow. By the time he reached the outskirts of the village, it had started to spit, promising another deluge was on its way. With arms outstretched, a gusting wind sent him sprawling into the road.

Another bright flash of lightning, accompanied by crashing thunder rattled the glass panes in windows. Houses and streets became bathed in a vast searchlight. Exhausted and bruised, he limped across the narrow streets and pushed the key into his front door with trembling hands. All thoughts of Lizzie no longer existed as he dried himself cursing every inch of the village to be turned to dust and washed into oblivion. All hope of sanity absent, he opened the kitchen cupboard and took out a half bottle of whisky. Before the hour was up he lay fast asleep, curled up on the floor clutching the empty bottle. The world could go its own way; he wanted no part.

CHAPTER NINETEEN

Rita Peters preferred the 'bob' to the other wigs. It made her look younger, she told herself, and a lot easier to keep in good order.

"I'll pay in cash if that's okay," she said to the hairdresser.

"No problem," the hairdresser smiled.

"Is it okay if I keep it on?"

"Of course, you need a little time to get used to wearing it; it suits you."

Rita Peters wasn't prepared for a direct compliment concerning her appearance; caught off guard she took a breath before responding.

"Thank you, do you think so?"

"Yes, it certainly makes you look younger. I hope you don't mind me saying so."

"No, of course not."

Rita Peters paused. She'd dressed and acted like a man for thirteen years and wanted to access the woman standing before her. Was she telling the truth, or were her words nothing more than empty sales talk?

"I've been ill for some time," she lied. "And now I'm fully recovered; I intend to live a little, enjoy being a woman again. Are there any good shops where a lady might fill her wardrobe?"

"You could try Trudees in the High Street. I'm sure you will find her a great help."

*

Five days had passed since Page drank himself into a drunken stupor. His front door remained locked, and owners with sick pets vented their anger by hurling insults. He'd have shot them where they stood if he owned a shotgun.

The sixth day was different. Startled by a car door slamming he immediately knew it was Cate. Nobody slammed car doors shut with such force they might separate from the vehicle. Seconds later, the constant ringing of the doorbell sent his temper into orbit. Slumped back in the chair, he covered his face with his hands and ignored the hot tears burning his cheeks.

"I know you are in there. A horse has been found half-dead on the edge of the forest. The police are waiting for you, so move yourself and stop sulking." Cate shouted through the letterbox.

Page groaned. He couldn't leave a horse suffering and, grabbing his bag, left the bungalow.

"My God, you look a mess. When was the last time you had a wash and shave?" Cate snapped.

"Shut up. And drive. I'm sick of the sound of you."

Cate's lips curled into a snarl. Her response burned on the tip of her tongue, but now wasn't the time to retaliate.

"I'm busy; Willow will give you directions."

Ten minutes later, Page pulled up next to a young constable taking a last drag from the filter-tip cigarette before tossing it on the floor and grounding it into wet earth with the heel of his boot.

"I'm the vet. What seems to be the trouble?" Page snapped.

"A horse with a broken leg is behind the hedge," he nodded. "If you would care to see the horse, sir, I'll fetch DCI Mattress."

"Do you know how the horse broke a leg?" Page asked.

"Seems it tried to jump the hedge and fell. Poor thing must have been scared to try and clear the hedge, much too high for a small horse, I reckon."

"Yes, these things always are," Page grunted, walking around the other side of the hedge. "Easy, girl." Page said softly to the stricken animal.

"Such a pity; she's a beauty," Det/ Insp Mattress spoke over her shoulder.

"Where's the rider? The constable believes the horse was spooked?"

"Yes, well, there lies the mystery," Mattress sighed. "A man's been found dead lashed to a tree and burned alive. A lady walking her dog heard him screaming and found him burnt to a cinder. She's on her way to the hospital suffering from shock."

Page blinked and shook his head.

"Has the man been identified?" Page muttered.

"We are certain it's Wellington Pennywise."

Page looked up and scanned Mattress's face for signs her words were a sick joke. Mattress stared back with a bland look covering her face.

"This won't go well with Lord Pennywise; he dotes on his sons. We won't hear the last of this for a long time."

Seldom during police investigations had a scene looked as gruesome as Wellington Pennywise's death. He might have been a brute of a man, but no man deserved to die in such horrific circumstances. Stripped naked and tied to a tree, a fire of bracken and wood had burned his body black leaving no recognisable part of his body.

"Good riddance if you ask me," Det/Sgt Down muttered. "This is how the bastard deserved to die."

"Now then, Down," DCI Mattress snapped. "That's no way to talk of the dead."

"No, ma'am, sorry, boss", Down mumbled, tugging out his notebook. "I've tried speaking to Lord Pennywise, and I can't get a word out of him. Real cut up he is, sits there picking his nose."

"How about Xander and Nelson?"

"Nelson acts as if he couldn't care less, and the way Xander carries on, you'd think he wanted Wellington canonised. Weird bunch, the whole bunch of them."

"Well, I'll be looking for some answers tomorrow," Mattress snapped.

"Roger that. No time like the present, boss," Down said eagerly.

"You're a bloodthirsty sod. No, we'll leave the family to mourn their loss and have a word with them tomorrow; I'll see you in the morning, Down, and for God's sake, grow up."

Horrified by her words, shame shook Page to the core. Borne away on an irresistible tide of conscience, he turned his head so that Willow didn't have to look at his face. Back in the car facing the sun, he squinted and wondered how he'd allowed himself to become mixed up in the tangled web of village life. Horses ripped open with a knife while still alive. His bungalow daubed with paint. And now a man burned to death tied to a tree. Would it ever stop? He could have sold his home a dozen times and left for a place he wasn't known. Those who ignored him and openly insulted him were the same people he'd been raised with. A man burned to death while tied to a tree; how the villagers would revel in that little episode while slurping beer in the Crooked Stick Inn. Enough was enough; there was no rebating his anger. His heart blackened and hatred burned in his body. His sanity teetered on the edge of a deep chasm from which there was no escape. Of course, he could hardly ignore his guilt; men don't regularly kill their wives. Or had it been jealousy, hatred, shame, or misplaced passion? He didn't dare consider an answer.

He'd forgotten about Willow seated by his side, her mouth gaping open. When he turned and looked at her, she stared back expressionless. Her following words knocked him sideways.

"Shall we go to church and pray for the dead man?"

Page's world collapsed. He wanted to return to his cell. Anywhere away from the plague of humanity that rotted and poisoned the ground they walked on.

"Church, why should we go to church? I've never thought of you as the religious kind," he mumbled.

"I'm not," she answered, "but you are."

"I don't know what you are blathering about."

"I've seen you enter the church no end of times, and only good people do that."

"You mean you follow me around without my knowing?"

"All the time. I like to know you are safe."

"And you," Page spluttered. "Are you a good person? Running away from home leaving people sick with worry about where you might be, wondering all the time if you are dead or alive."

"I don't know; how long is a mouse's tail?"

"Stop talking nonsense; it's time you grew up and acted your age."

Nothing stays perfect forever, he'd learned as a child. He knew he'd made a mistake the minute he uttered the words. His scowl of disapproval melted. He wanted to tell Willow he was sorry and didn't mean what he'd said.

"I know you're angry with me. Under the circumstances, I will ignore your outburst," Willow answered defiantly.

Words escaped him as he glared out the window like a man restrained from living.

"We're going home, the window men are coming today, and the furniture needs moving to allow them access." Page said, starting the engine and reversing from the narrow road.

"I don't feel well," Willow said quietly." I think it's the thought of that burnt body. What an awful way for a person to die. I'm going to be sick."

"Well, I'm not stopping now; I've had enough aggravation for one day."

"You're horrible, you are. And I thought you were a churchgoer?" she shrieked.

Her outburst amused him.

"We'll stop in the village for a fish and chips takeaway; will that make you feel better?"

"It might. How long is a mouse's tail?"

Half a mile on, Page leaned forward, eager

for a better view of four men dressed in green leather trousers and matching tops like people from past centuries. Each carried a longbow strung around their shoulders. Feathered hats like he'd seen in old Robin Hood films sat jauntily on their heads. Walking in single file, they slowed to allow him to pass by safely. He'd seconds only to stop and question the men if they knew anything of a man burned to death tied to a stake. As he drove level with the last man, they turned, pushed through a gap in the bushes and disappeared.

Willow grabbed his arm so tightly that he struggled to control the car.

"Don't stop; please keep driving," she said, releasing her grip.

"Do you know those men? Are they from your past? You seem afraid of them?"

She never offered her stock answer of how long is a mouse's tail. Instead, she sat back and nervously picked at her jeans.

"Well," Page continued, bent on having her answer his question instead of listening to her constantly ducking and diving.

Willow's mouth worked like she was chewing her bottom lip. She turned her head as if refusing to acknowledge his question. In that one small amount of time Page felt humiliated. Why did she behave in this manner? Hadn't he done enough to earn a little respect from her? And why did she follow him each time he left the bungalow? To make sure he was safe, she told him. And her on sticks to help her from one place to another. Since he'd left prison, all he'd ever craved was peace. Somewhere he could sit and think his thoughts. He wasn't opposed to helping people but disliked being tested each time he asked her a question. A cunning idea entered his head.

"Are all the stories you told me of your past true or a pack of lies? And don't ask me how long a mouse's tail is, or you can walk home, sticks or no sticks."

"Up to you whether you believe me. I don't care."

"Are you staying with Cate or coming home?"

"How long is a mouses tail?" she answered.

*

The early morning sun glowed over the four gleaming black stallions with black plumes bobbing in the breeze pulling the black carriage with dark-tinted windows through the village's turns and rises. Dressed in an immaculate black suit and matching top hat, the funeral director walked ahead of the procession with his head bent in respect. Those from the village who bothered to turn out and watch the spectacle of Wellington Pennywise's funeral wouldn't be enough to fill a single-decker bus. Elderly mourners unknown to the villagers came on sticks and walking frames clutching each other ready to collapse at a sudden waft of wind.

Behind them, the Pennywise Hunt mounted on horseback looked even more ancient and decrepit than those on foot.

Watching from the corner of the High Street, the funeral of Wellington Pennywise meant nothing to Willow. She knew nothing of the Pennywise family; her only meeting with Xander amounted to a brief interval of amusement in the Crooked Stick. Tired of watching proceedings, she tightened her grip on the leash.

"Come on, Lady," she said, bending down and stroking the dog's ears. "There's a good girl. Let's go home and feed the animals.

No one noticed the trim woman dressed in black with a black veil covering a stylish blonde 'bob' standing outside the newsagents.' She smiled through tight lips—the pupils of her eyes hooded by their lids. Rita Peters had taken her revenge on the man who had tried to kill her. She knew where he rode each morning and dressed in a short skirt and tight shirt; he almost fell off his horse to get to her. Spooked, the horse reared and galloped away. While recovering his dignity, Rita Peters leaned forward and jabbed the syringe into his neck. Now he was hers to do with as she pleased. The rest is history. Her next victim would be Xander, and after him, Lord Pennywise.

CHAPTER TWENTY

The next day Willow watched Page go about curing sick animals. Each time his gentle hands found the painful spot in an animal, he'd stop and whisper calming words in the creature's ear. Small dogs, aggressive cats, and even nervous hamsters reacted to his softly spoken words. But not everything was as it should be. The surgery was untidy and in need of cleaning. He'd slipped back into chaos, and she couldn't allow that, or everything he'd achieved since leaving prison would be lost. Without looking at him, she heard his deep, labouring breath as he searched for the correct medication beneath a pile of rubbish. She missed his mumbled words but knew his patience was ready to explode.

"Can I help?" Willow said quietly, hoping he would respond kindly.

"Make all the animals better, can you, or do you want to turn the place into another pigsty?"

Willow's heart hurt to think he didn't care.

"I spent weeks putting all the medication in

order, and since I left to live with Cate, the place has become a mess."

"I can manage, thank you, Page grunted.

"No, you can't. You want to learn to practise what you teach."

"Really, and just what does that mean?"

"For the animal's sake, I'm going to move back in this evening, and that's that."

"You needn't bother."

"It's no bother."

"You can be a real pain in the arse sometimes, can't you?"

"How long is a mouse's tail?" Willow grinned, grabbing her walking stick and shuffling out. "See you later, crocodile."

Page's mood lightened. Although he wouldn't admit it, he missed her constant chatter. The crazy ideas she had for her zoo, elephants, married before God and other mad ideas. He was not the kind of man to pass through a meadow and not see the flowers; he carried the feeling that whatever she chose to do, it would be a success. The promise of a hot meal that night increased his mood.

*

Rather than stay in the village, Rita Peters rented a small flat nearby. Brimming with confidence she wouldn't be recognised, she openly shopped and used the bars a lady might frequent. As far as alcohol was concerned, she was in the in-between place. Enough drink to help raise her confidence but not enough to be unreasonable. White wine mixed with a blue-label vodka was her favourite tipple. But tonight, flush with £50,000 Nelson had given her along with her savings, a few mouthfuls more of her favourite drink wouldn't cause her to become spiteful and destructive. The twenty-something kid behind the bar juggling bottles of brown ale like he was Tom Cruise raked the edges of her nerves. Three times he told her his name was Simon like he was the coming of the next Messiah. Next would be the all-devouring punchline. He'd insist on taking her home, expecting her to fall to her knees and thank him, certain what else she might do on her knees would follow.

"I finish in ten minutes," he whispered through his clasped hand across the bar. "Hang around after time, and I'll take you home."

"Really?" she said. "Room for two in your pushchair is there. I think it best you wheel yourself back to your nursery before the bogeyman gets you," she laughed, sticking fresh lipstick on her lips before walking out.

*

Things had improved. Page was happier than he'd been in weeks. True to her word Willow transformed the surgery with everything tucked away in the right places. What pleased him most was Willow getting around without using her crutches. She seemed more mature and grown-up than he'd noticed before. Her eyes shone with happiness. Her lips turned into a permanent smile.

"I think it's time you learned to drive. I'll book lessons in town for you, not the village; they have enough to gossip about."

"That would be great, thank you. But I don't own a car." She grinned.

"We'll worry about that later, shall we?"

"How long is a mouse's tail?" she laughed, throwing her arms around his neck.

*

Xander Pennywise stood in the room's doorway, unable to tear himself away from his father naked, apart from a baggy pair of tartan underpants. His left leg was heavily bandaged, and he held a large tumbler of malt whiskey in his left hand. Now Wellington was dead; his inheritance was the only thing on Xander's mind. Not that he'd dare mention his thoughts to his father and receive a tirade of insults for his trouble. Lord Pennywise lifted a jar of mint imperials and pushed a handful into his mouth. His face red with anger, he slurped and wiped the leaking saliva from his mouth with his wrist.

"Everything was peaceful until that fool Page was thrown out of prison: nothing but trouble since he returned. Even the damn villagers can't stand him," Lord Pennywise moaned.

"Oh, I don't know about that, father. Things have settled down, and those with sick pets are beginning to visit him."

"Really, in that case, we'll have to close him down."

Xander smirked.

"Well, you keep me out of your shenanigans. I want no part in upsetting the villagers. This place wouldn't run without them; be like cutting off your nose to spite your face," he said, shaking his head like an earnest child."

"For God's sake, grow a spine and stop acting like a useless turd. Penny to a pound of shit, Page had something to do with your brother's death."

"Rubbish, you know the kind of people that Wellington ran with? They'd burn their granny for a hard-on."

"Don't talk ill of the dead. Remember that Wellington was your brother."

A bubble of nervous laughter rose in Xander. Certain his father spoke out of anger; until now, he hadn't given his brother's funeral much thought. While outside the crematorium, some mourners crossed the grass to offer their condolences to his father. Aware of Wellington's lifestyle, others couldn't get away fast enough. Some looked perplexed when told there wouldn't be a reception; for most, free drinks and food were the only reason for attending the funeral. When Sylvia Gaunt, who owned a small garden centre, mentioned buds on the trees heralded the advent of spring, Lord Wellington told her to clear off back to her shop of common weeds. To make matters worse, someone he didn't recognise followed the funeral carriage with a bucket and shovel, ready to pick up shit the horses deposited. In a temper, Lord Pennywise tossed his top hat out the window and swore at the driver to get a move faster.

"Yes, father, how could I possibly forget that Wellington was my brother?" Xander said quietly.

"Never mind the sarcasm. I want Page out of the village. Are you listening to me?"

Yes, father, what do you propose we do? Tell him to be on the next bus or else?" Xander grinned.

It took Xander seconds to realise that his father was deadly serious. Not so much as a whisper in the air, Xander grimaced, wondering what direction his life was about to take. When he turned to leave, his father's voice reverberated across the room.

"Make yourself useful and do as I say, or you won't get a penny from me."

Xander stopped and turned to face his father. His legs trembled with anger.

"Stick your money up your arse. I'm sick of listening to your threats. If you want Page out of the village, tell him yourself."

"My God, you insolent waste of space. So do have the makings of a spine at last. Now get out of my sight and do what I told you."

When the door clicked shut, Xander leaned against the wall and recalled Wellington's suggestion that they kill their father. But things were different now Wellington was gone leaving him with Nelson as his partner in crime. Consumed by a mounting hatred, he visualised his father sitting in a pair of baggy underpants yards from where he stood. Teeth gritted, he weighed up the idea of returning to his father's room and suffocating him with a pillow. The police would put it down as a heart attack while mourning the death of his eldest son.

"In a bad mood, is he?"

The sound of Nelson's voice startled him.

"For God's sake, I wish you wouldn't creep around like a frightened mouse; you scared the shit out of me."

"Really?" Nelson sniggered. "Can't be much left of you then?"

"Piss off, you oversized girl's blouse."

*

The bitter winds that brought tears to Anton Page's eyes had subsided to a welcome mellowing breeze. Green shoots of early daffodils gently poked their heads from deep winter sleep. Spring had quickened, bringing colour and beauty to that which was cold and ugly. Sparrows, blackbirds, tits, and starlings searched for food before building nests. The small pond, overcome with thick clumps of algae a perfect place for the croaking frogs to start a new family.

A smile stretched the skin on Page's face. At last, the neighbourhood that had once shunned him slowly began to accept him back into the fold. But it cut no ice with him. He'd suffered the insults for far too long to forgive those narrow-minded villagers who'd gone out of their way to make his life miserable. To their embarrassment, he remembered those who owed him money and insisted on payment upfront before treating their pets or livestock. The sound of the front door opening and slamming shut woke him from his reverie. A sure sign Willow had returned from her third driving lesson.

"I drove in reverse today. It was easy. The instructor said I would make a good driver," she trilled, flicking on the kettle. "Tea or coffee, I'll start cleaning the surgery, and the cages need disinfecting."

"Coffee for me, please."

"Coming up," Willow laughed

"I want to talk to you about your situation here. Do you intend to stay or eventually move on?"

Sure she was about to hear bad news, her expression changed to apprehension.

"I want to stay here forever and learn to become a vet like you if you will have me. I thought you knew that?"

Pleased by her reaction, Page pushed his hands into his pockets and smiled.

"Remember when we spoke of you attending the veterinary college?"

"Yes," Willow answered softly.

"I want to train you as my operating assistant. Most pets suffer from bone problems, joints not knitting correctly, hip problems, or something they ate that might endanger their lives. Stick it out with me for one year, and I'll pay to put you through the veterinary college. It might come in handy when you open your zoo of dancing elephants. What do you say? Would you like to think about it for a few days?"

The offer might have daunted some people. Proud to be considered for such a post, instinct overrode all her other thoughts. Willow knew this was the beginning of something extraordinary.

"How long is a mouse's tail?" she laughed. "I'm ready to start right now. Thank you so much for helping me. My legs are growing stronger each day, and soon I can do without the walking sticks, and it's all down to you. Thank you so so so much. I won't let you down, I promise."

*

In the privacy of his room, Xander exhaled a long, drawn-out sigh. How could he force Anton Page to leave the village? Murder was out of the question without Wellington to guide him. His best chance was to find out what Page treasured most and take it from him. The thrill of breaking the law and being hunted by the police excited him. The thought passed quickly; there wasn't enough rebel in him to risk being locked up like a common criminal. He recalled the girl he'd met with Cate Page in the Crooked Stick. Her name was Willow, she'd told him. A plan began to formulate in his mind. He'd visit Anton Page's veterinary surgery and discover what Willow was to Page. Was she family? Did she work there? More importantly, how would Page respond if she were to disappear suddenly?

*

Rita Peter's eyes rolled with pleasure. Her new wig, dyed and cut into a striking style, hid her stick-out ears. Even better, when the beautician remarked the freckles made her look younger, she oozed newfound confidence. During thirteen years at Pennywise Mansion, not once had she applied face cream for fear of being called to attend one of the Pennywise family. Now free from their demands, she could become the attractive woman she'd always desired. Ninety minutes after a full facial, dressed in jeans and a white wool jumper, she glanced briefly at the occupants in the salon, then stepped outside into the warm spring air feeling certain the Pennywise family wouldn't recognise her in a month of Sundays.

*

Cate closed her eyes in frustration at the knowledge that when angry Willow's temper flew whichever way the wind blew. Eyes open, she ran a hand through her hair, turned from the window, and stared at the boxes waiting to go to her new address. Grabbing the phone, she punched Luke's number and received no answer.

"Shit," she moaned. "Why is the world so damned complicated?"

The front door swung open, and Luke walked in smiling from ear to ear.

"Hi," he said. "I thought I'd drop by and give you a hand moving the boxes."

"Do you own a white horse?"

"No, you know I can't stand horses, so why ask?"

"Cos you have just become my knight in shining armour."

*

Xander slipped the leash over Dylan's head, ushered him into the car's rear and started the engine. His destination, Anton Page's Animal Surgery and a meeting with the young girl known as Willow. Convinced that once he'd worked his overwhelming charm to disarm her, she'd be putty in his hands. If not, he'd set the place on fire and place the blame on Page.

*

When Page opened the doors for business, three ladies were waiting with sick dogs. Seated in one of the easy chairs arranged around a low coffee table, he decided to let them wait and poured another cup of coffee. To hell with them. Since returning to the village, his temper had burned on a short fuse. The death of Beau Legges had come as a shock. Of Wellington Pennywise, he thought little; the man was a pervert hated by the villagers. As for himself, he'd hidden behind the parapets of decency for months while the villagers defiled his name. He'd lost count of the times Cate told him he had a choice, remain in the village or leave and set up business elsewhere. But why should he be burdened with choices? Born and bred in the village, he'd every right to remain. Yet, he'd changed, grown resentful. The ligaments of hope had disappeared. He despised the villagers and yearned for revenge on those who made his life miserable and those who dared to offer him choices. The sudden appearance of Willow in jeans and a T-shirt helped loosen his mood. She'd painted her fingernails a light shade of pink and taken her time applying make-up. Hair tied into a ponytail suited the shape of her face. But what curled his interest most was how she moved freely without the aid of the two ever-present walking sticks.

"Good morning," she smiled. "Are we open for business?"

"Yes, there are three ladies in the waiting room. Ensure the lady in the khaki anorak pays the inspection fee before sending her to me. We don't operate a charity for scroungers."

Willow rolled her eyes, thought about answering, and then changed her mind.

"Looks like we have another customer. I saw him in the pub when Cate and I had a drink. He seemed cocky like he was God's gift to women."

"It's Xander Pennywise; what does he want? Send the three ladies in first; we'll see Xander together?"

Two ladies in the waiting room walked out when asked to pay the vet's fee. An elderly lady angry at being asked for money stared Willow in the face.

"How dare you, Mr Page, never charged me before."

"Things are different now. Mr Page has a business to run," Willow said, hands on her hips.

One of the two remaining ladies said she had left her purse on the kitchen table and hurriedly made for the door. The third lady smiled and paid the fee.

*

It was plain Xander wasn't there to have his dog checked over. The animal, a black retriever, looked in peak condition. His interest lay in Willow to such an extent that listening to him chatting her up became an embarrassment to Page.

"There's nothing wrong with your dog, and we are busy. I'd be grateful if you left," Page said sharply.

"I'm not leaving until Willow agrees to meet me for a drink."

"Get out of here; she's better things to do than meet with the likes of you." Page said, raising his voice.

"That's for her to decide. Or do you tell her

where and when she can go?"

"No, I don't. I don't want her mixing with the likes of you. You have only one thing on your mind."

"How about you, Willow? Would you agree to meet me for a drink?" Xander said, turning his attention back to Willow.

"If Mr Page doesn't want me to, the answer is no. Is that simple enough for you to understand?"

"Sorry I bothered you some other time, perhaps?" Xander said, slipping the leash over the dog's head. "Come on, boy, we aren't welcome here."

From the window of his surgery, Page watched a warm breeze drive the last of the dried leaves from the road. Spring had arrived, the month when the earth multiplied and nature prepared to offer her best. Then he noticed the woman wearing the khaki anorak standing in the middle of the road. With her feet apart, he saw the rage on her face. Page pushed open the window and stared at each other in silence. Raising a hand, she pointed at him as if selecting him for a painful death and then hurled a string of curses.

"Always did think you were high and mighty, didn't you? Bloody murderer, that's what you are. You'll get no money out of me."

Before Page had time to answer, the woman turned and walked away.

"What's her problem," Willow asked, inspecting her painted nails.

"I cared for her dogs for years and never received a penny. Damned if I'll start again."

Before they finished their conversation, the surgery door opened and closed.

"I'll get it."

"Thanks, Willow. Send them in."

"No probs."

The minutes passed without event until Willow entered Page's office with a smile.

"It's a man; he wants to speak to you."

"Send him in."

"He doesn't seem all there to me."

"What do you mean?" Page smiled.

"You'll see, he keeps stuffing liquorice allsorts down his throat."

"It's okay, Willow. Let him in."

Page looked at the man with open suspicion when he entered the office. Light on his feet in his mid-thirties, he was dressed in a camouflage shirt and stonewashed jeans with the knees slashed according to fashion. His sleeves were rolled up revealing the hairiest forearms Page had ever seen. His features seemed Mongoloid mixed with a hint of Chinese,

Page waved him to take the seat on the other side of the desk.

"What can I do for you."

The man leaned across the desk.

"You are Anton Page, the veterinary surgeon?"

"At your service, and you are?

"My name is Adlartok. Known as Toki to my friends."

"What can I do for you, Adlartok?"

"You can start by telling me how Beau Legges died and call me Toki."

Page swallowed hard and drew a deep breath. Toki leaned back in the chair, his deep-set eyes fixed on Page he began eating sweets from a box marked liquorice allsorts.

"You knew Mr Legges?" Page asked, labouring for his breath.

"We shared a cell in prison before he met you. I was with him when you phoned after his release. Tell me how he died and why?"

Page's hands started to shake.

"He was doing me a favour—he died in a vehicle accident in the village.

"He was doing you a favour in a village where everyone hated you, and for that, he died. What was the favour?"

"Putting the frighteners on those who trashed my bungalow and made my life miserable," Page whispered.

"Something you were too frightened to do yourself?"

"Yes, I wanted the villagers to like me."

"Strange way to influence people to like you, wouldn't you say?"

"Put that way, I suppose it would."

"You suppose?" Toki mocked, ramming sweets

into his mouth. "I've been in this village for two days, and I'm yet to meet anyone with the decency of a Nanook's arse, including you."

"No, you are probably right. I'm sorry. By the way, what is a Nanook?"

"A Polar bear in your language. Okay, Mr Page. I'll cut to the chase. I want to know who drove the vehicle that killed Legges and where I might find this person."

"All I know is a man named Onions was driving the van that accidentally ran Mr Legges down. He used to work at the Pennywise Manor until he left the village. Ask them; they might know where he is."

"Thank you. Good day, Mr Page. I'm certain we'll meet again before I leave. In case you wonder who I am. I am of the Inuit people you know as Eskimos. Mr Legge was a very dear friend of mine. We served together on many occasions."

Moments after Toki left, Willow entered Page's office. Shocked at the sudden change in his appearance, she ran an agitated hand through her hair. Page looked as if every ounce of blood had drained from his body as he fought to stay upright. He wanted to shout, to scream, to deny his existence. Enough was enough. His spectacles fell from his trembling hand and shattered on the floor by his feet.

"I'm calling the doctor, and don't argue," Willow said, keeping a consistent voice.

"No, no, I'll be fine in a moment. Just a bit of a shock, that's all." Page mumbled.

"I'm not arguing. I'm calling the doctor now."

Two hours passed when Doctor Wise told Page to remove his shirt. Ten minutes later, the doctor gave his verdict.

"Well, Anton, if I were a vet, I'd put you down and out of your misery. Are you in pain, your chest in particular?"

"All the time," Page answered, staring down at his feet.

"I'll give you some anti-biotics. Come and see me in seven days. In the meantime, take things easy and cut down on visiting farms. You need to rest. It must have been challenging for you in prison at your time of life."

"Life's never easy, is it?"

"No, I suppose not. Remember what I told you. I'll let myself out; goodbye."

CHAPTER TWENTY-ONE

Toki didn't bother to use a vehicle to visit Pennywise Mansion. With a heavy backpack strapped to his shoulders, he devoured the distance to the mansion like a trained athlete at a moderate gait. When he reached the large building, he hammered the wooden doors until they finally swung open.

"Are you deaf or too bone idle to get off your arse and open the door?"

Nelson Pennywise hesitated. Nervous at the sight of the big man.

"Neither, thank you. Whoever you are and whatever you are selling, goodbye; please don't call again," Nelson said, pulling himself up to his full size.

"I'm here to see Lord Pennywise. You tell me where he is, or I'll search every room until I find him."

Nelson blinked. Eager to break the everyday boredom, he stepped back and smiled.

"Follow me. I'll take you to Lord Pennywise's

office. I must warn you; he tends to masturbate with alarming regularity."

"He likes to slap the one-eyed serpent, does he? I've seen enough of that in my time. Lead on."

"Allow me to introduce myself. I'm Nelson Pennywise, Lord Pennywise's youngest son."

"Then you must have known this fellow, Onions?"

"Onions, yes, of course, I knew Onions. He left some time ago. No idea where he is now."

"Why did he run Beau Legges down? There must have been a reason."

"I believe it was an accident."

"I'm here to find the truth and will not rest until I do, however long it takes."

"Friend of yours, was he?"

"He was my unarmed combat instructor."

"Oh, I see; you are a soldier?"

"Ex Foreign Legion and SAS. I don't do it anymore. Death and killing do little for the mind."

Nelson raised his eyebrows at the answer.

"This is my father's office," he said, pointing to a large Oak door. "Would you like me to introduce you?"

"That won't be necessary," and leaning on the handle, Toki pushed the door open and stepped inside.

It was a large room shrouded in semi-darkness—heavy curtains were tightly drawn to keep out the daylight. A collection of soft watercolours hung from the walls. Toki took a liquorice allsort from the box and popped it into his mouth.

"Finished wanking, or are you about to start another round? I can wait. I'm in no rush."

Nelson covered his mouth with both hands to prevent laughing out loud, then turned and hurried away.

"Who the devil are you? What do you want?" Lord Pennywise grunted, pulling his bathrobe over his exposed body

"I want to know the whereabouts of the man called Onions."

"Onions? He's not a man. He's a woman, for God's sake. Get out of here, or I'll call the police and have you thrown out."

"Call Jack the Ripper for all I care. I'm going nowhere until I get some answers. The sooner you tell me what I want to know, the sooner I'll be on my way."

"Step closer out of the shadows where I can see you," Pennywise said, intrigued by Toki's attitude. "Don't get many specimens like you in our neck of the woods."

"Perhaps you should get out more. Tell more of this Onion fellow you say is a woman."

"Had me fooled for thirteen years, then walked in here as bold as brass and got his tits out. He even had the nerve to try and flash his fanny at me. It's a strange world we live in, unlike the old days."

"Did this so-called woman have a name?"

"Calls herself Rita Peters. I've no idea where she is; now clear off before l call the police."

"Rita Peters, eh, it's something to go on. Thanks for the help. You can get back to pulling your meat now. Try doing it under the bed; you'll find it much more interesting."

*

Rita Peters had paid a month's rent for the small flat above the Blue Moon Café. Her first choice would have been a room at an inn but that meant mixing with strangers. It would be better if she remained anonymous until she'd finished with Xander Pennywise. After brief consideration, she decided Anton Page would be her first target. Xander could wait. The fact that most villagers hated Page would work in her favour. She'd sympathise with him, tell him the villagers weren't worth the bother. Once she'd gained his confidence, she visualised no problem manipulating him to clear a path for her return to London's East End.

*

The sun descended from a dazzling blue sky at seven minutes to eight in the evening. Not a single cloud visible in the sky, Toki raised his gaze and looked across the fields and meadows at Pennywise Manor. Throughout his time out of his native home in Greenland, he'd never understood why people chose to spend their lives in old grimy dusty buildings. False turrets and battlements gave the Manor an air of Dracula and blood-sucking vampires.

He'd never needed anyone until he joined the military service. Being alone had always been the way for him since his parents passed away. He'd lived like that until the day he met like-minded people. The French Foreign Legion gave him the comradeship he'd craved. Later he left France and was accepted to serve with the SAS. At eight o'clock, he slung the backpack from his shoulders and erected a one-person camouflage tent. Thirty minutes later, he took the cup of water from the fire, added a fresh tea bag, opened a small tin of sardines and sat in front of the fire with a contented smile to enjoy his evening meal.

After finishing eating, he pushed two pills down his throat. The doctor told him the tranquillisers would help to subdue his fits of violent temper and uncontrollable rages. They didn't, but he took them convinced one day he might feel the benefits of modern medicine. At three o'clock the following morning, he stared up at the disappointing display of stars. It had been impossible to see the sky in Iraq and Afghanistan for the twinkling stars beckoning from far-off galaxies. His mood changed as his memory conjured up the four American soldiers he'd butchered for playing cards whilst on sentry duty in Iraq. Enraged by their arrogance and sloppiness towards the soldiers they were supposed to guard, three died of slit throats, and the fourth, a broken neck. The Americans blamed the deaths on a terrorist attack. Two days later, Toki was thrown out of the army to a life of violence and regular spells in and out of prison. The sound of a breaking twig brought him to full alert. Slowly breathing through his nose, he waited readily to pounce on the intruder. The sound of sniffing grew closer. Then he saw the fox licking the empty sardine tin. Reaching out, he grabbed the animal fox by the neck and, gripping the hunting knife in his other hand, drove the blade into the fox's brain killing it instantly.

"Thank you for the strength you are about to give me, Mr Fox," he mumbled, cutting open the animal's stomach and removing the entrails.

*

If Page had learned one lesson in prison, it was that some people do as they please and don't care what happens to others as long as it is good for them. To Willow's chagrin, he had several non-paying customers that day and managed to avoid them all. It was no secret he'd sent for Legges to chastise the villagers; the problem now was what mischief Toki might make that could be laid at his door.

*

With a great show of ceremony, Willow slipped off the latch and opened the cage containing the German Shepherd.

"Now, Major, the moment we have been waiting for, off you go and show me how well your leg has healed."

Major hesitated, looking into Willow's eyes to confirm all was well and his rear leg had healed.

"Well," she laughed. "Off you go; no need to be afraid."

Unsure, Major slowly left the cage, then turned and gazed at the open meadow. Ears pricked, he raced through the grass, stopped, and ran back and sat at her side.

"Good boy, good boy," Willow said, gently twisting the dog's ears.

"Fine looking dog, a little overweight, but nothing exercise won't cure," a deep voice called.

Willow stiffened and looked around for the voice. Seconds later, Toki pushed his way through a flurry of bushes.

"Sorry if I startled you."

Willow stared at him. His face was craggy like a man not given to smiling. His cheeks were hollow beneath high cheekbones, and his deep brown eyes staring.

"What makes you think you startled me," Willow answered haughtily.

"I didn't, then?"

"Didn't what."

"Startle you."

"How long is a mouses tail?" she shrugged.

"Been watching quiz programmes, have you? Don't believe all you hear on the TV."

Ill at ease, Willow looked around for Major. When she saw no sign of the dog, the muscles in her face jumped. Toki cocked his head to one side and watched her twisting and turning, hoping for an indication of the animal. Then pursing his lips, he let out a piercing whistle. Seconds later, the dog bounded across the fields and sat obediently at his side.

"Very good; I must learn to do that" Willow smiled, clearly impressed. "Do you live around here?"

"I live wherever I pitch my tent."

"Really, and where's that?"

"Over there, in the forest," Toki answered, nodding his head.

"This is Lord Pennywise's land. He doesn't like people wandering around his estate."

"He'll have to get used to it because I'm not going anywhere just yet," Toki answered, scratching his furry forearms. "How about joining me for breakfast."

"What is it?"

"Fox, I caught it last night sneaking around my campfire."

"Ugh, fox, no thank you, they taste like old string."

Her remarks stung him.

"A wildlife expert, are you? Know all about these things?"

"I lived with travellers once, and I know something of wildlife. I want a cup of tea if there's one going."

Toki struggled to hold himself together. Who did she think she was to lecture him on wildlife and then ask for a cup of tea? Yet he felt none of the anger that infused him at times like this. Instead, he felt relaxed.

"Yeah, I can run to a cup of tea, so long as the teabag is to your liking," he grinned.

Willow smiled.

"I'm sure it will. No need for the sarcasm."

They chatted about the countryside and the animals that lived within the boundaries. Slowly Willow told him of her past. That she never knew her birth parents and never wanted to. He, in turn, told her of his time in the army, omitting to mention his capture and torture by Iraqi soldiers. The moment he mentioned the name of Onions, the look on her face turned vacant. When she rose to leave, they shook hands and said they'd see each around. Before kicking out the fire, Toki waited until she was out of sight, then took two more tranquilisers washed down with tea dregs. Willow smiled. She liked Toki, his stories, and the easy way he laughed and hoped they would meet again. Toki wasn't so happy. Caught between hope and happiness, he wondered how he could find the woman known as Rita Peters. Was he searching for a man or a woman? Hands shaking, he pulled the bottle of tranquilisers from his pocket. Then changed his mind. A mouthful of pills wouldn't solve his problem.

Nor would a liquorice allsorts, but he ate one just the same.

*

Gripping both handles, Page hauled himself out of the bath. Recently installed the bath creaked as if it would split into two and flood the bathroom. Instead of wiping the steam from the mirror, he threw the bath towel over his skinny shoulders and shuffled into his bedroom sensing the world was against him. A beanpole, ginger-haired farmer had refused to pay his bill after Page had inoculated his herd of milking cows. When Page insisted on payment, the farmer laughed in his face and asked what Page intended to do about the outstanding bill. Seated on his bed, Page mumbled vicious threats and cursed God for deserting him. The faint sound of Willow's singing helped temper his foul mood as he dressed. By the time he entered the kitchen, the kettle had boiled.

"Coffee?" Willow called.

"Yes, please."

"I've been talking to that man who came to see you. Remember, Toki?"

"Oh, what did he have to say, still chasing the man who calls himself Onions?"

"I think so. We only touched on the subject. I like him. He seems genuine, unlike the mob that lives in this village."

"You be careful; we know nothing about him."

"Don't look upon everybody as you do the

villagers. You let them twine around you like unwanted weeds."

Flinching at her words, Page closed his eyes and turned his head away. She spoke the truth; he knew that and shivered. Daylight pressed against his closed eyelids, flooding them with tears.

"I shall go to the church tonight. You may join me if you wish."

Trapped in a feverish confusion, Willow tried to make sense of his words. She'd never stepped inside a church before. Would God accept her for what she was or punish her for her sins?

"I don't think God would like me in his church."

"The church is the house of God where all are welcome, sinners too," Page answered quietly.

"I'll come if you promise to stay by my side."

"I promise," Page smiled.

*

Eight o'clock that evening, arms folded tight to her chest, Willow followed Page through the village to the church. Each time she fell behind, she jogged a few steps to keep up with him. The same old thoughts nagged her, would God accept her or strike her down? When Page pushed open the church doors, she shrank back, fearful for her life.

"There's no need to be afraid. Be yourself. Let God see how good you are." Page smiled, waiting for her to enter.

Willow took two steps forward and stopped.

"Sounds like he's listening to the radio or playing records. Let's leave and come back when he isn't so busy," she said.

"What do you mean?"

"Listen."

Page stepped forward and strained his ears to the sound of 'Ave Maria,' The words resonated throughout the church as he stood rooted to the ground. "I've never heard that song sung so beautifully; it brings tears to my eyes."

"Is that God singing?"

"For God's sake, Willow, you must know something of the church. Of course, it isn't God singing."

"How long is a mouse's tail," Willow snapped, failing to think of anything better to say.

"Haven't you been christened?" Page said, sensing his anger rising.

"I don't think so. Does that make me a heathen?"

Before Page could vent his anger, the voice of Father Kevin boomed in his ears.

"Hello Anton, how nice to see you, and you have brought a friend with you."

"Sorry to disturb you listening to 'Ave Maria. Was it the radio or a tape, perhaps?"

"No, no, none of those things. I'm sure you have heard of DCI Mattress, our area's chief of police. Whenever available, she leads our choir at weddings and other holy events. Come and say hello. May I ask your friend's name?"

"Willow, this is Willow, my assistant at the veterinary surgery. I had no idea the DCI could sing like that; beautiful, one of my favourite songs."

"Do you sing, Willow?" Father Kevin smiled.

"I know a couple of Ed Sheeran songs. I don't know any hymns or church tunes."

"I like Ed Sheeran songs. Easy on the ear. I don't understand the lyrics these days; the singers tend to mumble. Not like Elvis, eh? Now there's a singer."

"Ah, Mr Anton Page. To what do we owe the honour of your company? A budding tenor, I hope,"

DCI Mattress had stopped singing and walking along the aisle and stood next to Father Kevin and Willow.

"You must be Willow, the young runaway I've heard so much about," DCI Mattress asked.

"I don't know why you have heard of me; I haven't done anything wrong."

"Then you have nothing to fear, have you?"

"How long is a mouse's tail? Willow shrugged.

"And what has a mouse's tail have to do with anything?"

"Nothing, it's just a saying."

"Well, it doesn't make sense to me."

"Does anything ever make sense to a policeman? Don't you deal in lies and twist the truth to get what you want?"

"No, young lady, we don't. We seek the truth

and twist the lies to get what we want. It's the kind of people we deal with."

Willow blushed a deep red.

DCI Mattress continued.

"I know you were born Jennifer Dove. Your mother gave you up for adoption the day you were born. At the age of six, adopted by Mr and Mrs Dominic Clark your name was changed to Kate Clark. Six years later, Dominic Clark, a cabinet minister of the Conservative government, was jailed for raping his daughter, and you ran away. The birthmark on your left shoulder will clarify my words."

Page stiffened and stared down the aisle at the altar. Father Kevin noisily cleared his throat and looked down at his shoes.

Shocked by the words, Willow's bottom lip began to tremble. For years, she'd strained against this moment, knowing that everything would turn against her one day. For the last few months, she'd felt reborn and pushed the fear of discovery aside.

"Will I go to prison?" she whispered, gripping Page's hand.

"Of course not. You haven't broken any laws. But you could have shown some honesty towards Mr Page for the kindness he has shown you." Mattress said.

Willow's fingers tightened around Page's hand.

"I'm so sorry, Mr Page," Willow whispered.

"Are you going to send me away?"

"Certainly not. I need you for the surgery. Anyway, I like having you around."

Page turned and faced DCI Mattress.

"Was all this necessary? The poor girl has been through enough without a third degree?"

"Perhaps, and perhaps not. This village is riddled to the core with secrets. Dead animals with their hearts ripped out. A local man burned to death tied to a tree. A stranger run down by a van and killed. The disappearance of Lord Pennywise's butler. Men with their little fingers cut off. All these things have occurred since you left prison, Mr Page. Perhaps you can explain why?"

Page looked about him. The air seemed suddenly thin and cold, and his breathing became shallow and laboured.

"You think I am responsible for all these things? Utter rubbish, all I want is a life of peace and quiet."

"Yes, everyone pleads innocence at times like this," Mattress snapped. "Do you deny the man called Legges was here in the village at your invitation?"

Father Kevin interrupted before Page could answer.

"We are in the house of God, not a police station. Stop this questioning immediately."

"Of course, Father. Forgive me," Mattress answered tritely. "I have work to do at the station. A good evening to you all. Mr Page, I'd like you and Willow to come to the station at 10 a.m. tomorrow."

"I have business tomorrow; can't it wait?"

DCI Mattress's face flushed red.

"Be there, or I'll take you in now, do you understand? Good night."

"Yes, of course, sorry, we'll be there," Page answered in a low, hoarse voice. "Come along, Willow; time we went home."

Followed by Willow, Page silently walked through the narrow streets towards home. Dizzy with fear of being questioned by the police, twice he stumbled and might have fallen if Willow hadn't caught him.

"Not far now," she said in a quiet voice.

With such briskness as his legs would allow, Page stopped outside his front door and fumbled in his jacket pocket for the key. When the door swung open, he stepped aside to allow Willow to enter. It was then a glassy numbness flooded his head with blackness. With all the strength he could muster, he wheeled around and walked back into the street. There was no sign of Willow; it was as if she'd melted into the darkness. All he could feel was the ache of cold air in his chest; his legs felt heavy, and his laboured chest constricted. The sound of cell doors crashing shut haunted his mind. The rattle of keys turning locks brought tears streaming from his eyes. The sense of calm that had helped him through such times had disappeared. Tomorrow, the police would come to take him back to prison and leave him to rot; he was sure of that.

Under the fading light of a half-moon, Willow made her way to Cate's flat. Hopeful she hadn't yet moved into her new house, she thought it best if Page were left alone. Suddenly everything turned to darkness. Rough hands pulled a cloth bag over her head and bundled her into the rear of a vehicle smelling of paint. Hands and feet securely tied she was pushed to the floor.

"No point struggling," a coarse voice said. "You ain't going nowhere for a while."

Uttering a strangled whimper, Willow struggled against the ropes.

"What do you want? Why are you doing this to me?"

"You'll find out all in good time, shut up and stop struggling," the course voice answered"

Thoughts of Page drifted across Willow's mind. Bewilderment mixed with an innate fear for his safety caused her to shudder. There could be no ridding of the dread swirling in the pit of her stomach. With no thought for her safety, she visualised the altar in the church and prayed for Page's safety. Why should he suffer for her sins, she asked herself silently. Minutes later, the vehicle stopped, and she heard the sound of muffled voices. The same rough hands dragged her from the vehicle and pushed her to the ground.

"Untie her feet; she can walk from here," a different voice called. "And keep the bag over her head; if she recognises us, we'll have to kill her and I ain't going down for murder for nobody?"

As hard as Willow tried, she failed to recognise the voices. Pushed forward, her shoulder collided with a doorway. The sound of running water pressed against her ears as the crown of her head scrapped against a low soft ceiling. Beneath her feet, the floor fell away and crumbled like loose cheese. The stomach-churning smell of sewage blocked her nose. Unable to protest, rough hands pulled her upwards and pushed her through a door when she fell to her knees. Seconds later, hands and feet untied, she pulled the bag from her head and listened to fading footsteps.

Eyes open wide, she stared at a newly furnished room with a TV, dining table and small kitchenette. On the floor was a soft white pile. A large sofa with two Zebra patterned matching easy chairs on either side. A mobile phone lay on a small coffee table next to a large four-poster bed, complete with a water mattress. After further inspection, she discovered the room had no windows. The only door in the room was locked tight; she was a prisoner, but who were her jailers? What did they want from her? Close to tears, she slumped down in one of the easy chairs and raked her fingernails through her hair. She imagined life if she stayed with the man she called dad. The open countryside, the warmth of the sunlight caressing her face, raised her emotions and she took a deep breath to regulate her breathing. She loved leaning over bridges, admiring the passing boats, waving to the crew members, and laughing when they waved back.

The warble of the mobile phone startled her. She slowly picked up the phone with cold and clumsy fingers and held it to her ear.

"Why am I being held prisoner? What have I ever done to you?"

"There's food in the kitchen to last a fortnight. All will be revealed later," a muffled voice replied.

"Who are you?" Willow shouted down the phone. "I'll call the police."

"You can't call out on this phone."

The phone clicked dead. The phone took incoming messages only.

CHAPTER TWENTY-TWO

Like most people, Anton Page never knew what to expect each time he opened his mail. Today was different. Dazed for the third time in as many minutes, he stared at the words written in neat capital letters. Without thinking, he opened the front door and peered down the road as if expecting to see whoever sent the letter hurrying along the pavement. His confidence hanging by a thread, not bothering with a coat, drove to the police station and demanded to see DCI Mattress, and no, he didn't want to take a seat and wait. Ignoring the desk sergeant, he strode down the corridor and entered the office with the DCI's name on a strip of white plastic fixed to the door.

"You're early. I said 10 am," Mattress said. "And where's the girl?"

"Read this," Page replied tersely. "It was delivered to my door not an hour ago."

"IF YOU WANT TO SEE THE GIRL ALIVE LEAVE THE VILLAGE AND NEVER RETURN,"

Mattress read the words written in capital letters aloud. "Did you see who delivered the letter?"

"No, of course not," Page said, studying Mattress through slitted eyes.

"I'll get this off to forensics. My God, Page, you carry a lot of baggage wherever you go," Mattress snapped.

Page turned his head to hide the scowl twisting his face.

"Don't blame me; blame the idiots that live in the village. What good does getting me out of the village do?"

"You could leave the village and save us a load of work."

"I'm sorry to disappoint you, but I'm going nowhere until I know Willow is safe. I'm confident she is being held somewhere in the village."

"Go home Mr Page, and stay there until someone contacts you. While we wait for forensics, we'll start knocking on doors and see what we can turn up."

Page tensed as if about to say something. Instead, he turned and left the office without uttering a word.

The intensity of his craving for revenge swelled inside him like a cancerous growth. If one single hair of Willow were damaged, he'd burn the village to the ground and listen to their screams as they perished in their beds. From now on, he'd carry a knife for protection.

*

Toki smelled the four men dressed as Robin Hood before he saw them. Hidden behind a beech tree, he watched two men smoking cigarettes; another drank from a flask, and the fourth man stretched out on the ground with his hands behind his head. Hotter than usual for the time of year, Toki rubbed his damp palms on his knees. Sweat gathered in the armpits of his cotton shirt and glued the thin material to his back.

"Good morning there," he bellowed, stepping into the clearing. Both men stubbed their cigarettes out on the ground. The man stretched out on the ground leapt to his feet, lost his balance and disappeared headfirst into a thorny bush. The fourth man climbed to his feet and tossed away the dregs of tea left in his mug.

"And who might you be?" he said, wiping his mouth with the back of his hand.

"Not the Sheriff of Nottingham, that's for sure," Toki grinned. "Why the fancy dress?"

"We're members of the Green Archers. Supported by Lord Pennywise, we keep an eye on his estate. There are forty of us in all, and we take turns to patrol the grounds and keep out travellers and picnickers from turning the place into a tip. We make sure gates are closed and streams aren't blocked. You do realise you are trespassing and liable to immediate prosecution?"

"Habit of mine," Toki smiled.

"Take my advice, and be on your way."

"I'll go when I'm ready," Toki answered, his smile widening.

The sound of a soft footfall to his left brought him to full alert. The man who'd fallen into the bush had disentangled himself. Toki turned to face him.

"On your way before you get my boot up your backside," the man growled.

"I'll go when I'm ready," Toki said, relaxing his shoulders and allowing his arms to dangle loosely by his side. "Please don't start anything you can't finish."

"Tough boy, are you? Let's see what you've got."

"Leave it, John; we're not here to fight, and he's doing no harm."

"I talked to a young girl yesterday," Toki continued. "She walks dogs here every day. Have you seen her today?"

"You mean Willow. She comes at all hours. She works for the village vet."

"Yes, that's her."

"No, we haven't seen her this morning. Right, we're off. Make sure you are gone when we return."

Toki waited until they were gone, then seated comfortably beneath the branches of a beech tree, he tore open a new pack of liquorice allsorts. Something tickled his neck, indicating that things weren't as they should be. The thought that it was better to know than not know had been instrumental in helping him stay alive in some of the world's most dangerous places. With his backpack concealed in the trunk of a dead oak tree, he set out for the village. His first stop was the vets where Willow worked. Thirty minutes later, disappointment fed his anger when he read the sign stating the vet was closed for the day. Reluctant to walk away, he made his way to the rear of the bungalow and saw the vet sitting next to a small pond filled with algae—his head in his hands.

"Good morning," Toki called.

Startled, Page leapt to his feet.

"So it was you that took her. What do you want, money? The police know what's happening; they're searching the village. Who paid you to do it? I hope you rot in hell."

"Easy old man, I don't know what you're talking about; I was looking for the young girl who walks the dogs by the Pennywise Manor."

"Damn liar, you were looking for answers concerning Beau Legge's death."

"Yeah, well, I'm not having much luck. I can't get a word out of the villagers."

"No, and you never will. Bunch of bastards, the lot of them."

"What's that got to do with Willow?"

Desperate for a friend, Page told Toki of the letter.

"Someone knew you were in the church and followed you when you left. You say Willow was behind you and never heard a sound?"

"No, when I turned, she was gone."

"There must have been more than one person involved if she never made a sound."

"Yes, that's possible."

"Do you have any enemies that might do this?"

"Enemies?" Page laughed. "The villagers hate me for what happened to my wife. They want me out of the village. Now summers on the way, they reckon the village will be full of morbid sightseers hoping for a glimpse of a murderer."

"And you refuse to leave?"

"I have no choice. I don't want any harm to come to Willow. I'll give the police a few days and then put the bungalow up for sale. One thing is for sure, whoever is doing this is local."

Toki cast a glance over Page's shoulder.

"Anybody else lives here?"

"No, just me and Willow. She has her rooms at the other end of the bungalow. I never go in there; she likes her privacy."

"Who lives in the big house on the edge of the village."

"That Lord Pennywise's place, he lives there with his two sons. There were three up to a month ago. His eldest was tied to a tree and burned to death. Keep away from that lot, a law to themselves they are."

Page looked as grim as any man Toki had ever

seen before.

"If I hear anything, I'll let you know. In the meantime, don't do anything silly. Let the police deal with it. Goodbye," Toki said, turning away.

Page never answered. The skies opened, and heavy raindrops beat down on the algae-filled pond. Instead of hurrying for cover, oblivious to the rain, Page remained seated with his head in his hands. Used to all kinds of weather, Toki ignored the rain and returned to the woods. When the rain ceased, he'd track down the four Green Archers. It would be them if anyone knew what went on in the area.

*

Rita Peters held the lead the way the lady at the animal rehoming centre had told her. Unfortunately, the lady failed to mention that the cocker spaniel had a mind of his mind and refused to budge.

"Come along, that's a good girl, and Mummy will give you a treat."

Rita Peter's temper rocketed off the gauge when the dog refused to move.

"Move," she bellowed.

Seconds later, the dog trotted obediently by her side as she made her way to Pages Animal Surgery. Gathering her calm, she rang the doorbell and received no answer. With no intention of leaving, hammering on the door with her knuckles, she stepped back and gazed in shock at the state of the man who'd opened the door and glanced at the door number to check she was at the correct address.

"Mr Page?" she asked.

"We're closed."

"I have an appointment."

"We're closed," Page said again.

"Oh dear, I think my dog is poorly; she isn't eating and refuses to exercise."

"We're closed."

"Yes, I heard you the first time. I must insist you look at the poor creature, and I'm at my wit's end regarding what to do."

Page faltered.

"You'd better come in."

"Thank you so much," Rita Peters said, pretending to sob.

"How long have you owned the dog?"

"She used to belong to my sister until she recently passed away. I couldn't bear to have her put her down, so I took her in."

" Does the dog have a name?"

"Of course, she's called Lady Jane."

"Then I suggest you change it; this dog isn't a bitch."

Rita Peters felt the heat rise on her face. Speechless, attempting to hide her embarrassment she rummaged in her shoulder bag. Then sat stone-faced afraid to meet Page's withering stare. This wasn't how the meeting was supposed to go. She needed to think quickly if she wanted to gain Page's confidence.

"How silly of my sister to make such a foolish mistake. Oh dear, I feel quite faint."

"That is the least of your worries. The dogs infested with fleas. I'll give you a spray and keep the animal away from other dogs."

"Yes, of course, whatever you say," Rita Peters said, sensing she was fighting a losing battle.

Red-faced and angry, Rita Peters left the surgery and headed for the Animal Rehoming Centre. Instead of entering, she left the dog outside the door and walked away. By the time she reached her rented flat it was raining. Her foray to gain favour with Page had failed miserably. But there was more than one way to skin a cat.

*

Along with the four Robin Hood lookalikes, Toki sheltered from the rain beneath two plastic corrugated sheets suspended from the branches of an oak tree.

"Don't you understand English?" Matt Capp, the leader, said.

"When it suits me," Toki answered. "I've been talking to Mr Page, the vet that employs Willow. She's been abducted and won't be freed until Page promises to leave the village. I wondered if you might have heard anything that might help me find her."

The four men exchanged furtive glances.

"When did this happen," Capp asked.

"A couple of nights ago."

"Two nights ago we saw a black van heading for Pennywise's mansion. Going like the clappers the driver was, wonder he got there in one piece. When we went to investigate, we couldn't find hair nor hide of the van."

"Have you seen the van before or since?"

"No."

"Can you think of any reason those living in the manor would want to kidnap Willow? Surely if they wish to get Page out of the village, there must be other ways. Seems a bit severe to pick on a young girl."

"Them Pennywises are a law unto themselves. Always have been; not much chance of the police asking questions up there."

"What are the chances of breaking in and looking around?"

"Who will be daft enough to do that?" Capp laughed.

"I am."

"Done this kind of thing before, have you?"

"Yeah, a couple of times."

"A burglar, are you?"

"Ex special services."

"Oh yeah, so what are you doing wandering around the village?"

"I'm searching for the truth about why a man called Beau Legges died here."

"I warned you there was something fishy about him, didn't I?" one of the men grunted. "I remember that weirdo Beau Legges running around cutting people's little fingers off. Mad as a hatter, he was."

Capp unscrewed the cap from a water bottle and took a long swig.

"You ever kill anyone?" he asked.

"That's the point of special services."

"If we decide to help, what do you want us to do that doesn't involve killing?"

"First, we must find the van you mentioned, then the driver. I suggest we start at Pennywise Manor."

"Not a good idea for us to wander around Pennywise's place."

"Draw me a map of the Manor, and I'll go alone."

*

Seated in an easy chair in front of the TV, Willow finished the salmon salad and started on the fruit and jelly dessert. Coffee and biscuits would follow later. Wherever she was, her captors made sure that she never went hungry. Not for one minute did it make her feel any happier. Most of the previous day, she'd pored over the room searching for a way out without any luck. After finishing the dessert, she lay back on the bed and wondered what she had to do to gain her freedom. Would Mr Page inform the police of her absence, or had he concluded she had returned to the travellers? It was obvious she couldn't remain a prisoner forever. Perhaps her captors planned to dispose of her. But why? What had she done?

*

Anton Page was hungry but couldn't bother cooking, which was just as well with an empty fridge. Worse, steeped in a lousy mood, he didn't feel like shopping at the tiny corner shop and having to listen to the snide remarks aimed at him behind his back. Unlike other times his anger conjured pictures of violence. A gun, a knife, no, a shotgun would close their cruel mouths for good. He'd watch them cower staring down both barrels. Better still, they wet their pants at the look as cold as a dagger's blade twisting his face. Despite the weed supposed to help him sleep, life's unholy clamour and chaos became a fixture in his mind. Had it not been for the dogs and the occasional friendly words from customers, he feared he might suffer insanity. Each time he thought of Willow and the trouble he'd caused her, tears sprang into his eyes. As midday approached, the thing he feared the most stared him in the face. A large silver coach crammed full of sightseers armed with cameras stopped outside his front door. The morbid and those of a sick mind jostled for position to get the best shot of a convicted murderer. Some clasped handkerchiefs to their mouths less they catch a disease that would lead them to commit murder. Others held their breath. Seconds later, sweat became visible on his forehead at the sound of someone beating their fists on the door.

"For God's sake, open the door and let me in," came the faint sound of Cate's voice.

Afraid his ears might play tricks, the lump in his throat bobbed.

"Open the damn door, now," Cate's voice sounded louder. "I know you're in there."

Page struggled to unclench his fists and fumbled with the latch before the door swung open.

"Have you called the police?" Cate rasped, fighting for her breath.

"Police? No, I haven't called anyone."

"Well, I will; this is outrageous. The villagers will be up in arms."

"Damn the villagers; I couldn't care less what they think."

Page uttered the words no sooner than he spotted a young woman framed in the window with a camera.

"Get off my property, you ignorant bitch. Who do you think you are?" Paged shouted at the top of his voice, trashing the room in temper.

The woman laughed and beckoned to those behind her looking for a photo.

"He's having a right old right fit in there," she called. "Looks like he's in the mood to commit another murder," she called.

The wailing of police sirens failed to disperse the crowd of people fighting and pushing eagerly for a picture to show friends and relatives.

"Whose, the driver of this vehicle?" Det/Sgt

Down demanded.

"I am," a short, balding, overweight man answered.

"Get this crowd back on your bus and get out of the village before I impound the vehicle for illegal parking and you lot locked up for causing a disturbance. And do it now," Down ordered. "You, madam, get out of the garden, or I'll do you for trespassing."

Mumbling and complaining, the sightseers bundled onto the bus threatening the driver to give their money back. Down waited until the bus was out of sight before he knocked on Page's front door and let himself in. The room looked like a tornado had ripped through it. The couch lay on one side, the TV was on the floor, and the curtains ripped from the poles.

Down ran his eyes ran over the mess.

"What the hell happened here?" he murmured.

"My father's not been too well. I'm afraid the intrusion pushed him over the limit. What were those people thinking of, and what did they expect to see?"

"Morbid curiosity. It always happens in my job; the more blood, the happier people are. Like throwing a bone to a hungry dog," Down said, eyeing the mess. "There's every chance this will happen again. My guess is that someone from the village has contacted the local tourist office and told them of your father."

"Any news concerning Willow?" Page asked quietly.

"No, sir, we are still conducting our enquires. We'll let you know the minute we have any news."

"I don't suppose you've made enquires at Pennywise Manor?"

"I'm afraid I can't tell you more, sir. We are doing all we can."

Page turned away with a look of resignation.

*

DCI Mattress beat a tuneless tattoo on the desktop with the end of a chewed pencil. Like it or not, duty said she must visit Pennywise Manor and question those who lived there. Old man Pennywise would rant and rave and promise her she'd be out of a job within the hour. The boys would find it a big joke and make it large with bitter sarcasm. But life isn't a box of chocolates. First thing tomorrow morning, she'd head for the Manor accompanied by Det/Sgt Down.

*

Early that evening, Toki carefully studied the map Matt Capp handed him.

"Hey, this is pretty good. I like the details," Toki smiled.

"Start at the rear of the manor. The stables are next to the building where they park their cars. Loads of doors in there have been locked for years.

"Pity we can't get hold of Onions. He knows

the building like the back of his hand."

Dressed in a black combat overall and his face blackened, Toki selected the tools needed to break into Pennywise Manor. At 3 am, beneath a moonless sky, he moved silently into the first stable taking care not to spook the horses. After checking out four stables without luck, he pulled aside two rickety wooden doors and flashed his pencil torch over a back van. Bingo, his senses rose at the sight of mud-dried footsteps leading from a door concealed beneath heavy canvas sheeting. The entrance was by a key. Toki studied a bunch of skeleton keys hanging from his multi-purpose belt and selecting the key he considered most suitable, pushed the key into the lock. His eyebrows rose as the tumblers fell into place and the door swung open to reveal a low tunnel and soft, crumbling earth beneath his feet. Cautiously making his way along the tunnel, taking care not to injure his head on the low roof, he faced a second door to the left of the door fixed onto the wall, an illuminated digital pad with the numbers 0 to10. To gain entrance, he needed access to the code. He hesitated and, disappointed, kicked the door. He had no option but to turn back. About to retrace his steps, he heard knocking from the other side of the door, followed by the plaintive sound of a girl's voice.

"Who are you?" Toki called.

"You know who I am. Now let me out," the voice answered. "Let me out, and I promise not to tell the police."

"Tell me your name first."

"Willow, you know that already."

"It's me, Toki; we have been searching for you. I can't open the door without the code. I'll have to go back into the village and inform the police."

"Hurry, I can't stand cooped up much longer."

"Be patient; I'll be back as soon as possible."

*

Anton Page's life consisted of little else but despair. Over and over, he debated whether to call more of his so-called friends he'd met in prison. They'd tear down the village without ethics or morals to help him find Willow. Blackness gripped him, turning over his insides. The taste of blood in his mouth where he'd bitten into his lips made him want to scream with anger and hate. His pulse beat frantically. The pain behind his eyes grew more potent by the second. From the notebook, he selected three names and, picking up the mobile phone with trembling hands made three calls. Hell in all its glory was about to visit the village.

*

Toki decided against his intended visit to the police. The police meant questions, and questions led to trouble. His best bet was to visit the vet called Page and let him inform the police of his findings. Of himself, he'd stay in the clear and move on to more convivial surroundings. Outside the Manor he paused before choosing the likeliest-looking route back to the village. Walking for about ten minutes, it dawned on him that he was lost. Before him a vast expanse of black water as glossy as polished slate; on one side, a wall rose in great slabs of black granite surrounded by ten great columns rising from the water. Metres away in a neatly attended clearing a cross buried upside down—gothic statues with tortured faces cast from molten brass dominated the clearing. Recalling his younger days spent in Polynesian islands during his time with the Legion, he recognised the smell of the occult and stood in fear for his safety. Instead of waiting, he turned and walked away. When he reached an area he recognised, he paused briefly to get his bearings before choosing the likeliest course and continued on his way back to the forest.

*

At noon the following day, Det/Sgt Harry Down finished typing his report and swallowed the last dregs of a cup of tea.

"Well, what's new?" DCI Mattress asked, plugging her mobile phone into a charger. "Did you find anything worth knowing?"

"Nope, nothing. Getting information from these villagers is like opening a can of beans with a paper tin opener."

"I guessed as much."

"I still think we'll find out what we want to know at Pennywise Manor."

"Yes, that's probably why the villagers aren't

talking. Too damn scared to open their mouths."

"But why?"

"Simple enough. Lord Pennywise owns all the land around here, including the village that pays him the rent on their houses. Any nonsense leads to instant eviction."

"I thought there were laws against events like that happening."

"Laws are made for the likes of us, not Lords. Get your coat, and let's get it over with."

*

Being confined to the room wasn't as bad as Willow first thought. Regular meals she could never afford in a restaurant were pushed inside the door. A shower twice a day and Sky TV made her life bearable. She had to wait until Toki informed the police, and she'd be free. Her main concern was for Mr Page and his health. Not a sound man, she knew an attack of nerves might do him permanent harm and leave her unemployed. Startled by the sound of the door opening, she stiffened, hoping to see police officers enter the room. Instead, she listened to the tray containing her lunch scrape across the floor, followed by the door slamming shut.

CHAPTER TWENTY-THREE

"When did you eat last?" Toki said to Page in a gruff voice.

"I don't remember," Page answered.

"How about sleep?"

"I don't have the time to sleep."

"Did you listen to what I just told you?"

"Of course I did; I'm not deaf."

"Then call the police or go to the station?"

"Are you sure it was Willow you spoke with? I don't want trouble with Pennywise and his crazy kids."

"Yes, I'm certain. Now get off your backside and get down to the police station."

"You go; you know where she's held."

"No chance. I'm not going down to any police station. What's come over you? Yesterday you were in a panic and afraid you'd never set eyes on her again. And here you are showing a complete lack of interest in her safety."

"I can't go to the police station; it's too late."

Toki stared at Page, unable to understand his

meaning.

"Too late for what?"

"I've spoken with friends, and they are on the way."

"Friends, what friends?"

"Friends I knew in prison."

"You're winding me up. What kind of friends?"

"Category one. Real bad people." Page shrugged.

"How many?"

"Three."

"And what are they supposed to do when they get here?"

"Find out where Willow is and return her home."

"You know where she is; I've just told you."

"Well, it's too late now, isn't it?"

Toki scanned Page's face convinced he'd lost his mind. Things were getting out of control and he wanted no part of the impending mess. But no way would he leave Willow to face the aftermath alone.

"Give me time to get her out of the Pennywise Manor."

Page shrugged.

"I can't promise that; they're probably on their way as we speak."

Toki's top lip twisted into a snarl.

"If anything happens to that girl, you will have me to deal with."

Instead of waiting for an answer, Toki wheeled around, walked outside and took three long breaths. His spirits suddenly sagged. He had some serious thinking to do and wanted nothing to do with the police. Caught between a rock and a hard place, damned if he'd go into action without a fresh packet of liquorice allsorts he popped one into his mouth. Then another followed by another until the package was empty. Although he could never turn feelings into thoughts or words, nothing would happen until he possessed another box of his favourite sweets.

Page flung open a window and gazed at summer sprawled across the lawn. Despite the warmth, coldness seeped into his bones. After twenty years locked away in prison he realised he was entering something far more dangerous than anything he'd ever encountered. He needed strength where there was none, a strong will he'd never experienced and a clear and trustworthy mind. He hoped the hate for him might one day pass and he'd return in body and spirit to the village he loved. But hope lingers and never lasts. Instead, he prayed that tomorrow would never come.

Toki wasn't the type to pray. He chose to look at things closely, glean as much information as possible and then plan a course of action. In the short time he'd spent in and around the Manor, he did not notice any sign of security. There was no sign of guards on the minimum wage and drawing a state pension while supping endless mugs of tea. Dogs? Instead, there were bound to be dogs hunting around for food scraps. Nothing a couple of chicken legs wouldn't bring to heel. Convinced, the entrance he'd discovered situated at the lowest part of the building wasn't the only way to reach Willow; he needed another way to get inside the manor. With time of the essence, he needed to be in and out as soon as possible. His best option was to grab Lord Pennywise and force him to lead the way to where Willow was held against her will. One of the rules he'd adhered to was it was an unwise man who went into battle on an empty stomach. Hardly eaten since he arrived, he needed a square meal. A sign outside 'The Crooked Stick Inn' advertised a basket of chicken and chips. Today, he'd take up their offer and sat at a table by the window overlooking the entrance. Two tables down, Rita Peters rolled the glass of gin and tonic between her hands. The man at the bar hadn't taken his eyes off her since she walked in and ordered a drink.

"Looks a bit hard-faced that one does, Arthur." Polly Parrott, the landlord, said with a wide grin.

"I shan't be looking at her face while I'm stoking her firebox; Arthur smiled.

"Pint to a tot of rum; you can't pull her."

"You're on," Arthur said, sliding off the barstool and heading where Rita Peters was seated

"Alright, darling?" he said." Can I get you a drink?"

Peters looked up, her lips set in a sneer.

"No, thank you. I'm fine."

"Can I get you anything else?"

"Yes, you can get me a one-way ticket to Miami, where I don't have to look at your fat ugly face."

"No need to play hard to get, is there?" Arthur said, sitting beside her and attempting to slip his arm around her shoulders. As she pulled away from him his watch bracelet tangled in her hair causing her wig to fall onto the table.

"Bloody hell, you're the one they call Onions, which works for old man Pennywise. Bit of a crossdresser, are you? You had me fooled; I nearly bought you a drink, you crafty sod," Arthur called aloud.

Every head in the Inn turned and focussed on Rita Peters, recognised as Onions.

"I don't want your kind in here. Got enough weirdos in the village without you joining them; go on, sling your hook before I throw you out,"

"Stuff you, and stuff this shithole you call a pub", Rita Peters yelled, pulling on the wig and stomping out, struggling to keep her balance on her high-heeled shoes.

Unable to believe his luck Toki climbed to his feet, dropped a ten-pound note on the table and walked out after Rita Peters.

"Hey, hold on a minute. I want to talk to you."

"Get lost. You've had your fun. Now leave me alone."

"I have a proposition concerning the Pennywise family you might be interested in."

"Really, why would they interest me?"

"I hear you have an old score to settle with the family."

"Old score? What are you talking about?"

"You and Xander, for starters. People in this village love the sound of their voices. It doesn't take much to get them talking about the Pennywise family."

At the mention of Xander, the blood drained from Rita Peter's face.

"I don't know you, so how come you think you know so much about me?"

A smile twitched at the corners of Toki's mouth.

"I want you to help me break into the Pennywise Manor."

Rita Peters stiffened and drew in a great breath. Her legs quivered like fiddle strings.

"And why do you want to do that?"

"I believe he's holding a young girl prisoner."

"That's not like the old man; he prefers middle-aged slags."

"So you know where she might be."

"She's probably in a room down in the cellar. Old man Pennywise spent a small fortune doing the place up. He calls it his love nest. Are you sure it's him that's holding this young girl prisoner? His two sons are capable of anything. Who is this girl, anyway?"

"A close friend of the local vet, Anton Page. He says he'd do anything to have her back safe and sound."

His words scattered through her mind. Maybe this was her opportunity to get into Page's good books.

"What's in it for me if I help you get inside the Manor and get this girl out?" Rita Peters said, sensing a spurt of motivation.

"Ask the vet; I'm sure he'd agree to some form of reward."

"Okay, let's go and see him."

"No, not until we have the girl out. We'll do it tonight. And get rid of that piece of horsehair you call a wig, or you'll have every dog in the county sniffing your arse. Do you have a car?"

"Yes."

"Good, meet me by the old windmill on the edge of the village at eleven tonight. And dress for hiking through the woods to the manor."

Toki watched Rita Peters disappear through the village's maze of streets and lanes. When she was out of sight, he purchased bread and a hunk of cheese before making his way into the woods where he'd hidden his tent. He'd been fortunate to meet Rita Peters; hopefully, his luck would remain throughout the night. If not, he had ways of making Mother Luck change her mind.

Rita Peter's scalp itched with excitement followed by a frantic thumping in her chest. When night extinguished the daylight, she checked her watch, tugged on a black canvas jacket and left her rented rooms. Her first thoughts were she'd arrived early until, out of the darkness, Toki laid his hand on her shoulder.

"Good grief, do you always sneak up on people?"

"Only when I want to frighten them," Toki smiled. "Once we reach the Manor, I want you to show me how to get inside. And remember, silence is of the essence."

"You'll never find the room on your own. It's like a maze trying to make your way through the building. I know where false doors are situated, so follow me closely. Once we have the girl, I know a secret passage out."

*

With Rita Peters leading, they entered the first stable.

"Help me move the straw; there's a trapdoor beneath which leads to the library, and try not to spook the horses."

Skin bristling with urgency, Toki did as he was told without uttering a word. Minutes later, he grabbed a metal ring, raised the trapdoor and followed Rita Peters down rusting iron steps into a pitch-black tunnel. The pale light of her torch threw a villainous shadow over the damp walls. The stench of sewage stifled Toki's breathing, and he felt his feet covered in wriggling vermin. Rita Peters pushed a small wooden handle protruding from the wall and opened a small door. Stepping through the door, she turned to Toki and raised her forefinger to her lips.

"Okay, we're inside the manor. The room we want is on the other side so we must be careful. Stay behind me; I know where the CCTV cameras are, so do everything I tell you," she whispered. "And stay close."

The precision of her words helped raise Toki's spirits. Used to working alone, he found taking orders from a woman complex. Ignoring the stirrings in his belly, he had confidence they would succeed in fulfilling the task ahead. Halfway along a corridor furnished with Victorian sofas and furniture overlooked by endless rows of portraits, Rita Peters stopped.

"The next room we enter is the library protected by CCTV cameras. We'll have to crawl on our bellies to avoid detection. On the far side of the library is a partition sealed by shelves of books; from there, we follow the stairs to the cellars and, hopefully, the room holding the young girl. The way out is easy."

Toki smiled.

"Lead on, madam. I'm right behind you."

"Remember to stay close," she said, throwing him a stern stare.

Her attitude angered him, and stubbornness held him back. He didn't want to move but knew he must. He'd come too far and risked too much to back out now. Flat on their bellies, they reached the partition concealing the stairs leading to the cellars. A dull glow crept beneath a wooden door. Impatience curled Toki's toes as he watched Rita Peters enter a series of numbers into the small electronic pad fixed to the wall. Seconds passed before the door swung open. After a thorough search, they found no sign of Willow. Frantic to find something connecting Willow to the room, Toki barged into the bathroom. Rita Peters crouched down and searched underneath the bed, then lifted the duvet over the mattress onto the floor. Both the rooms were empty.

"They must have moved her, but why? Did they know we were coming?" Toki growled. "The rooms look untouched, and I'm beginning to wonder if she was ever here."

About to answer, Rita Peter's body trembled when the door leading to the room suddenly slammed shut, plunging the room into darkness.

"What the hell is going on?" Toki yelled.

"Someone been following us from the moment we entered the manor," Rita Peters said nervously. "I haven't told a soul. Apart from me, the only other person who knew was you."

"Don't talk shite. Why would I do that?"

"What other explanation is there."

"I don't know, but I'm going to find out and you're coming with me."

Rita Peters shuddered. Things were going from bad to worse. If she wanted to return to London, she had no choice but to follow Toki.

"What do you intend to do?"

"Search every room in this decaying dump until I find the girl. We'll start with Lord Pennywise. Now get us out of here."

"I want no part of violence towards Lord Pennywise. He might be many things, but he wouldn't hurt the girl. If the girl is here, one of his sons brought her here. My monies on the twisted little bastard, Xander."

"Fine with me; I'm here for Willow," Toki grunted.

"There's another door in the bedroom leading to the garages. If we enter the manor by the main doors, I can reset the alarms and CCTV cameras and go where we like without being detected."

"Okay, we'd better move on while it's still dark."

*

Dizzy with exhaustion and lack of sleep, Anton Page attempted to close his eyes for the hundredth time. Each time his lids covered his eyes faces loomed out of the darkness. Heads on stalks like dandelions stared down at him through bloodshot eyes. Some he recognised as pimps and murderers he'd stood shoulder to shoulder in prison. The world hated him. God hated him; the only thing better than life was death. With one hand straining on the bed for support, he struggled to his feet and gazed through the window. The cold ache in his chest added to the laboured constriction of his beating heart. Through the darkness of the night, he felt the eyes upon him, relentless without mercy, as hot as burning coals. Gasping as his legs gave way, he almost fell. The darkness was so complete his hands searched for a hold to help keep him upright. The faces drew closer. He could hear their moans, the suck of their breaths. Perhaps he would die here, breathe his last breath among those who despised him. Fear choked him. He didn't want to die. He must not die, not yet, not until he knew Willow was alive and safe.

*

The first thing that caught Toki's attention was the black van parked in the garage. He remembered Matt Capp mentioning a black van heading at breakneck speed for the manor a couple of nights ago. That was enough for Toki to conclude Willow was still on the estate.

Time had slipped by when Rita Peters told him she'd fixed the CCTV cameras and alarms, allowing them to walk freely within the manor's walls.

"We need to hurry; it will be light in a few hours," she said calmly.

"Take me to Pennywise's rooms; we'll start with him."

*

The watery gravy from Lord Pennywise's stew dish slopped over his shirt and onto his pyjama bottoms when Toki entered the gloomy bedroom and settled comfortably on his bed.

"Who the devil are you walking around as if you owned the place" Pennywise stuttered, brushing the gravy from the front of his shirt. "And you, Onions, get me something decent to eat before I starve to death if you want your job back."

Rita Peter's smile lit up her face.

"You can stick your job where the sun doesn't shine. What have you done with the girl Willow?"

"Willow? I don't know what the devil you are talking about."

"Liar, you know everything that goes on around here."

"Once perhaps, but not now. I'm too old to worry about those blasted villagers and their constant complaints."

"Then one of your brats that have her then."

"How would I know cooped up in bed all day?"

"Come on," Toki interrupted. "We haven't got all night to listen to his ramblings. Show me where his sons are, and I'll get the truth from them."

"Please don't harm my sons; they are all I have in this world."

Toki's eyes glinted in the gloom. Convinced Pennywise knew more than he was letting on he considered slapping him to get the truth.

"If I don't get the correct answer from your sons you will never see them again."

"Don't intimidate me; my sons know how to look after themselves." Pennywise spat.

They left Lord Pennywise tied naked to the bed.

"We'll go to Xander's room first. He's a nasty piece of work with the scruples of a horde of starving rats," Rita Peters sneered.

Minutes later, Toki's shoulders drooped. Disappointed at Xander's empty bedroom his patience drained.

"More than likely he's shacked up with a woman for the night," Rita Peters remarked.

"Yeah, and that woman might be Willow. I don't suppose that crossed your mind?"

"She's too young; he likes his women more mature."

"You seem to know a lot about him. Talking from experience, are you?"

Rita Peters trembled at his words.

"You have a dirty mind. Try minding your own business, and remember, I wouldn't set foot in this place until you asked for help."

"I never meant to disrespect you. It seemed a harmless enough question," Toki said, scanning her face for a reaction.

Her pale face stared up at him, and he noticed the tiredness around her eyes.

"Do you want to carry on, or shall we call it a

day?" he continued.

"We'll give Nelson a visit; he's Pennywise's youngest son, although I doubt he'd know what's going on. Not five minutes pass without him having his nose stuck in a book. Follow me."

Relief spread across Toki's face. He'd given up hoping she wanted to carry on. Ten minutes later, Nelson raised his head from the book charting the directions of London's sewers.

"Glad to see you back, Onions, and you have a friend with you; that's nice. One mustn't spend too much time alone."

"Where's Xander?" Rita Peters snapped, staring at the tightly drawn curtains leaving the room shrouded in semi-darkness. Pulling the curtains open, light flooded in, illuminating the pale green walls. On every wall were shelves piled high with books—more books on the floor almost reached the ceiling.

"He's probably downstairs in the kitchen, filling his face. He never stops eating, but you already know that?" Nelson said without looking up from the book.

"You are certain he hasn't gone out without you knowing?" Rita Peters continued.

"It's as quiet as a grave round here. I'd have heard his car if he left."

"Thanks for that."

"Yes, goodbye; nice to see you again."

Back in the corridor, Toki's patience was at breaking point. He knew what he must do next.

"The one you call Xander is still in the building," he said quietly.

"How do you know that?"

"Who else closed the door in the room where we thought Willow was held?"

"Yes, of course, I never thought of that."

"We'll give it a few minutes and see if he returns."

"And if he isn't there?"

"Then he's somewhere else in the mansion and Willows with him."

*

Toki felt confused. Assisted by Rita Peters, they'd searched every room, every nook and cranny in the mansion for the last hour and found no sign of Xander or Willow. Outside, the sun rose over the horizon sending black shadows scurrying for somewhere to hide. Birdsong filled the air as Toki pressed his eyes shut hoping to relieve the pain hammering his temple. Drained of her strength, Rita Peters lurched by and leaned against a tree. There could be no ridding herself of it. The dread of failure hung like lead in the pit of her stomach. Would she ever walk the streets of London's East End again? Listen to the laughter in the public houses lining the crowded streets, the buskers and market traders pitching their wares while customers argued the price of a cutlery set made in China.

"What now?" she said, pulling up her collar.

"They're here somewhere; I can feel it in my

bones," and I won't rest until I find them. In the meantime, go back to your hotel and get some rest. I'll stay and see if Xander returns. I'll ring you when I have some news."

Rita Peters shook her head slightly.

"Don't do anything without telling me first; you've got my number, and watch your back."

"Why should I do that?"

"Believe me when I tell you a lot is going on in this village you know nothing about."

"Yeah, I'll try and remember that," Toki said, bemused at her words.

CHAPTER TWENTY-FOUR

The first of the three friends Page contacted the day before flicked the remains of his cigarette onto the garden. Glancing at a sign stating a scarecrow competition would be held the following afternoon, he paused and lit another cigarette. Changed his mind and stuffed the packet back into his pocket. Instead of knocking on the door to avoid the sheeting rain, he turned the doorknob and entered Page's bungalow unannounced. Startled, Page juggled a pack of pork sausages before they slipped from his hands onto the floor when Tommy King entered the kitchen.

"Hello Anton, it looks like I'm just in time for breakfast," Tommy King smiled, adjusting the neat knot in his tie.

"For God's sake, you frightened me; don't you ever knock?"

"Come come, Anton. Knocking on doors isn't part of a burglar's forte. You should know that by now. What can I do for you?"

Page frowned. What did he know about burglars? He took his time explaining the situation while King filed his fingernails, stopping to polish them on his suit collar.

"You're not bedding her, are you? She sounds a bit on the young side for an old boy like you."

"Don't be ridiculous, of course not."

"All right, no need to get uppity. Anything goes these days. I've met more honest people in prison than I'd ever meet on the outside."

The tinkling of the phone prevented Page from answering. Seconds later, he thumbed the red button and placed the phone back into the charger.

"Skinny Ling can't make it. He says he's too busy."

"That Chinaman must make a fortune removing bodies killed by London's underworld. The East European crowd have doubled the number of dead bodies since they came to town. As I said, there's no law anymore, is there? Do as you like these days. Anyway, what is it you want me to do?"

"The trouble is that Terry Gold is one of the bodies." Page continued.

"Now, that is a bit of a blow. I liked old Terry Boy, a good lad he was."

"Forget that; I want you to break into the manor you passed on the way here. See if you can find the girl; I'm sure she's being held prisoner inside."

"And if she is?"

"Bring her back here, of course. But I must warn you it could be dangerous and lead to violence."

"Whoa, I don't do violence. I'm a thief, not a hard case."

"All right, find her and let me know where she is, and I'll do the rest," Page said, agitated by King's refusal.

"You know something, mate; I want no part of this. I steal objects de art, not little girls. I'm off. Nice to see you again, Anton. Take care, and don't do anything silly."

King climbed to his feet. When he reached the front door, he paused and locked back at Page, biting his lower lip with his face buried in his hands. By the time Page had his mind under control King had disappeared through the front door. A frown corrugated Page's forehead. He loathed himself for being weak and calling on people like King to do his dirty work. Fists clenched, he remained seated and beat his thighs until he could no longer bear the pain. Tomorrow, he'd tell the estate agent to put the bungalow up for sale and find a property further south, far away from the village.

*

Toki waited until Rita Peters was out of sight before turning his attention to the mansion. He'd concluded she would be no further use to him after admitting she'd no idea why the door slammed shut while searching the room where they believed Willow was held prisoner. Someone had purposely slammed the door shut unaware Rita Peters knew of another exit. He paused to collect his thoughts confident Rita Peters knew who it was. He'd already checked out Lord Pennywise and his youngest son Nelson and felt sure once he found Xander, he'd find Willow. His brain accepted his thoughts without question. In the light of day, struggling to concoct a plausible excuse not to return immediately to the mansion, he settled beneath a thick clump of bushes and began eating his way through a fresh packet of liquorice allsorts. Hunger satisfied, he closed his eyes and drifted into a light sleep. His day was beginning.

*

Nelson's eyebrows rose like two caterpillars ready to go into battle.

"Are you deaf, boy, as well as useless?" Lord Pennywise raged. "I've been ringing the alarm for over half an hour; for God's sake, untie me before I die of exposure."

"I've checked the alarm. Someone had altered the code. That's why I never heard it ring."

"That damned Onion's work, I suppose. For some reason he's looking for Xander with his overgrown friend. Is the alarm code back to normal?"

"Yes."

"Then where the devil is that brother of

yours?"

"He's here somewhere. That's all I know."

"Find him and bring him to me."

"Perhaps he's seeking a wife who'll give him children, so he can claim all this money you insist on throwing around," Nelson replied flippantly.

"You saucy beggar, watch your mouth."

"Why should I? I've listened to your monocyclic rantings since the day I was born. And perhaps tell me why Onions is back. You never mentioned that before?"

"I didn't invite him back."

"Then why is he here?"

"How in blazes should I know what goes on around here? Now, do as you are told and find Xander."

"I'm too busy to find out what Xander's been up to. This afternoon, I'm judging the scarecrow competition at the village fete." Nelson replied.

"Really? Then try to choose one with more sense than any villagers; it shouldn't be too hard to do."

Nelson turned and left his father's room knowing why he hated him.

*

At noon, Toki rang Rita Peter's phone number three times and received no reply. Under the impression that she was a formidable woman with great inner strength, he realised the strain of the previous night might have drained her energy. After one more glance at the mansion, he decided he'd had enough for one night and returned to his campsite in the woods. Suffering from the pangs of hunger, after a strip wash and change of clothes, he headed for the village café and a large English breakfast. At the edge of the village green, he slowed and stared at a dozen life-sized scarecrows settled on wooden chairs the previous night by the villagers. The man he knew as Nelson was standing alongside DCI Mattress and Det/Sgt Down as crowds of onlookers converged onto the green, eager to watch the best scarecrow choose. Of little interest to Toki, he entered the café. After eating, the urge to call Rita Peters entered his mind. Still receiving no answer, he paid his bill and sauntered over to the gathering crowds surrounding the seated scarecrows. Kids were running around pulling faces at the straw effigies. Mothers placated the younger children, who shrank in fear at the painted faces and straw hands and feet. One of the elder children, braver than the others, ran forward, grabbed the small sackcloth that made up a face, stopped, and let out a high-pitched scream. Gasps rang around the green. Villagers stared in shock at the face of Rita Peters known to most as Onions, Lord Pennywise's butler. His eyes gouged out a thin line of blood highlighted his slit throat., His severed tongue hung from his mouth by a sliver of flesh.

"Call the station and get the SOCO boys down here and start moving the crowd back," DCI Mattress snapped at Det/Sgt Down.

Had Toki been born of a different matter, he might have displayed an ounce of remorse. Instead, a tiny smile played across his lips as he turned and headed for Anton Page's bungalow. During his connection to the military, he'd seen death in every guise possible, sometimes the impossible.

Page's appearance had hardly changed. He wore the same sloppy brown sweater with one sleeve longer than the other. His corduroy trousers were so baggy the crotch hung below his knees.

"Well," Page spoke in a scratchy voice. "Did you find her? Where is she?"

Toki decided to keep his answers detailed and precise less Page boiled up in rage.

"No, not yet, but I'm confident she's held in Pennywise Manor."

"Then it's best left to the police to find her."

"I think the police will have other things on their minds than Pennywise."

"What's that supposed to mean? What's happened that's not worth searching for a kidnapped young girl?"

"The man known as Onions has been found dead on the village green dressed as a clown."

"What in the blazes are you talking about?

Onions left the village weeks ago."

"Maybe, but it seems he didn't go far enough."

Toki went on to explain what he'd seen on the village green.

"This village is cursed. Full to the brim with nothing but death and misery. I'm expecting the estate agent later this morning. I can't get away from this place soon enough."

"What of Willow? Are you going to walk out and leave her?"

"What can I do? The people hate me."

"You can grow a pair of balls for a start."

"Oh yes, very wise."

"Give me a couple of days. I'm sure I can find Willow."

Page scratched the end of his nose with a bony finger. The rims of his eyes were red with tiredness. Everything about him displayed a broken man devoid of hope.

"Do as you please. But I warn you; I shall accept the first decent offer on this place and be on my way."

"Over my dead body. It's time you face the world instead of constantly complaining."

The shrill voice cut through the air. Page turned his head towards the open door and stared at his daughter, Cate, standing erect with a sneer twisting the contours of her face.

"Have you ever thought of anyone apart from yourself?"

Page pulled a face, angered at her words.

"How would you know what I've been through?"

"Me, me, the same old tune. If you had been brave enough to tell the truth about sleeping with that floozie while off your head with drugs, you might have given your defence lawyers a better chance of getting you off the murder charge."

Page shook his head. It was too much for him, the court case, prison, and the villagers' hatred. He stared at Cate as if she were a stranger. She ignored him and turned her attention to Toki.

"We don't get many Eskimos in the village, down to the lack of Polar bears, I suppose. So, you're the latest knight in shining armour straight from Her Majesty's prison pits to fight his battles for him? How much is he paying you while he sits here sobbing like a little school girl?" she said in a low voice, her eyes gleaming like beads.

"Who are you?" Toki smiled.

"I'm his daughter, you clown; who did you think I was, Father Christmas? And wipe that stupid grin off your face; it suits you."

Toki stiffened, raised his eyebrows and turned to leave.

"Wait," Cate snapped. "I haven't finished with you yet. Have you made any progress tracking Willow's whereabouts?"

"Some. I've been working on it," Toki said, turning to face her.

"Some? What the hell is that supposed to mean?"

Toki glanced at Page.

"For the sake of quiet, tell her what she wants to know," Page grunted.

"Well, I'm waiting," Cate snapped. "By the way, what is your name?"

"My name is Toki. Why do you ask?"

"I heard a strange man was in the village and assumed it could only be you. Are you from the same prison as my father?"

"No, my background is military, and watch your mouth. My past is none of your business."

"Oh, but it is if you are to help me find Willow."

"Your father is selling up and moving out of the village so Willow can be returned unhurt. Don't you ever listen? I need a glass of water if you don't mind."

"Help yourself."

Toki searched his pockets for his pills in the kitchen and swallowed two with water. Cate's attitude had aroused his temper and he needed time to gather his thoughts. He liked Willow; he enjoyed their conversations and smiled at her endless questions about the countries he'd visited. But that was all; she meant nothing to him. As for Page, he was so wrapped up in self-pity that he couldn't think straight. That became obvious when Cate asked him to help find Willow. Rita Peters dead dressed as a scarecrow meant he might become involved with the police, the last thing he wanted. The sound of someone hammering on the front door brought him to full alert. From the corridor he watched DCI Mattress enter, followed by Det/Sgt Down. Ears straining he listened to the conversation. Sweat began to form on his brow, and he grabbed the kitchen top with shaking hands to save falling to the ground. It would be another forty-five minutes before the pills took effect. Better he stayed away from anyone determined to apply pressure to his already troubled mind.

"I assume you know the man known as Onions has been found dead on the village green dressed as a scarecrow?" Mattress said in a loud voice.

"Yes, I heard a few minutes ago before visiting my father," Cate answered.

"A man was seen entering this bungalow thirty minutes ago. Is he still here?"

"Yes, he's in the kitchen."

Det/Sgt Down sucked in a deep breath, strode down the corridor and entered the kitchen.

"He's gone," Down shouted. "He can't be far away. I'll head for the forest and get a search party to scour the surrounding woods."

"What's going on? Why are you after this man? Has he done something wrong?"

"He and the deceased Onions were seen in Lord Pennywise's manor last night until early morning. I don't suppose you can throw any light on why?"

"In Pennywise's mansion? I find that hard to believe. The place is brimming with security cameras and alarms." Cate gasped.

"Apparently, Lord Pennywise and his youngest son Nelson spoke with him and Onions. They said they were searching for Xander and accused Pennywise of holding the girl known as Willow against her will."

"He's probably right, nasty piece of work that Xander is. If he harms that girl God help him; I'll see the bastard dead. You have allowed that family to ride roughshod over the villagers for years. How much does he pay you to leave him alone?" Page snapped angrily.

DCI Mattress's smile left her face.

"I'll ignore that remark, Mr Page. Pay attention to your demons before hurling accusations at others."

"Suggest what you bloody like; now get out of my house."

"Come on, Downs, we're finished here for the moment. As for you, Mr Page, let me remind you we are dealing with a murder case. Any information you might have, we'll be grateful to receive. We'll let ourselves out; good day."

Cate watched the two police officers leave before turning to face her father.

"Have you anything to do with Onion's death?" She said, a flash of annoyance lighting up her slanted eyes.

"Of course not. What on earth gave you that

idea?"

"Don't play the innocent with me. The village has been in a state of uproar since you left prison. People murdered. Willow's disappearance and one of your criminal cronies run over and killed by Onions, whose also dead. Now I have to watch a bunch of criminals walking around as if they owned the village. Where will it all end?"

Page looked as if he was holding a losing hand of cards. His face sullen he looked at Cate realising everything she said was true. Raising a thin bony hand he ran it over his balding head and sighed.

"I tried to seek forgiveness from those who hated me and received insults for my troubles."

"You're a convicted murderer. What did you expect, an invite for Sunday tea? I warned you not to
come back here but you wouldn't listen."

Page lowered his eyes to avoid Cate's withering stare. Startled by the sound of the rear door leading to the kitchen slamming shut, he jerked his head upwards when Toki entered the room.

"I thought you had left," Page grunted.

"What did the police want?" Toki growled.

"They're searching for you in connection with the death of Onions. Is it true you and Onions entered Pennywise's mansion without permission?" Cate asked, her eyes wide with surprise.

"We were searching for Willow. I know she's in there with Xander, and the quicker we find Xander, the better it will be for Willow."

Cate frowned.

"How could you possibly know that?"

"You'll have to take my word. Perhaps you can throw some light on why the Pennywise family want your father out of the village."

Cate pursed her lips.

"Yes, the same thing crossed my mind. My father's been in prison for twenty years and I'm inclined to believe something existed between him and Pennywise before he was sent down."

"I don't know anything about that," Toki said. "All I want is to see Willow safe. Ask your father; perhaps he knows more than he's letting on. In the meantime I'm heading back to the forest. Tonight I'm going back inside Pennywise Manor."

Cate remained stationary as Toki walked briskly towards the door. Tired of everything her father had thrown at her since his release she couldn't remember the last time she slept through the night.

"Wait," she snapped at Toki halfway through the door. "I'll come with you. I'm tired of standing around wondering what will happen next."

Toki stopped and turned, hands thrust deep into his pockets; he drew a deep breath. His decision took less than a second.

"Thanks for the offer, but I work better alone, and things might get rough," Toki said turning to face Page. "If you want to do something useful, get a few of your old jailbird friends down here. They can keep the police busy while I search for Willow. And make sure they stir up trouble in the local pub. In the meantime, contact the estate agent and tell him you are not selling the bungalow. You can do as you wish when Willow is safe."

Outside, the weather had changed. A sling of cold air hit Toki's face like a labourer's spade, and he shivered despite forcing his jacket tight around his body. The only bright spot in his mind was freeing Willow from the twisted family who lived on the hill. Dusk shrouded the trees when he entered the woods and followed the trail he'd marked leading to his backpack containing the small tent, a change of clothing and a mountain anorak. Settled in his sleeping bag, he listened to the silence like a stalking lion seeking an easy meal. Satisfied he'd had his fill of liquorice allsorts, he closed the carton and wriggled lower into the sleeping bag. Like always sleep came easy accompanied by dreams of home, the snow-covered Tundra and his family's smiling faces. He dismissed the never-ending poverty in the shanty village where he earned a meagre living as a courier for drug barons. Bullied by drug runners and fearing for his parent's safety, he skied mile after mile delivering bags of drugs concealed inside the bellies of dead fish. By the time he reached the last year of his teens, eager to see the world, he had paid for a one-way ticket to England. His first job in a large hotel was washing plates and cutlery. Months later, preferring the open air he worked as a street cleaner and became a regular victim of racial abuse. Forced into martial arts to protect himself, he found employment as a minder for a nightclub owner after eighteen months. The day he passed an army recruiting office, he stopped, turned around and, entering the office, signed up for twelve years in the British Commandos. Two years later, accepted for training with the SAS at Hereford, fearless under fire, he excelled in killing with or without weapons. Desperate for approval from senior officers until the death of a group of American sentries by his hand in Afghanistan, his service ended. He relished the idea of sneaking through the mansion and freeing Willow. But right now, there was something more substantial about a cheese sandwich with pickled onion. Afterwards, he'd eat liquorice allsorts. They made him feel sick, a burden he chose to bear to atone for the wrong he did in the eyes of God.

CHAPTER TWENTY-FIVE

Seated on a wooden bench overlooking the village green, Luke Warm ran his fingers through his straw-coloured hair and picked listlessly at a packet of unsalted crisps he'd bought from the village corner supermarket. Wincing in pain, he stopped and, leaning forward, pressed his fingers into his spine—an injury he'd sustained falling from a garage roof he'd robbed while surrounded by police.

"You'll get no peace until you die," his mother shouted at him across the court when the judge sent him down for four years.

He grinned and shrugged.

"Don't worry over me, Ma. I'm looking forward to the rest."

A professional agitator Warm was the kind of man who could stand alone in a room and start an argument with the wallpaper. Crushing a handful of crisps he threw them to sparrows hopping around looking for a meal. Then pulling out a flimsy piece of paper, reminded himself of the address and direction to the Crooked Stick Inn. Anton Page had promised him a payment of £700.00 to cause as much trouble as possible to keep the police busy. Satisfied he could remember the address he folded the paper, stuffed it into his jean jacket and headed for the Crooked Stick Inn.

Ranged along the bar the locals bought to Luke Warm's mind caricatures of Wurzel Gummage and East End gangsters. Men gave him suspicious looks when he leaned his elbows on the bar and ordered a pint of cold lager. Some stared as if he carried a plague to wipe out humanity. Seconds later he wiped a finger across the head of the drink and removed the foaming liquid from the glass-raised glass and swallowed a third of the drink. Then slammed the glass on the bar.

"Cold, I asked for a pint of cold lager not warm pig's piss," he snapped, pushing the glass away.

"Nothing wrong with the temperature of my beer. I reckon you'd be better sucking on your mother's teat. Anyway, you don't look old enough to be here so sod off and don't come back. Had enough of strangers coming in here causing trouble." Polly Parrott said, leaning on the bar and staring into Warm's face.

Warm turned his head to escape Polly's breath reeking of garlic. A smile split his features as drinkers moved away from the bar clutching their drinks tight to their chests.

"Nah, your lager tastes like wet shit. I must report you to the brewery for selling out-of-date drinks."

"Out-of-date drinks? Never heard so much crap in years," Polly blustered. "Who the bloody hell do you think you are?"

"An independent agent for local breweries. It's my job to report public houses selling sub-standard drinks to the public; it's obvious that you have been doing this for years."

"Bullshit, There's nothing wrong with my beer."

"I'm sorry, I'm afraid I must ask you to close the pub immediately."

Polly looked as if someone had pushed a hot poker up his backside.

"Over my dead body, you scrawny arsehole," he growled, taking a step forward.

"In which case, you leave me no alternative but to ring the police immediately. They will, of course, search the premises for other illegal activities; good day, sir," Warm said, turning to leave.

Before reaching the door to leave, he heard Polly's loud voice ordering everyone to get out before the police arrived.

"I always thought your beer was dodgy along with those packets of soggy peanuts you sell," a voice roared. "Gave me the shits more than once I can tell you."

"Wash your mouth out, you tight-arsed

country yokel. For the last seven years, I can't remember you ever buying more than one pint a night," Polly raged, grabbing the man by the collar and propelling him towards the door.

"Oi, stop pushing people around," another voice called.

Red with unreadable grey eyes Polly pulled himself up to his full height. The man who had called out to him trembled, aware his life hung on a shoestring. Mouth sagging open, he stared at Polly like he was a loose boulder from a mountain peak about to crush him.

"Settle down Polly; I was only joking. You know I like a laugh," he said, turning deathly white.

Like a greased piston, Polly's fist hit him square on the nose sending a sheet of blood showering those fighting to leave.

"That will put a smile on your face for a fortnight," Polly hollered, his grey eyes darting this way and that way. "Go on, bugger off the lot of you before I turn you into customers ready for cremation."

Pandemonium broke loose as men aimed punches at each other and fought to get out of the door

Sat on a bench seat beneath a parasol, Luke Warm smiled. All he had to do was wait for the police to arrive to break up the free-for-all inside the Crooked Stick Inn and then claim his £700 reward from Page. Not bad for a few minutes of work, he congratulated himself.

*

Satisfied with his selections, Toki finished checking his equipment. Two stun grenades, an incendiary grenade, a knife the size of a carving knife, and a garrotte. He left the 9mm handgun with a silencer in his kit bag; hopefully, there'd be no killing tonight. After checking his watch, he waited for the shadows to run across the countryside as the sun dropped dutifully over the horizon. Eyes accustomed to the dark, he set off for Pennywise Manor in a crouch. Minutes later, he stopped, sighed with disappointment, and shook his head at seeing the manor lit up like a summer fairground. Cursing himself for miscalculating, he withdrew to the safety of a copse of trees. He needed time to think and evaluate his position. If he were entering the manor with the intent to kill the occupants, there wouldn't be a problem. But this was an extraction, not wanton slaughter.

*

"Are you going to kill me?" Willow said, looking Xander in the face.

"Mmm, I'm not sure. It depends on whether old man Page has packed his bags and left the village."

Willow stared down at her feet.

"You won't get away with it; you must know that. The minute I'm out of here, I shall tell the police you held me against my will."

If the remark made Xander uncomfortable, it didn't show.

"You can tell them what you like. The police have heard it all before," Xander grinned.

Willow swallowed hard and made no reply as Xander continued.

"I don't wish you harm; money is my only motive for holding you here. I shall be rich the day Page leaves the village."

"Why is it so important he leave the village? What harm has he done to you or your family?"

"I'm afraid I can't answer that; you'll have to ask my father. He's the one that wants to see the back of him."

"You think holding me prisoner will give him cause to pack up and leave? He has a daughter. She won't let him pack his bags and disappear. I think you have stepped into a deep puddle which you can't get out of; that goes for your father too."

"Oh, for god's sake stop quacking. You give me a headache."

Willow moved her legs sideways from the bare mattress and stretched against the rope bounding her hands.

"What do you want for dinner tonight, fish n chips or a takeaway?" he hissed.

Dinner? He sounded like he might be her boyfriend, or someone more than just a casual friend. Perhaps it was his way of asking for a date. She'd never go out with him; he did nothing for her in a romantic way. True, he wasn't bad looking until you studied his mouth. The twist in his thin lips, ugh, who'd want to kiss them, be like kissing a piece of string.

"I asked you a question. Did you hear me?"

"How long is a mouse's tail?" she answered in a matter-of-fact voice.

"Must you act so childish?" he snapped.

"Look at the situation from my view and then see whose childish."

"Then go without; I don't give a shit."

"Nor do I, and you can shove your chips where the sun doesn't shine."

"Father is having a get-together with his bunch of geriatric hunt members downstairs. I'll bring sandwiches and cake when I return."

"Who cares?" Willow scowled.

She watched him leave, glad to have him out of her sight. It had taken little time before she eventually realised it was a thrill for him to lord it over women. He liked to act big like he was a kind of God, a gift to a world full of lesser mortals. She'd exact her revenge in gipsy fashion the day she was free of his clutches. As time passed, she heard laughter, the sound of knives and forks clinking over china plates —the tinkle of glasses against bottle tops. Time spooled, and the noise became louder. Laughter turned to wild screeches, voices raised to anger pitch. Her imagination began to work overtime as she thought of overweight men with thin moustaches tearing at the clothes of willing women, some more generous than others. At last, her eyelids flickered, and she finally surrendered to deep sleep.

*

Craning over a hanging branch, Toki peered at the mansion through the semi-darkness. No matter the risks, he was determined to enter the estate and search for Willow. If he failed to find her, he'd take someone he was sure knew where she was held against her will. Lord Pennywise was his primary target. Beneath the glare of twinkling lights from swaying candelabras, dressed in camouflaged tunic and trousers, he walked casually through the large doors, grabbed a tray of drinks from a bewildered waiter and made his up a flight of marbled stairs. Starting from the top and working the way down was his theory. It was faster and left room for a quick getaway if discovered.

A close inspection revealed the top floor was uninhabited. Most rooms were full of unwanted furniture; others empty, apart from giant spider webs. Feeling the hairs on his neck rise in the corridor, he stopped and stared upwards. High in the ornate ceiling, a chink of artificial light shone through a trapdoor. From the trapdoor hung a rope tied to a hook on the wall. Untying the rope, Toki tugged and watched the trapdoor swing down, followed by a steel ladder that settled on the floor feet from where he stood. A dull light poured through the hole left by the removal of the trapdoor. Toki reached out and shook the ladder to test its stability, snorted, and placing his foot on the bottom rung, began to climb the ladder. Like a tide, expectancy flushed in and out of his brain. Was it luck that brought or was it meant to be? Head tilted back, he continued climbing every few rungs to allow the ladder to stop from swaying lest he loses his balance and crashes to the ground. When he reached the top, he pulled a knife from his boot and slowly raised his head above the opening.

"Fish n chip shop closed is it, or has the Chinese takeaway run out of cats," Willow said, her back to him and thinking Xander had returned,

Toki couldn't stop the grin from spreading over his face.

"I've bought you a corned beef sandwich with a sprinkle of fairy dust," he said, still grinning.

Willow's body stiffened. Slowly she rolled over to face him. Tears gushed from her eyes as she struggled to free herself from the ropes holding her down.

"Toki, thank God you have found me. Please take me away from here. Something evil lives in this place; I can feel it in my bones."

Free from the ropes, Toki guided her to the opening leading to the ground.

"I'll go first, don't look down."

Eyes closed, Toki guided her feet onto the

rungs until they safely reached the floor.

"Now, we must find a way out; stay close. I think I can remember the way Onions showed me."

Twenty yards along the corridor, Willow stumbled and fell.

"I'm sorry. I can't get my legs to work after being tied up for three days."

"No problem, I'll carry you until we find somewhere safe."

Raising her in a fireman's lift, Toki moved swiftly along the corridor before descending a flight of stone steps. When they reached the room where Onions told him Lord Pennywise entertained his ladies; Toki gently laid Willow on the bed and began massaging her legs. After twenty minutes, she left the bed and stood unaided.

"I feel much better now," she smiled. "How did you know where to find me?"

"I didn't; it was luck. Not far to go now; how do you feel."

"Much better, thank you."

"Who locked you in the attic?"

"Xander, it was Xander."

"He needs to be taught a lesson."

"Really, and who might be foolish enough to try?" a voice boomed.

Willow stiffened and fell back on the bed. Toki tensed and crouched.

"Come out and show yourself," Toki called.

"And why should I do that? You won't leave this building alive."

"You don't scare me. You're no more than a mummies boy, a bully who likes to pick on young women."

Seconds passed in silence. Mesmerised, Willow struggled o breathe. A biting chill raised goosebumps on her skin. What did Xander mean they won't leave the building alive?

Toki saw the fear dart into Willow's eyes and laid a reassuring hand on her arm.

"He can't hurt us, or he'd have done it by now. He's frightened to show himself." Toki said out loud, hoping Xander heard his words. "The door leads to the garages; we're out in the clear from there. Remember to stay close."

Willow's eyes followed the direction of Toki's nod.

"Xander wouldn't have allowed us to get this far if that were true. He's playing with us."

When Toki tried to wrench the door, it stuck fast; they were trapped at Xander's mercy.

"Okay, we'll retrace our steps and return the way we came," Toki whispered.

"Sorry, but I can't allow you to leave," Xander's voice sang through the corridor. "It isn't part of my plan."

"How does he know where we are?" Willow's voice trembled.

"CCTV cameras, the building is full of them. If we can find one, we might be able to trace the cable and disconnect the feed."

Willow felt faint. Raising a hand to steady herself, she caught her finger on something sharp. During her chequered past, she had been involved in many events where lesser people would have failed. But under the threat of death, that was something else. She didn't want to die in some dark, damp corridor and be left to rot as food for rats.

"Here," she mumbled quietly. "There's a hole in the brickwork, be careful."

Toki pulled a pencil torch from his pocket and shone the beam onto the corridor side.

"Good work, you have found one of the cameras. If I dig it out from the wall, we can trace the wiring, and Xander won't know where we are."

Using his knife, Toki dug at the brickwork for fifteen minutes before releasing the bricks; pulling the camera free, he traced the cable feed concealed in the soft roof. One sharp tug and the cable fell free from the ceiling.

"Now it's us against him. First, I'll get rid of Pennywise's cronies downstairs. And I have the perfect answer to that small problem."

"No killing. I want no part in the murder," Willow said firmly.

"Who mentioned murder?" he said, turning his head to prevent her from seeing the glint of steel in his eyes.

She watched him move away, his silhouette

hunched like a bent hook. Somewhere deep in her mind, a flash of familiarity unnerved her. Whatever it was, it stopped her from bursting into tears. He stopped and turned to wait for her to catch him up, then made his way back to where she'd sunk to her knees. She looked up at him, her face pale, her mouth open as if gasping for breath. He wondered when she last ate a proper meal or had a good night's sleep. When he bent to pick her up in his arms, she murmured words he couldn't understand. She felt as light as a feather as he walked along the corridor.

CHAPTER TWENTY-SIX

With a face like thunder, DCI Mattress pulled off her grimy trainers and hurled them across the interviewing room in the police station. Det/Sgt Down managed to conceal his smile when she bent and rubbed her aching feet while cursing the villagers simultaneously. She'd forgotten how long she'd suffered the tingling pain in both her feet since her only relief was painkillers prescribed by her doctor, a young Asian in his early twenties. The trouble was the relief from the painkillers lasted approximately five hours, after which she perspired profusely in pain until she swallowed another tablet. Today was one of those days when she'd run out of pills and forgotten to slip a strip into her shoulder bag.

"Who the bloody hell is Tommy King, and what's he to do with us?"

"One of our coppers used to work for the Met. He picked up King for speeding on the edge of the village last night. He remembered King had been sent down for attempted murder on the evidence from a woman who swore under oath that she saw King holding a shotgun. He'd have walked free if it hadn't been for her statement. The evidence was flimsy, and the judge threatened to throw the charge out of court until the woman appeared late on the scene with new evidence. The woman was Rita Peters. We found her dead dressed as a scarecrow a couple of days ago, remember?"

"Of course, I remember. I'm not stupid. Nothing unusual about a revenge killing; those London villains are at it all the time?"

"King says he'd never recognise Peters after his years in prison. He was visiting his old prison mate, Anton Page."

"Anton bloody Page, I should have known he'd be involved. The village has never been the same since he returned. Get round to his bungalow and find out what's going on. Any trouble, cuff him and bring him to the station."

"Not much room in the cells after the bust-up in the Crooked Stick. Half the men in the village are locked up."

"Serves them right; they'll survive for a few more hours."

"Right, boss. By the way, my mate's friend knows a chiropodist. He reckons having a man suck your toes might help to relieve the pain."

"Get out of here; Down, you dirty-minded little sod, before you end up sweeping the roads."

"Just a thought, boss," Down grinned, heading

for the door.

*

Page's world had turned upside down. Since leaving prison trouble had followed him tighter than a shadow. Cate had become a stranger threatening to ignore him until he sold the bungalow and moved where no one knew him. Heartbroken with worry over Willow, he began to lose weight, and events went from bad to worse as the days grew longer. Ignoring the loud rap on the front door, he turned up the volume on the TV set and slurped down the dregs of a cold mug of tea. A sudden shower sent large raindrops pattering on the windows. He wondered why the rain zig-zagged down the window instead of running straight from top to bottom. The world could go and take a running jump. The heat in his face raised a notch as the rap came again. It had to be the law; only police officers rip door knockers off trying to gain an entrance.

"Yes, what is it now? The police station run out of milk?" Page growled, opening the door and staring at Down.

"Does the name Tom King mean anything to you?"

"It might do; why do you ask, aren't I allowed friends now without you lot knocking on my door every few minutes?"

"Do you mind if I step inside, we're enquiring about Tom King's presence in the village?"

Page closed his eyes, sighed, and stood aside to let Down enter.

"Kings on his way to Scotland Yard accompanied by two police officers charged with the murder of Rita Peters, also known as Onions, who worked for Lord Pennywise as his butler."

"Why would he do that? He's not a murderer?"

"Peters gave false evidence at King's trial after he was caught red-handed stealing jewellery from luxury apartments in Canary Wharf. He might have gotten off with a slap on the wrist until Peters swore he was responsible for a dozen other crimes under oath. The judge sent him down, and King became one of many looking to get revenge on Peters."

Before Page could answer, the front door burst, revealing Froggie Spawn, a dairy farmer from the other side of the village.

"You'd better come quickly; there's something wrong with my herd of milkers," Spawn gasped, struggling for breath.

Page's lips stretched tight into a sneer.

"Why tell me? Since I left prison, you have made my life miserable, insulted me, blackened my name and constantly referred to me as a murdering bastard to anyone prepared to listen to your poison. Piss off, Spawn; I don't have ten seconds for the likes of you. Get out of my house and go and find a vet."

"You murdered your wife; what did you expect, a gold medal? Think what you will of me, but don't let my cattle suffer."

Down blinked slowly, watching and waiting for Page's response. Page stared at his feet and then turned to gaze at the raindrops running haphazardly down the windows. He hated Spawn and the rest of his farming cronies driving around in their flash Range Rovers and acting like Gods.

"I'll be over when the rain stops, and I want payment upfront. I've had my fill of your lot refusing to pay their bills. A bunch of ten-a-penny wankers, the lot of you. Now get out before I ask this policeman to throw you out."

Spawn's face turned scarlet. A man who believed he was above others stiffened beneath Page's verbal onslaught. Without answering, he turned and left, closing the door gently behind him. Page turned his attention to Down.

"Well, are you finished with me, or do you intend to arrest me for inviting Tom King to my home to help find Willow?"

Down pushed out his bottom lip like a child's pout.

"Under the circumstances, you should check the trouble with Mr Spawn's herd of cattle. We can talk later."

"Stuff Spawn, he's had in for me since I seduced his wife two days before they married. Sour grapes, that's what it is."

Down pulled in his lip and smiled.

"Village life, eh? Anything goes."

Minutes after Det/Sgt Down left, the rain ceased, and Page stepped into the garden and smelled the freshness in the air. The scent of lavender, thyme and rosemary filled his senses. At that one moment in time, he wished it could be over, and he could sleep in a place where there could be no dreaming. It took several minutes before he decided to check Spawn's herd. Reluctantly grabbing his bag, he fired the engine in his car and left for the twenty-five-minute drive.

*

"How much longer must we go to be safe?" Willow asked in a muted voice.

"I don't know; it's daylight, and look at them prancing around like naked headless chickens. There can't be one of them under sixty," Toki said, not bothering to keep his voice low. "Can you stand?"

"I don't think so. I feel so weak."

Toki didn't answer; instead, pulling a packet of liquorice allsorts from his pocket he slipped one into his mouth

"Right, be prepared for fireworks; before we go any further, I need to move that load of drunks out the way," Toki said, pulling the pin from a flash-bang grenade and rolling it down the stairway. When the grenade exploded, Ignoring the screams, he raised Willow onto his shoulder and ran down the stairway towards the exit. Once safely outside, he lowered Willow to the ground and tossed an incendiary grenade into the room where the guests' coats were held; at the same time Xander stumbled from the building.

"You blasted fool; you'll pay for this," Xander screamed, raising an arm to block the heat from burning his face

"When I've seen this lady to safety, I'll be coming for you," Toki answered.

"You don't frighten me," Xander sneered.

"You've been warned. If you have an ounce of sense, you'll be out of this village before the police beat me to it."

Xander stopped dead in his tracks at Toki's words.

"The police? You must be joking; we own the police."

Toki gazed over Xander's shoulder.

"Let's hope you own the fire brigade, too; it looks like your building is about to collapse in flames."

Xander turned. A look of horror twisted his face as orange flames leapt skywards engulfing Pennywise Manor.

"Oh my God, my fathers in there. He'll never get out alone."

"Then you'd better get your arse into gear before he's burnt to death, and remember what I told you," Toki said, smiling at the naked bodies pouring from the burning mansion. "As for you, lady, let's get you home."

After ten minutes, Willow told Toki she was strong enough to walk unaided. He stopped, gently lowered her to the ground, pulled his arms away, and waited for her to climb unassisted to her feet. Once upright, she raised her arms and stretched out the stiffness in her bones.

"Thank you, Toki. I thought I was going to die."

Toki smiled, pulled a paper bag of liquorice allsorts from his pocket, and rammed two into his mouth.

"Return to your friends. Tell them nothing of me and live your life accompanied by happiness," he said.

"What do you mean? I wouldn't be here if it weren't for you; you saved my life."

"What's done is done; I wish to return to Greenland, the land of my ancestors. There I will protect the Polar bears and wildlife from extinction. Take care, little lady."

Before Willow could answer, he disappeared into the woods.

"Don't go, please; I owe you so much," she called, holding her hand tight to her heart and gasping for breath.

Toki hesitated in the shadow of the trees, then chewing his bottom lip lengthened his stride. Surrounded by the silence of the woods, Willow made her way to the village. Page's car was missing from the drive. Too tired to worry about others, she entered her bedroom, slumped on the bed, and fell fast asleep.

*

No matter how much Page disliked Spawn, he tried not to sneer. When he eventually spoke, it was in such a considered tone that Spawn knew something wasn't how it should be.

"I need to take blood samples from your cattle and get them analysed immediately."

A cloud passed over Spawn's face.

"Messing me about, are you? Want revenge because I didn't shake your hand and buy you a drink for what you did to Lizzie?"

Page didn't answer right away. When he did, it sounded like he was reading a passage from a book.

"I think your cattle are suffering from leptospirosis. It causes anaemia and liver and kidney failure. If I'm right, you could lose the herd."

Spawn rested his chin on his chest and scratched his head.

"You're bluffing."

"I'm deadly serious, Spawn. I can take six examples while I'm here and have them analysed later this afternoon. The decision is yours."

Spawn turned his head and gazed across the open fields before answering.

"Do what you have to do."

"And if you fail to pay me up front, I'll let your animals die in agony and report you to the agricultural authorities for failing to listen to a qualified vet."

Spawn looked at him dumbstruck.

"Do what you have to do," he said quietly.

It took Page twenty-five minutes to take samples from infected animals.

"I'll be back later. In the meantime, keep the herd away from other cattle."

"The money will be here when you return with the results."

"It better be, or I'll finish you as a farmer." Page sneered, pleased at having the last word against a bully like Spawn.

CHAPTER TWENTY-SEVEN

It seemed to Willow she'd closed her eyes just minutes ago when the shrill sound of a passing fire engine woke her. Immediately, Pennywise Manor filled her thoughts. Neon numbers blinked the time on the radio clock. Sat in thoughtful silence on the edge of the bed with her hands resting on her lap; she crossed her ankles and tried to tidy her mind over the last few days' events. Engulfed in her thoughts, a soft evening light spread over the village. The sound of the front door jerking open failed to rouse her from her thoughts. Someone laid an arm on her shoulder and pulled her tight.

"Oh, my poor dear, thank God you are safe," Cate's voice sounded distant.

Willow blinked and opened her eyes to allow her tears free reign as they tumbled down her cheeks.

"Am I a bad person?" she whispered.

"Of course not," Cate answered softly.

"Then why do bad things happen to the people

I care so much for? Why didn't my mother want me? Am I cursed? Where is my father? Perhaps it would be better if I were dead."

"Now you are talking nonsense. You have made a lot of people happy since you arrived in the village. And the animals, look how much they love you when you care for them. I don't believe my father would have survived the hatred in the village were it not for you."

"You are only saying these things to make me happy."

"Listen to me, Willow; I cannot answer your questions. What has happened has happened. You must face your past and use it to guide your future. I think of you as the little sister I never had. My father treats you as his daughter. Think of the good things in life, and the bad things will disappear."

"Toki saved me from Xander. After setting fire to Pennywise Mansion, he has gone forever back to Greenland."

"What a shame; I quite liked him. I thought him quite handsome."

"Did you fancy him? You did, didn't you?" Willow shrieked, staring Cate in the face.

"A little bit, perhaps."

"A little bit? I bet you wanted to bed him; go on, tell the truth."

"Well, you soon recovered; what a terrible thing to say," Cate laughed, squeezing Willow tighter. "Get a shower, and we'll talk later."

*

"Unfortunately, your findings were accurate. The tests show leptospirosis. Spawn's herd must be isolated and given antibiotics. It could take anything from three days to three weeks before we see any sign of recovery; if there's no change, the herd must be destroyed," Steve Weir said.

"Such a shame that a man's livelihood is gone in a few days."

"Yes, if you can wait half an hour, I'll prepare the antibiotics."

"Yes, of course, I'll wait."

Darkness had fallen when Page returned to Froggie Spawn's dairy farm. Surrounded by his two sons and a daughter, Spawn threw a black look at his wife Sonia, when she offered to make Page a pot of tea.

"He's more important things to do than sitting here slurping tea."

"Learn to show some manners," Sonia snapped at her husband.

"Thank you, Mrs Spawn, later perhaps, when I have finished injecting the cows," Page smiled.

"I wouldn't reckon sitting on your arse all night. The farms split into two halves, ninety cows in the top and a hundred and ten in the lower fields," Spawn grunted. "We have rigged up searchlights so you can see what you are doing."

Page's smile disappeared.

"I never realised you had so many cows. It's a good job I ordered more than enough antibiotics.

I could do with some help, though."

"That's your problem," Spawn grunted again. "You'll get no help from us; if anything goes wrong, the insurance company won't pay us a penny using unqualified staff. One of my boys will drive you to the top field and help as much as he's allowed. Give us a ring when you're ready for the bottom field. Oh, by the way, here's your money."

Page took the money and, without looking at Spawn, stuffed the envelope in his pocket. He'd made a mistake not checking on the size of the herd. Injecting two hundred cows would take all night and the best part of the following day.

*

Four hours later, just after midnight, Page was ready to give up injecting the cattle. Billy, Spawn's youngest son was more intent on keeping his new pair of trainers dry and free from cow's dung than being of any help.

"For God's sake, Billy, get a move on, or we'll be here for a fortnight and lose both herds at this rate. And don't forget to paint a cross on the rump of each cow treated." Page said, angrily pulling the ringing phone from his pocket. "Yes, I'm busy; who is it?"

"It's Cate; where are you? Willows returned safe and well."

"Thank God for that. I'm at Froggie Spawn's farm, and I could do with some help. Get up here as soon as possible."

"What!"

"You heard. I haven't got all night, and bring Willow with you," Page said, closing the call.

Cate turned and looked at Willow. Freshly showered, pale-skinned and with big green eyes, her gelled hair scraped back into a flowing ponytail; she looked a fraction of herself.

"That was my father; he needs help at Spawn's farm. Do you feel up to it, or would you rather wait here?"

"No, I want to help."

Billy looked at Page through quizzical eyes.

"Why do people call my dad Froggie? Is it because he's big staring eyes like a frog?" he asked.

Page smiled.

"No, lad, nothing like that. After winning the long jump on school sports day for three years on the trot, the boys said he could jump further than any frog in the world, so they called him Froggie.

*

The moment Cate set eyes on her father, she sucked in a great breath. It was clear he was at the end of his tether. He tried to stand straight and erect and then, like a sad tortoise, lowered his head into the neck of his anorak. Wearing no make-up or trinkets, Cate set her jaw firm.

"What are you trying to prove by helping Spawn of all people? He's responsible for half the misery in this village?"

"I'm not interested in him. I'm trying to save

his cattle from suffering and dying."

"Look at you. You can't even stand straight, let alone treat cattle. What is wrong with them?"

"They need antibiotics, or they will die."

"I know how to do that. I read it in one of your books. The jugular vein is behind the ear; it's easy," Willow said, stepping forward.

Page raised half a smile.

"It's good to see you safe and sound. We were worried you had gone away and left us,"

"I'd never do that. Shall we get started? We can do two simultaneously while Cate and Billy herd the animals into the pen."

Too tired to argue, against his better judgement, Page nodded his head towards Billy.

"What do you say, Billy? Will you tell your father Willow offered to save his herds?"

"Nah, I won't say a word. I'm not interested in farming anyway. I want to be a plumber, not walk around up to my knees in cow shit for the rest of my life."

"Then let's get started," Page said in a hoarse voice, followed by a bout of coughing and spitting.

It took four hours before Billy splashed a white cross on the rump of the last animal to pass through the pen. When Cate turned to congratulate her father on a job well done, he'd collapsed in a heap on the ground surrounded by milling cattle. Cate knelt and, cradling his head in her hands looked into his eyes. His face was thin and pale, his eyes distant as if he stared into another world.

"I'm taking you to the hospital; damn the cows, they can wait," she said fiercely.

Page jerked himself into action. Not for the first time, he wished he could sleep in a place where dreaming was banned.

"No, I'll be alright; the cows come first. I gave Spawn my word," Page said in a low voice.

"To hell with the cows," Cate snapped angrily.

Pushing himself reluctantly upright, Page climbed unsteadily to his feet.

"Billy," he called. "Take us to the bottom field, and let's get this job done before morning."

Billy bit his bottom lip and glanced at Cate. Cate puffed out her cheeks and let out a long breath.

"Do as he says; we don't have the time to argue."

With tears pricking at the corners of her eyes and one arm around Page's waist Willow helped him into the vehicle waiting to take them to the bottom field. Climbing into her car, Cate gritted her teeth and negatively shook her head.

"Show me where to stick the damn needle. I don't care what Spawn says or thinks. My fathers had enough for one night," she shot at Willow.

Willow glanced at Page, then turned to face Billy.

"Do it; I'm freezing my balls off shoving these cattle into the pen," Billy grunted.

The sun was making its way to its zenith when Cate pushed the needle into the last cow. As if on cue, Spawn arrived while Cate and Willow busied themselves loading Page's instruments in the back of his car.

"All done then?" Spawn shouted. "They'll be trouble if I lose any cattle."

Cate spun round to face Spawn.

"Shut your stupid mouth, you pig-headed moron. And get on your knees and thank this man for saving your herds. If it were me, I wouldn't trust you with a newborn kitten."

Red-faced and mouth hanging open, Spawn didn't answer when Willow pushed the car into gear and drove away.

"Drive to the hospital, Willow," Cate said firmly.

"Yes, of course," Willow answered.

CHAPTER TWENTY-EIGHT

Pennywise Manor wilted beneath the surge of flames eager to feed its insatiable hunger. The sky glowed bright red as Nelson lowered his father gently onto the wet ground. Close by, fire engines operated by solemn-faced firefighters followed by a posse of ambulances with wailing sirens and blue flashing lights screeched to a stop. Men dressed in heavy polyester cotton two-pieced suits tumbled from the back of the ambulances as firefighters reeled out long hoses ready to combat the licking flames.

"My father, can someone help my father, please? He's swallowed a lot of smoke and can hardly breathe."

"The horses, save the horses and the cars," Lord Pennywise stuttered, trying to suck air into his burning lungs

"Step aside, sir," a gruff voice called as someone clamped a plastic oxygen mask over the elderly man's face.

"Is anyone still inside the building?" a

different voice called.

"I'm not sure. A party was in progress to honour my father," Nelson whispered.

"Can't see many surviving the fire now the fire has taken a firm hold," a firefighter called.

Nelson looked up at the Manor disappearing beneath a cloud of black smoke.

"I'm sure all the guests manage to escape to safety, but my brother Xander might still be in there," he whispered. "My father's suffering from exhaustion."

"Sorry, sir, we are doing all we can to rescue anyone trapped inside," the firefighter said over his shoulder as he quickly moved away allowing Lord Pennywise to be lifted onto a stretcher and taken to a waiting ambulance.

Nelson blinked as a camera flashed in his face followed by another to ensure the photographer had the picture he wanted. From the corner of his eyes he saw half a dozen people staring at him. He recognised the woman from the village newsagent, then caught sight of the greengrocer standing next to the landlord of the Crooked Inn public house. Their disparate faces staring at him and judging him made him nervous. He knew they were wondering how the Manor had caught fire in the middle of the summer months. A young girl dressed in a school uniform glared at him without embarrassment through glacial blue eyes. A woman wearing a baseball cap leaned and whispered in her ear. Seconds later, the young girl turned and skipped away to her place of learning. It was then that Nelson realised he had nothing. He had no money, home, clothes and, as things stood, more than likely no family apart from his invalid father.

"Will someone help me free the horses in the stables and help me to move cars from the garage," he cried, searching for any response from the gathering crowd.

A man in his mid-twenties wearing a white T-shirt over a muscled torso stepped forward,

"I know where the stables are; you get the cars," he called.

Without pausing to speak, both men sprinted to the rear of the manor not yet fully affected by the fire. Minutes later the horses galloped to safety screaming and whinnying with fear. With two vintage Rolls Royce clear of the building, one black and the other white, Nelson returned for the maroon Bentley. Beaten back by the advancing flames he stood helpless as the roof collapsed burying a new Ferrari and a BMW motorcycle.

"There's someone trapped in the stables," the man wearing a white T-shirt wheezed.

"Oh my God, it must be Xander. Thank God he's still alive; we'll have to get him out as soon as possible before the building collapses," Nelson gasped

"You can't go in there; you can't see anything for flames."

"He's my brother. I'll die for him if I have to. There's a canvas roll in the corner; help me get it over my head."

Pulling the piece of loose canvas over his head, Nelson forced his way into the garage.

"Xander, where are you? Can you hear me?" He shouted.

A sheet of burning plywood moved to Nelson's right. Sucking a great breath of air Nelson stumbled towards the plywood and pulled it to one side.

"Beezulbub, what are you doing in here?"

The old grey donkey climbed to his feet and trotted out of the stable."

"What was that?" the man in the white T-shirt said.

"That's Beelzebub, my elder brother's donkey. He tells him about his troubles and swears blind the donkey gave him good advice. Thank you for your assistance; if there is anything I can do to help you, please let me know. We would have lost the horses and the cars without your help."

"No problem. Perhaps I'll see you around."

*

"Over there, can you see the black smoke? Somethings on fire," Cate said excitedly, pushing her foot down on the accelerator.

"It looks like Pennywise Manor," Willow said in a hushed voice. "Let's go and take a look?"

Twenty minutes later, Cate and Willow stared in silence at the burning rubble once known as Pennywise Manor. Eventually, Cate found the strength to speak.

"I can't believe it. It's been there since the day I was born. Most of the villagers work the land and care for the forest. Such a shame."

Willow remained seated, desperately trying to think of something to say. Shaking, she sank into the seat deep in her thoughts. She held no affection or respect for the building or those who dwelled between the walls. Only hours ago Xander Pennywise had held her life in his hands as if she were a toy. Resting her hands on her lap she recalled Toki's words to Xander, threatening he would return and make Xander pay for his crimes.

"We'll find out soon enough what happened. In the meantime, let's get my father to the hospital."

Two hours had dragged by before Cate and Willow were allowed to visit Page. Cate observed her father from the doorway of his private room where he lay propped up in bed. With an oxygen mask covering his mouth and nose, and a drip running into his thin right arm, Page looked skeletally thin. He seemed to have aged almost beyond recognition. Willow didn't react immediately. She wondered if he might be sleeping and prayed he was. Unsure he could receive visitors, she remained by the door and watched Cate step closer to his bed.

"Hello, dad, how are you feeling?" she asked in

barely a whisper.

When Page never moved or displayed any sign of consciousness, the tears burst from Cate's eyes and ran in streams down her face. Caught up in the scene of deep emotion, Willow began to sob uncontrollably.

"You called me dad," a faint voice slipped from Page's mouth.

"Thank God you are alive," Cate blubbered, blowing her nose.

"You called me dad," the faint voice came again.

"Well, you are my dad, aren't you? Please don't tell me you object to me calling you dad."

If Page had the energy to answer her question, it never showed as he remained still with closed eyes. Cate's shoulders slumped as she let out the most mournful cry Willow had ever heard.

"He doesn't like me, he never wanted me, and now he tells me on his death bed that I mean nothing to him," Cate wailed, tipping the contents of her shoulder bag over her lap and onto the floor while searching for a clean tissue.

"He never said any of those things. He said he was pleased you called him dad. Come to think of it, I have never heard you refer to him as your dad," Willow countered.

"Because he is my dad doesn't mean I have to call him dad."

"Yes, you do; it's good manners."

"Where do manners come into it?"

"Because they do," Willow said, struggling to find a suitable answer. "Go on, call him dad again."

"He won't answer; I know he won't."

"Try it."

"He won't answer."

"Bloody hell, try it and stop moaning all the time. You're enough to make a saint curse at times."

"Don't you swear at me, young lady?" Cate said, trying to make a joke to puncture the absurdity of their conversation.

"How long is a mouse's tail?" Willow said in frustration, raising her head and staring at the ceiling.

"Alright, alright, I'll try it once only," Cate said, inclining her head close to her father. "How are you, dad? We are worried about you."

When Page's lips moved, Willow leaned forward and raised the oxygen mask from his face.

"I feel better knowing you are here. You bring light into my life," Page whispered.

"Oh, dad, I love you so much."

"Yes, I know, and I love you."

*

"Open the cells and let them out," DCI Mattress barked at Det/Sgt Down. "And tell them if I hear any more nonsense from the Crooked Stick, I'll have the lot of them before the magistrate."

"Do you want me to ask who started the trouble," Down asked.

"No, they are all as bad as each other. Get me a car; we'll visit Pennywise Manor and see what's happening."

"Okay, boss, I'm on it," Down said, striding from the office.

"You watch too much television," Mattress shouted after him and shook her head.

*

It was a coincidence Lord Pennywise was placed in the room next to Page. Sooner or later, when one of them began to feel better, he might take it upon himself to visit the other. By the time Lord Pennywise arrived accompanied by Nelson, Cate and Willow had left the hospital and made their way home.

"You can come and stay with Luke and me until we sort things out," Cate said.

"No, now your father is in the hospital; someone must care for the animals."

"Of course, I never thought of that," Cate answered.

*

Fortunately, the only animals in the surgery were two small dogs and a cat with a bandage over its right eye. Willow was overjoyed the fridge contained eggs, bacon and sausages. She hadn't had a decent meal since Xander captured her and locked her in Pennywise Manor. Pulling out the frying pan, she ate until she could eat no more. After finishing a mug of steaming tea, she busied herself reading Page's notes, fed the animals, and hesitated whether to carry out the required treatment for each animal.

*

Struggling to concoct a plausible excuse not to close his eyes and sleep, Page stared at the running crack in the ceiling of his room. He scarcely needed reminding if he allowed his body to rest; dreams of his past would fill his mind. A shaft of sunlight teased him of another world that lay outside the grim walls that held him like a wild animal unfit to walk with decent people. He recalled the time a cocky young scouser asked a heavily built black man for a cigarette and received a beating that almost killed him for his cheek. The piercing screams of a French teenager caged for pushing harmful drugs to disco users when three East Europeans lined up to enter his backside. Caught in the semi-conscious limbo between sleep and awake his dreams merged with reality, and he drifted confused through imaginary encounters and hidden anxieties.

Lord Pennywise slipped his hand down the front of his pyjamas in the room next door and began to caress himself. His mind clear of wrongdoing and filled with the erotic, his body jolted by the explosion the moment he ejaculated. Free of all other thoughts and his head resting against the iron headboard he relaxed and waited for his heartbeat to return to normal.

Three days passed before Lord Pennywise entered Page's room unannounced. Page pulled himself up between the sheets and placed the magazine of country wildlife on the bedside cabinet.

"What do you want, Pennywise?" Page said, making no effort to disguise his sneer.

"I have a title, you know. Show some respect for your betters,"

"Betters? You are nothing but a lowlife. The whole of the village knows that."

Pennywise smiled.

"The same old Page. A convicted murderer and son to a couple of cheap artefact robbers."

"And you, a bullying arsehole who can't keep his hands off his cock because no woman would give you the time of day."

"Oh, I don't know about that. We both knew someone who couldn't keep her hands off me, didn't we?" Pennywise grinned. "You know your trouble, Page? You suffered delusions. Saw yourself as the village's saviour, always throwing a few pounds here and there to the needy hoping it would improve your standing. But your wife made a laughing stock of you. If you had an ounce of gumption, you would have left the village without your wife and never returned. But you wouldn't do that, would you? Instead, you copied her and began sowing your oats with anyone who wanted free treatment for their pets.

You embarrassed the village and its history with your cheap antics."

"Go and tell your stories to a deaf man, Pennywise. You disliked me because I stood up to you and your moronic sons for bullying everyone and throwing people out of their houses. You owned their properties and if they refused to work for you for a pittance you had them evicted. As for your medical appliances, they're not worth the plastic they're made of."

"Gentlemen, we can hear your voices in the wards. Lord Pennywise, please return to your room?" A young nurse said with an Irish lilt through the partly open door.

"Be glad of the opportunity to give my nose a whiff of fresh air," Pennywise grunted.

"That's because your nose is stuck up your arse, Pennywise," Page retorted.

"Goodbye, Page. I'm sure we shall have the misfortune of speaking again."

"I wouldn't hold my breath if I were you."

"Oh dear, how could you possibly be like me? You are lowborn."

"Jesus, will the pair of you shut it and grow up?" The nurse snapped.

When Pennywise disappeared, Page laid his head on the pillow, closed his watery eyes, and pinched the bridge of his nose, hopeful it would ease his splitting headache.

Lord Pennywise sat on the edge of his bed with raised eyebrows and looked about him before slipping two large tablets into his mouth. His throat was uncomfortably dry and his water jug was empty. Intending to find a nurse he left his room and shuffled along the corridor. He'd barely covered half a dozen steps when something soft struck the back of his neck. Stumbling forward with his arm outstretched, he cannoned into a stainless steel trolley full of used bed pans and fell flat on his face.

"That's where you belong, Pennywise, up to your neck in piss," Page hollered. "You can keep the slipper and shove it up your arse."

An hour later, two male attendants wheeled Pennywise into a mixed ward, leaving him between two women complaining of pain after hip replacements.

"What in blazes do you think you are doing? I paid for a private room. Now take me home immediately," Pennywise bellowed at the attendants.

"Sorry, sir, I'm afraid it's the only available space in the hospital," one of the attendants answered. "And I'm afraid you no longer have a home."

CHAPTER TWENTY-NINE

When the doorbell chimed, Willow had just finished bathing the springer's eye. Wiping her wet hands down her smock, she dropped the damp lint into the wastebin, made her way through the bungalow and pulled open the front door.

"Can I help you?" she smiled.

John 'Boy' Ladd returned her smile, his greedy eyes devouring her figure.

"Play your cards right, and you might get lucky," he smirked, displaying a set of stained teeth. "I'm looking for my old mate Anton. Is he about?"

"No, he's in hospital," Willow answered, gripping the edge of the door tightly.

"He ain't gone and kicked the bucket has he? He owes me seven hundred quid."

"I'm sure he'll pay you when he leaves the hospital. If you give me your name, I'll make a note of it."

"Nah, I can't be giving my name to strangers.

You might be the police for all I know. I'll pop back tomorrow. Live here on your own, do you?"

"No, there's six of us," Willow lied.

"Shame, it might have been your lucky day. Never mind, eh, can't win them all?"

Willow breathed a sigh of relief when he turned and walked towards the village with his hands shoved deep in his pockets. The sight of Cate's car added to Willow's relief. Wrinkling her nose, she waited on the doorstep, her long fair hair straddling her shoulders down to her small breasts. The thumb of her left hand tucked loosely into her waistband, her features relaxed when Cate waved and smiled. Willow's lips formed a broad smile. She'd not mention the man who refused to leave his name to Cate while Anton was recovering in the hospital.

Still afraid to close his eyes and visualise haunting memories of the past, yet desperate for sleep, Page threw back the bedclothes and sat on his hands at the bottom of the bed. Accompanied by the steady ticking of the clock on the nurse's table he stared up at the ceiling with unseeing eyes. Pennywise had tormented him without mercy. Manipulated him into thinking he was nothing. When a picture of Lizzie appeared in his mind, he reached for the glass on the bedside cabinet ready to smash it into her face leaving her scarred for life. But she was gone leaving his thoughts to ease his anguish. Instead, he felt contempt for himself. Because of his deep love for her he'd allowed her to use him and become an unwanted obsession. But like cancer, he became addicted to her and unable to free himself.

"Come along, Mr Page. Time for your sleeping pill. After a good night's sleep, you'll feel better in the morning."

He didn't know where the voice came from or remember drifting into a deep sleep, but knew the dreams would come.

*

"The hospital informed me father can come home tomorrow," Cate said, wrapping her long fingers around the mug of coffee.

"You're doing it again," Willow said, staring directly into Cate's eyes.

"Doing what, now what's put a bee in your bonnet?"

"Calling him father instead of dad."

Cate's lips parted to display her milk-white teeth. The fingers of her left hand fiddled with her necklace of black balls.

"Why is it so important to you?"

"How long is a mouse's tail?" Willow snapped, losing control of her mug of coffee and quickly climbing to her feet. "Now look what you have made me do."

Cate frowned and shrugged her shoulders. She found it annoying being constantly reprimanded by a girl old enough to be her daughter. Page was her father and had no business with Willows. It made her realise Willow was far more insecure than she first imagined.

"Willow, Anton is my father, and I shall refer to him in any way I please without being disrespectful."

Willow fidgeted and looked uncomfortable.

"Yes, of course," Willow answered softly. "I shouldn't have spoken the way I did. I'm sorry."

"Well, we don't want to make a mountain out of a mole hole, do we?"

"No. Don't you mean molehill?"

Cate ignored her remark.

"Has it ever crossed your mind to call him dad?" she whispered.

There was an awkward silence. Cate knew the important thing was to stay calm. Willow had other thoughts and, without warning, leapt to her feet.

"How long is a mouse's tail?" she cried, rushing from the room leaving Cate with her mouth sagging open and juggling with a mug of coffee to prevent it from spilling onto the floor.

The front door slamming shut drowned out any chance of Cate responding.

*

The following morning, Willow turned the shower on and adjusted the thermostat. She intended to get as close to the hot water as she could bear. Giving little thought to the warm sunny day outside, she recalled the spat with

Cate. She first noticed that she and Cate were drifting apart when Cate made it plain that she'd pick up her father from the hospital alone. On top of that, any conversation between them had become meaningless. Altering the angle of the showerhead, she stepped into the bath when the doorbell rang. Although it might be anyone, the thought it might be an injured animal seeking attention sent her scurrying for her bathrobe before opening the door and peering through the small gap.

"Are you the lady that helps the vet?" Nelson said, pushing an untidy lock of hair from his eyes.

"Yes, I was just about to climb in the shower. Is it important?"

"Well, I'm sorry, but I think it might be. One of my brother's dogs was caught in the fire up at Pennywise Manor. I'm afraid he's badly burnt and might be blind."

"Give me a minute to get dressed and bring the dog into the surgery."

"Thank you; you are very kind. My name is Nelson; no doubt you have heard of me?"

Willow didn't reply immediately. She took in his unruly mop of black hair and earnest brown eyes. Baggy trousers that need six inches cutting off the bottom and hiking boots that had never seen a tin of shoe polish with the lid off.

"Yes," she answered eventually. "I've heard the name mentioned before. If the dog belonged to your brother, why didn't he bring the dog himself?"

"Ah well, the dog belongs to my brother Xander, and we don't know where he is."

Twenty-five minutes later, after injecting the dog in the manner Page had shown her many times before, the animal lay asleep as Willow began to cut away the burnt hair.

"A qualified vet must administer other treatments, and I'm afraid he is in the hospital recovering from a mild breakdown. I can trim the dog's eyelashes, remove the burnt hairs from his eyes, and use eye drops to ease the pain when he wakes. Does the dog have a name?

"Dropper, he can't hold anything in his jaws for more than a few seconds. He's the only remaining dog of nine; the rest perished in the fire."

"Your brother, Xander, do you think he might also have perished in the fire?" Willow asked, stumbling over the words and crossing her fingers.

"It's possible, I suppose. I never gave it much thought."

"You don't sound too bothered. Was anyone else in the house?"

"My father and a few of his friends managed to escape, thank God," Nelson answered casually. "The best thing to happen to the house was watching it burn. Not a happy place at any time. If you can do anything for Dropper, please do it; I don't want him to suffer."

"I'm not qualified to do what I have done already."

"But you do know what to do?"

"Well, yes, I do."

"Then do it. Money isn't a problem; if anything goes wrong, I promise not to say a word to anyone."

"You are quite fond of this dog, aren't you?"

I'm fond of all animals. The world wouldn't exist without them. Did you know that?"

His words took Willow by surprise and she found herself warming to him. There was a long pause, and she watched Nelson's expression turn to deep concern. She resisted the temptation to tell him to leave until Page returned from the hospital fit enough to take up his position as a vet. The electronic tone of his mobile phone interrupted her thoughts. Pulling the phone from his pocket, he caught his finger on a loose thread from his jacket and the phone fell to the floor.

"Sorry, silly me," he grinned, pressing the phone to his ear. "No, I'm busy and will be for most of the day. It will have to wait until later."

A long pause followed, and with eyes closed, he waited until the voice on the other end became quiet.

"I don't care. I told you, you'll have to wait; goodbye," he growled, pressing the red button to end the call.

"That was my father. He wants me to pick him up from the hospital in his Rolls Royce. He is such a show-off. At times he's unbearable. Now, about more important things, what are we going to do about Dropper?"

"I don't know," Willow said, shaking her head.

"Let's forget what is right or wrong and concentrate on what is best for Dropper. He requires urgent treatment, yet we seem to have come to a barrier forbidding us from doing the right thing. Don't you agree?"

"Well, yes, I suppose so," Willow answered, meeting his gaze without blinking.

"Then we must forge ahead and forget all about rules and regulations. They are for the weak-minded."

"Disobeying regulations isn't always the right direction to go. We must think of Dropper; as I pointed out, I am not qualified to treat him. Perhaps you would feel better if you took him away for treatment?"

"I can't do that."

"Course you can. Didn't you tell me qualifications count for nothing?"

Nelson looked at her through squinted eyes, then rammed his hands into his trouser pockets and pushed his arms out sideways until he looked like a clown in a circus ring. Willow burst out laughing at the sight.

"You tricked me, didn't you?" he grinned red-faced and cleared his throat. "Please help

Dropper, please."

"Okay, but I shall need your help. First, we'll remove Dropper's burnt fur and massage soothing cream onto his skin. Later, his paws will need bandaging. Then we'll concentrate on his eyes and pray the fire hasn't left him blind."

"Thank you. I will never forget the kindness you have shown to Dropper."

"You will; they all say that."

Instead of answering, he took in her straw hair lightened by walking recovering dogs on hot sunny days. Her perfectly shaped nose and deep glacier-blue eyes gripped his interest, and he stared at her longer than he intended to. Her jeans and black T-shirt hugged her tight figure as if made to measure. Not by any means a ladies' man himself, he thought of Xander and involuntary curled his top lip at the thought of him forcing himself on her.

"You weren't born in the village; otherwise, I'd know you?"

"No, I wasn't born in the village. And if I was, perhaps I didn't want you to know."

"Where were you born?"

"How long is a mouse's tail?" she grinned at his endless questions."

"Which mouse did you have in mind?"

"You choose," Willow smiled, eager to see how he would wriggle out of the question.

"The long-tailed fieldmouse in Europe, north to Scandinavia and east to Ukraine, has an unusually long tail. Then there's the short-tailed hopping mouse from Australia found near Alice Springs. Hunted by cats and foxes they are almost extinct."

Willow looked at him in amused suspicion and shifted her weight from one foot to the other. He was lying. How could he possibly know such things? He'd made it up to impress her. She looked at him differently, he wasn't a rocket scientist, but he was no fool either."

"Now it's my turn to ask a question," he said, taking his hands out of his pockets. "In what month in 1932 did the Mona Lisa fail to smile for three hours?"

Willow creased her forehead. How could she possibly know the answer to questions such as that? Things were going from bad to worse, and her anger began to soar out of control. He was laughing at her, treating her as a fool. She felt helpless and caught in a trap of her making.

"Over there in the cupboard are fresh bundles of lint. Can you pass me one, please?" She said, annoyed at the shrill sound of her voice. "A few more minutes and I'll be finished after which I'll treat Dropper's eyes and let him sleep."

"You have done an excellent job, thank you. I have enjoyed your company immensely. It is a rare privilege to meet someone intelligent in this God-forsaken village."

Willow shrugged, feeling too highly strung and unpredictable to continue in his company, but at the same time, she liked him. Full of facts one minute, the next relaxed and amusing, she found him easy to get along with. However, forgiving him for knowing so much about a mouse's tail might not be easy. Tugging his phone from his trousers pocket, he pushed it tight to his ear.

"Yes, father, I shall be at the hospital within the next thirty minutes, and no, I won't be in the Rolls Royce. The police have cordoned off what's left of the manor whilst the fire investigators do their business, including the garage and cars."

Nelson pressed the red button to cut off the call and turned to Willow.

"I can't thank you enough. Would it be okay If I pop by now and then to see how Droppers is coming along?"

"Of course, feel free anytime, "Willow said, smiling.

*

DCI Mattress stood next to the window attempting to shrug off the pain throbbing in her feet when Det/Sgt Down entered the room puffing and panting.

"They have found a body up at the Pennywise Manor," Down said, struggling for breath.

"Then I suppose we'd better get up there," Mattress winced.

"I wouldn't bother. The pathologists have taken the body for an autopsy. We'll know more this evening."

"Penny to a pound they have found Xander."

"They reckon the body is a woman and been there for some time."

Visibly shocked, Mattress fiddled clumsily with the laces on her trainers.

"In that case, we'll go to the mortuary. If this is a murder case, I'm not hanging around all night waiting for a pathology report while they sit around drinking tea. Get a car and wait for me at the front."

Downs enthusiasm for his chosen profession nosedived. It was the second time that week he'd bought fish and chips and been forced to leave them uneaten in the knowledge the gannets around him would finish them off the moment he left the station. He exchanged half-smiles with Helen, the office typist.

"They're yours, unopened," he said, pushing the plastic container onto her desk.

"Thanks, I'll save you some," she grinned.

"You're all heart," Down grunted.

It was a twenty-five-minute drive to the outlying town and mortuary, and the pathologists were never happy to have the police tramping around asking questions. Overlooking the table where the blackened corpse lay, Down pulled out a handkerchief and held it to his mouth. Mattress concentrated on the pathologist's monologue.

"Time of death approximately three years ago. No flesh left on the body, probably eaten by rats.

No sign of violence or broken bones. Discovered in a small, bricked room with a single unlocked door, I think this woman lost her way in the maze of tunnels beneath Pennywise Manor and perished. Her handbag, with credit cards and club membership cards, was found by her feet bearing the name Agnes Chane. Correspondence in her handbag shows she was also known as 'Daisy' Chane, a high-class prostitute from Kensington, London."

"Sounds like she was trying to escape from someone, and we all know who," Down muttered.

"Enlighten me with your wisdom," Mattress asked, standing on her heels to relieve the pain in her feet.

"Old man Pennywise of course. The village knew his orgies with his hunting cronies and call girls from London."

"Contact the hospital and see if he's left. If he's still there, post a man outside his room until he's fit enough to be questioned.

"Yes, boss, roger that."

*

Willow spent the night into the early morning hours talking and soothing Dropper until he eventually fell asleep. Rather than allow him to wake and panic in a strange environment, she curled up on the floor next to his cage and listened to his uneven breathing. Her mind returned to Nelson Pennywise. Unlike his brothers, he seemed likeable with a sense of humour, and she hoped to see him again. Dawn was breaking when she became caught in the semiconscious limbo between sleep and awake and drifted into the welcoming arms of oblivion.

*

"I find it strange that Willow couldn't find the time to visit me in the hospital," Page muttered, grabbing the edge of the bed to regain his balance before leaving the hospital with Cate.

"I'm sure she was too tired after the time spent together injecting cattle. It seems the whole village knows of it."

"Damn the villagers. I can't wait to get out of the place."

"You don't mean that."

"How can you say that after telling me to leave the village?"

"Things might be different after what you did at Spawn's farm."

"And cows might jump over the moon. To hell with Spawn," Page's voice hardened.

*

Notebook open and pen in hand Det/Sgt Down's jaw dropped when the hospital informed him Lord Pennywise had discharged himself and left with his son Nelson an hour ago, leaving no forwarding address. DCI Mattress was bound to rebuke him until she turned red in the face and no longer felt the pain in her feet. It wouldn't be the first time she left him shaking like a schoolboy caught peering under the doors in the girl's toilets. He considered calling in sick. But that would leave him up to his neck in tedious paperwork when he returned. Reaching inside his jacket pocket for his warbling phone, he held it close to his ear.

"Forget the hospital. Pennywise is in the Sherwood Hotel with his son, Nelson. Grab some lunch, and then come to the station."

Grab some lunch and then come to the station; the words spiralled around Down's mind. Something was wrong, or she'd found a magic potion that cured her aching feet. Damn her; he'd play it cool, stay in the restaurant, and finish his fish and chips followed by a double portion of apple pie.

*

Willow didn't have a clue of the time when the sound of the front door crashed open as again Page had lost his balance. Fingers locked she reached up for the ceiling, yawned, and gazed at the clock on the wall. It was 11.55 in the morning, and Dropper lay silently on his side. On the verge of panicking, Willow knelt and, grabbing his ears sighed with relief when he beat his tail twice against the metal cage.

"Good boy, let's get you fed, shall we?" she cooed, gently stroking his neck.

"Hello, Willow," Page said, looking at Dropper. "Good grief, he looks as if he's been barbecued."

"He was trapped in the fire at Pennywise

Manor, the only one of nine to survive. Under the circumstances, I did the best I could during your absence."

"Looks a fine job. You will make a fine vet one day."

Willow felt a burst of pride as the heat burned into her cheeks. For a brief moment, she didn't know where to look.

"I'll put the kettle on," she mumbled half to herself.

"Good idea. Cate's getting my stuff out of the car, and I could murder a hot cup of tea. Shame about the dog. Who owns him?"

"Nelson Pennywise."

"Oh, does he, did he give you any trouble?"

"No, quite the reverse; his only concern was for the dog, and he couldn't have been nicer."

"Good, I won't have any nonsense in the surgery, especially from the Pennywise mob."

"Ooh, I'm bursting for a cup of tea after that dishwater the hospital serves up in those machines," Cate declared, looking at Dropper and smiling at Willow. "Got a new visitor, have we?"

"Yes, he came in last night.

"Keeping the business going, that's what I like to hear."

Willow remained quiet while making the tea and keeping a close eye on Dropper. The first time she'd treated an animal, it was vital he recovered safely.

"Well, now that Pennywise Manor has burned

to the ground, what will happen to the village?" Cate said. "The developers have been eyeing the land for years. Before we know it, the place will turn into a concrete jungle, heaven's preserve. No longer work around here for farmers or people working the land."

"That won't bother me and serves them right. I don't intend to be here much longer," Page said, slurping his tea under a withering stare from Cate.

"You won't be going anywhere until properly rested, and that's final," Cate said in a sharp voice.

"That suits me. I can sit in the garden and watch the world pass by," Page smiled.

*

Lord Pennywise sat upright in an armchair and looked around the room. To his right was a small flat-screen television, a window with a panoramic view across the small bustling town consisting mainly of tourists. In the far corner, a small drinks cabinet in need of refurbishment. Frail and bent, he stared at his one remaining son with an inconsolable look attached to his face.

"Damned if I'll stay here longer than necessary, like living in a rabbit hutch," he muttered loudly.

Nelson smiled.

"You own the hotel. Where else would you live?"

"I own a string of hotels. But you didn't know

that did you?"

"No, and neither do I care."

"Suit yourself. What's happened to Xander? Why isn't he here when I need him?"

"No idea; the police think he perished in the fire."

"Perished in the fire? Not Xander; he's too damn crafty to let that happen before he gets his grubby hands on my money."

Nelson looked at his father and shuddered.

"Is that all you ever think of, money? It's brought this family nothing but misery with your childish accusations. Have you ever thought of being a father instead of a bitter old man? Since you drove mother to an early death bed, we have waited on your hand and foot and bore the brunt of your foul temper day after day," Nelson said, his voice rising as he spoke. "Do what you like with your money. I couldn't care if I never set eyes on you again."

Pennywise worked his mouth without sound as Nelson closed the door and, taking two steps at a time down the staircase walked out of the hotel and into the street. He was free, the shackles of misery lifted from his shoulders. With a newfound spring in his step and breathing easy, he checked his gold wristwatch and with an image of Willow clear in his mind made his way to his car.

*

"His Lordship left strict orders he doesn't

want to be disturbed? Now that is a crying shame, isn't it," DCI Mattress said, sarcasm drooling from her mouth. "The number of his room, please, now, or I'll have this place shut down unsuitable for human attendance."

"Room 39, and if I get the sack, I'll sue the police for every penny I can get," the receptionist said, disappearing through a door behind the reception desk.

"Don't just stand there gawping Down, warn Pennywise I want a word with him. Tell him any nonsense, and he'll be down the station," Mattress said, trying to control her rising temper as the pain in her feet increased. "No, on second thoughts, we'll use the lift and surprise him."

Twice Det/Sgt Down rapped on door number 39 and received the same answer on both occasions.

"Clear off. Don't you understand English?" Pennywise raged.

"Step aside. I'll have no more of this," Mattress said, twisting the door handle.

The second she entered the room, her mouth dropped open and she closed her eyes.

"Get dressed, Pennywise, you damned pervert, before I take you down the station and charge you with indecent exposure.

"Good grief, woman. I'm in my hotel room, and I own the hotel. Damn police, I've seen more brains on a butcher's apron. What in blazes do you want?"

"Is he decent?" Mattress said, staring at Down. "And take that silly look off your face, or you'll be directing traffic next week."

"Yes, Boss, he's decent."

"Well, get on with it. Whatever it is that's festering in your tiny mind," Pennywise snapped, staring at Mattress flip her notebook to a new page and crossing his legs.

"Does the name Agnes Chane mean anything to you?" Mattress began.

"No."

"She was also known as 'Daisy' Chane."

"Preposterous name, what is she, a child. And what does it have to do with me?" Pennywise answered, uncrossing his legs.

"Her body was found in the ashes of Pennywise Manor. It had been there for three years, give or take a few months."

"Really? Nothing to do with me; why should it?" Pennywise snapped.

Mattress stiffened and raised her eyebrows.

"A body eaten by rats has been found in your house, and you have the nerve to say it's nothing to do with you. What do you take us for, fools?"

"If the cap fits, wear it," Pennywise grunted, twisting and writhing in the armchair.

Mattress felt the urge to wrap her hands around his throat and wring the truth out of him. But the police manual frowns on such behaviour. Instead, gazing from the window, she watched a young woman trying to reverse into a free parking space while holding up a stream of honking traffic.

"Perhaps it's something to do with my sons. I can't watch them every minute of the day," Pennywise said, sensing Mattress's anger. "And there lies a problem: one dead, another missing, and the youngest born with a brain fit for a zombie."

"Brain fit for a zombie. Hmm, I'd say that just about sums up the whole family. Put your coat on; I'm taking you down the station for further questioning," Mattress said, staring directly into Pennywise's eyes. "Give me trouble, and I'll arrest you for suspected murder."

"Arrest me? Don't make me laugh. Do you know who I am? I'll be out of your station within minutes, and you'll be looking for a job, you stupid woman."

Mattress shook her head from side to side.

"Read him his rights Down, then take him downstairs and bundle him into the car."

"Yes, boss," Down grinned. "Be a pleasure."

CHAPTER THIRTY

Hugh Pong, of Chinese parents, weaved a path through the village's crowded streets and lanes, trying his best to avoid the barging shoulders. Mid-summer, the army of tourists studied mobile phones equipped with a sat/nav occupied every table and chair. Kids with long faces and bored-to-tears tongued multi-coloured ice creams. Outside Page's bungalow, he pushed the doorbell and tapping his left foot against the step waited for the door to open.

"Hello, I haven't seen you before. I'm looking for Mr Anton Page," he said, smiling.

"Who shall I say is calling?" Cate said, looking at him through narrowing eyes.

"Tell him Hugh Pongs here. He knows who I am."

"Wait there, please."

"No probs, but I ain't got all day."

With a worried brow, Cate explained to Page that a man called Hugh Pong was at the door.

"Of course. Give him this, and offer my

deepest thanks," Page said, withdrawing a brown envelope from a drawer by the window.

"You don't want me to ask him in?"

"That won't be necessary."

"He's that Chinese man that's been going around the village loosening wheel nuts on vehicles isn't he? Even tractors and other farm vehicles weren't safe. The silliest thing I've ever heard and dangerous."

"Serve the villagers right now; please give him the envelope."

The second Cate handed Hugh Pong the envelope without uttering a word, he turned away and walked toward the village.

Page observed his daughter from where he was sitting. Not about to let the appearance of Hugh Pong rest, he could see that she wanted to know more by the look on her face. To question him until he became irritable and blurted everything out. But this time, he wasn't going to bite.

"Come along, Willow and tell me all about this dog you are treating," Page said, getting up off the chair and entering the surgery.

"His name is Dropper. He can't hold anything in his jaws without constantly dropping it. As you can see, the fire burned most of his coat from his body. Nelson Pennywise thinks the dog might lose his eyesight."

"Hmm, continue with the eye drops three times a day, and we'll check his progress. And put a plastic collar around his neck to stop him from licking his wounds. You have done a fine job; now, we must wait and see what happens. As for me, I feel I could sleep for a month."

*

Lord Pennywise was angry after being dragged down the police station against his will.

"I'm not some two-bit criminal, you fools; I demand I speak to my solicitor. My God, heads will roll before this day is out," he ranted, spittle running down his chin.

"No problem, sir. Second door on the left you'll find a phone. One call only. We must keep to the rules," Det/Sgt Down said with a twinkle in his eye.

"Enough of your insolence; whom the devil do you think you are?"

Down turned to Pennywise, his head inches from the Lord's face. He'd had enough of the constant insults and complaints.

"Perhaps you'd like one of your fancy high-class prostitutes to keep you company while you are waiting for your bent solicitor," he hissed. "Now shut your mouth, or I'll lock you in the cell next to the three drunks we arrested last night."

"That will do, Det/Sgt Down," DCI Mattress snapped, entering the room. "Go home for the rest of the day. I'll see you in the morning."

Down forced himself to be calm and think clearly. Offering no response, he buttoned his jacket and walked out of the police station.

Horse racing from Newmarket was on TV that afternoon; he'd have a lucky fifteen, treat himself to a can of cold beer and put his feet up. To hell with the likes of Lord Pennywise. His kind could murder Peter the Apostle and walk away with a slap on the wrist.

*

Almost breaking into a run, Nelson Pennywise slowed to an even pace trying to figure out why he should be attracted to the vet's assistant at the surgery. Just conversing with her, he knew she'd never received a high education. Yet she possessed a quality he found fascinating. She asks silly questions like how long is a mouse's tail, then looks puzzled over his ridiculous question concerning the Mona Lisa. Has she read a book from cover to cover and flicked through the Times crossword in minutes? What did it matter? Had he fallen in love? That would amuse his father. Not that he was without cash, but when he heard Wellington had died, he crept into his room and stole his life savings hidden behind a set of pine drawers that wouldn't close properly. It wasn't a king's ransom by any means, but £11,750 is not a sum to be sniffed at, along with the £37,000 he'd stashed away over the years by living frugally. A hundred steps from the surgery he slowed to a halt. What if she wasn't there and he'd wasted a journey? Or perhaps she was there and couldn't be bothered to see him. What if Dropper had recovered sooner than expected dashing all hope of ever seeing her again? All these things sat uncomfortably on his mind. The closer he became to the surgery the more nervous he became. God, he wished he'd changed his baggy trousers. They were okay for lounging around reading books or memorising poetry but entirely unsuitable for courting a pretty girl.

At last, he was there facing the door that held her inside. Before he could raise his hand to knock on the door it unexpectedly burst open. Lost for words, he stared into her deep blue eyes. Fear kept his mouth shut. He wanted to speak, tell her how pretty she looked but the words wouldn't come. He recalled Xander's description of people he didn't like. Like a spare cock at a wedding, he used to say. Thank God he wasn't present to ridicule me; Nelson shivered.

"Hi, so good to see you again. Dropper is coming along fine, but there's still a long way to go before he's back to his old self. Come in and say hello to him; he'd love to see you."

"Um, er, yes, what a good idea," he mumbled.

Willow squinted at him, wondering if he was suffering from a sore throat.

When Nelson entered the bungalow he noticed Page sitting in a chair with his mouth set in a disgusting line. As fleeting as the moment was, it stuck in Nelson's mind. He knew his father hated Page but had consistently failed to consider why. He fidgeted and looked around the room, hoping to glimpse Dropper. As if Willow could read his mind, she slipped her arm through his.

"Here he is, bless him," she said softly, dropping to her knees and gently tugging his left ear.

Nelson sensed the warmth of Willow's touch and prayed it would never go away. She glanced up at him with a frown of concentration on her face.

"Well, say hello to Dropper. I'm sure he's glad to see you," she said quickly, her voice impatient.

"Yes, yes, of course. Hello Dropper, how are you, boy? Feeling better, I hope. Remember, you are in good hands and soon be up and running around."

"And where will he be doing that, might I ask?" Page interrupted. "His days of running around Pennywise Manor are over."

"There's plenty of places unaffected by the fire, Mr Page, as you know."

"Maybe there is, but you are not the open-air type, are you? You would rather have your nose stuck in a book."

"That depends on the contents of the book."

Willow looked at Nelson and then at Page. A knot formed in her stomach. It took little thought to realise an argument was brewing between Nelson and Page.

"Don't you think he looks better?" she said, her eyes fixed on Nelson. "Mr Page says I have done an excellent job caring for Dropper."

"Yes, indeed I do. If Mr Page says so, then you are to be congratulated. He is the expert. And I'm very grateful to him."

Page cleared his throat.

"You may visit Dropper anytime you wish, and we will keep you informed of his progress," Page said through clenched teeth.

"Thank you, sir. I shall no longer trespass on your time. Good day," Nelson replied in a clipped tone and let himself out.

Willow sucked in a great breath and exhaled slowly.

"Why do you paint everyone with the same brush?" she flared at Page. "He is nothing like the rest of his family. He cares for Dropper, or he wouldn't have brought him here."

"I have known that family longer than you, so please don't make statements about things you know nothing about. They're trouble. Remember, one of them kept you a prisoner in Pennywise Manor, or have you forgotten?"

"Of course, I haven't forgotten; how could I?"

"Then hold your tongue. I'll brook no nonsense from the likes of you. You have been here for five minutes and are already telling people how to run their lives. Now go to your room. I'm tired and need to rest," Page roared, red in the face.

Eyes filled with confusion Willow stiffened. He'd never spoken to her in this manner before.

She wondered if she had outstayed her welcome. Had she pushed her mannerisms too far? She'd had her way in all things, a roof over her head, food, and clothes free of charge.

On top of that, Page had been over-generous with pocket money. Guilt thinned the blood in her veins. Pale and trembling she twisted the seam in the leg of her jeans with long nervous fingers trying to think of something to say. But Page was in no mood for turning.

"Did you hear what I said? Go to your room and count your blessings. Do you have any idea what defines a person? No, of course not. Well, I shall tell you. It isn't fate or luck, nor decisions. It is opportunities that shape a person's life. Take them or lose them; the choice is yours. What happens to the rest plays only a small part in our lives. But you, you seem blind to the obvious. And please don't tell me you are sorry."

Willow raised her eyebrows but didn't reply. Page and his daughter Cate had been supportive since she appeared out of nowhere and made a nest for herself. Now nineteen years of age, after failing to mention a birthday a month ago, she needed to consider her relationship with Page and Cate. Cate offered her a box of tissues as tears bubbled and ran down her cheeks.

"I understand the last few days have been traumatic for you, but life goes on," Page snapped.

Willow raised her bloodshot eyes, sniffed and

entered her bedroom without uttering a word.

Page gritted his teeth wondering if he'd been too hard on her. She'd been through a lot for someone so young. He decided he'd wait and see how she reacted, hopeful that things might change for the better, then remembered his promise to leave the village

Elbows resting on her knees and her face cupped in her hands, Willow stared at the trees gently swaying in the breeze as if conducted by an orchestra. Opportunities, he'd said. She'd never had the luxury of choice and took the meagre offerings without complaint. Told by the man she called Dad that she was going blind and forced to walk with crutches, she'd accepted that her life had collapsed like ashes in a dying fire before it had even started. Then everything changed; her chance encounter with Page gave her hope; at last, God had smiled on her. Everything she had ever wanted had fallen at her feet. She viewed Page as a father and Cate, his beautiful daughter, as her sister. Surrounded by love and animals, her prayers were answered in full. But now Page was leaving the village; her assistance would be surplus to requirements. Filled with determination, she wiped away the tears and began to back her belongings in her small backpack.

Seated on the edge of his bed in his featureless bedroom, Page stared unblinking at his chewed fingernails. His heart filled with anger, compassion, and something else he didn't understand started the makings of a violent headache. In a moment of a fleeting daydream, he wished he could take one small step upwards and enter into heaven. There, he'd search for Lizzie and force her to tell him the truth about the night of her murder. Did he do it? If he didn't, then who did? Knowing that one person in the village lived a life riddled with guilt was a small consolation. No amount of tears and heartache could make his wish come true. He'd never steal back the twenty years cooped up in a cell. Those missed Friday nights in the Crooked Stick Inn laughing and joking with the same people who sneered and cursed him at every opportunity. How many animals suffered or died during his forced absence?

Horses lost their foals, cows, calves, sheep and lambs. Why couldn't he have been a carpenter, painter, decorator, or car mechanic? As a boy, he'd always tinkered with engines. No more calls at night to help a mother give birth to piglets or humanely put down an animal unable to bear the pain of living. His life seemed cursed from the day he slipped from his mother's womb. His marriage was a farce. She wanted any man but him, yet he couldn't stop loving her. Then there was Willow. Like a breeze of fresh air, she'd entered his life with a smile to conceal the hurt of being given away to strangers at birth. Kicking off his shoes, he wiggled his toes.

Nobody knew how he felt, and nobody needed to know. Nothing would change; nothing needed to change. In his mind, he repeated the words in the knowledge it would be futile to think otherwise. Everything had already changed, and more was about to appear on the horizon. The squeak of his bedroom door opening gave him cause to look up at Willow framed in the doorway.

"I'm leaving now, thank you for everything you have done for me, and I'm sorry for all the trouble I have caused you," she said quietly.

He stared at her, wondering how such few words could evoke his feelings. He opened his mouth to answer her. Instead, he bit into his bottom lip. His cheeks flushed. He wanted to cry, to let it all out in one gushing moment. Instead, he held his nerve.

"I don't want you to go," he said. "I want you to stay."

"Can I call you dad?"

"Yes, of course, if you want to."

"I'll stay then," she said, turning around and disappearing from his sight.

Page shook his head at the simplicity of her words. It had all happened so quickly that he wasn't sure he understood the situation. He'd gained another daughter, and the thought pleased him.

*

Lord Pennywise had spoken the truth. Minutes after being placed in a cell, the duty sergeant opened the door and told him he was free to go. With ten minutes left on his shift, the sergeant would be gone before DCI Mattress discovered the truth and put the station through hell. There would be no forgiveness for those present, no possibility that heaven ever existed. But it was not to be. When the new duty sergeant informed her of the event, she smiled and told him to make her a cup of tea and one for himself. Five minutes later, Det/Sgt Down entered the police station, stopped in his tracks and stared goggle-eyed at Mattress and the duty sergeant chatting over a cup of tea.

"Don't stand there staring like a pregnant goldfish Down," Mattress said with a sweet smile. "When you have finished your coffee, get back up to Pennywise Manor, I want the burnt timber cleared away and a thorough search made for hidden tunnels. I have sent a couple of young constables to look around and ensure they do their job properly. I'll have Pennywise before a judge if it's the last thing I ever do."

Down tapped the side of his left leg with nervous fingers. When you have finished your coffee, she said. Something was wrong; she was on drugs. Worse, she'd fallen in love with one of the young constables recently attached to the station.

"Everything all right, boss. You seem to be in a good mood this morning?"

Mattress noisily swallowed the last of her tea.

"For the first time in months, my feet aren't killing me. The doctor recommended surgical stockings, and they have worked a miracle."

"Surgical stockings, eh? Perhaps I can help you out there. My mate deals in lady's underwear, and he'll do you a lacy black suspender belt with red bows at a knockdown price."

"Forget the coffee, Down, and get out of my sight, you degenerate," Mattress hissed through clamped teeth.

"Right boss, Roger that, I'm on my way. Pennywise Manor, you said?" Down grinned, fighting to keep the smile off his face.

The moment Down stepped from his car he overheard the argument between a young policeman and one of the firefighters damping down the remaining wisps of smoke from the fire.

"Got a problem, lad?" he said to the young policeman.

"Hello, Sarge, we've found a doorway blocked with loose bricks by the exit to the Manor, but they won't allow us to remove the bricks."

"What's the problem?" Down said, turning to the firefighter.

"We don't know what's behind the bricks, and it might be dangerous to poke around."

Down couldn't contain his impatience any longer.

"We are dealing with a murder case and need to investigate thoroughly. I'll take full responsibility. Okay, constable, show me where this doorway is. And what's your name?"

"Thyme, Sarge, Mark Thyme."

PC Mark Thyme quickly found what he was searching for and, stepping back, allowed Down to inspect the bricked-up hole closely. Down stepped back and picked up a water pipe from the heating system.

"Right, let's see what's hidden behind the bricks," he said, ramming the pipe into the bricks and stepping back as clouds of black cinders flew into the air.

Down repeated his efforts until the bricks clattered into a pile, leaving a gaping square hole.

"It seems to be a manufactured tunnel large enough for a man to pass through. Pass me your torch," Down said, itching with excitement.

In front of the pool of light from the torch, Down gagged at the foul dank air. Thyme felt the smell rising and nausea gathering in his throat. Feet rolling in the mud, he tried to keep pace with Down. When a damp chill crept into his bones, he wished he'd kept his mouth shut instead of blabbering to everyone he'd found a secret entrance. Further along the tunnel Down hesitated to wait for Thyme to catch up. About to continue their journey through the stinking tunnel, Down swung the torch on something white. The image of the swollen flesh of a body remained fixed in Thyme's mind.

"Jesus," Down whispered.

Thyme's adrenaline spiked, and he turned allowing his vomit to rush freely from his mouth.

"Get back here, you dumb clown, and hold the torch while I get photo's on my mobile," Down shouted.

"No, no, I'm getting out of here," Thyme shouted back, feeling his screams rising in his throat."

With the torch between his knees, Down struggled to find his mobile phone. The torch fell to the floor. Sickened and confused, he knelt in the muddy water, striking out with his hands while searching for the torch. The body was there; he'd seen it. Tugging out his phone and using the torch app, he found the body and took random photos. No longer able to bear the rancid stench mustering the last of his strength, he picked up a rotting handbag close to the bodies and fought his way back against the current of the dirty stream. Outside in the fresh air, ignoring the gathering crowd he scrolled through the pictures on his phone. A shiver clattered his bones. There could be no ridding the images of the two bodies lying side by side.

"Get the area cordoned off, and don't let anyone, regardless of who they are, near the entrance to the tunnel, Constable Thyme," Down said. "Pull yourself together."

The tip of Thyme's tongue flickered over his lips.

"I'm sorry, Sarge. I panicked; it won't happen again."

Down removed his shoes in the back of the police car, tossed his wet socks into a hedge, put his boots back on and called Mattress.

"Good work, Down, stay where you are. I'll send someone over to ensure no one tries to get down the tunnel. In the meantime, I'll inform the chief to get the bodies removed and taken to the mortuary. We'll wait and see what a post mortem reveals. When you return to the station, bring the handbag, I want a detailed record of Agnes Chane's, aka Daisy, movements for the last five years and anyone who knew her. Check with all the East End police stations and high-class escort agencies. And well done; you have done a great job, excellent police work."

"Thanks, boss; about that suspender belt?"

"Don't push your luck, D/S Down. The Met's looking for beat bobbies to cover London's parks."

*

Page rose early the following morning unaware Willow was in the kitchen working her way through a second helping of porridge.

"Good morning," she said brightly.

That was a first, Page thought, raising an eyelid.

"I'm glad you are up and about. I want to run a few things by you to ensure we don't get our wires crossed in the future.

Willow stopped eating and placed her spoon in the porridge. Eyes open and alert, she said nothing.

"First, I will pay you a salary of £12,500 per anum while you live here; of course, you will pay no rent, food or bills. Does that sound fair?"

"I'm happy to work for nothing; you have given me a home I never thought I'd have."

"Your hours will be from 9 am to 6 pm, Monday to Saturday and Wednesday off if we aren't too busy. How does that sound?"

Her tears came so quickly that they took him by surprise. He waited, unsure of what to do next. He wondered if he should hold her, tell her not to worry. Instead, he changed the subject.

"From what I can gather, you seem to like the Pennywise boy, Nelson, I believe. It's quite alright with me if he visits you occasionally. I promise to make him welcome. He seems to be the best of the bunch. Now finish your breakfast and see to Dropper?"

"I did it before I sat down for breakfast."

"Yes, I thought you might. In which case, we'll sit and drink tea until our next patient arrives.

"Yes, dad," she said, drying her eyes with the cuff of her sleeve.

CHAPTER THIRTY-ONE

Tiredness pushed aside, Det/Sgt Down worked through the day until early evening, tracing friends of 'Daisy' Chane. London's East End police stations had little on her movements apart from the fact she worked through various agencies as a high-class call girl under the title of an escort. With several addresses of local escort agencies provided by Hackney Police Station, it would be better if he called in person rather than over the phone. Existing on the fringe of the law agencies were reluctant to answer questions concerning the girls that worked for them.

"Best we wait for the pathologist's results before we go any further," DCI Mattress said. "Both bodies were clothed and carrying handbags, and God knows what they were doing in the tunnel."

"I still reckon they were trying to escape and got lost," Down said, tapping a pencil on the desktop.

"Escaping from what? If we knew the answer

to that, we could all sleep at night knowing Pennywise is safely behind bars at night."

Down dropped the pencil on the desk and yawned.

"You're convinced it was Lord Pennywises work, aren't you?"

"Who else could it be?"

"Pennywise had three sons. It could be any one of them. It wouldn't surprise me if all four were mixed up in something unlawful."

"Maybe, time will tell," Mattress said. "I want every brick and piece of charred wood removed from the site of the mansion and men with shovels and forks to fine-comb the area. And this time, I want it done properly."

*

Det/Sgt Down's vision of London's East End amounted to little more than pearly kings and queens, down-to-earth humour and Del-boy selling dodgy watches out of a suitcase. Instead, faced with a multicultural society and a sack full of languages he'd never heard before, he counted his blessings that he lived in the country. Litter choked the gutters and drains. Street market stalls selling everything from Asian saris to used mobile phones lined the roads. Young girls in short mini-skirts tottered on six-inch heels after a night out on the tiles as they made their way home. Dogs gathered around the rear of stalls looking for something to eat. A fleeting glimpse of Del-boy might have helped to settle his nerves, but it wasn't to be. One thing was for sure; Down had no intention of remaining in the city one minute more than he needed to.

Armed with three addresses supplied by London's Metropolitan Police, Down's first stop was 'Hollies Hot Lips Escort Agency' on Mare Street, Hackney, situated between a deli and pizza shop. Sturdily built with mild acne, with a brass ring through her left nostril and in her late teens, the receptionist wore slashed khaki trousers with pockets down each side and a black T-shirt.

"Good morning, sir; my name is Kylie. We insist our clients fill in a short form telling us of their needs before we go any further," she said, flashing a warm smile, her East European accent barely noticeable.

"That won't be necessary," Down said, flashing his police identity card and waiting for her reaction.

"Ere, I ain't done nothing wrong since I got out of nick a couple of months ago. I'm straight now. My mum ain't too well and needs me."

Down grinned, ignored the sudden change of accent, and watched her nervously shuffling papers, her face like a cornered poodle.

"Going straight? You're having a laugh. You'd go down for a couple of years running a place like this."

"I don't run the place. I only work here."

"Okay, Kylie, do me a favour, and I'll look the

other way this time."

"Do you a favour? You ain't getting a free blow job off me, you dirty sod. All the same you lot are."

"Does the name Agnes Chane mean anything to you?"

"Daisy, everybody knows Daisy. Game for anything for a few quid, she is. Ain't seen her for years; she must have settled down. Mind you, I've been banged up for six months."

"Do you keep records of the girl's jobs?"

"Yeah, she'll be on the computer somewhere. I'll have a look if you want me to."

"Do that, and I'll be grateful."

"I told you once, didn't I? You ain't getting your leg over for free."

"You got ten seconds, and then I'm running you in."

"Bastard," she spat at him, running her fingers over the computer keyboard. "Dirty bastard."

Lips slightly parted, Down's smile changed to a grin.

"Here she is. Her last job with us was four years ago for some geezer called Wise at the Crooked Stick Inn near the New Forest.

Down pursed his lips and sucked in a long breath of air. Battling excitement, he reeled off the names of the two women he'd discovered in the ruins of Pennywise Manor.

"Try Helen Hellfire and Nancy Twist, and I'll get out of your hair. That's a promise."

Kylie spent the next few minutes tapping her fingers on the computer keyboard.

"Here we are. Helen Hellfire is a fire eater, and Nancy Twist is a bodybuilder with muscles to spare; she can turn men on within seconds, a popular choice at parties. Their last assignment with us was at the same place as 'Daisy' Chane four years ago, and we haven't heard from them since. Does that answer your questions?"

Down's grin turned to a smile. At the first attempt, he'd discovered that all three women had been at the Crooked Stick Inn approximately four years ago. An hour later, in a motorway service station on the M4, he paid for a plastic breakfast washed down with coffee made with warm cow's piss. He'd be DCI Mattress's best boy for at least a day.

In the police station that evening, Mattress became so excited Down worried she might ruin his sex life.

"As fine a piece of police work as I've ever seen. Down, my lad, you are a genius," Mattress said, grabbing Down's buttocks. "At last, Lord Pennywise and his family are about to pay for their crimes. Everyone down the pub, I'm paying; tonight, we have something to celebrate."

*

Willow raised her eyebrows pointedly.

"I can manage," she said to Page, applying liberal doses of cream to Droppper's skin. "Please sit down and rest. You look tired, and the doctor said you must take things easy."

"Rest? Life is too short to rest. What would happen if we suddenly had an intake of sick animals, eh? Have you thought of that?

"There are other vets available. I'll close the surgery and go shopping if you don't sit down. There's nothing in the larder and the fridge is empty."

"Are you serious?"

"How long is a mouse's tail? Try me if you don't believe me."

Face flushed; Page left the surgery confident she would do as she said.

"I'll make some coffee," he muttered to himself.

Seconds later, the doorbell rang. Abruptly reverting to calm Page tugged open the front door.

"Ah, Horatio, isn't it?"

"No, sir, my name is Nelson. We met a couple of days ago."

"Really? My memory isn't too reliable these days, old age, you know."

"My father suffers the same. He has a job to remember his name at times."

"Your father, do I know him, what is his name?"

"Lord Pennywise."

"Pennywise?" Page exploded. "If ever a man deserves to suffer, it's him. I remember you. Come to court Willow have you? She's in surgery treating your dog. And mind you keep your hands to yourself."

"Yes, sir," Nelson blinked, and, with a look of anger contorting his face instead of entering he turned from the bungalow and strode down the street.

That evening Nelson stared sullenly at his supper, a limpid pork chop and potatoes surrounded by half a tin of faded green garden peas. Later, if he were in the mood, he'd finish tiling the kitchen floor with stone tiles. The house belonged to his father's estate, and when the former tenant, a tree surgeon, moved away to seek steady employment Nelson took it over as a haven to escape from his brothers. Each month he paid the rent leaving no one any the wiser. With the Manor burned to the ground, he lived comfortably surrounded by his loving books rather than move into the hotel with his father.

"Willow," he said slowly, letting each letter melt on his tongue. "Sweet Willow, will I ever get to know you?"

A smile spread across his face. How silly of him to think she might come like him. He, old-fashioned and boring, dressed like a tramp with hair like a grenadier's busby and as interesting as a mouldy pork pie. If his father had the slightest iota of his son's feelings for Willow, he'd probably hire an assassin to save him from further embarrassment. Pushing away his plate, he contemplated her being his wife. He visualised her face sparkling like a cut diamond whenever she smiled, how her long yellow hair met the curve of her waist whenever she stood erect. Naked in bed, she'd roll over and murmur soft words in his ear as her hands explored his body. He'd close his eyes and wait for her to kiss his eyelids. In a fraction of a second, his expression changed to hopelessness. Enough of his foolishness, he blurted out loud, hurling the plate of uneaten food into the sink.

*

Lord Pennywise bowed his head and raised a hand to cover his eyes. DCI Mattress stared at him with distaste distorting her face. The longer Pennywise's breath rattled through his throat, the angrier she became.

"What do you mean you have never heard of them? she barked, tasting the blood where she'd bit into her tongue. They were found dead on your property. "At this moment, I have men turning over the ground searching for bodies. For once in your miserable life, Pennywise, tell the truth or by God, I'll see you rot in prison."

"Find Xander. He knows more about these things than I do," Pennywise said, staring up at the ceiling, reluctant to answer Mattress's questions.

"Tell us where he is, and we'll do that. He is still alive, I presume."

"Who knows where that boy is? He's a law unto himself."

"Really? I have him down as a murderer. Something you would know about. If he is alive, we'll find him."

Pennywise kept his eyes hidden behind his hand. A vein in his neck jumped. Blackness crowded his concentration. Why am I here, he wondered. What have I done wrong? Why am I in this tiny little room that reeks of age and the closeness of death?

"For the moment, you will remain in the hotel with a police guard on the door. No visitors apart from your solicitor," Mattress scowled, reading his mind.

CHAPTER THIRTY-TWO

Matt Capp looked down at his tired uniform modelled on the outfit worn by Errol Flynn during the making of the film Robin Hood.

"Damn it, I've torn a hole in my tights," he muttered.

"God help you when the missus finds out," someone in the band of Green Archers laughed.

"We've got more things than your tights to worry about now the manors burned to the ground. With Lord Pennywise holed up in his hotel under police guard, there ain't much use for us anymore. I'm not working as an unpaid litter picker. I've been thinking of joining the bowling club," another voice called.

"Settle down," Matt Capp shouted. "If we find Xander, he'll sort things out."

"Not much chance of that if he's under a pile of ashes."

"Not that wily devil. He's around here somewhere. You can bet your Sunday socks on that, probably hiding in the forest."

A melee of voices came thick and fast.

"Funny you should say that. The milkman told my missus someone had stolen a dozen eggs, two loaves of bread and two pints of milk off his float a couple of days ago. That's never happened before, and there no travellers around here or we'd have seen them." Someone with a squeaky voice called.

Matt Capp rubbed his chin thoughtfully. He too had heard rumours of a man living rough in the forest.

"All right, all right, settle down. There are a dozen of us here. We'll split into groups of three and start searching the forest. If it is Xander, he'll know the best hiding places, so stay alert."

An hour and thirty minutes of searching produced nothing. Capp was about to abandon all hope of finding Xander Pennywise when a shot rang out. Barely time to fling himself to the ground, the bullet exploded into a shower of splinters as it struck a tree trunk. Paralysed with fear, he lay listening to his heart pumping as a trickle of sweat ran down his back. At last, gathering a fraction of his senses, he called out to the remaining band of Green Archers and received no answer. He shouted to warn the others twice more and again received no reply. The cowards had deserted him to face the shooter alone. A second shot shattered the same tree sending fragments of dead wood showering his head. Fear straightened his legs. Hands clasped over his ears his brain screamed at him to run away and hide. Minutes seemed like hours as salty sweat stung his eyes. The sound of rustling branches added further fear to his trembling body. He didn't want to die alone in the forest as food for hungry animals. Despite being scared more than ever, he pulled himself into a sitting position and debated whether to run for safety. Then froze as the rustling noise grew closer.

"Who are you? Why are you shooting at me? Don't you know you're on private property?" Capp called in a forced voice.

"I own the property, you fool. Who are you, and what do you want?"

Before Capp could answer, the shape of a man framed against the sunlight rose from the undergrowth. With the sun in his eyes, Capp could barely make out the silhouette of a man of average height wearing a pair of green nylon overalls and sunglasses with a blue tint. Squinting against the sun's rays, Capp tried to make out the man's features covered with a mask a special forces soldier might wear.

"That's no reason to shoot me. If you own this land, then you must know who I am. More to the point, who are you, and why are you wearing that mask?" Capp said, slowly climbing to his feet.

The man pushed through the bushes until a couple of yards from where Capp stood. Capp gasped and reached for his breath. Still blinded by sunlight, he heard the man snigger.

"I know you," the man said.

Capp waited. If he had the slightest drop of common sense, he'd have figured out who the man was.

"Xander, is that you? What are you doing out here trying to kill people?"

"You know as well as I do the police are looking for me after the fire at the mansion. I hear the bodies of two women have been discovered in the maze of tunnels beneath the building. If that's true, the police will be better off talking to my father."

With a thoughtful look, Capp lowered his guard before answering.

"If that's the case, you have nothing to fear. Go to the police and tell them about your father's activities."

A sudden gust of wind swept through the trees. The rifle slipped from Xander's hands as he reached out to prevent himself from falling. Seizing his chance, Capp grabbed the weapon and levelled the muzzle at Xander's head. Close enough to reach out and touch Xander, he saw the charred flesh protruding from the edge of the mask. Unsure what to do next, Capp waited, expecting a monologue of threats explaining what Xander would do to him if he didn't return the rifle. Instead, Xander sighed and sank to his haunches.

"Go on, do it; put me out of my misery. I don't

care if I live or die. My life is over."

Full of loathing, Capp stared at Xander, the great bully, the beater of women close to tears because life hadn't worked out the way he wanted. His finger tightened around the trigger. One gentle squeeze and the scourge of the village would be no more, and he'd be the toast of the village for years to come. But he wasn't a killer, nor did he want to be a hero. He was an ordinary man with a deep love for the countryside and everything nature provided for the world to marvel. Reaching out, he returned the rifle to Xander, noticing the charred black skin on his hands.

"Do as you wish. I want no part of this," Capp said quietly, disappearing into the bushes.

Pushing his way through the deep undergrowth, Capp heard Xander demanding that he return or pay later. The further he went, the sound of Xander's maniacal voice grew dimmer. Entering the village, he went to the police station and asked for the duty sergeant. An hour later he signed a written statement describing the meeting with Xander Pennywise. That night his wife watched with an open mouth as he stuffed the Robin Hood uniform into the barbecue and set it on fire

"Are you feeling well, dear?" she asked.

"I'm thinking of joining the pub's darts team, dear," he said.

*

DCI Mattress couldn't look happier. Everything was falling into place. The sooner the Pennywise family were out of the village the better it would be for everyone. At last, after years of being forced to ignore their disregard of the law she had them plumb centre in her sights.

"You're certain it was Xander?" she said to Capp, looking at the photographs and posters of Errol Flynn dressed as Robin Hood hanging from every wall of his front room."

"Oh, I'm certain I'd know him anywhere."

"And you remember where this meeting took place?"

"I do. I know this forest like the back of my hand."

"It will take time to get men together to begin a search. Is there anywhere he might hide if he gets wind we are onto him?"

"He already knows you are on to him. He mentioned something about bodies found in the remains of the manor. Said the police would be better talking to his father."

"How did he look?"

"In a bad way, I'd say. Covered in burns from top to bottom."

"Hmm, he'll require hospital treatment then?"

"I'd say so; he didn't look well to me."

"Thank you for your help, Mr Capp. Just one more thing. Would you show my sergeant where you last saw Xander Pennywise?"

"I'll take you as close as I dare; as I said, he's

armed and dangerous."

"Down, take two men and accompany Mr Capp into the forest and find out where Xander was last seen. I'm going to Pennywise's hotel for a little chat with his lordship. "

"Copy that, boss. If you'd like to follow me, Mr Capp, We'll get this done as quickly as possible, and you can go home. Thank you for being so helpful."

*

The shutters were closed in the upstairs hotel room where Lord Pennywise was being held until further notice, and the curtains were pulled shut. A pair of matching table lamps burned so ardently the brightness hurt the eyes. A TV in the middle of the room flickered an old black and white film from the fifties. Seated three feet away in a worn easy chair, wearing glasses with thick lenses, Lord Pennywise squinted at the screen through rheumy eyes.

"Come to release me, have you? By God, you'll rue the day you locked me up in one of my hotels," he said in a squeaky voice.

Mattress's eyes fluttered with distaste. She said nothing, noticing a plate of sandwiches, each half eaten and a pile of crumbs littering the floor.

"We'll be picking up your son Xander later today. He suggests we talk to you about the bodies discovered in the burned-down manor. What have you to say to that?"

"I have nothing to say. I'll leave the talking to my solicitor."

"You don't frighten me. You are a big bag of wind and bones ready to be thrown into a prison cell and left to rot along with the scum you call a son."

"How dare you talk to me in this manner. Do you know who I am?"

"Nothing. You are unfit to hold the title, Lord. How many more victims will we find? Another two, a dozen maybe."

"Victims, get out of here, or I'll call the police," Pennywise said, gasping for breath.

"Poison, perhaps?"

"I never poisoned anyone," Pennywise's voice rose to a scream.

"Drugs, was it drugs, or did you spike their drinks before abusing them until they could stand no more and hid in the depths of the manor where you left them to die?"

"It wasn't me. Ask Wellington. He knows what happened."

"Wellington is dead. Did you kill him too, or did you get that malformed son of yours called Xander to do it?"

"Xander isn't my son, not my real son. He's the son of Lizzie Page, the whore wife of that stupid veterinary Anton Page."

Stunned, Mattress pulled a tissue from her pocket and dabbed her brow. Pennywise shrugged carelessly.

"Does Xander know who his real mother was, and how on Earth could her pregnancy go unnoticed by Page? And who is Xander's father?"

"I'm his father. Of course, he doesn't know Lizzie Page is his mother. Page was in Africa for twelve months helping rehome orphan gorillas when she fell pregnant."

"Why didn't you tell him?"

"What good would it do?"

"Then who killed her? Was it you or one of your brats?"

"You'd better ask Page that question. He served time for her death."

"But he didn't kill her, did he? And Page doesn't know Xander is his dead wife's son. Which I believe makes him Page's stepson. "

DCI Mattress was walking on thin ice but felt confident that sooner or later, Pennywise would slip up and reveal what happened the night Lizzie Page died.

"According to the jury, he killed her," Pennywise said, visibly shaken by Mattress's words

"You are hiding something, Pennywise. The more you try hiding something, the more people become curious."

"Oh dear, taken to grabbing at straws, are we?" Pennywise cackled.

Despite mustering all her guile, Mattress knew he was right. She was grabbing at straws. Unsure which direction to take, she had one more card to play.

"I assume you are the father," she said in a level voice. "How else can you explain Xander living under your roof and using your name."

"I told you, I'm Xander's father. Where else would he live?"

Mattress pushed her feet tight against the ground and stared into his eyes. He stared back, his toady eyes unblinking. She needed time to regroup and to make sense of his words.

"In which case, you'll have no objection to a DNA test."

"I'll be a party to no such thing. How dare you threaten me?"

"I'm not threatening you, Pennywise. I feel we will meet again quite soon."

*

DCI Mattress woke the following day feeling elated. After a breakfast of toast and thick marmalade, seated by her house's rear door, she watched birds fight over the food she'd spread the night before. After twenty minutes with Pennywise the previous day, her head was still spinning. How on earth had he the gall to believe he ran the world as if he were the only person who counted and others existed merely to serve his needs? In the eleven years she'd served the surrounding villages, time after time, the name Pennywise cropped up whenever a crime occurred. Particularly against defenceless young women. Not that she considered the bodies unearthed from the manor to be innocent, far from it, but nobody deserved to die in the manner they did. Suspicion lurked around every corner of her mind. Lord Pennywise was going down whatever it took, and his son skulking in the forest with him. It would be no easy task with the case littered with a tissue of lies and unverified facts, along with Lord Pennywise's clout in high places. With her head full of misleading simplifications, she set course for the forest, hopeful Det/Sgt Down had apprehended the man assumed to be Xander Pennywise.

"No sign of anyone ever being here, Boss. Searched the area three times," Down said, waiting for a blast of her temper.

"Then get more men, I want this man in custody before nightfall. And call the local hospitals and doctor's surgeries to be on the lookout for a man seeking treatment for burns."

"Copy that, Boss. Do you think I'll need to call out the army?"

"Grow up; Down. I'm not in the mood."

CHAPTER THIRTY-THREE

Nelson Pennywise sighed in a reflective mood, picked up the half-full cup of coffee and drank it in one go. His venture into the frail world of fashion left him staring into the full-length mirror and his mind overloaded with doubt. Gone was the bushy hair that bounced whenever he moved; in its place, a neatly styled modern haircut. The slim-fit jeans beneath the black T-shirt clung to his legs as if designed especially for him. The garish multi-coloured trainers bought a flush of red to his face. Not bothering with socks made him feel half-dressed. But none of that mattered. The crux was, would the beautiful Willow approve of his efforts?

Unsettled by past events, Willow thought twice about exercising the dogs left in her care. Recently cracks were beginning to show in her stubborn attitude. Despite mustering all of her positive thinking, she had difficulty performing the tasks that were once second nature to her. In the past, time and time again, Page told her that animals always come first. But the feeling of not knowing what might happen to her had shackled her mind. Drawing a deep breath, she counted her blessing that only two dogs required exercising that day. Minutes later she guided the dogs along the busy High Street with their leads securely attached and headed for the park. The park gardeners were always busy at this time of the year, and if she kept them clear in sight, she felt confident no harm would come to her.

His mind scrambled like an unfinished jigsaw puzzle; twice Nelson undressed and then dressed again. Aware Willow would laugh at him for trying to attract her attention, dressed like a court jester, he slammed the cottage door shut. Chin tucked tight into his chest and hands deep in his pockets he made his way along the High Street. Halfway across the road to the park, the air left his lungs as a car slowed, and the driver shouted to him to return to the circus. Metres from where she stood, Nelson gripped the metal bars of the gate leading into the park. One of the dogs in Willow's charge stopped and cocked a leg. Willow waited, then turned to face Nelson entering the park. Nelson prayed for a magic wand that he might make himself invisible. The joints in his legs froze.

"You look different," she said, smiling.

"I just thought I'd smarten myself up, get back in the groove. You know how it is?" Nelson stammered.

"I thought you looked cool the way you dressed before. You didn't need all that expensive modern rubbish. Be yourself, not what others want you to be."

Nelson paled and prayed silently for a deep hole to jump in. Then, feeling his leg warming looked down at one of Willow's dogs relieving itself against his right leg.

"See, what did I tell you? Even the dog disapproves of your dress," Willow laughed. "Now, you must go home and get out of those clothes."

"But I wanted to talk to you," Nelson answered sheepishly.

"We'll wait for you by the gardener's shed if you hurry."

"Thank you, thank you so much. I'll be back in a second."

Willow's smile widened as she watched him break into a run. She knew he was older than her but enjoyed his company. One minute he could make her laugh without trying; the next, he held her spellbound with a pearl of wisdom. Full of high humour and spirits, he congratulated himself for having a theory for everything.

*

Xander Pennywise's stirrings of anxiety grew more potent by the second. The burns on his chest and arms were blistering, and pus leaked from open wounds. If he tried to stand it would make him feel dizzy, so he stayed where he was.

Knees ablaze with deep burns and arms wrapped around his chest, a sneer plucked at the corners of his mouth. They will pay, every one of them, he whispered to himself as if afraid of being overheard. Tonight, while the village slept, he'd break into the small chemist on the corner of the High Street for bandages and medicines to treat his burns. Then he'd make his way to the site where Wellington, his deceased brother, held orgies and practised devil worship. A place where villagers were frightened to go, he'd remain there until well enough to wreak his vengeance on those responsible for burning down his home. Top of his list was Anton Page. Since his return from prison, the village had been in an uproar. Secrets that had remained unspoken for years hung loose on lips, his name to the fore. Strangers appeared from out of nowhere, intent on causing mayhem, and the name Pennywise dragged through the gutter. When the searchers, accompanied by dogs tugging on sturdy leads, came looking for him, using a dead fox, he laid a trail away from where he hid in a small bunker beneath the undergrowth. The handlers would lose control of the dogs and the search called off for the day. Tomorrow he'd go to ground until healed and ready to emerge and wreak havoc.

*

Placing a record on the turntable, Page sat on the patio with his back to the open door. At first, he began tapping his fingertips on the plastic table, then rocking his shoulders side to side listened to the Stones singing Satisfaction. The makings of a smile played across his lips remembering how Lizzie hated the Stones and loved the Beatles, John Lennon in particular. One day soon he'd get someone in to clear the pond of algae and place a pump to provide a fountain, the sound of running water an excellent method of helping him relax. Willow would choose the fish. Carefully checking his watch, he wondered why she was taking so long exercising the dogs, then scolded himself for worrying over petty matters. It was Sunday, long since he'd last visited the church, joining in the flat voices singing hymns and later chatting with Father Kevin. Twenty minutes later he inhaled a deep breath to compose himself, then closed his eyes and tried to shut down his brain to prevent it from leaping from one event to another accompanied by a pessimistic attitude. The doctor insisted on rest but resting the body and mind were two different things. How could he sleep without thinking, and how could he not believe while resting? No matter how often he spoke the words, none of it made sense. Without warning, his sight blurred, and he stiffened at the sudden pain in his chest. His strength leaked from his body, and he slumped back sensing the pain growing more intense. Seconds later he lost track of time and didn't know where he was.

Forty minutes had passed when Cate entered

the bungalow and began making coffee. Mug in hand, she walked out onto the patio. Then stopped abruptly, allowing the cup of coffee to slip from her hand. Using what senses she had, she called 999 and asked for an ambulance to take a man suffering from a suspected heart attack to the hospital. Then kneeled beside him and squeezed his hand.

"It's alright, dad; the ambulance is on its way; no need to worry," she whispered, ignoring the tears flowing down her face.

Curtains twitched and front doors edged open at the sight of Page carried to the waiting ambulance on a stretcher. Cate's face twisted with rage.

"Crawl back under your rocks, you twisted bunch of mongrels," she shouted, entering the back of the ambulance.

She waited in the corridor for two long hours, rotating her feet in anxious circles until a lady doctor approached with a practised smile creasing her face.

"Your father has suffered a mild stroke and is resting. We shall monitor his progress for the next few days. By all means, call the hospital if you need an update, but we are confident he will recover. Of course, he will need to change his lifestyle. No more running around farms treating animals, unfortunately. He needs rest, or the chances are he may suffer a serious heart attack."

From the moment Cate left the hospital, she hadn't the capacity to dwell on the unpleasant things in life. Her time on Earth had not been without its hardships. Her father imprisoned for murder before she reached her teens had left a permanent mark. But there was little purpose in wishing the facts away. A face as expressionless as the painted face of a toy soldier, she made her way back to the bungalow. There she'd confront Willow, after which she had no idea what Willow intended to do next.

Before entering the bungalow, the howls of suffering dogs filled her ears. A search produced no sign of Willow. After feeding and watering the animals, she sat and sighed at the quietness of the surgery. For something to do, she busied herself washing dirty cups and plates and cleaning the sink top. As time moved on her anger began to fester. Where the hell was Willow? Why wasn't she in the surgery caring for the animals? Had she been abducted again? Question after question raced through her troubled mind when the front door swung open, and Willow entered, smiling from ear to ear.

"Where the hell have you been? Weren't you told never to leave the animals for more than a few minutes?

"How long is a mouse's tail?" Willow snapped back.

"Grow up and stop talking like a big wet kid. Fathers in the hospital suffering from a stroke,"

"Oh dear, a stroke this time, is it? It seems he gets something different every other few weeks."

"How dare you, after all he's done for you?"

"You know what he's like, always complaining. He's like a man that wears wellingtons in the middle of a heatwave."

"Well, aren't we seeing your true colours today? Is anything else wrong with us that you don't like? How about me? Do I get on your nerves? What is wrong with you?"

Willow dropped the latch on the last cage that held the dogs. The intensity of her words frightened her. How could she say the things she said? What had come over her? Why was her spittle sour and metallic, her short-breathing gasps struggling to leave her lungs? She looked into Cate's face, pale and lined with creases she'd never seen before. Blackness gripped her and twisted her insides.

"I'm sorry. I don't know why I said those words. I didn't mean them, honest."

"Really, well, they sounded genuine to me. Who are you, Willow? Where did you come from, who are your birth parents, and why did they give you away?"

"How long is a mouse's tail," Willow said, twisting her lips into a smile. "I'm going to bed; I have a bad headache."

"I can assure you this isn't over; I'll speak to you later, young lady."

Willow hesitated. It didn't matter what Cate

had to say. All she wanted was to be alone.

Sat on the edge of the bed, she lay back and covered her head with the pillow to hide the tears. How could she tell Cate that she'd tried to kiss Nelson Pennywise, and he'd pushed her away when she fondled his privates? Under the impression it was what every man wanted, his response left her confused and wondering what she had to do to please him.

"Are you gay?" she asked in innocence.

"No, I am not gay. How dare you make such accusations and talk to me like I'm some pervert off the streets? I suppose you want me to pay for your attention, but you won't get a penny out of me."

"But…."

"Don't but me. I hope I never see you again."

Tears flowed from Willow's eyes. In her naivety, she'd misjudged Nelson. Before she could explain her actions, he'd walked away in long hurried strides and disappeared into one of the narrow lanes. The stench of embarrassment mixed with failure reached her nostrils.

"Come on, boys, time to go home," she sobbed, tightening the dog's leads. "Stuff him; I hate men, all of them. I've never yet met one worth bothering about."

Back in his cottage, Nelson felt the sun pour in through the windows and heat the room until he could barely breathe.

"What kind of a fool am I?" he cried out loud.

"How could I have been so stupid to rebuff a beautiful woman for showing her feelings?"

CHAPTER THIRTY-FOUR

After two days of scouring the forest for rabbits, Det/Sgt Down felt tired. The blame lay squarely with DCI Mattress for insisting he take a couple of days off from solving crimes leaving him to grapple with his brain the best way to spend the time. He felt misled with no sport on the TV and nothing interesting in the village besides the grotty little pub full of yokels. Too hot for fishing; a light breeze from the south via the Isle of Wight and ripe fruit falling from overladen trees promised a perfect day.

Not the kind of man who sought solitude, there were times when he revelled in his own company, and today was one of those days. Jumbled together with the occasional cries of animals and calls of birds, the further he pushed into the forest, the darker it became beneath the dense cloak of trees. Moving deeper, he followed the tip of the village church steeple visible above the tree tops and stopped in a small clearing. From out of nowhere, a figure emerged from the semi-darkness. Dropping to a crouch and gripping his rifle tight to his chest, the smell of fire invaded his nose. Locals knew fires in the forest were strictly taboo. Common knowledge prevailed that local magistrates dealt severely with those foolish enough to start campfires.

Tonguing his lips and sucking in a deep breath, Down rose, stepped forward, lost his balance, and plunged to the ground. His rifle slipped from his hands into the thick undergrowth. Rolling to one side, he massaged his ankle and heaved a sigh of relief at the gun butt visible in the long grass. Minutes later, he stumbled on the source of the fire, the ashes extinguished by water. Empty bandage packages lay strewn next to used tubes of ointment suitable for burns. Convinced he'd found Xander Pennywise's hideout, he dropped to one knee and considered his next move. It made sense to call for backup and wait for reinforcements. He didn't want a shoot-out in the forest if Xander was armed. High overhead, the sun swung round in the sky, blinding him, and he shuddered as something zipped by his head. Sure it wasn't a bullet by the lack of gunfire; shaking with nerves, he wondered what he should do next. A second zip followed by breaking twigs sent his nerves soaring. Vigorously wiping away the sweat stinging his eyes, he stared at the broken arrow lying feet away on the ground. The last time he'd had a run-in with Xander, Xander carried a rifle. The Green Archers used bows and arrows.

"Capp, you fool, what the hell are you doing shooting your blasted arrows at me?" he shouted. "Do you hear me?

Another arrow rebounded off the trunk of a nearby tree.

"Matt Capp, what the hell is wrong with you?"

Still no answer. On hands and knees, Down started crawling in the direction which the arrows came from.

"Stay where you are, copper. Or the next arrow will go into your right eye."

Down froze at the sound of the voice. It wasn't Matt Capp. Working the saliva in his dry mouth, he forced the words from his mouth.

"Give yourself up, Xander. You aren't going anywhere. You are making matters worse for you and your family.

"Stuff my family; they mean nothing to me. Lay your rifle on the ground, empty your pockets, and step back."

Down sighed, rattled that Xander, armed with a bow and arrows had the drop on him.

Confusing thoughts of a way out of his predicament twined around his mind like weeds. He didn't have to do anything dangerous or courageous. He couldn't see Xander, so how could Xander see him enough to put an arrow in his eye? Follow your instincts, they told him at the police training academy. Right now, his instincts told him to run. But police officers don't do that; they don't run from trouble. Their job is to apprehend troublemakers and protect the people. The feeling of not knowing what to do next began to eat into his bones. He could wait until Xander gave away his position and then make a dash for safety.

"I won't tell you again. Put the rifle on the ground and step back."

Xander's voice sounded ragged and closer than before. To Down's left, the branches of a bush shivered. Panic threatened to choke him. Only a fool would wait until an arrow struck his eye. In a sudden dash to safety, his foot struck a rock and he stumbled head-first onto something soft. In a blind panic to get to his feet, he slipped and stared at Matt Capp's dead body. Capp's eyes were wide open, staring into the sky, a neat bullet hole in his forehead. Vomit poured from Down's mouth. Gripping the rifle, on hands and knees, he forced his way through the thick undergrowth ignoring the thorns tearing the flesh from his face. A coldness penetrated his body. His body shook uncontrollably. Wiping the blood from his face, he vowed silently to end the life of Xander Pennywise, no matter the cost to his safety. The hunted was to become the hunter. No quarter given, and none asked.

No longer able to stand upright because of overhanging branches, Down dropped to a crouch as another arrow became embedded in the trunk of a nearby tree. Convinced that Xander was waiting for him to break cover, he began to circle closer to where he thought Xander was hiding. Seconds later another arrow narrowly missed his neck as he plunged through the underwood, then slowed and forced himself to walk with caution. A surge of water rushing into a gully rode above the top of his boots and pressed against his ankles. The further he went, the more his hate for Xander grew until his lips formed a permanent sneer. The sound of beating wings startled him, and he stopped and held his breath. Five metres away, Xander was stringing another arrow with his back facing him. Down raised the rifle and without hesitation fired at Xander's right shoulder. Xander screamed in pain, dropped the bow and fell to his knees clutching the back of his neck.

"You're under arrest for the murder of three women found dead at your father's manor and the murder of Matt Capp. I won't bother to read your rights; you're not worth the time."

"What do you want, copper, money? I can get you money. All you have to do is let me go." Xander smirked.

"I don't want your money. I want to see you serve the remainder of your life behind bars along with your twisted father."

"In your dreams, you thick copper."

Down let the remark pass, ramming another bullet in the breach he put another shot into

Xander's knee.

"I'm going to tie you up and leave you here," Down sneered. "Pray the forest animals don't find you first, especially wild pigs. They'll eat you, bones and all."

"What, you can't do that? You're a copper. You have to take me in," Xander screamed.

"Is that right? Pity, it's my day off."

Refusing to allow his conscience to get the better of him, Down tied Xander to a tree stump, gagged him, and set course for the village without looking back. Despite the sun's warmth, the air seemed thin, like the atmosphere on top of a high mountain. No matter how hard he tried, his breathing became laboured. Over and over, he asked himself why he'd done the things he'd done. A man of good character, he chastised himself for allowing his temper to dictate his mood. Why had he allowed his police training to disappear without a trace?

Over a hot mug of coffee in his rented apartment, he wrote out his resignation from the force, bundled his uniform into a bin bag and dropped them off at the police station. Behind the wheel of his car, he sat deep in thought. Then, with a grim jaw set course for Dover. From there, he'd drive to Costa Brava, Spain, and his sister's beachside house overlooking the sea.

CHAPTER THIRTY-FIVE

The first time DCI Mattress read Down's letter of resignation, confused, she missed breakfast and lunch. No matter how hard she searched for a reason to explain his sudden departure, she could only contemplate the cause that made a first-rate Policeman such as Det/Sgt Down disappear into the blue overnight. It wasn't until she read the letter for the fourth time in as many days she became aware of Det/Sgt Down's sudden decision to leave the force. Picking up the phone, she composed her thoughts.

"Where is Xander Penntwise's body now? She murmured, folding the letter and pushing it aside.

"What's left of him is on the way to the mortuary," a voice cackled.

"Does Lord Pennywise know his son, Xander, has been found half eaten by forest creatures?"

"No, I thought it would be better coming from you."

"Yes, good work. I want a full report on my

desk within the next two hours," Mattress said, tapping her fingers on the desktop. "And deliver it personally."

She pressed the off button on the phone and waited for a shift of emotion. It never came. Instead, she knew Lord Pennywise's face would buckle with grief and despair as the message sank into his mind. For a brief moment, she considered writing a note and having a Police Constable deliver it by hand. But why do that? She wanted to look at Pennywise and watch him suffer while screeching threats to anyone in sight. That way, she could find a form of revenge for the countless insults he'd taken pleasure in hurling at her in the past. Later he could wallow in the misery he found great pleasure in bestowing on others. In a better frame of mind, she left for the hotel beaming like a cat drowning in a tub of cream.

Pennywise sat sprawled in his armchair like it was a throne. He held his head back as if ready to deliver a sentence of death to some poor unfortunate lacking all form of defence. Eyes clouded, DCI Mattress had no intention of holding back when she told him of his son's dreadful death.

"What do you want this time? Come to ask me some more of your stupid questions; how often do I have to tell you to speak with my solicitor? Now get out of my sight," he said in a hoarse voice raising in anger.

Mattress struggled to keep the sneer from her face. Anger pressed her mouth into a thin red line. The golden flecks in her eyes flashed with fury.

"The body of your son, Alexander, has been found in the forest half eaten by animals. Sometime today, you will be required to identify what's left of the body at the mortuary. I shall have a car at your disposal. Good morning; enjoy your breakfast."

Mattress never waited to see the growing despair crumple Pennywise's lined face or the tremble that threatened to toss him out of the chair. Bypassing the lift halfway down the stairs, she heard his high-pitched howl echoing throughout the hotel. Her sigh was long and drawn out; at last, the village would no longer live in fear of Pennywise's cruelty. What would become of him and his one remaining son, Nelson? She neither knew nor cared.

*

Willow knew she had a whole load of serious explaining to do. Not just a casual word asking forgiveness, but comments straight from the heart. Cold sweat gathered on her brow and armpits. Sickness tumbled in her belly. Her conduct the night before had been inexcusable and she prayed Cate would accept her apologies as sincere. Alternatively, she'd have to leave the surgery and find employment elsewhere. The thought caused her to vomit in the handbasin.

Moments later, the phone ringing yanked her out of her lethargy. The name on the lighted screen read Anton.

"Cate will be at the surgery in a couple of minutes to keep an eye on things. I want to speak to you at her house. Please leave when she arrives."

"Yes, of course, thank you," Willow mumbled quietly.

Turning off the phone, she began pacing the room like a caged animal. Anton hardly used his phone, preferring to take messages on the answering machine. And why couldn't Cate have delivered the message? Resigned to being asked to leave for shooting off her mouth, she dried her tears. Seconds later, she listened to Cate pulling up on the drive.

"Dad's waiting for you, and don't take all day; he's not as strong as he used to be," Cate snapped, leaving the front door partially open

"Yes, of course," Willow answered, wincing at Cate's severe tone. "I'll leave immediately."

The result of a bad night left Page feeling lost. Memories of prison invaded his thoughts relieving him of a mind of his own. On a warm sunny day outside, inside, the air was dry and icy cold as if summer had abruptly surrendered to winter. However hard he tried, he failed to assemble his mind in order; everything was a tissue of lies and unverified facts. The sound of the front door slamming shut startled him. Eyes closed, he cursed mildly at the clumsiness of women. When he opened his eyes, Willow stood before him. Hands clasped behind her back, she looked pale and constantly tapped her right foot on the bedroom carpet as though suffering a nervous complaint.

"You wanted to see me?" she said.

"Did I? Oh yes, I remember now. Cate and I have decided you need a holiday. Go away on holiday, abroad, if you want to. I have asked too much of you. I am sorry."

She stared at him huddled beneath the bedclothes and shivering from head to toe. For the first time, the spirit of friendship teetered on the edge of an abyss. A holiday he'd said. What did he mean? Was this how people were sacked? Told to go on holiday with no mention of return? Tension cranked up between them. Unable to find the words to answer, her foot tapping increased. The seconds drifted into minutes before she finally found her voice.

"I'm sorry I wasn't able to meet your expectations. Perhaps I'm not cut out to be a vet. I'll get my stuff packed and leave this afternoon. Thank you for taking me in and giving me a chance to better myself; goodbye." She said, holding back her tears.

"For goodness sake, stop trying my patience. What are you talking about? Not cut out to be a vet? You will make a great vet. Cate tells me I am working you too hard, and you need a break. I'm closing the surgery for a few weeks until I feel better. Now off you go, and don't forget to send a card."

Christmas Day, the 5th of November, St. George's Day, Willow didn't know what time of the year it was. Elation pumped the blood through her veins at breakneck speed. She wanted to grab Page and hug him, smother him with kisses of gratitude, tell him he was the best thing since peanut butter on toast. Instead, she leaned forward and kissed him lightly on the forehead. Seconds later his heavy breathing turned into a gentle snore.

*

Nelson Pennywise stuffed his new tight-fitting jeans, black T-shirt and fancy coloured trainers into a bin bag and dropped them into the wheely bin against the wall next to the front door. Stuff fancy clothes, they hadn't helped to impress Willow. Thirty minutes later, he returned to the wheely bin and retrieved his clothes mumbling about plenty more pebbles on the beach apart from Willow. A lonely child, as he grew into adolescence, he fantasized about having a real family full of noisy siblings, jolly aunts and uncles with exciting stories to tell, and doting parents. Instead, imposed on a family of macabre thoughts, he kept himself to himself, reading book after book of far-off places and useless information. Finished hanging the clothes back in the wardrobe, he rolled his eyes at the mobile phone on the tabletop. Then, as his patience drained, he snatched it up and punched in Willow's number.

"I'm sorry," he said.

"So am I," she answered.

"I'm more sorry than you are."

"No, you're not. What are you doing?"

"Nothing,"

"Meet me in the park in five minutes."

Shaking with excitement, Nelson slipped into his baggy pants and ruffled his hair with his fingertips. No point in pushing my luck, he giggled.

*

"Come," DCI Mattress called, seated behind her desk and wincing at the pain in her feet.

"The report you asked for, ma'am," the police lady said, dropping the folder on the desk.

Intrigued at the accent, Mattress looked up from rummaging through her desk drawers.

"I haven't seen you here before," she said to the tall, unnaturally thin woman standing before her.

"No, ma'am, I have been here for seven weeks. Straight from training at Hendon. I'm from Tobago originally."

"I never could understand why you leave such a beautiful tropical island to come to the wet and windy UK. What is your name?"

"Precious, ma'am, Precious Jones."

"And what is it you do here, Jones."

"Fetch and carry, make tea and wash dirty cups and saucers, ma'am."

"Do you know what policing is all about? It's no job for people in their right minds. It's a job for people with schizophrenia, an activity that requires mental dissociation. To be a policewoman, you must be inside the world and outside it simultaneously."

"Or, in my case, starve to death or become a prostitute at twelve and dead before I reach my thirtieth birthday," Jones answered quickly.

Mattress fluttered her eyelids and opened the folder as Jones turned to leave.

"Wait, I have to go to the scene where Xander Pennywise's body was discovered and then to the mortuary. Have you ever seen a dead body before?" she asked.

Jones stopped in her tracks and swung round to face her.

"I've seen death in all its forms," Jones answered, her eyes boring into Mattress's face.

"Good, get your coat and come with me. I must visit a crime scene and need a new assistant."

For a brief second, Jones felt lost, adrift in a fog at her good fortune; she mumbled her words.

"Yes, Ma'am, straight away."

*

"Seventy per cent of the body covered in burns; Xander Pennywise must have died in agony. The pathologists will be able to tell you more. Sorry I can't help," the senior investigating officer told Mattress

"Was he dead before the animals got to him?" Mattress asked, surveying the scene of Xander's death.

"I'd say he was still alive, poor bastard. Who could be sick enough to do this to another person?"

"Hate and revenge come in many forms. Thanks for your help. Come on, Jones, let's see what the mortuary can come up with."

Jones hesitated.

"Something is not right. I sense death all around us," Jones said quietly.

"Sense, what do you mean, sense?" Mattress said impatiently.

"There, over there, that is where the men must search," Jones said, pointing to a thick clump of bushes."

Mattress frowned.

"Not a load of mumbo jumbo from Tobago, is it?"

"Unfortunately, I don't find death amusing. Suit yourself with what you do. I can only tell you what I sense."

Mattress stared at Jones. Tall and rigid, her eyes were as large as pickled onions and veined red.

"If it makes you happy, I'll have a couple of men search the bushes before we leave."

Twenty minutes later, five corpses dressed in

Green Archer's uniforms were pulled from the bushes and placed in body bags.

Mattress's mouth gaped open.

"How on Earth did you know?"

"Perhaps it was black magic. Much better than probing around for details all day long," Jones smiled.

*

"He was shot in the shoulder from behind, then again in the knee facing his assailant," the pathologist at the mortuary said. "Time of death, approximately three to four days ago."

"The gunshots didn't kill him?" Mattress asked.

"No, judging by the position of the animal bites and the expression on what's left of his face, he probably died of shock."

"How about the five bodies?"

"Four were shot with a Lee Enfield .303 rifle, the kind used in World War Two. The fifth died with an arrow to the neck. At a guess, I'd say the assailant ran out of bullets after killing the first four and used a bow from one of his victims to kill the other. How he managed to drag the bodies into the bushes is a mystery. I'll get a full report to you later in the afternoon."

"Thank you, doctor," Mattress said, then turned to Jones. "Right, Jones, you have some answering to do."

"Yes, ma'am," Jones smiled.

Halfway between the town and village,

Mattress told Jones to pull over into a small layby and wound the window down.

"How did you know there were bodies concealed in the bushes? Or was it just a lucky guess?"

Jones didn't answer straight away. Instead, she stared through the windscreen at a young woman herding cattle through a fence into a field. Finally, she spoke.

"No, it wasn't a lucky guess, nor was it mumbo jumbo," she said, sounding irked. "If you believe that you are in the wrong job."

"Watch your mouth, Jones, or you will be back washing cups and saucers in the station. Come to that; I've never seen a saucer at the station."

"That's because you never bothered to look. If you or the scene of crime officers paid attention, they would have noticed the broken branches and tracks where someone had dragged the bodies into the bushes."

"So it wasn't black magic?"

Jones pursed her lips, gave a deep sigh and shrugged.

"My mother could read the future by doing what we called throwing the bones. She tried to teach me the skill, but I wasn't very good or interested. Years later, I discovered I could sense death. Frightened I was possessed I decided to leave the island to be free of the devil, but he followed me. So I joined the police force, hoping it would frighten him away. But he's still inside me. You might mock what you call mumbo jumbo, but I can tell you that this village is drowning in the stench of death. I can sense it all around me."

The words blurred Mattress's thoughts, followed by a long silence her forehead folded into creases. Startled by the revelation and Jones's readiness to admit to something others might find unbelievable, she endeavoured to keep her voice steady.

"Have you told anyone else of this gift, or whatever you wish to call it?"

"No, they would laugh in their ignorance."

"Then take my advice, keep it to yourself, or find another job."

"I'm happy in what I am doing. I don't want another job."

Mattress sat back and clasped her hands. She wasn't foolish enough not to realise what a great help Jones would be in helping to solve outstanding murder cases.

"I require an assistant. Would you be interested in acting as an unpaid sergeant on probation for six months?"

Jones felt the hairs on the back of her neck rise and pulled her teeth over her lower lip.

"Yes," she said, unable to think what to say next.

"Yes, is that all you have to say?"

"Yes."

"Well, don't go overboard with gratitude,"

Mattress smiled, pressing the green button on her mobile phone. "I'm on my way," she said, thumbing the red button to end the call. "We've got a call to go to the Sherwood hotel in town. Do you know the way?"

"Yes, ma'am."

"Then, move on and stop saying yes every time I speak to you."

"Yes, ma'am," Jones answered.

CHAPTER THIRTY-SIX

Anton Page stared up at the ceiling and groaned as he swung his legs from the bed with great deliberation and struggled to his feet. Ignoring the silver thread of saliva looping from his mouth and settling on his arm, he tugged on his dressing gown.

"Damned if I'll lie in bed all day; to hell with the doctors," he muttered, struggling to make his way through the bungalow door leading to the patio.

Seated on the metal seat, he leaned his arms on the tabletop and gazed across the countryside through half-opened eyes. A small creeping smile altered his features at the sight of a red tractor pulling an empty trailer across a freshly harvested wheat field. Birds twittered and rose from the bushes as a magpie settled on the tree branch in the garden's centre. The soothing sound of falling water from the newly installed fountain in the pond helped to ease his mind as he leaned back and slowly closed his eyes.

*

Willow couldn't care less who watched as she threw her arms around Nelson's neck and kissed his cheek. Nelson's lips trembled as he pulled her tight to his chest.

"Anton says I must go on holiday and take a break. We can go together, you and me. If you want to, of course." Willow said, laughing with joy.

"Where, where shall we go?"

"Seaside, I love the sea and the clean fresh air."

"When shall we go? I'll have to let my father know, or he'll have a fit," Nelson said quietly.

"Oh my God, he won't want to come with us, will he?"

"He might; he loves the seaside and eats candy floss all day when he isn't scoffing cockles. "

Willow's face dropped.

"I'm joking," Nelson said, bursting out laughing.

*

PCW Jones followed a few feet behind as DCI Mattress strode purposely to the reception desk.

"What seems to be the problem with Lord Pennywise?" Mattress asked the receptionist, busy filing her nails.

"May I ask who you are?" the receptionist answered, inspecting her nails.

"DCI Matthews, and look at me when I talk to you," Matthews snapped, producing her warrant card as proof of identity.

"I'm afraid Lord Pennywise is refusing to see anyone. A policeman sent to take him to the mortuary to identify his deceased son is waiting outside his room."

"How long is this been going on?"

"Since nine o'clock this morning, almost six hours ago."

"Do you have a spare key?"

"Yes, of course," the receptionist said, taking a key from a cupboard.

"Come on, Jones, let's get this nonsense sorted." Mattress snapped.

"Do you mind if I use the toilet first? I'll be with you in a few minutes. Nature calls," Jones said.

"Well, don't take all day. I've enough to do as it is."

Jones waited until Mattress disappeared into the lift before turning her attention to the receptionist.

"Where is the fire escape?"

"Through the door marked private," the receptionist pointed. "Then straight on, you can't miss it."

"Thank you," Jones said, inhaling a deep breath.

Ten minutes passed before Jones entered Lord Pennywise's room through the slightly ajar door.

"Ah, you made it then?"

"Yes, ma'am, sorry."

"No matter," Mattress scowled. "It seems

Pennywise has done a runner right under the staff's nose. Worse still, no one saw him leave."

Jones swallowed noisily.

"I'm afraid not, ma'am. His body is at the bottom of the fire escape. It seems he committed suicide."

Mattress's cheeks flushed red, and she stared hard at Jones as if sizing her up, judging the truth of her statement.

"Another one of your feelings, was it? You didn't need the toilet, did you? You knew he was dead."

"I didn't know what else to do. I had to be sure before I told you to prevent you from laughing at me."

Mattress glanced at her watch and shook her head.

"You are going to take a lot of getting used to. Show me where the body is, and then close the hotel."

From the top of the fire escape, with teeth gritted, Mattress looked down at the twisted body of Lord Pennywise below. A feeling of relief blocked out all forms of pity she had for the man lying on the hard concrete floor. Ever since she arrived in the village, the Pennywise family had been a constant thorn in her side. Now only Nelson remained. A bookworm whose world consisted of written words between two book covers. Thumbing her phone, she called the station and asked for the SOCO team and pathologists to get to the hotel asap. Afterwards, she'd find Nelson Pennywise and tell him of his father's death. From experience, she didn't expect wails of mourning and floods of tears from Nelson. She paused for a moment and weighed the situation up in her mind. Since Pennywise Manor had burned to the ground, she had no idea where Nelson was living.

"Wait here and make sure no one tries to enter or leave the hotel. This is a murder scene. And please don't find any more bodies lying around," Mattress said with a small smile.

Three times Mattress drove around the village, and each time she failed to see any sign of Nelson. Unwrapping a chocolate bar, she leaned back and gazed at the cars parked on the side of the road out of habit. A blue Fiesta with a flat front-off-side puncture belonging to Holly Foyle, the woman who used to drive the mobile library van caught her attention. Leaving the uneaten chocolate bar in the glove compartment, Mattress walked along the garden path to Holly Foyle's house and rapped on the front door. A young man in his early twenties opened the door.

"Can I help you?" he said, stepping back and frowning.

"Just a courtesy call," Mattress said, flashing her warrant card. "I noticed your car has a flat tyre

Before Mattress could finish her question, the young man smiled, turned around and called out.

"Mum, it's the police."

The sound of saucepans crashing to the kitchen floor echoed throughout the house.

"Please, dear God, not after all this time," Holly Foyle wailed, appearing in the kitchen doorway. "I knew one day you would come. I didn't mean it. She was such an evil woman. I caught her doing it with Lord Pennywise in her garage the night I came to collect her outstanding library books. I told her she was a disgusting whore. She laughed and told of the time she seduced my husband. Livid with anger I lost my temper, grabbed a garden spade and struck her with it. Twice I did it. Then rang Mr Page, and minutes later, I called the police. I don't remember where Lord Pennywise went. When I saw Mr Page pull up in his car, I panicked and ran away. I didn't mean for him to go to prison for twenty years. I'm so sorry."

Mattress swallowed noisily, wondering if her ears were playing tricks.

"You are talking of Lizzie Page's murder?" she asked nervously.

"Yes, isn't that why you are here?"

"No, I dropped by to tell you your car has a flat tyre."

Holly Foyle stared wide eyed considering the words. Then blinking, she fell to her knees shaking her head from side to side. The moment's intensity transported her back to the time of the event. She vaguely remembered grabbing the spade, raising it above her head, and sending the sharp blade into Lizzie Page's neck. Gripped in a frenzy of temper, she repeated the process until her victim's head hung limp.

"Tell Mr Page I am so sorry," she sobbed.

Devoid of pity, Mattress curled her lip.

"I don't think being sorry will be enough, do you?" she said in a low voice. "I'm arresting you for the murder of Lizzie Page. Do you understand?"

"Yes, I understand," Holly Foyle said, turning to her son. "I'm so sorry, Winston; please forgive me."

DCI Mattress shivered as a cold spike ran up her spine. Wellington, Alexander, Nelson, and now Winston. Would the curse of Pennywise ever end?

Stiff as a stone statue, Winston remained upright. His face pale, his lips a shade of blue.

"All those years, you let a man who cared for sick animals rot in a cell and never said a word. As for my father, who left us years ago, I hope he rots in hell. I hate you both," he sneered, kicking open the door and disappearing into the kitchen.

Holly Foyle had finished her written statement when a knock on the interrogation room door interrupted proceedings.

"Nelson Pennywise has been brought in," the duty sergeant informed her.

"Put him in the interview room. I'll be along in

a moment. In the meantime, put Mrs Foyle in a cell.

Two minutes later, Mattress faced Nelson across the wooden table. The look on his face made it difficult for Mattress to judge his mood.

"Your father was found dead in his hotel this morning. At the moment, we are treating it as suicide," Mattress said, staring across the table at Nelson's face. Nelson licked his lips and fidgeted. Leaning back in the chair, he slipped his hands into his trousers pockets.

"I suppose you expect me to burst into tears. Or wring my hands in anguish?" Nelson said, smiling.

Mattress watched him. The sign of a man who cared little for the time he didn't wear a watch. No rings adorned his fingers. The collar of his jacket was worn and tattered, and his shirt bordered on grubbiness.

"I expect nothing from your kind. I couldn't care less how your father died or why." Mattress snapped, vexed by his attitude.

"In which case, I assume I'm free to go?" Nelson said in a gentle voice.

"As far away as possible; I don't care."

Nelson pulled himself up and stared directly into Mattress's eyes.

"I know you tar all the Pennywise family with the same brush. At times, you and the villagers have had every right to do so. However, discard me from your feelings, and I might add my family has left me disgusted by their actions on more occasions than I care to count."

Mattress shuddered at Nelson's unexpected broadside and peered at him through half-closed eyes. Then climbed to her feet.

"We are finished," she said, opening the door and disappearing into the corridor.

"If I'm wanted, I'll be at Anton Page's bungalow. Better he hears of Holly Foyle's confession from me," she told the duty sergeant.

*

Willow's face twitched when Nelson told her of his father's death. She had expected a reaction, a sign of remorse or sadness at the news. Instead, he said it like he had a tiny splinter in his hand, and a slight tug would release the pain.

"Aren't you a little sad?" she asked.

"Not really; he wasn't a good man like a father should be. Not like Anton is to you."

"Anton isn't my real father."

"No, but he could be. I've seen how he treats you; it's plain he loves you like he loves Cate, his natural daughter."

"Is it plain to see how much I love you?" the words gushed from Willow's mouth, her face bright red with embarrassment. "Oh my God, I didn't mean to say that; I'm sorry."

Before she could catch her breath, Nelson pressed his lips tight against hers.

"Don't be sorry. I love you more than anything in this world," he said, pulling back his head.

"Let's get married."

Lost for words, Willow leaned forward and kissed him again and again.

"We must tell Anton first. He's at home resting."

"Let's go now before you change your mind and leave me an old, embittered man," Nelson laughed.

*

Twice, Mattress rang the doorbell at Page's front door and received no answer. She turned at the sound of laughter and watched Nelson and Willow make their way along the garden path.

"Can I help you?" Willow said. "I hope we haven't done anything wrong."

"It's essential I speak with Mr Page," Mattress answered, ignoring Nelson.

"He's rather poorly at the moment. Is it so important it won't wait?"

"Unfortunately, no, it won't wait. It might be better if you were present when I speak to Mr Page."

Willow glanced at Nelson, then turned and unlocked the door.

"I'll wait here," Nelson said.

"Are you two an item?" Mattress asked.

"Yes, we are," Willow said.

"Then it's better if you were both present."

"What is it you want? You are beginning to frighten me," Willow said.

"Oh, it's nothing to fret over, quite the

opposite. Today I'm the bearer of good news."

Willow entered the bungalow first and went to Page's bedroom, expecting to find him asleep or reading a magazine concerning wildlife in some far-off country. Peering through his bedroom window, she saw him sleeping on the patio with his head on his chest.

"He's outside on the patio, fast asleep. Seem such a shame to disturb him."

"What on earth is going on here?" Cate interrupted, standing in the doorway. "Where's father, and why are the police here?"

"I need to speak with your father urgently. Someone wake him, please."

"Father, there's someone here from the police to talk to you," Cate said, striding out onto the patio. "Come on, dad, wake up."

When he didn't respond, Cate leaned and shook him by the shoulder, then jumped back when his head rolled to one side as he fell onto the table.

"Dad, are you all right? Stop messing about."

Mattress reached out, laid her fingers on his neck, and then turned to Cate.

"I'm so sorry. I'm afraid your father is dead."

"No, no, he can't. He'd never leave us," Willow's wails turned to screams. "Please tell him to wake up, Cate; please ask him to wake up.

"Sit down, Willow. He won't wake up," Cate said, trembling from head to toe as Mattress called for an ambulance.

"Is there anything I can do?" Mattress said quietly.

"No, we need time to come to terms with his death. He was a fine man, regardless of his past."

"It's that I came to see him about; Holly Foyle has admitted to murdering his wife, your mother. We have a written confession."

Cate's face paled as tears flooded down her cheeks. Unable to gather the strength, her legs buckled, and she fell to the floor.

"I hate this village and everyone in it," she raged. "It's so full of evil even the devil wouldn't live here. "May God strike it from the face of the earth. For twenty years, he suffered someone else's crimes without a word of complaint while that evil woman lived her life as if butter wouldn't melt in her mouth."

The moment the ambulance arrived, the medics turned their attention to Willow. Unable to breathe and as white as a penguin's bib, she writhed on the ground kicking and shouting words no one could understand. Under sedation and seated next to Anton Page's body, the ambulance took her back to the hospital.

"And what do you want? There's nothing here for you; clear off," Cate sneered, turning to Nelson. "It's your family responsible for most of the misery in this village. You should have burned with the rest of them."

Nelson stepped back at the force of Cate's words. He knew the words she spoke smacked of the truth and turned and left without uttering a word. For most of his life he'd wanted no part of his family; now, the only time he'd felt truly happy, everything was in danger of being dashed from his hands. He had little recollection of his childhood or mother; his life existed around his father's iron will. His only escape had been to bury his head in words written by people he never knew. But he'd met Willow; they were kindred spirits, detached and ignorant of their past; she was something he must hang onto and never allow to slip through his fingers. People could say whatever they wanted; he didn't care. Aware the villagers could spread gossip faster than a sewist could spin thread, he recalled when as a child, he'd fallen asleep in church one Sunday morning. By the time the gossipers had finished, he'd snored so loud the vicar, unable to hear his sermon, threw him into a freshly dug grave awaiting the burial of a village councillor. Heart pounding against his ribs and ignoring the sudden outburst of the rain bouncing off the pavement, he decided to drive to the hospital where he could be close to Willow. He would be her rock on which she could anchor her emotions and feel safe.

Fortunate to find a parking place close to the hospital he turned off the engine, slumped back in the seat and gazed through the passenger side window at Willow. Alone with her head bowed, she sat on the wall next to the hospital entrance.

"I'm so sorry to hear of Anton's death. I know you cared for him deeply," he said, sitting beside her.

"I loved him like a father. Nobody was as kind to me as he was. I shall miss him for the remainder of my life," she said quietly.

"If there is anything I can do, you only have to ask. You know that, don't you?"

"Yes, of course," she answered, taking his hand and giving it a slight squeeze. "I need you more than ever now."

Nelson felt a surge of relief. In her grief, she hadn't ordered him to go away and leave her to mourn alone.

"Shall we go to my place? It's quiet there, and we won't be disturbed. Best you ring Cate and tell her you are fine before she gets worried."

"Whatever you think best," Willow answered, pulling out her phone and punching Cate's number.

For the remainder of the day until sunset, Willow sat and stared at the ham sandwiches. Though she wore only a cotton shirt, sweat gathered in her armpits and glued the thin fabric to her back.

"A penny for them?" Nelson said quietly.

Willow blinked and smiled.

"I was wondering what will happen to me now Anton has passed on."

"You'll stay here with me, of course. Don't worry over such trivial things. Now eat your sandwiches, please."

"Whatever you say."

Nelson frowned and, studying her face, feared she was losing the will to think for herself. Already dark circles were beginning to form around her eyes.

"Would you like something different to eat? An omelette; I'm good at cooking them. Egg on toast, perhaps?"

"How long is a mouse's tail?" she muttered.

Nelson turned his attention to the rows of books covering each wall. Somewhere, one of the books would have the answer to his predicament. But which one? The light had drained from the sky leaving the small room in semi-darkness.

"Would you like the lights on?" he asked.

"How long is a mouse's tail?" she muttered again, but this time not so distinct.

"Would you like a takeaway from the Chinese restaurant," he said, his voice tinged with desperation.

"How long is a mouses tail?"

She touched his arm and murmured something he didn't catch, then folded her arms on the table and laid her head on her hands. Her eyes closed. Her breathing became uneven as she began to sob. Reflexively he stroked her hair tracing the contours of her slender neck. During his lifetime, there had been many times when he'd felt uncertain and awkward. But never like this. For the next two hours, he sat beside her waiting for her to wake and smile at him. Then cautiously, with stiffened arms, he raised her from the chair and carried her into the bedroom. As he lay her on the bed, his body ached with his love for her. The intensity was unlike any other experience he'd ever felt before.

The following day while Willow slept, Nelson answered her ringing phone.

"Where the devil is, Willow, and why are you answering her phone? If anything has happened to her, God help you." Cate shouted down the line.

Nelson ignored her outburst, gave her his address, and pressed the red button to end the call. Before the kettle had boiled, Willow appeared at the bedroom door.

"Good morning," she smiled.

"Hi," Nelson grinned. "Coffee?"

"Yes, please."

"How are you feeling this morning?"

"Fine, why shouldn't I be? I'm going to see Anton later this morning; we are low on dog food."

Nelson's heart jumped a beat. The room was shrouded in semi-darkness. The curtains were so tightly drawn he struggled to see the contours of Willow's face.

"Ah well, good luck," Nelson said, moving towards the windows and pulling back the curtains to allow the light to flood in. "I shall be here all day if you need me."

For a brief moment, Willow remained where she stood, her lips slightly parted, revealing flawless white teeth. Then turned and entered the bathroom. Nelson sat at the table with his head in his hands. He couldn't think of one justifiable reason to accompany her on the wasted journey to Anton's bungalow. Nor could he fathom the reason for her actions unless she refused to believe that Anton Page no longer existed. In which case it would be wiser for her to visit a doctor. The thought brought a smile to his face. Willow would swear there was nothing wrong with her and refuse his suggestion.

Her phone on charge Willow started to dress ready for her visit to the surgery. At the same time, she wondered why Nelson hadn't asked if they could go together. She liked to have him close; it gave her a renewed feeling of security that he loved her and she him.

CHAPTER THIRTY-SEVEN

No matter how often CDI Mattress considered DS Down's sudden departure-she couldn't arrive at a suitable conclusion to ease her mind. Although unproven, it stood to reason he was responsible for the death of Alexander Pennywise. The crux of the matter was, should she inform her superiors of her suspicions or sweep the issue under the carpet and be grateful that the Pennywise family, apart from wimp Nelson, no longer existed to make her life a misery? Against her instincts and training, she chose the latter.

"Good morning, ma'am," Police Constable Jones trilled, entering the office without knocking. "How are your feet this morning?"

Mattress looked up from her desk and frowned at the question.

"Actually, they feel better than they have for months," she answered, startled by the question.

"My grandmother taught me how to mix a potion to relieve pain in the legs and feet. Perhaps you would like to try it sometime?"

"Oh my God, don't tell me it's some witch doctor's magic potion made from bat's wings and fleas off a cockatoo's arse. No, thank you, I'll give it a miss if you don't mind."

"Such a shame," Jones smiled. "I've been putting a spoonful in your tea for the past four days. Now you tell me the pain in your legs is easing. A bit of a coincidence, wouldn't you say?"

"There are times, Jones when you overstep the line. Can I trust you to make me a fresh cup of tea without adding concoctions from a West Indian witch doctor?"

"Of course, ma'am."

"Then please do so. Wait, is this magic potion all gone?"

"No, ma'am."

"Best not to let it go to waste; you might as well slip a small spoonful into my tea."

"Yes, ma'am, very wise."

*

The sound of barking dogs bothered Cate. The absence of Willow added to her anger. Now her father had passed away, the surgery would be run differently. No more sloping off whenever the mood took Willow. Now, she must pull her socks up if she wants to remain or leave.

Seconds after feeding the dogs, Willow entered the room looking dejected.

"Is Anton still unwell? I thought he'd have the strength to feed the animals.

Cate leaned back against the sink and folded

her arms, struggling to keep her temper under reasonable control.

"Running around after you is like looking after a kid. Wake up and get a grip on yourself. My father is dead, and you know it, so stop acting stupid." Cate fumed, red in the face. "Pull your weight, Willow, or leave. The choice is yours."

Willow stared at Cate petulantly.

"That's up to Anton; you can't ask me to leave."

"Anton is dead; bless him. Learn to accept it."

"Stop saying that. Anton's here somewhere caring for the animals. I'm not staying here listening to your evil words." Willow sobbed, turning to leave.

Halfway along the garden path, Willow slowed and looked at the crowds of people milling around the gate. As she grew closer she saw the bunches and bouquets of flowers leaning against the hedge.

"Hello, dear," a woman Willow didn't recognise said. "It's the best we can do after the dreadful mistake that sent Mr Page to prison for something he never did. The whole village, along with the outlying villages, is ashamed of itself. The poor man deserved better."

Even as the woman spoke, more and more families arrived clutching bunches of flowers.

"Willow," Cate's voice sounded softly behind her.

"Willow turned and wrapped her arms around Cate's shoulders."

"I'm sorry, I'm so sorry," Willow sobbed.

"What is done is done, and life must go on," Cate whispered.

*

Two weeks later, at the reading of Anton Page's will, Cate was awarded a sum of money so significant she became on the verge of passing out. The bungalow, including the surgery, was to be shared equally between Cate and Willow. Should Willow decide to leave, the house's value would be shared between them.

Nelson, the sole existing heir to his father's fortune, inherited the staggering sum of 138 million pounds made up of public houses, girlie clubs, a racing stable, private houses, a manifesto of gold shares in South Africa and an astonishing amount of money deposited in banks throughout the world.

After three days, attended by the whole village seeking atonement, Anton Page was laid to rest in the cemetery behind the Church of St Luke. Included in the congregation, people from nearby towns and cities came to watch the burial of a man who had served twenty years in prison for a crime he never committed nor complained.

CHAPTER THIRTY-EIGHT

Two years later, Nelson and Willow were married at the village Church of St Luke. Instead of choosing someone to give her away at the altar, Willow raised her arm to allow Cate to lay a folded tie belonging to Anton Page on her arm. With her arm in the linked position, to gasps of admiration from the packed congregation, a radiance seemed to envelop her as she walked dressed in white alone to the altar. Dropper, the yellow retriever, acted as best man with the ring tied loosely around his neck. After the service, DCI Mattress left everyone spellbound with her rendering of 'Ave Maria.' Father Kevin later remarked it was the happiest marriage he'd ever conducted.

As a wedding gift, when Nelson asked what Willow would like more than anything else, she answered a zoo.

"Then it will be so," Nelson replied, smiling.

For a further two years, the land Nelson received from his father's will began to take shape. Fields became pastures for animals to wander freely. Buildings to shelter animals were erected for donkeys, horses, pigs, cattle and other unwanted creatures. Four Llamas, three peacocks, and two ostriches given as gifts from a large northern private house were quickly housed. The land on which the Pennywise mansion once stood became a huge boating lake, complete with an island for monkeys. A restaurant and a café were erected next to a children's play area where parents could keep an eye on their children.

Last but not least, a large illuminated sign above the entrance read 'Anton Page's Adventure Land.' As time passed, a house of mirrors became a great favourite for adults and children, as did a maze of hedges. Nelson hired two qualified vets and the staff to allow Willow time to attend the veterinary college. For three years, she studied hard and eventually passed with honours.

On the day she accepted her doctorate she was six months pregnant and later gave birth to twins, a girl and a boy. They named the boy Anton, and the girl, Paige. Instead of building a large home in which to raise the children they remained in the bungalow. Nelson said the closeness would help them to remain a family with their feet firmly on the ground amidst their wealth and privilege.

Nelson tried his hardest to keep from reading every minute of the day, and to fill his days; he took to writing. Twelve months later, his novel, 'Life as the son of a Lord,' became a best seller.

Once a month they visited Anton Page's grave and gazed silently at the simple grey marble cross.

"A man amongst men is how I would describe him," Nelson spoke quietly.

"He was a father to me," Willow whispered, turning her head to listen to a blackbird singing his song in a nearby hedge.

THE END

I hope you have enjoyed reading this story as much as I enjoyed writing it. I would be most grateful if you would consider leaving a review.

Thank you…

BOOKS BY THIS AUTHOR

Coming Home

The Art Of Evil

All In

The Dancing Boy

Pennies In A Pound

Hidden In Plain View

Secrets Never Sleep

Echoes Of Madness

Hell With The Lid Off

Printed in Great Britain
by Amazon